"YOU FLEA-B[...] GET OFF ME!"

Her temper caught fire like dry kindling.

"I would if you'd shut your mouth long enough." Cale's body tensed, his thighs closing tighter around hers. His gaze seemed to fondle her as his eyes slowly traveled from her breasts, up her slender neck, to the senuous curve of her jaw. "Are you going to behave?"

Mutely, she nodded.

But there was one thing he had to do before he let her go. His mouth descended upon hers . . .

Praise for HEART OF THE WILD by Donna Stephens:

Other **AVON ROMANCES**

ALMOST A LADY *by Sonya Birmingham*
FORBIDDEN FLAME *by Selina MacPherson*
THE LILY AND THE HAWK *by Marlene Suson*
LORD OF THE NIGHT *by Cara Miles*
SAGEBRUSH BRIDE *by Tanya Anne Crosby*
SUNSHINE AND SHADOW *by Kathleen Harrington*
WILD CONQUEST *by Hannah Howell*

Coming Soon

MASTER OF MY DREAMS *by Danelle Harmon*
PASSIONATE SURRENDER *by Sheryl Sage*

And Don't Miss These
ROMANTIC TREASURES
from Avon Books

MASTER OF MOONSPELL *by Deborah Camp*
THEN CAME YOU *by Lisa Kleypas*
VIRGIN STAR *by Jennifer Horsman*

WIND ACROSS TEXAS

DONNA STEPHENS

AVON BOOKS  NEW YORK

WIND ACROSS TEXAS is an original publication of Avon Books. This work has never before appeared in book form. This work is a novel. Any similarity to actual persons or events is purely coincidental.

AVON BOOKS
A division of
The Hearst Corporation
1350 Avenue of the Americas
New York, New York 10019

First Avon Books Printing: August 1993

AVON TRADEMARK REG. U. S. PAT. OFF. AND IN OTHER COUNTRIES, MARCA REGISTRADA, HECHO EN U. S. A.

Printed in the U. S. A.

RA   10   9   8   7   6   5   4   3   2   1

To my critique group:
Velda, Patti, Judy, and Colleen

To the memory of Jim Roginski,
agent extraordinaire

To Lyssa Keusch, my editor,
who is a joy to work with
and who keeps me on my toes

Chapter 1

Dallas, 1865

Cale hated cheaters. He had been in enough poker games to know when someone was dealing cards from the bottom. The fat son-of-a-bitch rancher across the table from him was doing just that.

He'd been in one gunfight back in Mississippi; he didn't want to draw his gun on another man if he could help it. He prayed for the rancher's sake there was another way. He was a good shot. In fact, he was better than most. He didn't want to make a name for himself, but neither would he back down from a fight.

He fingered the revolver strapped to his thigh. The Civil War had aged him. He had wanted to fight on the side of truth, which to him meant enlisting in the Union army. Now, at thirty-two, he simply wanted to forget all the killing, maiming, and death he had experienced. He yearned for a quiet place untouched by the war. Wyoming loomed in his mind. He was drawn to the land, to the peace it represented and to the freedom he had cherished before he joined the fighting. His peace of mind depended on his getting home.

The saloon hummed with a mixture of sounds. A piano's off-key tinkling competed with clanking mugs, shuffling cards, and raucous laughter. Pungent odors punctuated the musty air: a combination of tobacco smoke, spit, stale liquor, and unwashed bodies.

His blue eyes narrowing, Cale looked at the men around the poker table and inwardly groaned. It was late. He had drunk too much and his head hurt. He massaged his brow beneath his wide-brimmed hat and leaned back in his chair, glancing at the cards he held close to his chest.

How had he come to this? It had been two months since the war ended, but at the moment it felt like two years. As a major, he'd been responsible for his men, but now he only wanted to be responsible for himself.

What he hadn't figured on was winding up in Texas without much money to his name. Most of his meager supply lay in the center of the table before him. He had always been a good card player and he had hoped to double his funds to see himself home.

The man to Cale's right leaned forward and tossed a bill onto the pot. "I'll call you, gentlemen. I figure my pair of eights is worth something."

Without a second look at his hole cards, Cale regarded the aces in front of him on the table before matching the gentleman's bet.

"I call," Cale said, tossing money onto the pot.

The one remaining player did the same.

With a slight curl of his lip, Slocum touched his revealed seven and nine. "I'll take you on." His eyes locked with Cale's.

Cale read the challenge. Instinct warned him that the rancher was planning something. But what? He'd be patient and let Slocum make the first move.

Across the crowded room, Brad Alexander observed the poker game. He leaned nonchalantly against the edge of the bar, sipping his beer.

Watching the rancher deal himself another card from the bottom of the deck, Brad curiously eyed the man sitting across from the weasel.

He wore mostly black: dusty black boots, adorned by silver; a black leather belt topping black trousers. His blue shirt contrasted with the rest of his garb. A darker blue bandanna hung loosely around his neck, and a black Stetson rode down upon his brow.

But it was the stranger's gun belt which held Brad's attention. Slung low across his hips, the belt nestled a Union army–issue revolver. A returning soldier passing through Dallas like himself. A Yankee among a hornet's nest of Rebs. The stranger would need help to leave—alive.

Brad smiled and took another sip. Yep, this evening was going to be real interesting all right.

He strolled to the table, beer mug in hand. "Mind if I watch?"

Cale looked up from his cards. The speaker appeared to be in his early forties, his face lined and his hair graying at the temples. He had the look of a man who had been in the war. Cale recognized the haunted glaze in his eyes—eyes that had seen their fair share of dying and destruction.

"No objections," Cale said.

The man sipped his beer, returning Cale's regard over the rim of the mug. He wiped his mouth on the sleeve of his shirt. "The name's Brad Alexander."

Cale inclined his head in answer, his eyes never leaving Slocum.

Slocum ignored the newcomer and turned his hand over, revealing aces and kings. Laughing, he raked in the pile of money.

Cale gritted his teeth.

Another hand was dealt.

"Well, what's it gonna be, boys?" Slocum asked.

One of the other men put down his cards. "I'm out. This is getting too rich for me."

Cale accepted Slocum's dare. "I'll see you." He tossed a dollar onto the pile.

"Let's just see where this ends." Confrontation echoed through the rancher's statement.

Slocum laughed as the others folded, tossing their cards onto the table. Everyone conceded, except Cale.

"I figure your luck just changed," Cale drawled.

"I don't think so, friend," Slocum responded, looking very pleased with himself.

Slocum dragged the final card he'd dealt himself to the table's edge to steal a look. He checked his cards close to his chest and gazed about the silent group of men.

Obvious satisfaction as to the likely outcome of this game caused the rancher's cheeks to warm. He tossed more bills onto the pile. "It's up to you."

Outwardly, Cale appeared calm. Inside, his guts twisted. His trained eye had caught Slocum's movement from the bottom of the deck again. He didn't enjoy gunplay, but if he were backed into a corner, he'd come out fighting. And he knew how this one would end. He wasn't leaving the saloon without his rightful money.

A carefully schooled expression hid Cale's anger.

Cale answered the bet with more money. "Yeah, I guess it is," he replied in a detached manner. "Let's get on with it. I want to see what you've got."

Slocum laid down his cards. "Aces high."

Cale tossed down his cards. "I can't beat that."

He removed his hat and ran his fingers through his shoulder-length black hair. He readjusted his hat. Indifferently, he rose to his full height of six feet two inches and straightened his broad shoulders.

"At least, I can't beat that without cheating." His blue eyes never left the man across from him.

Amid crashing chairs and scattering glasses, the other two men scrambled away from the two adversaries.

Slocum stopped raking in the money. He curled his hands into fists atop the table. "I must have heard you wrong."

The entire saloon went silent. No one moved.

Tension flashed across the room like brushfire.

"No, you heard right. You've been dealing cards from the bottom for most of the night," Cale said in a voice level with conviction.

Red-faced, the rancher boomed, "I'll be damned if some drifter is going to call me a cheat. You'll apologize, or me and the boys will see you leave here feet first." His eyes cut to one side where some of his cowboys lounged against the bar.

"That might be, but I'll take you with me." Cale's hand rested on the butt of his revolver. "The only way I'm going is with my money."

The rancher slowly stood, hooking his jacket behind the top of his holster. "Then, by God, you won't leave at all."

Out of the corner of his eye, Cale saw movement.

"I don't believe this is a fair fight," came Alexander's voice. "Looks to me like the odds are stacked."

"Just who the hell do you think you are interfering in my business?" Slocum asked.

"Bein' in the Union army has made me a bit touchy toward unfairness. I guess war does that to you."

"Stay out of this, boy. It ain't your affair," Slocum said.

"I'm gonna make it my business. I've been watching you and you've been stacking this game in your favor for the last hour." His voice hardened. "Why don't you just admit your mistake and I'm sure my friend here will forget the whole thing. Providing he gets his money, that is."

Slocum's neck veins protruded. "I said stay out of this."

Alexander shrugged, all the while settling his hand on his own weapon. "Better odds, two against seven."

"The name's Breland," Cale said out of the side of his mouth.

The rancher sensed a shift in the momentum. "Then you'll be dead like your friend," he said to Brad.

"That's a chance I'm willing to take," Alexander replied smoothly.

Sweat broke out across the rancher's forehead. "Both of you can meet your maker."

"If the devil doesn't get you first," Cale growled.

Within the span of a heartbeat, Cale and Slocum locked gazes.

Slocum went for his weapon.

Cale drew down on the rancher.

There was an explosion of sound. Smoke cleared. Slocum smiled at Cale, then his brow wrinkled. Slowly shock spread across the rancher's face as he clutched his chest with his left hand. His right hand released his gun, sending it clattering to the floor.

"I never figured you to be that fast," Slocum said in bewilderment.

Then Slocum pitched forward, face down in the sawdust, his body twitching in the throes of death.

From the corner of his eye, Cale saw movement. He dropped to one knee and dispatched one of the rancher's hired hands before the man's gun cleared leather.

From the direction of the bar, several bullets whizzed by his head.

Cale sought cover and joined Alexander behind an overturned table.

"Damn, Breland. . . . You're either one brave bastard . . . or the craziest man I've ever seen," Alexander groaned.

In front of them, four of Slocum's hired hands had holed up behind the bar and were squeezing off shots.

Alexander gestured with his head. "You cover me," he said. Then he rolled onto his stomach to one side of the table and fired. A piece of lead slammed into his arm, shattering his elbow. He slumped to his knees in agony, blood covering his arm and clothes. He briefly looked at Cale before his eyes rolled back in his head and he lost consciousness.

At that moment, Cale made his move. His pistol gleamed in the lantern light, and again it spat deafening fire and smoke. A thud was heard as a second cowboy hit the floor.

An unnatural silence descended.

"Don't shoot. This ain't our fight," came a voice from behind the bar.

Four cowboys rose from their sheltered spot. Pitching their guns away from them, they stood, muttering and cursing under their breaths.

"You'll be sorry you murdered Mr. Slocum," one of the hands said, his voice ringing in the oppressive silence.

With narrowed eyes, Cale watched them back out of the saloon slowly, taking their fallen comrades and their dead boss with them. He made sure they got on their horses and rode out of town before he turned his attention to the man beside him.

He knelt beside Alexander and gently rolled him onto his back. Cale lowered his head close to Alexander's face as he listened for breathing.

Cale's mouth slashed downward. Alexander was alive. But he was losing a great deal of blood. Cale looked up as a shadow crossed him.

A redheaded woman stood above him, concern mirrored in her eyes. When she got a good look at Alexander's face, she paled beneath her artfully applied makeup and her voice caught in her throat. "Take him upstairs to my room."

Cale untied his bandanna and tried to staunch the blood gushing from Alexander's arm. "He needs a doctor. He's losing too much blood."

"I'll send one of the other girls for Doc Harrison." Her gaze fell to the hinged front doors. "Hurry."

"I reckon we haven't got much choice."

Cale bent and retrieved his money off the floor, stuffing it in his pants pocket. He took only what belonged to him and left the rest. He didn't want money bought with blood.

Then Cale hoisted Alexander across his broad shoulders. "I'll follow." He grunted, signaling with his head for the woman to go ahead.

As he carried Alexander up the stairs, Cale felt blood dampen his neck and back. He hoped the poor bastard didn't die before the doctor came.

The woman stopped at the second door and opened it. She hurriedly scooped clothes and other articles off the bed, tossing them into the center of the room.

"Put him here," she said, smoothing back the covers.

She fetched the washbasin, water pitcher, and a pair of scissors.

Cale did as he was told and backed away.

With deft fingers, the woman cut away Alexander's shirt. She began cleaning the wound.

"What's your name?" Cale asked.

"Maggie."

Just then Doc Harrison burst through the door, bag in hand. "What happened?" he asked the woman as he began working on his patient. "John Slocum's dead."

"A gunfight. Slocum got caught cheating."

The doctor kept working, but whistled through his teeth. "Tell that to his sons."

Cale observed the woman. He supposed the war hadn't robbed everyone of a spark of decency.

Cale pulled her to the side. "How is he?"

"Holding on. The shot cut an artery looks like."

"Can he hear us?"

"He won't come to for a long time. You'll be gone by then. You don't want to hang around too long because if Slocum's sons get wind of this soon enough, you won't make it out of town alive."

"Where can I take him?" Cale didn't voice his concern over Alexander.

"There's a place outside of town. I have friends. They'll take care of him. As soon as Doc Harrison is through, you need to get Brad out of here. Neither of you want Sheriff Harper to find you. Slocum owns half of this county, if you get my meaning."

"I do."

Two hours later, Doc Harrison had removed Alexander's arm from the elbow down and had wrapped the stub. Shortly after, Maggie acquired a buckboard for Cale and he was on his way.

As he rode out of town with Alexander, Cale regretted not thanking the woman from the saloon for all she'd done.

It wasn't the first regret he'd had since he'd ridden into Dallas.

Several days later, Cale found Brad resting, although the grimace on his face declared the repose far from comfortable. A tight smile formed on Cale's lips until he saw Brad's wound. Only a stump packed in white bandages, blood-red spots here and there, remained.

Remorse filled the pit of Cale's stomach. If he hadn't gotten into that argument with Slocum, none of this would have happened. It could have been him lying flat on his back. Damn. Cale's ill-used conscience caused his head to ache.

"Why're you looking so grim? I'm going to be fine. Doc says I won't be in this bed too long."

Cale sat in a nearby chair. He smiled at Brad to ease the brief flash of fear he saw in Brad's eyes.

"I reckon you'll be good as new before long."

Cale sensed Alexander's discomfort at his choice of words and watched him turn his eyes away.

"Look, Alexander, I'm sorry."

After a moment, Brad looked back at Cale. "Call me Brad."

"All right, Brad."

"A man's got nothing to do but think when he's on his back. And I've been doing plenty of it lately. I want you to go to my ranch with me."

It was Cale's turn to look uncomfortable. "How'd you come up with that?"

"I could use a friendly hand on Twin Creeks."

"I don't know. . . ."

"Where you from?" Brad asked.

"Wyoming."

"Have you got enough money to get back home?"

Brad's question hit a raw nerve, and Cale barked, "No, I damn well don't."

"Then you need a job. Come work for me on the Twin Creeks. When you've earned enough, you can go back to Wyoming."

Cale couldn't argue with logic, nor with the man who had saved his life. "All right. I'll give it a try."

After the last of the mourners had gone, Jared and Henry Slocum stayed behind, staring at their father's grave.

The taller of the two bent down and picked up

a single flower from atop the black dirt. Jared spoke to his younger brother. "Pa didn't deserve to be shot down like a dog." He snapped the flower stem in two.

Henry's jaw tensed, the muscles in his cheeks outlined clearly. "I spoke to Sheriff Harper and told him we wanted the man's name who did this. And quick."

Jared looked at his brother. "We'll give Harper a short spell. Then he'd better have some answers."

"Whoever murdered Pa didn't know who he was dealing with."

Jared crammed his hat atop his head and turned away, heading for his horse. "When I find the son of a bitch he's gonna know. My face is gonna be the last thing he sees before I send him to the devil."

Overhead, a diamondlike Big Dipper and its smaller companion shone brightly against a backdrop of black velvet. The June night air was warm and humid, and the breeze blew gently. In the distance, a horned owl hooted in the darkness.

A campfire, with its bright shades of orange, red, and yellow, tipped with blue, glowed against the black sky, illuminating two men who sat nearby. The ashes settled with a soft rush and the glowing warmth reached out to touch and warm the two travelers.

Cale stretched his long legs and leaned against the soft side of his upturned saddle to enjoy a cup of steaming coffee. As he sipped the strong, bitter brew, Cale regarded his traveling companion over the rim of the cup.

At first, it had seemed right to accept Brad's offer of work, but the closer they came to the ranch, the quieter and more apprehensive Brad grew. Something was wrong. And Brad wasn't talking.

Cale took another sip of coffee. Well, he'd give it a try, but if it didn't work, he'd be on his way. All he wanted was to earn enough money to get back to Wyoming and start his own spread. Life seemed simpler that way. And he was a man who didn't want complications.

Brad's words broke into Cale's thoughts.

"I'm not much on words myself, but, Breland, you've got me beat." Brad laughed.

"Haven't had much to say."

Brad poured himself a cup of coffee. "You haven't said two words all day."

Cale's brow drew down into a frown. "Just thinking."

"About us being two survivors of the war? Or going with me to Twin Creeks?"

"Going to your ranch."

"I wish you'd put any doubts out of your mind. I invited you, and my brother isn't going to have anything to say about it."

The way Brad said "my brother" made Cale even more uneasy. He had to be honest and express his misgivings. "Somehow, I doubt that. With the war over, he's probably got enough mouths to feed without another one. And me a blue belly."

Frustration soured Brad's voice. "Dammit. Don't make any judgments until you get there. Besides, what's really eating at you is the fact that you feel indebted to me for saving your life."

"Maybe."

"Don't be."

"Easy enough for you to say."

Brad laid a hand on the knob that had once

been his elbow. "I'm not holding you responsible for what happened. I'm only offering another soldier the chance to make enough money to get home on."

Cale shook his head. "I've never known a man to refuse to take no for an answer. You're as stubborn as a Missouri mule."

"I've been called worse." Brad laughed.

"I can understand why."

"Know me pretty well, do you? Wait 'til you meet my niece, Shay. You think I'm stubborn? You haven't seen nothing yet."

Cale groaned. "Heaven help me."

For the first time, genuine warmth came into Brad's voice and expression. "Believe me, you're going to need it."

"Sounds like the type of woman I always try to avoid."

"If Shay sets her mind to it, you won't be able to avoid her. But I don't think you've got much to worry about. Never known her to show much interest in men."

"What's the matter? She wear glasses and have buck teeth?"

Brad's mood changed to a solemn one. "No. As a matter of fact, she's probably too beautiful for her own good by now. She was fifteen when I left and a beauty then. No one takes a pretty girl seriously. They're not supposed to have brains, but Shay's far from stupid. Sneed is the problem. My brother has caused his own daughter to distrust men."

"That's quite a cynical view."

"Yeah, but you see, she saw her mother abused." Brad paused. "No need to raise a brow. Not physically beaten but made to feel she wasn't good enough. That's why Lela ran away. Couldn't take any more of my brother and his hurting ways."

"Aren't you worried about your niece?"

"Why do you think I'm anxious to get home? We should be there tomorrow, if traveling's good."

Cale had found that the present was hard enough to deal with. Tipping his hat over his eyes, he tried not to think of tomorrow.

With her gloved hands on her hips, Shay eyed the colt warily. "Look, you might as well give in, or it's going to be a long afternoon. For both of us."

The black defiantly tossed its head and pawed the paddock ground as if to say it had no intention of cooperating.

"Fine. Have it your way, but you're going to let me saddle you. I guess I'll have to do this the hard way," she muttered.

Tucking her thick red braid inside the back of her shirt and adjusting her cowboy hat, she stepped forward and grabbed the halter rope. "You need to remember who's boss here."

Shay pulled. The colt tugged back.

Shay widened her stance. The black planted its feet.

Shay gritted her teeth. The horse snorted and reared back, pulling on the rope.

Then Shay blinked, and the confrontation was over. She lay sprawled, face down, in the soft paddock earth.

Slowly, she rose, wiping the dirt from her eyes, nose, and mouth, and righted her hat.

"Of all the ornery, darn-fool things to do, you lunkhead. I ought to sell you."

The colt snorted, tossed its sleek head once more, and trotted to the far side of the corral.

Suddenly, Jasper, Shay's white cowdog, rounded the corner. He wagged his burr-tangled tail, sat and cocked his old bent ears in the black's direction.

Shay watched his movement with wary interest. "I've got enough trouble without you starting any." She waved an arm. "Get going."

The dog didn't budge.

Shay threw up her hands. "Now I've got two beasts that don't listen."

She eased past the dog to the colt and took the halter rope in hand. When she maneuvered around the old cowdog with the black in tow, Jasper nipped at the horse's rear fetlock.

A blur of white and black erupted around Shay. She was jerked off her feet and dragged helplessly like a rag doll halfway across the paddock. Dirt clogged her mouth and nose. She couldn't breathe or cry for help.

Suddenly, somewhere amid the snorting and barking, came a strange man's voice. "Christ, man! Let go!"

Her fingers, numb from gripping the rope, wouldn't comply with the harsh directive.

"I said let the hell go," the baritone voice thundered.

Friction from the rope heated her gloved hands as the hemp was jerked, then ripped, from her grasp.

Shay lay motionless, trying to catch her breath. Somehow, she rolled over, pushed her hat up, and looked at the sky. She blinked her eyes, trying to clear her vision.

Her widening green eyes met intense blue ones. Very intense. And disquieting. Within the span of a heartbeat, Shay felt as if she knew him, yet knew she couldn't.

Her first impression took the form of several disjointed words. Rough. Coarse. Masculine. Rays of sunshine streamed down on him from a cloudless sky and cast his figure in an intimidating silhouette.

His tight trousers clung to well-defined calves and thighs. Spurs were hooked to his dusty riding boots. His shirt, of sweat-stained, faded red homespun, hung carelessly open at the neck with a blue bandanna tied there. His face was partially shadowed by a wide-brimmed hat pulled low.

Despite the fact that trail dust covered him from his hat to his boots, despite the fact that his features were covered with several days' growth of beard and shadowed by his hat, and despite the fact that he gave her a typical male look of superiority, he was the most handsome man she had ever seen.

For one giddy instant, she wondered what he thought of her. And for an even wilder moment, she wished she looked more like a lady than one of the hired hands. Just as quickly as those musings entered her head, they left. What did she care what he thought—about her or anything else?

However, the stranger was far from speechless.

He put his hand beneath her shoulder blades and lifted her to a half-sitting position. "Of all the stupid things to do. You could have gotten yourself killed." He ran his hand up her leg. "Anything broke?" His hand traveled to her chest. "A rib?"

There his hand froze. On one of her small rounded breasts.

As if burned, he let go of her and shot to his feet. Her head fell back with a soft thud.

She used her elbows to push herself up. The look in his eyes told Shay that he'd had no idea she was a woman, but that didn't extinguish her kindling anger. No man had ever touched her in such a familiar way or treated her so rudely.

She lashed out in defense and mortification. "Excuse me, but I don't remember asking for your help, whoever the hell you are." She threw her hat off and pulled her braid from the back of her shirt.

The rigid set of his jaw betrayed his own irritation. "Next time, I'll let you break your damned neck."

"And I'd like to put a rope around yours for interfering. I could have managed."

The man's blue eyes, fanned by tiny wrinkles at each corner, narrowed. He chuckled, a low, humorless rumble from deep inside his chest. The sound was decidedly masculine, resonating through her person.

She didn't like his effect upon her or his insult. "Why don't y-you . . . just leave?"

Shay always stuttered when she became angry. She could never express herself around her father and she had learned to hide her emotions as a matter of survival—except she couldn't hide the unwanted habit of stuttering when she was mad.

"Temper, temper, miss. . . ."

To Shay, the way he drawled the last word sounded more like ridicule than a respectful address. She remained still and quickly made a mental inventory of herself. She certainly didn't look like any lady with her dirty pants and shirt, her smudged face, and her tangled hair. But that didn't excuse him.

Slowly, she got to her feet. She was going to relish putting this man with his impertinent ways in his place. "The name's Shay Alexander. And my father owns the ranch you're trespassing on."

His reaction didn't disappoint her. He straightened his broad shoulders and tipped his hat back, his sun-bronzed complexion paling slightly. His blue eyes seemed to pin her to the spot.

"Should've known," he drawled.

Now what was *that* supposed to mean? she wondered. Nevertheless, she drew herself to her full height of five feet ten inches. "That's what I said. Shay Alexander. But I didn't catch yours."

"Didn't give it."

"Look, tell me who you are or I'm going to have you thrown off the Twin Creeks faster than you can spit."

He gave her a devil-may-care grin. "You can try."

Shay had intended to show him who was in charge here, but she failed. The notion didn't do anything for her present state of mind. This man was a burr under her saddle.

"Mister, I'm not usually so disagreeable with strangers, but you're forcing me to make an exception."

He tugged the brim of his hat. "The name's Cale Breland, Miss Alexander."

Even the way he said her name made her mad. And that smirk lurking behind his eyes. Ooh! she fumed silently. Vile names twisted like snakes inside her brain, each slithering across the next.

Then everything flew out of her head as she caught sight of her uncle coming into the paddock. Her green eyes widened and her throat thickened, making it difficult for her to swallow. Briefly, her mind registered the missing arm, but her thoughts skipped across the waters of her memory.

Uncle Brad was home. The one person who loved her unconditionally. Nothing else mattered. Her practiced defense of coolness evaporated. Tears clouded her vision and she ran blindly toward him.

She threw herself on him, twining her arms about his neck. "Oh, Uncle Brad. I can't believe you're finally home." She kissed his cheek.

He hugged her with his good arm. "It's been a long time, Pumpkin," he whispered against her hair.

They reluctantly parted, each drinking in the sight of the other.

Tears freely spilled down Shay's cheeks. Her uncle meant more than life to her. God had given him safe journey and she was thankful.

"There were times when I wasn't sure I'd ever see you again." Her voice caught with emotion.

He wiped his eyes with his sleeve. "There were times when I wasn't sure I'd ever make it home."

Her gaze went to the stub of his left arm. "How?" The single word drifted hauntingly on the breeze, conveying all her heartfelt grief.

"I'll tell you about it later. I don't want to spoil my homecoming. Have you met my friend from Wyoming, Cale Breland?"

Shay turned and looked in the direction of the

paddock. "Yes, I've already had the pleasure." Her voice conveyed all the sweetness of a persimmon.

Chuckling, Brad draped his arm across Shay's shoulders and pulled her along. "I invited him to Twin Creeks. He needs the work."

"Just what I need," Shay groused.

"What was that?"

"Oh, nothing. You always were softhearted, Uncle Brad. I'm surprised you didn't bring home half the Union army."

"I don't think Sneed would have approved of that," he muttered.

Shay felt her uncle tense beside her, but she chose not to say anything. Uncle Brad and her father would come face-to-face soon enough.

"Shay tells me you two have already met," Brad said to Cale, giving his niece's shoulder a squeeze.

Shay cut her eyes to Cale and gave him a go-to-hell look.

A lazy grin spread across Cale's whiskered face in response. "Yeah. I reckon we did at that."

"I know you'll be wanting a bath and a shave, Cale." Brad looked at his niece. "Shay, why don't you show Cale to the bunkhouse? I'm going to the house."

Shay wanted to tell her uncle that she certainly didn't want to have anything to do with Cale Breland, but out of deference to his homecoming, she remained silent and merely nodded.

When Brad had walked out of hearing, Shay said between her teeth, "I don't have to be polite, but I'll do what Uncle Brad asked." She tossed her head in the direction of the bunkhouse, situated behind the barn. "C'mon. I'll show you where you can stow your stuff."

Cale picked up his saddle and roll and slung them over his shoulder.

With a stiff set to her frame, she walked in front of him. Dressed as she was in tight pants and a shirt tucked in at the waist, Shay inadvertently drew Cale's attention to the soft sway of her rounded hips and bottom and to the gentle swooshing of her long red braid down her slender back. Cale couldn't help but admire what he saw.

Despite his irritation with her behavior, he had never seen so intriguing a young woman. It wasn't her comely face and definitely not her sullen disposition that piqued his curiosity. Yet something about her held his attention.

They came to the weathered bunkhouse built of graying planks with a small porch and a single window near the door.

Shay knocked once before entering. "Cotton? Roper?" she called.

No one answered. She stepped inside, with Cale close behind her.

"Cotton, Roper, and the other hands must still be out riding fence." She glanced about. "You can take that one," she said, pointing to a vacant bunk.

Cale walked over and dropped his gear atop the bed. "Where could I find water to wash up?"

"Out back. There's a rain barrel with a basin on a bench next to it. The men do their washing and shaving there."

Shay felt itchy and wanted to leave. Being alone with Mr. Breland made her extremely uncomfortable. "The men will probably be back about sundown. Anything else you need to know, you can ask them." With that she walked out.

As she made her way to the main house, her

thoughts lingered on Cale Breland. Despite their set-to, something about this man kindled her interest. Although she thought him rash, he possessed some hidden quality which excited her. Perhaps in time she'd find out what, but for the present she'd steer clear of him as much as possible. Her life was muddled enough without some cowboy making it worse.

Chapter 2

Brad stood inside the hallway. Removing his hat, he took a deep breath and inhaled the scent of fresh-baked pies. His stomach growled. Aromatic fingers beckoned, each tickling his senses, pulling him along the corridor toward the back of the house.

It would be wonderful to have a slice of home-made pie and a cool glass of milk. Countless times during the war he had thought of those very things as he lay in innumerable ditches.

Thoughts of home got him through the war. It made his skin crawl just thinking about all he had endured, from vermin-infested clothing to dysentery. Being home was all that mattered.

His thoughts shifted to Lela's sister, Nettie. Her presence on the ranch, after Sneed drove his wife away, had been a downright blessing. A smile surfaced. How shocked she would be to see him again after all this time. He imagined her small mouth rounding into an O before she hugged him.

Brad stopped inside the kitchen door. Just as he had envisioned, Nettie stood at the table in the middle of the room, laboring over piecrust. She stopped and pushed a renegade strand of hair back into the bun she wore at the nape of her neck.

In the corner, the middle-aged cook, Sally, looked up from where she sat, peeling potatoes. Her eyes grew round before she broke out into a grin, her smooth black skin wreathed in happiness. She opened her mouth to speak.

Smiling, Brad silenced her with a finger to his lips. He crept closer to Nettie, intent on giving her the biggest bear hug she had ever had.

Within the space of a breath, he remembered his lost arm, but refused to allow the thought to spoil his homecoming. He crept forward, stopped, and seized the unsuspecting woman around her waist with his good arm.

Nettie screamed and whirled, dropping the rolling pin on the wooden table. Her mouth opened a split second later as recognition registered and she squealed her delight and hugged him.

"Merciful Lord, Brad. You're a sight for sore eyes," she said breathlessly, fingering the wisps of gray at his temples.

They hugged for a few moments longer, then they parted.

He held her hand at arm's length. "You're mighty pretty on the eyes yourself, Nettie. Haven't changed a bit."

"Still the liar," Nettie teased.

For the first time her gaze dropped to his left shoulder and followed its natural course downward to the stump of his elbow. Her gaze flew back to his face. "What happened?"

Brad attempted to brighten her mood with a smile. "I lost it in Dallas on my way home. But there'll be plenty of time for details later." He

pulled a chair over to the table and sat down.
"Ever since I set foot inside this house, my
mouth's been watering for some of that peach pie
I smell."

Sally came forward. "It sure is good to see you,
Mr. Brad. I'll fetch you a piece of that pie right
now." She went over to where two pies were cooling and cut Brad a generous slice.

Brad felt as if he had died and gone to heaven
as he dug into the treat. The ripe orchard peaches,
cooked in sugar and their own juices and wrapped
in golden, flaky cinnamon-sprinkled crust, tasted
wonderful. No one made a better pie than Nettie.

With sweet juice dripping down his whiskered
chin, he said, "Just as good as I remembered. You
don't know how often I've thought about this."

Tears misted Nettie's eyes. "Quit talking and
finish your pie."

Moments later, Brad pushed away from the table, feeling full and content. "I couldn't eat another bite."

Nettie picked up his empty plate and empty
milk glass. "By the looks of you, that's exactly
what you needed. You've lost weight."

He wiped the milk mustache from his upper lip.
"You spoiled me. After you, the Union army
couldn't compare."

Nettie's countenance turned serious. "When are
you going to see Sneed?"

Brad's own expression clouded. "I suppose now.
Might as well get it over with." He stood. "Where
is he?"

"Going over accounts in the library." Nettie
placed a hand on his arm. "I better warn you.
Since you left for the war, his drinking has grown

worse. Sometimes I don't know him at all. Be careful."

At Nettie's concern, Brad said, "If nothing else, the war taught me to look after myself. Sneed won't easily intimidate me."

Brad hoped that was the case as he made his way to the library. He stood in the open doorway and waited several minutes, but Sneed didn't look up.

He hadn't faced Sneed in five years. He knew their meeting wouldn't be easy, but he hadn't counted on it being so damned hard.

Brad stepped inside the richly adorned room unaffected by the war. "Is this any way to greet your long-lost brother?"

Sneed remained behind his desk, seemingly engrossed in the papers spread before him.

The clock on the fireplace mantel ticked away in the ensuing silence.

Brad took a chair in front of the large desk. "You can't ignore me. I know we've had our differences in the past, but I had hoped we could start over."

At this, Sneed glanced up, his teeth clenched. "Differences? Is that what you call it? I call it having a brother who turned traitor and fought for the Union while I broke my back trying to supply beef to the Confederacy."

Brad felt his own temper rising but fought to stem it. He didn't want a scene the first day back. "We both made choices," he said evenly.

Sneed wasn't appeased. His gaze slithered over Brad. "So you thought you could just waltz in here as if nothing happened?" He slammed the desk top with an open hand. "Well, you can't. As far as I'm concerned, I don't have a brother." Lowering his gaze, he scoffed, "And don't think because you lost your arm I'm going to feel sorry for you."

Brad's anger bubbled at his stupidity and wishful thinking. He had truly hoped they could be civil to one another, but plainly that wasn't going to happen.

"Sympathy is the last thing I want from you. And, like it or not, you do have a brother and I'm not going anywhere. This ranch is as much mine as it is yours. Pa saw to that, and there's nothing you can do about it." Brad stood and looked down at his brother. "It's me who feels sorry for you, Sneed, because you haven't changed one bit. If anything, you're harder than when I left."

He pivoted, took two steps, then turned again. "By the way, I brought someone with me. His name's Breland. I told him he could work at Twin Creeks a while."

Brad didn't waste a backward glance as he strode from the library.

Shay sat in the kitchen, perched on the back of a chair, eating an apple. Sally pulled two pans of corn bread from the oven.

"I can't believe Uncle Brad's home. It's like a dream come true," Shay said, crunching on her apple.

"It sure is wonderful," agreed Sally, setting the pans on the table nearby.

Shay eyed the corn bread and inhaled appreciatively. "Hmm. That smells good."

"Don't go asking for none 'til suppertime."

Shay looked innocently at her. "Now, would I do that?"

Sally chuckled. "You sure would. And don't be batting them eyes at me, Miss Shay."

"Oh, Sally. You don't let me get away with anything."

"I do my best." Sally went to the stove and stirred the pot of creamed peas. Drifting columns of steam wafted in the air, causing perspiration to dot her black skin. Rubbing her forehead against her shoulder, she wiped the moisture from her face without letting go of the wooden spoon.

Shay came to stand beside Sally and peered into the pot. "What else are we going to have tonight?"

"We's gonna have fried chicken, mashed potatoes and gravy, peas, okra, corn bread, and some of those peach pies your auntie baked."

"Can't wait."

"Miss Nettie tells me that Mr. Brad done brought somebody with him," said Sally, still attentive to her chore.

Shay's face darkened, and she moved to the door and lounged against the frame. She looked out across the yard toward the bunkhouse. "Yeah. A man by the name of Cale Breland."

"Where's he from?"

"Wyoming is what Uncle Brad said. For the life of me, I can't figure why he didn't head straight back."

"Men gets the traveling lust."

Shay frowned. "What do you mean?"

"They just ups and leave. They can't stay in one place long. It's like they got a fierce burning in their soul to wander."

"You mean they never put down roots?"

"Something like that."

"Well, I don't like him," Shay said impulsively.

"What's he done to you?"

What had he done to her? Shay wondered.

He was rude.

He was bold.

He was . . . handsome.

"There's just something about him that I don't care for," Shay responded heatedly, annoyed with herself for finding him attractive. Annoyed with herself for thinking of him at all.

Sally laughed knowingly. "Sounds to me like you're hiding from yourself, but that's okay. You don't have to tell me nothing."

Shay didn't know why, but she felt jittery. She pushed off the doorjamb. "Sally, I want you to use your sight."

"Now, Miss Shay, what'd I tell you about that?"

Shay gazed directly into Sally's eyes. "Please?"

Sally put down the spoon and wiped her hands on her apron tail. "All right. But then you leave me alone so's I can get this cooking done. Your pa's gonna skin me alive if I don't have supper ready on time." She walked to the table, wiped a spot clean with a rag, and motioned with her hand. "Go ahead."

Shay spit on the indicated spot.

"What'd you want to know?" asked Sally.

"Why do I feel so restless?"

Sally intently studied the spittle. Seconds passed. Her pleasant expression changed by degrees into a concerned look.

Glancing from Sally's face to the table, Shay asked, "What is it? What do you see?"

"There are a lot of changes coming for you."

Goose bumps cropped out across Shay's skin. "What?"

"I can't say for sure, but your life is gonna be

different. Different from anything you've ever known," Sally answered slowly. "You're gonna give up what you love for something you'll love more."

Sally's tone troubled Shay. "What do you mean?"

"Everything will be turned upside down. You'll be fearful of change, but only because you don't understand what's ahead of you. You've got to learn to be brave and walk that unknown road. You'll know what to do when it's time." Sally wiped away the spittle with the tail of her apron and returned to her work. "Don't ask me any more 'cuz I can't tell you, Miss Shay. The spirits don't want you to know everything."

"Why?"

"You ask too many questions, Miss Shay. A body's not supposed to know everything about their future. Only what they need to know at certain times."

Shay went to the door and gazed out. Inside, she felt a strange combination of excitement and dread. What did Sally's vision mean?

The sun rode low in the sky, casting long shadows across the yard, casting shadows across her spirit. Shay didn't want her father to ruin her uncle's homecoming, but she sensed things would never be right between them. They hadn't been for as long as Shay could remember. No one would ever talk to her about the trouble between the brothers. All she knew was it had something to do with her mother, Lela.

Sally's voice behind her disrupted Shay's thoughts. "I want you to take this soap to the bunkhouse. The men ran out yesterday. They'll be coming in and wanting to wash up."

"Do I have to?" Shay asked, not wanting to see Cale Breland.

"It's because of you I'm behind on my cooking." Sally handed Shay a big bar of lye soap and gave her a shove out the door. "Now get going."

Shay drew out her steps. The one time she'd come in contact with Breland had been nothing but trouble. She didn't figure this time to be any different. Something about that man rankled her and at the same time intrigued her. Whatever it was made her jumpy.

Then an idea came to her. She'd slip around back and leave the soap on the bench by the rain barrel. A smile came to her lips. She didn't have to see Cale Breland at all!

Shay walked around the corner of the bunk-house, intent on leaving the soap and quickly heading back to the main house, when she came up short.

There at the washstand stood Cale Breland, shirtless, with a razor in one hand, lather covering part of his face, and a towel tossed over his shoulder.

With each pass of the razor, his corded arm muscles rippled beneath his skin and the breadth of his shoulders bespoke inherent strength. His damp hair touched the top of his shoulders and droplets of water trickled down his chest.

His rib cage arched above the flat plane of his stomach. Highlighted by the fading sun, his skin was golden from his back to his smooth chest.

All she could do was stare. With difficulty, she shifted her gaze. It swept across his black hair, across his lean, rugged features, past his straight nose and strong jaw, settling on his firm mouth. And there it remained.

Shay had no idea how much time had passed before she managed to give herself a mental shake. What the blue blazes was wrong with her standing here gawking at the man? Or worse yet, wanting to touch him? Her stomach tightened at the idea of running her hands across those smooth, tanned muscles.

Cale wiped the lingering suds from his face and tossed the towel onto the bench. "Can I do something for you, Miss Alexander?"

His tone implied something Shay couldn't quite grasp. "I—I," she began.

Cale grinned.

Damn, she was stuttering! She gritted her teeth. "I brought soap."

His eyes danced with amusement. "I had my own."

"I—I mean Sally sent me." She put the bar beside the towel.

He picked up a clean blue shirt and slipped his arms into the sleeves. "Who's Sally?"

"Our cook."

"I see."

Damn, again! This was going from bad to worse. Every time she opened her mouth, she sounded childish. He probably thought she didn't have a brain in her head.

Just leave, Shay told herself.

"I should go," she said lamely, but she couldn't make her feet move.

"I reckon you should," Cale replied, his eyes traveling from her head to her toes.

Trapped by his bold stare, it felt like an eternity before Shay was able to move. Finally, she spun on her heel and walked away. His laughter followed her.

* * *

Cale gathered his shaving things. Shay Alexander was certainly interesting in more ways than one. He couldn't put his finger on it, but there was something about her that he found appealing. Some part of him, on some level, was drawn to her.

Cale didn't take the time to analyze his feelings, but instead went inside the bunkhouse.

He had just cleared his gear away when two men walked in.

They joked with each other until they caught sight of him. They stopped in their tracks and looked at each other, then back to Cale.

One of them, a man in his late twenties, came forward. He pushed his hat back, revealing sandy blond hair. He stared at Cale with intense brown eyes. "Who the hell are you?"

Cale took several steps forward and extended his hand. "The name's Breland. Brad Alexander hired me. You might tell me who you are."

When no gesture was made to return the proposed handshake Cale lowered his arm. Trouble's coming, he thought to himself.

"I'm Cotton, the foreman on Twin Creeks, and this here's Roper." The first man indicated the second, a tall, thin man who appeared to be approximately the same age as the foreman.

"Where you from?" Cotton asked.

"Wyoming."

"Wyoming? What're you doing here?" Cotton's expression turned thoughtful. "Did you fight in the war?"

"I fought for the Union, if that's what you mean," Cale said, wary of the direction this conversation was taking.

"A stinking blue belly." Cotton's countenance hardened, along with his voice.

"You fight for the Confederacy?" Cale demanded in return.

"Nope."

"Then the way I figure it, you have nothing to say about anyone who fought in the war regardless of which side he chose."

The veins alongside the younger man's neck stood out. "You got gumption talking to me like that."

"Look, Brad Alexander hired me. So we're going to be working together for a while. I don't want any trouble. Why don't we just stay out of each other's way as much as possible?"

"Fact is, Brad Alexander ain't here." Cotton moved closer to Cale. "That means you're a liar."

Cale's temper flared, but he struggled to control it. He'd give these two bumpkins the benefit of the doubt since they obviously didn't know Brad was home.

Yet he intended to set them straight. "You're wrong on that count; I arrived with him this afternoon. But if you insist on calling me a liar, then I reckon I've no choice but to prove you wrong."

Roper moved forward. "Nobody challenges us."

The three men squared off.

Cale flexed and unflexed his hands, itching to throw the first punch, but he refrained. He instinctively didn't like these two, but he had to work with them. He'd let them throw the first one.

At that moment the door opened and in walked Brad.

Cotton and Roper both turned.

"Brad, didn't know you were back." Cotton's voice registered surprise.

"Sorry to disappoint you, but I made it home," Brad returned. "Well, Cotton, Roper, I see you've met the new man, Cale Breland."

They backed away, but Cale noted the look in their eyes and knew they meant to finish this later. That was fine with him.

"When did you get here?" Cotton asked.

"This afternoon." Brad addressed the other man. "Roper, you and Cotton can show Cale what to do tomorrow."

"Yes, sir." Roper's voice was taut.

Brad turned to Cale. "If you have any questions or problems, let me know."

When Brad left, Cotton turned to Cale. "Don't think nothing's changed just 'cause you're on friendly terms with the boss. You're still a Yankee lover."

His stay at Twin Creeks might be shorter than he'd figured, Cale thought to himself. Or seem longer. He didn't know which.

The following morning a cry shattered the calm. "Miss Shay! Come quick!"

Shay whipped her head around, her mane of red hair settling about her shoulders like a fiery cloak. She rose from the wooden table. "What is it?"

Her green eyes grew round with alarm as Sally burst into the kitchen and halted inches from her. They stood toe to toe.

Sally gasped, gesturing with her arms and hands. "Hurry, Miss Shay. Your pa is gonna whip Jerome 'cause he done took and et one of your pa's chickens without asken'." She tugged on

Shay's rolled-up sleeve. "Hurry. Your pa done gone and got hisself a buggy whip and I'm afraid he's gonna skin Jerome alive."

"Dear Lord," Shay breathed, and dropped her half-eaten biscuit to race after Sally out of the kitchen and across the yard toward the barn.

Shay ran so hard that she developed a stitch in her side, but she ignored the pain and pressed on. She had to reach her father. She just prayed she was in time.

Inside the barn, the smells of hay, manure, and horse sweat permeated the air. Along with fear. And hatred. The look on her father's mottled, twisted face as he stood before a stall and cornered Jerome made her insides grow cold. Two ranch hands stood farther back, watching.

Shay couldn't help but cry out when her father raised his arm, whip positioned above his head, and prepared to strike. "Papa! Don't!"

She quickly formulated a lie. Anything to save Jerome. She didn't want murder added to her father's list of sins. "I told Jerome he could have the hen," she said in a raspy rush of words, her breath a hard knot in her throat.

Sneed Alexander froze. He cut his gaze toward his only child, his eyes narrowing. Shay had never seen such fury. Black fury.

Out of the side of his mouth, he snarled, "Oh, you did, did you? By whose authority, might I ask?"

"I'm sorry. I should have asked. I just didn't think."

Sneed glanced at the men behind him. He threw the whip down and advanced with menacing steps toward his daughter. "I take it you deliber-

ately chose to ignore my orders. No darkie is to
have extra food. I give them enough as it is."

"I said I didn't think."

He stopped inches from her. The whiskey on his
breath caused her skin to crawl. "So you didn't
think. I didn't know I'd raised such a simple-
minded girl."

Shay had seen that expression before, and it
boded ill for her. Yet she couldn't back down now,
not when a man's life was at stake—even if it
meant enduring the consequences of her father's
wrath.

Giving her father a pleading look, Shay hooked
her arm with his and tugged. "Let's go into the
house and we'll talk about this. I'm the one who
made the mistake."

Sneed jerked out of her grasp. He took a deep
rumbling breath and fixed her with an icy glare.
"No child of mine interferes with my punishing
one of the darkies, no matter who's to blame."

He lifted his hand, and Shay's eyes widened
momentarily before her father delivered the blow.
Her lithe body swayed and her head snapped to
the side.

Her cheek felt on fire, and she laid trembling
fingers to her burning skin. Tears welled in her
eyes, making it difficult to see, but she fought
them back. This was not the sober, gentle man she
loved, but the drinking, hard man she despised.

Not a soul moved or spoke. All eyes were
trained on father and daughter. The atmosphere
in the barn grew heavy and charged, moist with
hostility, like a thunderstorm about to burst.
One ranch hand nudged the other in the ribs
and the two men nervously shifted toward the

barn door, obviously in haste to make their exit.

Sneed reached out and grabbed Shay by the upper arm, twisting her around to face the hired hands. "No one defies me. Not even this conniving wench who calls herself my daughter," he said to the men. "And you can tell that to anyone in doubt."

Sneed thrust Shay ahead of him and out of the barn.

Ominous silence pulsated in the room like a living, sinister presence, stretching Nettie's nerves taut. She knew why she had been summoned to the study to stand before her brother-in-law. She recognized the gathering winds of fury about to be unleashed upon her.

And her absent niece. What had Shay done this time to warrant her father's displeasure? But then again, Sneed's dissatisfaction over his daughter's activities was an ever-increasing occurrence. Especially when he drank.

Nettie regarded Sneed's austere countenance as he glowered at her from where he stood behind the ornately carved desk, looking every bit the intimidating Texas rancher. His mouth was a thin line chiseled in a face of stone and his large hand was white on the chair's back. She offered a quick prayer that he would listen to reason; yet, he seldom did. Many times she had seen the mark of his irritation upon her niece's cheek.

Nettie clasped her slender hands in front of her and steeled herself for the fray. She thanked God Brad was sleeping upstairs. If he knew what was about to take place there would most probably be

murder committed this day. No one loved Shay
like Brad did.

Sneed's honed words sliced through the silence,
cutting into Nettie's thoughts. "I won't tolerate
Shay making a fool of me any longer."

Dismayed, Nettie took a step forward. "Tolerate?"

"Yes, tolerate. She's stuck her nose in my business for the last time."

"You're her father! Why can't you act like one?"

"I can't as long as she continues to be so defiant." His voice boomed, seemingly shaking the
paneled walls, and his meaty fist crashed down
upon the top of the desk.

"And what exactly did that sweet child do that
was so terrible?"

"She interfered with my punishing one of the
niggers. Those darkies have got to learn that just
because the war is over, they're not going to get
away with anything. They'll not cheat me of an
honest day's work. And to add insult to injury,
Shay sympathizes with the darkies."

"I hardly find Shay's actions so awful."

"You wouldn't." Sneed sniffed disapprovingly.
"Your niece has the misguided notion that the
blacks are our equals and worthy of friendship. It
galls me just to think of how she acts around
them. Why, she gives them extra food . . . clothes
. . . anything she thinks she can get away with.
There's no telling how much that child has cost
me over the last few years."

Nettie thrust her chin forward. "Why does it all
come down to a dollar figure with you? You judge
everything by money."

Sneed looked incredulous. "And why not?
Money talks."

"Decent folk don't listen to that kind of talk." Censure colored Nettie's voice.

"Hah! You and your pious ways. You're not going to stop me from treating my daughter, and my property, the way I see fit."

Nettie's own sense of justice came to the fore. "The war has been over for months now. You don't own those people anymore, Sneed."

"I paid good money for them, and I say they're still mine."

"You can't keep them here by force much longer. Someone's going to find out and do something. It's against the president's order."

"Lincoln was a fool—and worse, a Yankee. And no Yankee tells me how to run my affairs." Sneed all but shouted the last words.

"Still as pompous as ever."

"Practical."

Nettie's expression softened. "At least your daughter has a sense of right and wrong. Your beliefs go against the teachings of the Bible."

"You can judge me all you like, Nettie, but I know what's best for my daughter. She should be wearing frills and trying to catch a suitable husband instead of doing things best left to men."

Nettie threw her hands out in disgust. "Best left to men, is it? Women are not inferior creatures to be ordered about."

Sneed moved to the front of the desk and crossed his muscular arms on his broad chest. His green eyes stared at her from beneath heavy black brows. "We would be a might better off if they'd take orders instead of having their heads full of nonsense. Women are not, and never will be, as smart as men."

Nettie pushed graying strands of brunette hair back into the bun at the base of her neck, straightened her thin shoulders, and returned Sneed's direct regard. "Rubbish."

"Whatever you think of my views, Nettie, is of no concern to me. I have decided that Shay should marry. I want you to take her to town. It's high time she started wearing dresses instead of going around in pants. I want you to buy whatever she needs, but I want her looking like a proper young lady, not a cowhand."

"There's nothing wrong with the way she looks. It's not the clothes that make a person. It's what's inside that counts."

"No man will consider marrying her looking like she does."

"Marry? So she'll be off your hands?" Her full mouth twisted into a parody of a smile. "You're the one who's tried to make her into the son you always wanted. And now you condemn the child for being what you've made her. What a hypocrite you are, Sneed."

The dimple in the cleft of his chin deepened as he clenched his teeth. "I never intended her to be so rebellious, so headstrong—so unpredictable. She's not at all what a father wants in a marriageable daughter. I sometimes think she enjoys being at constant odds with me."

"So marriage is the answer?" Nettie nearly choked on the words.

"It's the best one I can think of."

Her green eyes narrowed and she gritted her teeth. "And who's the lucky man?"

"Cotton."

"Why him?"

"Because he's ambitious, with a good head on

his shoulders for the working of this ranch. When I'm gone he'll be more than capable of taking care of Twin Creeks. And he appears to be man enough to give me heirs."

"Is that all you can think of? Someone to run this ranch? What of your daughter's happiness? She's not a brood mare. What of love?"

Sneed's mouth twisted. "She'll learn to love him."

Nettie was beside herself. "You only want someone who is loyal to you and takes orders. That's it, isn't it, Sneed?"

"Yes."

"You can't do this! Not to your only daughter."

Sneed started for the door. "Spare me, Nettie. I doubt that she's my daughter."

"When will you give up this obsession, Sneed? You know she's yours, and not Brad's."

He stopped and turned slowly to face Nettie. "Don't talk to me about Brad."

She felt a small measure of satisfaction at rankling Sneed. "Why? Because he fought for what he believed in?"

Sneed's body grew rigid and seemed to sing with tension. "Because he's a damned traitor to his country and his family."

One corner of Nettie's mouth lifted. "Well, the Union won. Seems you've been on the losing side."

"I've built this ranch into the most prosperous one in central Texas."

"You've built it on the misery of others." Nettie's voice rose a degree.

"I don't call it misery when I've kept body and soul together in troubled times. Others haven't done so well," Sneed countered defensively.

"But they've still got their pride."

Sneed's expression soured. "Pride! Hah. Pride won't fill their bellies when they're empty, or keep them warm in winter when their clothes are threadbare."

A hint of sadness crept into her voice. "Misery is a terrible price to pay for a full stomach and warm clothes."

"I've no regrets. I did my part by supplying beef to the Confederacy."

Her tone hardened once more. "And got rich doing it."

"Don't change subjects on me. I intend to see Shay married. And soon."

"So the mighty Sneed Alexander has spoken, is that it? Have you no regard for your daughter's feelings?" Nettie walked to him and placed a placating hand on his forearm. "Don't make her marry a man she doesn't—or couldn't—love."

Sneed's gaze, hard and icy, paralyzed her. "You heard me, Nettie." He jerked his arm away and stalked out of the parlor, slamming the door in his wake.

Nettie trembled with anger. How dare the man shun his own daughter as if she had the plague!

Damn Sneed and his Scottish temper. And damn his dependence on the bottle. He'd never been the same since Lela had left, but then Lela hadn't been able to tolerate his weakness for liquor either. Drunk, he had beaten Lela, sometimes badly. No one knew when Sneed changed, but some inner demon had transformed him from a caring, sensitive man to the person he was now.

And surely, as there was a God in heaven, Sneed Alexander would pay. And pay dearly. For all his

wealth, losing Shay would make him a poor man
indeed.

She needed a breath of fresh air. At the window,
she spied Cale Breland, arms laden with firewood,
as he moved around the side of the house. How
much had he heard? she wondered.

Cale had heard plenty. He hadn't meant to
eavesdrop, but it had been impossible not to have
heard the voices raised in anger.

He swore beneath his breath. Anger radiated
from every inch of his trim, powerful frame.
Now he knew exactly why Brad had pushed
himself to get back home. How could Sneed Alexander treat any human being the way he
treated his daughter? The man probably handled
his horse better.

Shay sat on the edge of her bed, tracing the
stitching on a quilt square. Her mouth puckered
into a frown. Her father had always considered
blacks to be inferior, but Shay couldn't condone
his way of thinking.

Blacks were human beings, too. God never intended them to be someone's property—including
her father's. And God never intended for one human to mistreat another. That was something Shay
would fight against as long as she had breath in
her body, even if it meant fighting her own father.

Her finger outlined the wedding ring design
for the second time. She hadn't been close to her
father since she was a small child. For longer
than she cared to remember, he had acted as if
he couldn't stand the sight of his own daughter.

Shay gazed at her mother's picture on the

dresser. She remembered her mother's lovely green eyes, her curling red hair, and her tall, willowy frame. Her mother was a lady. Shay didn't feel she resembled her mother at all. Instead, Shay thought herself too tall and awkward to be graceful. Her feet were too big to be dainty and her hair was too riotous to be fashionable. Shay lifted a tentative hand to her still-smarting cheek. Pain throbbed across it. The marks from her father's hand were indelible in her brain. But she loved him, and would forgive him as she had so many times before.

A lot of their quarreling seemed to be her fault. After all, she couldn't stop from being herself any more than she could stop breathing. Why would God give women brains if they weren't supposed to use them?

Shay mentally listed her shortcomings: defiant, stubborn, and impulsive. Her father constantly argued her role on the ranch, but she only wanted to use her God-given gifts and intelligence. Was that too much to ask?

She knew the answer. It was too much to ask of her father. He seemed to thrive on his control over her. Time after time, he reminded her that she should be grateful for having money and all that it could buy. But what Shay wanted more than anything wasn't something money could buy. She wanted back the kind father she remembered from her early childhood and the love he was no longer capable of bestowing.

Shay released a quavering sigh. For all her twenty years, she had known only this ranch, and thoughts of leaving the Hill Country scared her. For better or worse, Twin Creeks provided all the security she knew. Life beyond these boundaries might be far more frightening. Yet, there were times when she would stare off into the northern sky and feel a melancholy pull toward an unknown place. She wondered if the emptiness within her would ever be filled.

She bit her lower lip. No, she'd probably never leave Twin Creeks, and would die an old maid unless her situation changed. What man wanted a tomboy for a wife? Besides, marriage, as Shay knew it, only resulted in pain. Her parents had been an example of such. No, she would never allow herself to become too close to a man. A relationship would lead only to hurt, and she'd been hurt enough already.

Shay brushed aside the tear trickling down the side of her face. Being a fighter, she hated self-pity in others and abhorred it in herself. She'd allow no one to soften her backbone. A Texan didn't know the meaning of defeat. Or retreat.

A knock intruded on her thoughts.

"Who is it?"

"Aunt Nettie. May I talk to you, Shay?" came the soft, lilting voice from behind the wooden panel.

Shay knew her father had talked to her aunt. Why else was Aunt Nettie's timing so in keeping with the day's events? Yes, Sneed Alexander had already made his displeasure known to her aunt. The only thing Shay wondered was what punishment her father had decided upon.

"Come in. The door's not locked."

Shay watched the door open slowly, revealing the wispy figure of her aunt in the opening, her bright yellow dress in stark contrast to her dour facial expression.

"That bad," Shay said matter-of-factly, but her

insides were far from calm. She'd never seen her aunt look so grim.

Nettie stepped into the room and sat beside Shay on the bed. "I'm afraid so." She took her niece's hand in her own. "He plans to marry you off."

Shay inhaled so quickly that she nearly choked. "He what?" she gasped.

"He's decided that the only way to handle you is to make you someone else's problem."

"Am I expected to wear fancy clothes and parade in front of the county's eligible bachelors?"

Nettie nodded. "Something like that. He's mentioned Cotton."

"What?" Shay sprang from the bed and started pacing. "I can't believe Papa's come to this!"

"Oh, I can. Your father doesn't know how to deal with you. So this is his solution."

"Well, if he thinks I'm going to lie down and take this, he's got another thing coming. Cotton indeed. He's too stuck on himself to suit me, besides fancying himself a ladies' man. I've heard the other hands talk."

"Your father's beyond that. He's convinced he should have done this long ago. He believes all you need is a strong man to put his spurs to you and make you settle down."

Furious, Shay thought she would scream. "Well, I'm not some mare to be put to bridle. I won't have it. Do you hear me, Aunt Nettie, I won't have it! I'm not a child anymore."

But that's how Shay felt—like an unwanted and unloved child. She tried desperately to mask the anguish she felt beneath the surface of her anger. She hadn't thought her father could hurt her any more than he already had, but she had been wrong.

Shay's chest tightened with emotion. "I've allowed his drinking and his anger to control me for too long. I've learned when to speak and when not to for fear of making Papa mad. I try to stay out of his way when he's in one of his moods because if I don't he'll take it out on me."

Shay drew a ragged breath. "But this is too much to ask of me. I'm not willing to sacrifice my life to a loveless marriage. I want more than that. I've always been afraid of leaving Twin Creeks because it's all I've ever known. But whenever I have talked of leaving, he throws my financial dependence on him in my face. I don't know how many times he's told me that I couldn't make it on my own, that I couldn't find a job to support myself."

Shay's voice dropped to a whisper. "But I'm beginning to think that nothing could be worse than this. I've almost given up hope that Papa will ever change. I love him, but I have my own life to live. I'm not going to end up like Mama."

"You're going to have to keep a cool head until an answer presents itself, Shay. Something will come up. Be patient a little while longer."

"I'll wait, Aunt Nettie, but not until it becomes too late."

"Your father is a foolish man who is throwing away happiness with both hands. He can't see the treasure he has in you."

A wistfulness stole into Shay's voice. "I'm glad to know that someone has faith in me as a human being."

"A great deal of faith, honey. You're the only

completely honest person I know. Don't ever change."

Wistfulness transformed into determination. "It's a little late for that."

Nettie's gaze reflected her misgivings, but she spoke reassuringly. "I know I can't change your mind, but I'll support you in whatever you decide. Just consider what you're doing carefully, Shay. I don't want to see you hurt any more than you already have been."

Shay hugged her aunt. "You're a treasure, Aunt Nettie. And I love you."

Moving onto the bunkhouse porch, the two cowboys looked to the main house.

Cotton reached in his trouser pocket and pulled out a plug of tobacco. He bit off a hunk.

"I don't hold with strangers," he said, shifting the wad in his mouth. "And I don't hold with people with fancy airs getting themselves invited to supper at the big house."

Roper regarded his partner. "How come ya let him talk to ya the way he did? Never knew ya to take no guff off anybody."

"Don't you never mind. What was I supposed to do with Brad coming in and all?" Cotton's eyes narrowed. "I plan on taking care of that fella in my own good time."

"What ya gonna do?" Roper asked.

Cotton smirked. "Don't rightly know just yet, but I'm gonna make sure he remembers me. Things are fixin' to change around here and mighty fast."

"What d'ya mean?"

"Something I've been working real hard at for

the past two years. Looks like I'm gonna get what I want after all."

Roper looked puzzled. "You're already foreman. What else ya want?"

"I want to own this place someday. And the boss has just made that possible."

"You've lost me."

Cotton spat a brown stream onto the ground beyond the wooden planks. "I've been offered the sweetest prize of all. The boss wants me to marry his daughter."

Roper's mouth dropped open. "You're joshing."

"Took me aside today and told me I was the son he never had and how he wants me to take good care of the ranch after he's gone. But before he goes, he'd like a grandson to carry on his name." Cotton grinned knowingly. "There's nothing I'd like better than to ride that filly. I've been wanting her for a long time."

Roper scraped the mud from one boot. "You're one lucky cowboy."

Cotton snorted derisively. "Luck's got nothing to do with it. Who do you think makes sure the boss has his whiskey when he wants it? When he can't think for himself, I help him a little is all. It was my idea about marrying his daughter. All I had to do was wait for the right time. He was ripe for the picking."

"So you get the ranch and a real looker in the bargain." Roper paused as if considering some great question. "But what if she says no?"

Cotton leaned his tall frame against the post. "She's no different than half the women in this county. Once she's had a sample of what I've got to offer, she'll want me, all right."

"Maybe, but I wouldn't want to be caught in her

drawers before the wedding. The boss would make short work of you."

"Shay's gonna come to me before it's all over with. I'm gonna make her want me—and real bad." Cotton grabbed himself. "This is gonna be easy now that I've got her papa's blessing."

Chapter 3

With her mouth screwed up, Shay looked at herself in the mirror. She gazed at the peach muslin dress, with its fitted waist, small puffed sleeves, and ribbon-trimmed neckline. Her waist-length hair was pulled back with a single matching ribbon.

God, how she hated dressing for supper! It was a rule of her father's that she come to supper dressed as a lady. Why couldn't she just be plain Shay, with no frills? But her wearing a dress wasn't worth incurring his wrath.

After one last look, Shay left her bedroom and walked down the hallway.

At the top of the stairs, she heard her father's voice raised in argument. "What do you mean you invited him to supper?"

"This house is as much mine as it is yours. I'll invite who I want to supper." Brad's voice held mild hostility.

Shay tiptoed down the stairs. Her stomach tightened. She remembered how she hated it when her father argued with her uncle. Their fighting tore her apart. It seemed all her hopes for a brighter future were dwindling rapidly.

"Since when do the hired hands eat with family?" Sneed boomed.

"Lower your voice, Sneed. I won't have you embarrassing me or my friend."

"Friend, hah! Some drifter you picked up in Dallas, you mean."

When Shay reached the bottom stair, she glimpsed her father and uncle in the hallway.

"No, what I mean is the man who saved my life," Brad replied, his posture clearly evidencing his displeasure.

"Bah. Do what you want, but I don't have to talk to him." Her father's footsteps echoed on the wooden floor as he walked away.

Brad turned around and spied Shay. He came to her. "How long have you been there?"

"Long enough."

"I'm sorry you had to hear that."

"I don't care. I'm just glad you're home," Shay said, her face wreathed in smiles.

Brad hugged her. "You're a poor liar, Shay, but I love you anyway." He stepped back and looked at her. "My, you look pretty, Pumpkin."

Shay blushed and dropped her gaze. "I still don't like wearing dresses, but Papa insists."

"Yeah, I know." Brad's voice reflected his feelings. Then his tone brightened. "Someday, you're gonna like having a man tell you how beautiful you are."

Nettie came upon the two. "Are you two going to stand in the hall all night or are you going to join us in the parlor?"

Brad winked at his niece. "Coming." He draped his arm over Shay's slender shoulders.

They entered the drawing room. Lantern light bathed the room in soft, golden tones. The com-

fortable atmosphere made this one of Shay's favorite rooms. The interior reflected quiet shades of
green, blue, and gold. Floor-length, light green, tie-
back drapes dressed the windows. A fireplace
dominated the wall opposite the doorway. A white
Chippendale camelback sofa flanked it on the
right and in front sat a Queen Anne mahogany
game table. A Chippendale corner chair with cab-
riole legs faced the table. Two rose-colored wing
chairs with Chinese fretwork rims were placed directly opposite to the left of the grouping.

The furniture contrasted with life in the Texas
Hill Country, but her mother had imported each
piece from England, via Galveston. And Shay
loved each piece because her mother had loved it
all.

When Cale caught sight of Shay, something inside him clenched. He couldn't believe this was
the same young woman. She was beautiful. But
since when had he been attracted to hellcats?

Shay walked over to her father, who sat in a
chair near the fireplace. When she leaned over to
kiss his cheek, Cale nearly groaned aloud at the
sensual display of her breasts above the neckline
of her dress.

He felt himself harden. This damn well might be
the longest evening of his life, he thought.

Shay and Brad sat near Nettie. To the side sat
Sneed Alexander.

As the conversation flowed between her uncle
and Aunt Nettie, Shay's attention was repeatedly
drawn to the man from Wyoming.

When she didn't think he was looking, she
glanced at him. His clean clothes, closely shaved
jaw, and freshly washed hair presented him in a
different light.

Her cheeks grew warm. Oh, how she remembered the way he'd looked by the washstand. The feeling had left Shay shaken. She didn't like what this man did to her.

His mouth lifted in an amused smile.

Abruptly, Shay tore her gaze from him as she realized she had been staring. A second wave of heat washed over her.

Ooh, damn him! she thought. Why couldn't he just go away?

Sally appeared at the door. "Y'all best come on before the food gets cold."

Everyone moved into the dining room. It was no less attractively decorated, with blue drapes and green-and-blue carpet. A massive Queen Anne table dominated the center of the room.

A snowy white linen tablecloth adorned the large table and was set with delicate china and silverware. The centerpiece consisted of freshly cut red roses from the garden out back.

Sneed sat at the head of the table. He glared at his sister-in-law. "Nettie, why all the fuss?"

"I wanted things to look nice for Brad's homecoming," Nettie defended.

Sneed replied with a snort.

Brad regarded his brother. "Makes me feel good seeing the house like it used to be."

Shay felt the tension in the air and knew by the look on Uncle Brad's face that he referred to her mother and dared Sneed to say something in front of everyone.

A wistfulness stole over Shay. She missed her mother desperately.

When her father's gaze sliced over her, she carefully schooled her face to hide her emotions. She kept quiet.

Nettie waved her hand. "*Gentlemen*, please be seated." She said pointedly, "We don't want our guest to get the wrong idea about us." She glanced at Cale and smiled.

"Why hide the truth, Nettie?" Sneed asked, looking pleased with himself. "This fella's gonna find out fast enough that this family doesn't get along."

Nettie looked sharply at Sneed. "It would be nice if we could try and get along for one evening."

Brad seated Nettie at the opposite end of the table from Sneed, then seated his niece across the table from himself and Cale.

Sally promptly served the food.

During the course of the meal, Shay listened to her uncle and Cale talking.

Her uncle was an intelligent man, she thought proudly. He also was a sensitive, caring man, and she loved him with all her heart. He represented all the things her father didn't, and that hurt Shay greatly because her father had once been that same kind of man. She looked up. Her uncle's approving gaze warmed her before it returned to his friend.

"Where in Wyoming do you come from, Mr. Breland?" Nettie asked between bites.

"Jackson Hole," Cale replied.

"How was it you came to Texas?"

"Nettie, aren't you getting a bit personal?" Brad interjected.

Cale turned to him. "I don't mind. I figure if I'm going to be on Twin Creeks for a while, a person's got a right to know something about me." He directed his attention back to Nettie. "After the war was over, I just started traveling west, trying to get back to Wyoming. Ran out of money in Dallas."

Nettie sipped her wine. "What do you think of Texas so far?"

"It holds a man's attention."

Nettie's eyes were lit with interest. "What did you do before you left your home?"

"Worked on a cattle ranch."

Brad looked at Sneed, who had not spoken since the meal began. "See, he's suited for the job. We always need good hands on the spread," Brad said.

Sneed said nothing, but glared coldly at his brother.

"I'll only be staying long enough to earn money to get back home," Cale said, wiping his mouth with his napkin. "I've got plans for a spread of my own."

His deep voice resonated through Shay. She sipped her wine, willing herself to master her nervousness. He would soon be on his way. Somehow that thought had a disturbing effect upon her, although she didn't know why.

And if her reactions weren't bad enough, when she glanced at her father she saw his eyes flash with resentment at Breland.

For the first time, Sneed entered the conversation. "Tell me, Breland, did you take sides during the war?"

Cale was thoughtful. "I fought for the Union."

Sneed's next words hung over the group like a pall. "That figures if you teamed up with my brother. Should've known you were a blue belly, too. It's hard to stomach people who fight for the wrong cause." He gulped down a large portion of his wine.

"And what cause was that?" Brad baited, his annoyance clearly indicated by the hard set to his jaw.

Sneed clenched his hand beside his plate. "You know perfectly well what cause."

"The only cause you know, Sneed, is yourself," Brad replied.

Shay's fork froze near her mouth. She held her breath, waiting for the explosion.

Nettie must have sensed the impending outburst, for she came to her feet. "Please, not here. Not tonight." She looked imploringly at Brad, then Sneed.

Stress strained Shay's nerves. She had to do something. "Yes, Papa, please," she added, wanting to smooth the friction.

Sneed turned on his daughter. "You stay out of this! I'll not have you telling me how to act."

Shay flinched and dropped her gaze. She didn't want anyone to see the anger and hurt in her eyes.

Brad unshackled his outrage. "Don't talk to her as if she's a child. She was only trying to help."

"Keep your nose where it belongs."

"I won't let you treat Shay like you did Lela."

At this, Shay jerked up her head. She looked at her father.

Sneed's face turned red and the muscle in his jaw tensed. Shay thought he would leap across the table and strangle his brother. But instead he rose and tossed down his napkin. "To hell with you. I'm going to bed." He left the room.

Nettie looked sheepishly at Cale. "I'm sorry you had to witness that."

"No problem, Mrs. Grisham," Cale replied.

Brad glanced at Nettie, raising his eyebrows, then at Cale. "Why don't you take Shay outside on the front porch, Cale? I'd like to talk to Nettie in private."

Shay wanted to scream her refusal, but couldn't bring herself to tell her uncle no. She was embarrassed at having a stranger observe her family's discord.

She walked ahead of Cale to the front porch. There she chose the swing. Cale sat on the top step, his back against a post, looking out across the yard.

The night was typically warm for June. A gentle southerly breeze stirred the air and the wisps of hair brushing Shay's temples. Crickets made their nightly music in the bushes surrounding the house. Overhead, a full moon bathed the yard and the surrounding buildings in silver. Stars dusted the sky.

Neither spoke.

Sighing, Shay pushed off the railing with her foot and began to swing. With each swaying motion, tension left her body. This was her favorite place to sit in the evenings, swinging and thinking about nothing.

Cale plucked a twig from a nearby bush and chewed on the end. He glanced at Shay as she stared into the night. Her rocking motion pulled her into the shadows, then into the light. Her red hair appeared shot with silver. His fingers curled as he thought about running them through the silky strands.

He envisioned her green eyes—the color of spring grass. Eyes that made a man forget himself. But not this man.

He reckoned Shay Alexander was going to be trouble from the get go. In the first place, she was pleasing to the eye. How was a man supposed to go about his work with a woman like her around, knowing he couldn't touch her? And in the second place, her father had already made plans for her—plans which didn't include him. His thoughts turned to the foreman, Cotton. What a waste and a shame to saddle such a fetching piece of woman to a man like that. Yet he wanted to know more about her.

During supper, in an unguarded moment, Cale had glimpsed the specter of old pain in Miss Alexander's eyes. He had learned over the years that no human being was completely submissive. The war had more than emphasized the point. He wondered what untamed currents flowed within Miss Alexander.

Cale broke the silence. "You always lived on the Twin Creeks?"

The breeze carried Shay's voice to him. "I was born here."

"Ever wanted to leave?"

Shay sighed. "Oh, I suppose there are times when everyone would like to see the world."

"But what about you? Do you want to see the world?"

"I always wanted to travel. I've never been outside Texas."

"Why?"

"Papa said I wasn't old enough, and then the war broke out." She looked intently at him. "Why do you ask?"

"Must get lonely out here with only your aunt for company."

"You're wrong. Besides Aunt Nettie, there's Sally—"

"I mean someone young. Don't you miss having friends your age?"

Shay frowned. "Why are you asking so many questions?"

"Because I want to know more about you."

"There's no need for that."

"No need for what?"

"I know what you're doing. You're being nice to me because of what happened in there. I don't want your pity."

"I'm not giving any."

She stiffened. Something about his probing questions excited and aggravated her at the same time. She didn't want him to know anything about her—and yet she did. She wasn't sure what she wanted from Cale Breland.

"You shouldn't ask so many personal questions."

Just how deep were Miss Alexander's traditional values buried? Unable to resist digging for the answer, Cale asked, "What do you care?"

"Because it's not polite. We don't know each other well enough," she snapped, annoyed with herself and him.

Cale laughed. "Funny, I could have sworn you weren't a person who stood on formality."

Shay responded to his laugh in kind. "You're right. I'm not."

"Do that again."

Shay cocked her head to the side. "What?"

"Laugh."

"Why?"

"I like the sound of it. You should do it more often."

"I would if I had more to laugh about," she said solemnly.

She was a different person when she let her guard down. Uninhibited, carefree. Cale wanted to know that person very much. "Why don't you want anyone close to you?"

Only the night chorus could be heard in the following minutes.

Cale wondered if she'd answered him honestly. Was she willing to allow another to glimpse inside her?

She chewed on her lip. "Because it means pain."

"Have you been hurt so much then?"

"It hurt me when my mother left. It hurts me because my father doesn't approve of my behavior." Her voice possessed a faint tremble. "It hurts me because my father and uncle don't get along."

For an unexplainable reason, Cale revealed a part of himself he had never shared with another person since he was a boy. "I know what you're going through. My father was a drunkard, too."

"I don't suppose it would do any good to deny it."

"No. I've seen it too many times."

Shay turned her face. "Don't," she whispered.

Cale gazed at her moon-bathed face as the swing moved forward. "Don't what?"

She looked around and returned his stare. "Be nice."

"Why?"

"Because I don't want to like you." There was a silent moment as her words faded into the night.

"You've got nothing to fear from me, only from yourself."

Shay stopped the swing, her features hidden in the shadows. "You're wrong. To a woman, you're a very dangerous man."

The hushed syllables of her words rolled across Cale like a gray, sullen rain cloud, drenching him in dark desire. His mind had conjured agonizing visions of her supple body ever since he'd glimpsed the sweet perfection of her breasts above the neckline of her dress. He had wanted her then. He wanted her now.

She set the swing back in motion. He looked again upon her pleasing face, soft with moonlight. She was so vulnerable, he thought. The realization that his attraction to Shay went beyond the physical brought him up short. This was leading to no good.

Cale stood. "If you'll excuse me, Miss Alexander, I'll turn in now."

Shay watched him walk to the bunkhouse. He moved with sensual grace for a man of his height and build.

She remembered when she had come across him shaving and had stared at him with fascination. He had regarded her in a removed, alarming sort of way. The way he looked at her made her intensely aware of herself as a woman—something Shay had suppressed for a long time.

She recalled the sound of his voice—low and compelling, and most decidedly masculine. Not having known a man like him before made it impossible for her to gauge her reaction to him. Just being near him was very disconcerting. He possessed qualities that made him as intensely virile as he was compellingly handsome.

Irresistible. . . .

Stop right there, Shay told herself. She wasn't a schoolgirl, but a grown woman capable of controlling her emotions. She had learned to hide her feelings very well these past years because of her father.

She shivered despite the muggy night. What had Sally said? Her world would change?

Shay went inside and upstairs.

Alone in her room, she undressed and donned her nightgown. She sat at her dresser and brushed her hair. With each stroke, her thoughts wandered to supper. Her throat constricted and her eyes suddenly stung. She gazed, her eyes watering, at her image in the mirror.

Her father was so unfair. Why couldn't he treat her like a beloved child instead of an unwanted orphan? He was always so quick to ridicule and taunt.

Her hopes had been to remain on Twin Creeks, to be an important part of his life. But those hopes were drying up like a calfless cow.

Shay laid her brush down and walked to the window, looking out across the moonlit landscape. A soft breeze wrapped around her. An intense feeling of wanted something just out of her reach assailed her. She instinctively knew the answer lay beyond, in the great unknown. Excitement coiled inside her. Soon she would find the courage to leave Twin Creeks and claim the life that awaited her.

She blew out the candle and crawled into bed. Pulling the covers up to her chin, she settled down into the bedding and eventually fell asleep.

The next morning Cale set about his task of cleaning out the stables.

He didn't mind physical labor. In fact, he welcomed the chance to exert himself. When he was busy, he didn't have time to think, and he didn't want to think about Shay Alexander anymore.

Last night, he'd lain awake, remembering how pretty Shay had looked. She tempted him with her natural beauty and uninhibited ways. She was like the Texas Hill Country, untamed and proud.

He had been glad she couldn't see his face clearly last night, or she would have seen the hunger in his eyes, and that would have been disastrous—for both of them.

No, she wasn't for him.

She had a home and family. He had no one and no place to call home.

Oh, he had plans for a place of his own, but those plans were only a dream right now. He had to have money first, and that was his reason for working on Twin Creeks.

Shay had loved ones—her aunt and uncle—who cared about her. Caring for anyone scared the hell out of him. He wasn't sure he could ever care about someone like that—not the permanent, until-death-do-you-part kind of love.

His mouth turned down. How well he remembered Janet and how she had stepped on his heart. He had been young and head over heels in love with her. And she had taken that love and thrown it in his face. He had vowed at the time that it wouldn't happen again. Love was for fools. He didn't intend to be one again.

No, Shay Alexander wasn't for him.

He reined in his thoughts. Why the hell did he think about her at all? He'd stay on the ranch long enough to make some money, then he'd be on his way, leaving Miss Shay Alexander as far behind as he could. But would he be able to forget her? Cale mentally shook himself and concentrated on his work.

Shortly, Cotton entered the barn.

"Well, I see our yeller belly found work suited for him." Cotton laughed. "Shoveling horseshit."

Cale didn't look up.

Cotton drew near. "I came to check on your work, Yankee lover."

Still, Cale refused to acknowledge the other man's presence. Cotton was spoiling for a fight, grasping for any reason to have him fired. Cale wasn't going to play into his hands. He was sick to death of small men trying to act big. He'd seen enough of it during the war.

Cotton produced tobacco makings and rolled a cigarette. Finished, he struck a match on the sole of his boot.

Holding the lighted match, Cotton said, "I'll be back later to make sure things are done right." He flicked the match into a pile of manure-filled straw at his feet. "Remember, I'm the foreman and what I say goes."

Cale scooped up the dirty hay and tossed it on the match . . . and Cotton's boots. "What you are is full of this."

Cotton drew back his fist. "I'll show ya."

Just then Shay entered the barn carrying a bridle. She approached her horse's stall, oblivious to the tension between the men.

Cotton dropped his hand and said out of the corner of his mouth, "This ain't finished between us." He approached Shay, tugging on his hat. "Morning, Miss Shay, can I help you saddle your horse?"

Shay turned to him. "No, thanks. I'll do it myself."

"I really think you ought to let me help you. We're going to be helping each other a lot in the future."

Shay turned on him. Her eyes burned with disapproval. "Don't go getting any ideas. I have no intentions of marrying you."

Cotton gave her a crooked smile. "That's not what your pa tells me. The way I figure it, he's already got things worked out."

"I've done fine without you in my life. I can manage a few more minutes. I'm sure there's more important things that need your attention. I suggest you get to them."

Cotton visibly bristled at the dismissal. He glanced from Shay to Breland, but said nothing further and walked out, leaving Shay and Cale alone.

Shay turned her thoughts to her horse. She tried to bridle her mare, but the Appaloosa kept tossing its head and moving about the stall.

"What's got into you today?" Shay said, sidling around the animal.

She made another attempt to grab the horse's mane, but missed. "Stand still or I'm gonna knock you between the eyes."

The Appaloosa looked at her as if to say, "No you wouldn't."

"You're right, I wouldn't, but I'd like to," Shay countered.

"Need a hand?" came a familiar voice from behind her.

"No, *thank you*," she said between gritted teeth. "If I can manage without Cotton, I can manage without you."

Cale shrugged and leaned against a pole near the stall. "Suit yourself."

"Don't you have chores to do?"

A slow grin spread across his tanned face. "Just finished up for now."

Shay redirected her attention to the Appaloosa.

She managed to slip the bridle on, only to have a strap break. "Damnation." Nothing was going right. And why did Breland have to keep staring at her like that?

Breathing deeply, she mentally counted to ten. She didn't know which made her madder, the cantankerous horse or the obstinate man.

She had handled horses all her life. Now, she'd be darned if this wasn't the second time since Cale Breland's arrival that something like this had happened.

Shay looked around for something to use instead of the broken bridle. Her gaze settled on a length of rope curled atop the feed box and she fetched it. She began making a series of half hitches in the rope, preparing a makeshift bridle.

Slowly, approaching the mare, Shay said, "You thought you were going to get out of this."

The Appaloosa tossed its dappled head and snorted.

Shay managed to slip the rope about the horse's head, but a knot slipped and the bridle slid off.

Cale pushed off the pole. "You're not using the right knot."

Frustrated, Shay dropped her hands and cocked her chin at him. "And I suppose you're going to show me how."

He laughed. "You never give an inch, do you?"

He was right, Shay thought. She couldn't help herself. Ever since his arrival, it seemed, she'd been on the defensive.

She managed to maintain a hold on good manners. "I'm sorry. I usually don't have so much trouble."

"No need to apologize. Just let me do my job." Breland moved inside the stall and took the piece of hemp from Shay. He made his own bridle and eased it over the horse's nose and ears.

He handed the rope end to Shay. Their hands touched and goose bumps broke out along Shay's arm. A powerful yearning took hold, clutching her insides. She stared at his handsome face, into his hypnotic blue eyes. There was danger of losing herself in those eyes. He wanted something, his eyes said so, but what?

She watched his gaze shift to her lips and linger there, making her extremely self-conscious, making her tingle all over. He was so tall and muscular, so alluringly handsome, so close. . . . Too close. For one wild moment, she thought he meant to kiss her. And shamelessly, Shay hoped he would.

Suddenly, horse hooves pounded up to the barn door. Shay moaned, a strange combination of relief and regret, for in that suspended moment she had hoped Cale *would* kiss her. And was afraid of what she would have done if he had.

Sneed Alexander dismounted and walked toward them. "What the hell are you doing?" His gaze slid from Cale to Shay.

Shay grew uneasy beneath his scrutiny. "Nothing, Papa. Mr. Breland was just helping me with my horse."

"Well, I'm not paying him to stand here and do nothing." He jerked his thumb over his shoulder, toward the entrance. "Walk my mount and cool it down."

Cale did as instructed, leaving Shay and her father.

"I don't want you keeping that man from his chores," Sneed said.

Shay felt guilty somehow for being caught alone with Breland. She averted her eyes. "Yes, Papa."

Taking her elbow, Sneed steered Shay toward the door. "Where were you going?"

"One of the brood mares was having a difficult time down in the bottom paddock. I was going to help."

"That's a man's work. Stay where you belong . . . out of the way!"

Shay temporarily forgot herself. "Why? I'm just as capable as any of the hands."

Sneed stopped and gave Shay a jerk. "Don't talk back to me. You get these foolish notions from your aunt. She shouldn't fill your head with rubbish."

"Since when is it rubbish to think and act for one's self?"

Sneed's eyes took on an inner glow. "Not another word, Shay."

Shay knew when to back down from her father. It was useless to argue when one of his moods came over him, which was most of the time.

She gently extricated herself from his grasp. "I'll go to the house and help Sally."

Shay hurried out of the barn, not wanting Cale Breland to witness her humiliation at the hands of her father.

Chapter 4

Brad watched Shay walk to the house. Sneed emerged from the barn a moment later. The scowls on both of their faces told Brad that something had happened.

His jaw tensed. He didn't approve of Sneed's treatment of Shay. Sneed had bullied her ever since Lela left. It was time it stopped. The past was dead and needed to be buried.

Intent on lightening the oppressive atmosphere, Brad approached his brother. "Been looking for you. Thought we'd go over the accounts."

"Later," came the gruff reply.

"All right," Brad said slowly. "I'll spend some time with Shay then."

"Leave her be."

Brad's temper rose. Sneed didn't own his daughter like a piece of livestock. "Why can't *you* leave Shay alone?"

Sneed made an attempt to shoulder past his brother. "It's none of your concern."

"That's where you're wrong," Brad said, stopping him with a hand on his arm.

"Get your hand off me, Brad. Now." Sneed's implication coiled like a deadly rattler.

Brad tensed, ready for a fist in his gut. "Why? You planning on punching me?"

"Maybe."

Brad removed his hand. "That's right, Sneed. You always resort to violence when things don't go your way."

"You may be my brother, but I don't owe you anything." Sneed's face reddened as if the words choked him.

"Except respect."

"You don't know the meaning of the word."

"I know more than you ever will."

"Why don't you just stay out of my way?" Sneed said.

"I can't when you mistreat Shay. I might have been gone for the last five years, but I'm home now. I worry about her."

"Why? Because she's yours?"

"You're talking crazy." Impatience peppered Brad's voice. "Lela was never unfaithful to you." He raked his fingers through his dark hair. "Lord knows, you gave her every reason to be. But she was a good woman and a loyal wife to you."

"Ha. All she did was lust after you."

"I treated her kindly. You never gave her any affection or encouragement."

"First, you tell me how to treat Shay. Now, you want to lecture me on how I handled my wife. You've gone far enough, Brad."

Brad's stomach churned with anger and frustration. "Dammit! You're not being fair to your daughter."

"Don't tell me how to deal with her. I've allowed Shay to run unsupervised long enough. Things are going to change. I've decided it's high time she got married."

"And how does Shay feel about that?"

"She has no say in the matter."

Brad gritted his teeth. "Oh, no, you don't. I'm not going to allow you to marry Shay off unless that's what she wants."

Sneed ignored his brother's challenge. "I've got work to do. Tomorrow we begin the head count on the cattle, or have you forgotten?" He walked away.

"You're the one who never forgets," Brad said to his brother's back.

Having eaten, Shay stepped outside, dressed and ready for roundup. She enjoyed the morning coolness against her face and breathed deeply. From a nearby oak tree, she heard the soft coos of a dove.

She stopped to scratch Jasper behind his ear. "Stay out of trouble while I'm gone."

He whined in return and licked her hand.

"I'm going to miss you, too." She laughed.

Shay tucked her braid inside the back of her shirt and pulled on her hat. She quickened her step, not wanting to be the last one mounted. Her spurs jingled as she walked to the barn. The sounds of men preparing for the roundup grew louder as she approached.

Inside, she hummed as she saddled her Appaloosa mare.

"What do you think you're doing? You're not going anywhere," Sneed thundered.

She turned and faced him. Her eyes reflected her confusion. "What?"

He moved closer. "I said you're not going."

"Why?"

His stiff posture told Shay it was useless to argue. "It's time you started behaving like a proper young lady. And a proper young lady doesn't go on roundup with the men."

Roundups were something Shay looked forward to. She enjoyed being outdoors and sleeping beneath the stars, eating beans out of a tin plate and drinking strong coffee. Now she couldn't even do that.

"Papa," Shay cried, "why are you being this way? What have I done?"

For a fraction of a second, Shay thought she saw regret—and something else—flicker across her father's face. "Don't defy me on this, Shay. I've made up my mind and that's final." Sneed turned his back to leave.

Shay grabbed his arm. "I want to go, Papa. Please?"

Sneed hesitated. "You look so much like your mother." His words were softly spoken and the stony glint in his eyes faded briefly before hardening once more. He jerked his arm from her grasp.

Sneed proceeded to walk outside. Shay followed.

There, the men of Twin Creeks were mounted and waiting.

At that moment, Brad and Cale came up, leading their horses.

"You're late," Sneed groused at his brother.

Brad raised a brow. "Am I?"

Sneed pointed his finger at Cale. "He's staying."

Cale tensed but remained silent.

However, Brad spoke up. "What's this?"

"Someone needs to stay behind with the women." Sneed didn't look at Shay beside him.

Brad remained thoughtful for a moment before

turning to Cale. "It might be best if you did stay. At least I won't worry about Shay or Nettie if you're with them."

"You're the boss," Cale replied.

Incredulous, Shay stepped forward and stared hard, first at her father, then at her uncle. Surely, they were joking. She couldn't be expected to stay here with Cale Breland!

She flung out her hands in frustration. "You can't mean that. Leave someone else here."

Sneed whirled. "I've said all I'm going to, Shay."

With that he mounted and rode toward the lower pasture. The men followed.

Brad lingered a moment. "You'll be fine. I'll make this up to you later." He winked at Shay, reined his horse around, and trotted after the others.

Both Shay and Cale were left standing in the middle of the barnyard, staring at the retreating riders.

Shay whirled and pinned Cale with her gaze. He stood too close to suit her.

She moved back.

He moved forward.

She tried to sidestep him.

He blocked her path.

Shay knew it was childish, but she took her disappointment and anger out on him. "Don't think to try anything while they're gone," she said heatedly.

Cale pushed his hat back on his head. "What am I supposed to think about doing?"

Indignation filled Shay. He knew perfectly well what she was talking about. Surely, he didn't expect her to come out and say such vulgar things. She had read in her novels what men did to unsuspecting women. He wasn't going to catch her unawares.

"I'm not about to answer you," she said.

Cale released his breath slowly. "It doesn't matter, because I'm going to do my job anyway. I've been ordered to look after you and Mrs. Grisham, and that's what I'm going to do."

Shay knew by the determined set of his jaw that he meant every word. But she wasn't going to back down either. "That may be, but it doesn't mean I have to like it. Just stay out of my way."

Cale moved to stand in front of her. His face loomed near hers and his breath whispered across her face as he spoke. "Can you stay out of mine?"

She didn't answer. Her gaze fell to his mouth and his full, sensual lips. Suddenly, the impulse to kiss him rushed over her. She remembered reading about passionate embraces between men and women, and she wondered how Cale's arms would feel about her, pressing her close, his lips on hers.

"I'm waiting for an answer, Miss Alexander."

Half appalled at her brazen thoughts and half aching with curiosity, Shay forced her thoughts to propriety. "Don't forget your place."

As she walked back to the house, she wondered if she had forgotten hers.

Shay found her aunt in the parlor dusting.

When she heard footsteps Nettie looked up from her task. "I thought I heard horses leaving earlier."

Shay plopped down into a chair and swung one leg over the arm. She removed her hat and sent it sailing across the room. "You did. Papa decided he didn't want me going. Something to do with my behavior as a proper young lady."

Nettie lowered her duster. "I'm afraid this time he's not going to change his mind."

Shay whacked the chair's arm with her fist. "Why can't he just let me be? I can't be the person he wants me to be." Angry tears trickled down her cheeks. She thumped the chair again.

"I was hoping with your Uncle Brad's return that your father might see things differently. I was wrong. They're only getting worse."

"Maybe I should just marry like Papa wants and get on with things."

"Unless it's someone you love, you'd be more miserable than you are now."

"But what about Papa and the way he treats me? I do what he asks. At least, what I can. And nothing's ever good enough. He always wants more from me. I'm not sure I've got any more to give."

Nettie walked over to Shay. She gently placed her hand atop Shay's head. "You've got a great deal to give to the right person. Just wait for that man."

Late that afternoon, Shay searched for the new litter of kittens in the barn and found them in the hayloft.

She climbed the ladder, then stealthily crawled to the place where she heard their soft meowing. In the right corner, just out of view from below, three kittens were searching the straw for their mother.

They were adorable, each one a calico. Their eyes weren't open yet, and they made quite a fuss trying to find their absent mother.

Shay carefully picked up one and cradled it against her cheek. "Ssh. It's all right," she crooned.

Time passed quickly as she lay on the straw and held the kittens until the missing mother appeared. Then Shay was content to simply watch the babies nurse.

After some time, Shay realized she'd best be getting back to the house. Just as she prepared to descend the ladder, Shay heard someone coming. Cale. On impulse, she scrambled back to her spot and lay stomach down on the hay and peeped over the edge. He carried a pitchfork. Apparently, he had come to rake out the stalls.

From her vantage point above, Shay watched him work. With each lift of the pitchfork, the muscles in his arms rippled beneath the fabric of his shirt. His shirt was unbuttoned to his waist and his chest gleamed with sweat.

A peculiar sense of familiarity came over her. It was as if she knew what it felt like to touch his smooth, golden skin. Her body wanted to do things her mind couldn't fathom.

She moistened her lips. What had begun as innocent fun was turning into sweet torture. And there was no way out. She had to remain hidden until he left and then she could slip down. She'd die of mortification if he knew she had been spying on him. She should have come down the ladder when Cale had first entered. After all, she didn't owe him any explanations. But she did now. Embarrassment pinkened her cheeks.

Shay was inching backward, intent on waiting him out, when her foot struck another pitchfork positioned against the wall. The pitchfork fell and clattered against the wooden planks. It seemed to Shay that the sound ricocheted off the barn walls.

She froze and held her breath. Maybe if she were lucky he hadn't heard it.

No such luck.

"Who's up there?" came Cale's voice from below. "Come out and I won't shoot."

She heard his steps on the ladder and the distinctive sound as he cocked his pistol.

There was nothing to do but reveal herself. Her thoughts skidded to a halt. What was the matter with her? She had nothing to hide. To hell with what he thought. This was her family's ranch. She straightened.

Before she could call out, Breland had reached the top of the ladder. Smiling, he checked his gun. "Should've known it was you up here making all that noise." He moved closer.

Shay rolled her eyes, annoyance at his self-assured manner etched in every line of her face. "Well, as you can see, there's nothing to be concerned about."

She made to move around him, but lost her footing in the hay and stumbled into him. They went down in a heap with Shay atop Breland.

Shay's breath left her. Her mouth was a mere inch from his. The musky scent of him, tobacco, hay, and leather assaulted her. His shimmering blue eyes encompassed her and his arms tightened about her. His body heat passed through her. He rolled over, pulling her with him, until she lay beneath him.

She was intensely aware of the intimate positions of their bodies. She felt his sinewy, taut length pressing her to the ground. His weight was oppressive, yet at the same time erotic. Part of her responded involuntarily to his nearness, and she felt a throbbing in her lower regions.

The look on his face caused Shay to go still. Her eyes widened. She swallowed—and waited.

Cale straddled her prone form. "Damnation! What were you doing? And why didn't you answer when I called?"

She wanted to get away from Breland. His nearness caused something to blossom within her, but fear kept her from examining the feeling—she was too scared of what she would find.

She fought her fright the only way she knew how. Her fist thudded against his chest. "This is my ranch and my barn. I don't have to tell you a damned thing!"

Cale caught her wrists and forced them to her sides. "I think you owe me an explanation and I'm not letting you up until you give me one."

"I'll scream."

"That wouldn't be smart. How are you going to explain getting yourself in this position?"

Shay knew he had the upper hand, yet she refused to surrender to his demands. "Get off me."

"Not until you explain yourself."

"Like hell I will," she spat out.

"Then you're not getting up."

Shay opened her mouth to scream. In the blink of an eye, he had her hands secured above her head with one hand, and her mouth covered with the other.

"I warned you," he said softly.

She bucked beneath him, trying to throw him off. Her senses were assailed by the touch and feel of him. Her response scared her. She didn't want to be attracted to him.

When she realized she wasn't going to budge him, she grew still. Her breasts rose and fell rapidly from the exertion, and she tried to steady her breathing.

"Are you going to tell me?" he asked.

She shook her head from side to side.

"This standoff could take some time," Cale said.

Shay had little time. How soon before someone came looking for her? She didn't want to be caught with this man in such a compromising situation. Something had to be done.

She bit him.

He inhaled sharply, jerked his hand away, then swore a blue streak. His eyes narrowed, and he clenched his teeth. He slowly raised his hand.

She cringed, awaiting the blow. It never came.

Instead, his fingers wound themselves in her hair. He stroked her cheek with the thumb of his other hand. "Why don't you make this easy on both of us?" His voice was smooth as old, worn leather as he moved his hands away.

"I'm not about to make anything easy for you," Shay countered.

Cale stretched over her and once more held her arms above her head, his hand covering her mouth. He maintained a small space between their bodies by raising himself on his elbows.

His eyes burned into hers, blue flames, blazing brightly. "Christ, woman, you try my patience. Now will you be still?"

Shay groaned her frustration. Damn him and his infernal ways! He certainly put a kink in her tail.

He leaned over. His breath warmed her cheeks. "I reckon your aunt is going to be looking for you any time now. What are you going to tell her when she finds you?" His white teeth contrasted with his golden skin.

Mentally, Shay dug her heels in. He wasn't going to get the best of her.

Cale lifted his hand from her mouth. "Don't make a sound, all right?"

When she nodded, he removed his hand.

She gulped in air, intent on crying out.

He clamped his hand back over her mouth. "I said not to make a sound." He sighed. "You're the most pigheaded female I've ever run across."

Me! she screamed silently, her eyes widening. Why, he was the most insufferable . . .

He laughed softly, correctly reading her expression. "You're right. I am. Guess that makes two of us."

She mumbled against his hand and tasted the saltiness of his skin. The taste and feel of him on her lips was surprisingly intimate, and the sensations left her giddy. And she loved the feel of his hard body pressed against hers. Shay grew angrier at her traitorous responses. She didn't need or want this. Did she?

"Let's try again. But this time, don't scream. Okay?"

She blinked her understanding.

He drew his hand across her mouth and away.

Shay licked her dry lips. "And what are you going to tell her when she finds you atop me in the hayloft?" She groaned at her careless question.

"The truth," he replied. "What are you going to tell her?"

Her temper caught fire like dry kindling. "You flea-bitten mangy dog, get off me!"

She should have exercised caution, but he could rile her faster than any man she knew.

His nostrils flared. "I would if you'd shut your mouth long enough."

His body tensed, his thighs closing tighter around hers.

Shay renewed her struggles. Her shirt became unbuttoned as she rubbed against his chest. Her breasts, covered only by a thin cotton undergarment, touched his skin through his open shirt. The contact was like heat lightning, sizzling through Shay's entire body. She went stock-still and she closed her eyes.

The seconds ticked by with each beat of her heart.

His voice sliced through her like a knife through warm butter. "Are you going to behave?"

Mutely, she nodded.

Releasing his hold, Cale sat and straddled her hips once more. His gaze fastened on her barely concealed breasts.

Shay blushed with mortification. And something more . . .

His eyes darkened to the color of lapis. With distressing purpose, his gaze slowly traveled from her breasts, up the slender column of her neck, to the attractive curve of her jaw and cheeks, across the dusting of freckles atop the bridge of her small straight nose, to her long-lashed eyes. His gaze seemed to touch her, to fondle her.

Her breathing sounded unnaturally loud to her ears. What were those funny feelings churning inside her stomach?

The quickening of his breath and the flare of his nostrils signaled his painful awareness of their contact. Her trembling legs felt hot and liquid, and her hips burned where he straddled her. Her nipples ached and strained against her cotton undergarment. As she moistened her dry lips, his eyes tracked her action. She squirmed against him, but he didn't move.

"I don't advise you do that," Cale warned.

Cale's senses sharpened and his pulse raced. God, he was aware ... all too aware ... of her nearness, her heated scent, the flawless perfection of her beauty, and his attraction to her.

Damn, he wanted to kiss that tempting mouth of hers.

He wanted to do more.

To desire Shay with such intensity was dangerous, because longing and affection stripped a man of his defenses. Something he should guard against.

Desire grappled with his sense of decency. His body urged him to take her now—in the hay—but his conscience demanded he release her.

There was one thing he had to do before he let her go. . . .

Still straddling her, Cale crushed Shay to him. Her eyes widened as his strong hand pressed intimately against the small of her back, while the other cupped her chin and held her face. His mouth descended upon hers.

The feel of his lips upon her own opened the gates of her senses; the will to fight him drained from her. And within that contact, Shay fleetingly wondered if this was what she had been searching for. The texture of his mouth and the searing heat of his kiss frightened Shay; yet she didn't want him to stop. She felt as though she were suffocating, overwhelmed by the assault of sensations that tried to rob her of coherent thought. Cale's handling of her had brought on the most intense sensual awareness she had ever experienced with a man. What would it be like to experience a more intense intimacy?

In a last effort to stop Cale before they reached the point of no return, she twisted her face away and glared into his glittering eyes. "Get off me, you varmint!" she rasped.

"When I'm ready." His deep voice sounded oddly breathless. "Not before."

Shay's reply was lost as his head dipped again.

Shoving futilely against the rock-hard wall of his chest, Shay felt his corded muscles ripple beneath her hands. The heat of his powerful body threatened to envelop her completely.

"Stop it!" she entreated against his mouth.

Cale ceased his actions and released her. She fell back against the hay. Looking up at him as he knelt over her, she wondered what he meant to do.

Cale reached for her and began buttoning her shirt.

She must never allow him to know how close she had come to surrendering to him. She erected a wall of hostility for safety.

Shay knocked his hands away. "You've done enough already." Pushing him off her, she sat up and finished the job.

She stood and glowered at Cale. "I don't want you coming near me again. Do you hear?" Her voice quivered and she hated her body's weakness to his proximity.

Shay turned and descended the ladder. Cale was right behind her.

She had started toward the barn door when Cale's voice stopped her. "I'd stay away from the hayloft for a while. Never know what kind of varmints you'll come across."

The gleam in his eyes promised that the next time they were alone they would finish what they had begun.

Shay walked to the house, feeling as if her last breath had been squeezed from her lungs.

She found Sally in the kitchen, cleaning turnips.

"Where you been?" Sally asked, glancing up from her task.

Not wanting Sally to suspect anything, Shay answered a little too quickly. "In the barn, playing with the new litter of kittens."

At the explosion of words, Sally stopped. With a strange light in her eyes, she looked at Shay. "You must've been playing hard, because you still got hay in your hair."

Shay hated lying, and knew she wasn't good at it. Perhaps the truth would serve her better. "Oh, it's that man!" she groaned, pulling the straw from her red locks.

Sally commenced peeling again. "How so?"

Shay plopped down in one of the chairs, agitated with herself and with Cale Breland. "He riles me faster than all get out." She plucked another piece of straw from her hair, stuck it in her mouth, and chewed.

Sally laughed softly. "Maybe that's because you likes him."

Aghast, Shay spit out the hay. "You can't mean it. Me? Like him? Your brain's going soft, Sally."

"There's nothing wrong with my thinking. It's your eyes I'm worried about."

"There's nothing wrong with my eyesight."

"Then, what you call it when you can't see what's in front of you?"

"There you go again." Shay came to her feet and

paced. "Always trying to tell me what I'm thinking or feeling."

"I only tells you what you already know. You just won't admit it half the time."

"I guess that goes back to your gift of sight," Shay huffed.

"Goes back to me knowing you since you were young. I was the first one to diaper you. I knows you pretty well." Patience wove itself through Sally's soft voice. "If you'd just listen to what your heart tells you, you wouldn't get yourself in messes all the time."

"I don't see how that's got anything to do with that man."

"That man's got a name. Why don't you use it?"

"Because I don't like him."

Sally shook her head. "You're acting mighty foolish. Sometimes, I wonder what goes on inside your head."

"According to my father, nothing happens. You'd think I didn't have a brain at all."

"You have a brain. You judge a man for yourself."

Shay walked to the back door. She picked up the dipper in the water bucket and drank. Finished, she wiped her mouth on her sleeve in her tomboyish manner.

She faced Sally. Resignation threaded her voice. "I suppose you're right. But I don't know how to act around men who aren't Papa or Uncle Brad."

Understanding entered Sally's eyes. "You know how to behave around the other hands. Why's this one different?"

Shay chewed her bottom lip. She had been in

the arms of a virtual stranger, and she had delighted in the familiarity. What was happening to her?

"I wish I knew," Shay said softly.

Chapter 5

The next morning, as Shay set about her chores, she lingered in the cool air that caressed her skin, and she breathed in the sweet scent of morning glory and honeysuckle. Ambling toward the garden to pick vegetables for Sally, she stopped momentarily by the corral and saw Breland feeding the horses.

Thoughts of the day before washed over her. Within the space of a heartbeat, Shay replayed the scene in the hayloft. Regardless of how hard she tried to erase it, the memory clung to her like perfume, sweet and titillating. Her cheeks burned. Pressing a cool hand to her face, she turned away.

Shay kept walking, her boots kicking up tiny puffs of dust. Once in the garden, she commenced picking tomatoes, trying to keep her thoughts anywhere but on Cale Breland.

She managed to lose herself in her task until she heard Breland's voice. "Sally said you needed help."

Blast his cantankerous hide! Why did he have to show up now?

Shay straightened, pushing a strand of hair out

of her eyes. "Sally?" She tried to check her temper, which she was losing too frequently since Mr. Breland's arrival. "I don't know why she told you that. I always pick the vegetables."

"That's a good place for you. Out of people's way."

If she would have paid closer attention, she would have noticed the teasing tone of his voice. Instead, she was troubled by his nearness, reinforcing remembrances she was trying desperately to erase. She didn't want to recall his intoxicating kiss, nor the feel of his strong arms around her, nor her near surrender.

Her irritation swelled and she snapped, "Who made you God to criticize people?"

Breland quirked a brow. "Are you always in a good mood, or is it me?"

"I would have thought you'd figured that out by now," she said tartly.

"What I've figured is that you need a lesson in manners."

Shay should have ignored him and gone about her work, but she couldn't. "As if you have any."

"I know a lady when I see one." He rubbed his chin. "You could use some work."

"Why don't you just go on? I can manage by myself."

"Maybe."

"You're a conceited ass."

To her consternation, his gaze traveled downward. "Hmm," he drawled, his eyes lit with wry amusement. "You've got a nice one, too."

"Ohhh! Darn you!"

Breland grinned. "No need to thank me."

"That's not what I had in mind," Shay said between gritted teeth. She wanted to call him every vile name she knew.

"What did you have in mind?" he asked.

"Telling you to go sleep with a polecat."

Breland clucked his tongue. "And leave you alone? Unprotected?"

"You don't have to put on an act for me."

Some of her newfound self-confidence dwindled at his unsettling gaze. He had a way of looking at her that made her feel soft inside.

"Maybe. Maybe not." His voice was smooth as silk.

She marshaled her senses. "Just leave me alone."

"I would if that was what you really wanted. But after what happened yesterday, I know that's not what you mean. Whatever there was between us, we both felt it."

"You're not listening. How many times do I have to tell you?"

"Then tell me again."

"Why do you have to make this so hard?"

"Because life's not easy."

"I can't believe you're so thickheaded that you don't understand."

"You can explain it to me anytime—in depth." He moved closer. "I'm a very good listener. Among other things."

His meaning was not lost on Shay. At first, she couldn't find adequate words to express herself because of his nearness—and the intense look in his eyes. Part of her wanted to answer the challenge in his blue gaze and part of her wanted to issue a challenge of her own.

When she was capable of speech, her voice came out in a raspy whisper. "I need to get back to my chores."

"I would never keep you from doing what you need or want to do. Provided you know exactly what it is you have to do."

"I suggest you remember your place while working on this ranch."

"I'd say it's up to you as to how much I remember."

Shay clenched her hands at her sides. "Will you stop playing games with me?"

A smile touched his lips. "I have every intention of ending the game when it's time."

"If you aimed to irritate me, then you've succeeded."

"Sorry, but when it comes to you, I have other plans."

The soft cadence of his voice stroked her in secret places—places best left unexplored. Again, memories of the day before poured over her—memories she was doing her damnedest to forget. It was more than she could stand. The situation was slipping from her control. Frustration swelled in Shay like yeast-risen dough. She wanted to wipe that knowing expression from his face.

She cast her gaze about. It settled on the basket of tomatoes. In the blink of an eye, she picked up a tomato and hurled it at him.

Splat! The tomato hit him square between the eyes.

Time became suspended.

Wiping the red bits from his face, Cale looked at her.

Shay held her breath and waited for retaliation. You've done it now, Shay Elizabeth Alexander, she told herself. You won't see your next birthday.

His stony expression revealed nothing. She wished to God he'd do something and put her out of her misery. Then his eyes crinkled at the corners, and he burst out laughing.

Shay couldn't believe it. He was laughing at her, and she didn't have a clue as to why. "What's the matter with you?" she asked irritably.

"You're not like any woman I've ever met," Breland said, his shoulders shaking.

Suddenly Shay saw the humor and the absurdity of the situation. Here she was, a grown woman of twenty, acting like a giddy schoolgirl, throwing tomatoes at another person.

"We seem to bring out the best in each other," she teased.

"Indeed."

Recklessly and good-naturedly, caught in the spontaneity of the situation, she picked up another tomato and heaved it at him.

This time he ducked.

He straightened to his six feet two inches. A lazy grin spread across his face. "I'll have to teach you a lesson."

Ever so slowly, Breland bent and picked up a ripe tomato of his own. He rolled it around in his large hand.

Shay's eyes grew round. "You . . . w-w-wouldn't," she stuttered.

He tossed the fruit into the air a couple of times. "Oh, wouldn't I?" He took a step toward her. "I'm going to enjoy this."

"You stay away from me with that," Shay squealed, backing away.

"And miss my fun?" His teeth flashed against his tanned skin. "I don't think so."

Shay turned to beat a hasty exit and tripped on a mound of dirt. Arms flailing, she yelped and sprawled face down on top of a pile of tomatoes.

She rolled to her back, covered in tomatoes, and stared up at him. He towered above her, feet spread wide, one hand on his hip, a tomato in the other hand. He wore the devil's own look as he grinned at her.

Breland reached for her and pulled her to her feet. "It's time to pay the piper."

"Don't do anything . . . y-y-you'll be sorry for." Damn, she was stuttering again.

He stepped back and assessed her openly. "I'm only sorry we didn't have fun sooner."

A smile tugged at her mouth. His remark pleased her. "We have had fun, haven't we?"

A sobering thought cautioned her not to enjoy herself too much.

"It's not over."

Her stomach tightened. What did he mean? She watched him tear into the tomato with his fingers. Juice dripped down his long brown fingers, hands, and strong forearm. Inside her, something delicious trickled down her spine.

She tracked his movements as he raised his hand and licked away the juice from his fingers. Shay ran her tongue across her own lips. His actions were doing unspeakable things to her insides, making her feel as soft as an eiderdown quilt. He had the uncanny ability to make the most common actions take on a sensuality of their own—something Shay hadn't ever been aware of. Until now.

He took a bite of tomato, then pressed the piece to Shay's mouth. "Have some."

The silky contours of Cale's voice brushed over Shay's heightened senses. She took a bite of the ripe fruit. Pleasure pulsated through her as she thought of her lips being where Cale's had been. Juice dripped down her chin and throat.

His blue eyes dark with unspoken emotion, Cale lowered his head. His tongue lightly ran across her chin, then down her throat, causing her to tingle all over.

Cale broke the contact. "How does it taste?"

Taste? It was all she could do to focus her thoughts. Sweet yearning streaked through her body.

Shay stared at him, her mind unable to coherently frame a reply. Her womanly instincts told her what the look in his eyes meant. She closed her own eyes. Within the span of a heartbeat, she allowed her imagination free rein, something she couldn't allow her body. She pictured him kissing her, his lips firm yet gentle, then his tongue doing sinful things to her mouth, teasing, tasting, seeking. If this were torture, it was the sweetest torture she had ever endured.

Shay's breath left her. Her mouth was a mere inch from his. His shimmering blue eyes encompassed her. He took her into his arms with surprising gentleness, except there was nothing frail about the well-knit muscles holding her. They were finely woven into a hard and unyielding frame. Any notion of protest or escape scattered on the winds of sensuality.

"This is where I've wanted you since I first saw you." His breath, warm and light, whispered against her lips.

Shay couldn't deny that she, too, had had such a fantasy. But they were entering dangerous territory and she couldn't allow him to explore any further. Regardless of how right it felt to be in his arms, their actions were nevertheless wrong.

A thin ribbon of coherence held her thoughts together and she managed to weave a single thought. "I think you should let me go."

Breland lowered his arms and a faint scowl traced across his features. Shay didn't want this to end on an angry note.

She gave him a saucy look. "I hope you've had your fun."

His eyes went from her head to her feet and the frown disappeared. He laughed. "More than enough."

Shay, too, laughed, revealing straight white teeth. "I must look a sight."

A sight indeed. She was the loveliest woman he had ever seen. Too damned beautiful for her own good—and his. Her natural innocence heightened his attraction to her.

Cale's lighthearted mood lifted. He needed to put distance between himself and Shay. He didn't want her to look at him with such passion.

He didn't want to desire her.

Yet, Cale couldn't stop himself from reaching out and taking Shay in his arms and kissing her again. Her lips were soft and yielding beneath his. His tongue eased into her mouth. Desire, patent and raw, burst inside him. God, he wanted her.

Shay was helpless to resist. She leaned into him, her hands flat against his broad chest. Her blood raced through her veins like a young colt.

Somehow clinging to sanity, she pulled away. Her lips still felt heated and moist from his kiss. She took a deep, steady breath before she looked at him. Words failed her.

Instead, she turned and walked toward the house. Halfway, she stopped and said over her shoulder in an offhanded manner, "I liked being kissed."

Cale watched her as she continued her stroll. There was something dangerously potent about Shay's innocence, something that worked its way under his skin. He could tell by the way she kissed that she had no real experience with men. Pleasure rushed through him at the knowledge. She had the sweetest mouth, like a tree-ripened peach—luscious, temperate, soft. He wanted it for himself.

To Shay, the distance from the garden to the house seemed longer than it had been before, although she knew it was the same. She prayed she'd be able to sneak to her room without anyone noticing her. How was she going to explain the tomato residue? Or the stain to her cheeks resulting from the kisses of a man who elicited baffling emotions from her?

Her prayer wasn't answered. As Shay started up the stairs for her room, Aunt Nettie caught sight of her.

Aunt Nettie's eyes were wide with wonderment. "Whatever happened to you?"

Shay shrugged. "I had an accident."

When Nettie got closer, her nose wrinkled. "You smell as if you've been wallowing in tomatoes."

"I tripped and landed on some. Guess I should be more careful."

What she wanted to say was that she should be more careful around Cale Breland.

Nettie pointed a finger to the top of the stairs. "Well, get yourself upstairs this minute and get out of those clothes. Then I want you in a tub. You can't go around smelling up the house."

"Yes, ma'am."

Shay took the stairs two at a time.

Once in her room, Shay shucked off her clothes and tossed them into a corner. At that moment, she glimpsed herself in the full-length mirror. What a sight she was. She felt as dirty as she appeared. How could she have allowed a man she scarcely knew to take such liberties with her? Strange things were happening to her, and she didn't know how to stop them. She couldn't lie to herself and say she hadn't wanted him to hold her and to kiss her. Since the day Cale Breland arrived, she'd been dishonest with herself, denying her fascination with him. Funny thing, though, she hadn't fooled anyone except herself with her deception. But more sobering, she had ignored his dangerous allure and had allowed herself to blindly walk into situations that could have ended in disaster, because secretly she had hungered for a taste of passion more than she had adhered to morality.

Distressed, Shay sat at her dressing table and buried her face in her hands. Even if her family never learned what she had done, she couldn't hide from the fact that she had betrayed her moral upbringing for a few moments of passion.

Shay donned her robe.

Sally made several trips, hauling buckets of hot water for Shay's bath. Shay watched her empty the last two buckets of steaming water into the tub located in the corner of her room.

Finished, Sally regarded Shay. "You sure is getting clumsy these days."

She gave Shay no time to reply, but walked out, carrying the two empty buckets.

Shay shrugged off her robe and eased into the

hot bath. The steaming, rose-scented water reached her chin, and her tense muscles relaxed, one by one.

She leaned her head against the tub's rim and closed her eyes. She became frustrated with her inability to banish Cale from her consciousness. As if his image rose from the steamy water, he clouded her mind, a lingering vision, sensual and taunting. Her hands navigated the course her mind charted across her torso beneath the surface of the steaming water.

Cale's hands were large, strong, callused by work, but his touch could be agonizingly gentle. What would it feel like to have his powerful hands touch intimate, undiscovered places?

Her hands came to rest on her breasts. Shay tingled as she remembered how she felt when her breasts had rubbed against Cale's chest.

The tingling blossomed into yearning. Her hand traveled the slender column of her neck, followed the ridges of her rib cage, curved around her small waist, then traced her thighs and her calves. Her lips formed a tiny smile at the wanton feeling that streaked across her body, like a shooting star, as her hand touched red curls. If his kiss drove her beyond distraction, what would his hand do to her if it found this same sweet place?

Twin red spots stained her cheeks and she removed her hand. Taking the bar of soap, Shay vigorously scrubbed herself. At one point, she slapped the water with both hands, sending it spraying about the room.

Hell's bells! Her life was changing, and she didn't know whether to be excited or scared.

* * *

Later that evening, Shay went to the kitchen. At least she wouldn't have to suffer Breland's attentions at the supper table—he had eaten with them the first night only because he was a guest of Uncle Brad's. This house was her sanctuary from him. How could she face him after she had wantonly admitted she enjoyed his kisses? What had caused her to say such a thing? What must he think of her?

When she entered the doorway, her heart leapt into her throat. It couldn't be him! Not here. Not now.

At the table sat Cale Breland talking with her aunt. He had washed and changed clothes. His neatly combed black hair hung about his collar in damp waves.

Why couldn't he have been uglier than homemade soap, instead of being unnervingly handsome? she wondered as she studied his features, so aggressively male and so forbiddingly compelling.

Aunt Nettie glanced up, cutting short Shay's reflection, and smiled at her. "There you are. I was beginning to think I would have to go upstairs and get you."

Breland looked at her. Uncertainty lurked in his eyes.

Well, at least he wasn't so sure of himself either, Shay thought. She might have a chance of coming out of this without making a fool of herself—for the second time that day.

Despite their earlier encounter, Shay mustered her manners, determined to be polite in front of her aunt. "I didn't realize you were waiting on me."

"It's perfectly all right." Nettie gestured with

her slim hand. "I've asked Mr. Breland to join us. With the others gone, I didn't see any reason for him to eat alone."

That was her aunt, always taking care of everyone, Shay groaned inwardly.

Breland's blue eyes glittered with challenge. "Perhaps I bother Miss Alexander and should leave," he said, half rising from his seat.

Before Shay could respond, Nettie chimed in. "Nonsense. Sit down. Shay doesn't mind." Her aunt looked at her. "Do you, dear?"

What could Shay say? No, she didn't want him here because she found his company unsettling. Or, yes, he did bother her—in more ways than she cared to acknowledge.

Shay sighed. "If that's what you want, Aunt Nettie, then it's all right with me." She sat across from her aunt, with Breland to her left. It was far from all right with her, but she'd keep quiet.

Nettie began spooning potatoes onto her plate. "Sally's gone to a great deal of trouble cooking all this. Shall we eat before the food grows cold?"

"Sure looks good," Cale said, helping himself to ham, biscuits, and potatoes.

When all had filled their plates, Nettie paused. "Mr. Breland, will you say the prayer for us?"

Shay noticed his hesitation and wondered if he knew one.

Cale bent his head and folded his hands. "Thanks for the food and for the company. Amen."

"Amen," the women intoned.

Cale looked up at Shay. His smile told her that he was certainly enjoying her company.

They began eating.

As the meal progressed, Shay was thankful that her aunt kept the conversation flowing.

"Tell me, Mr. Breland," Nettie asked, "how are things going?"

"As well as can be expected. Some of the men don't hold with my fighting for the Union, but I can't say I blame them. It's hard for them to accept that the Confederacy lost."

"You certainly have a great deal of insight."

"Not insight. Just understanding."

"If you don't mind, tell me something about yourself. About your family, perhaps."

"I was orphaned at three. I don't remember much about my ma or pa. Except what others told me."

"How did you survive?" Nettie asked between bites.

Shay looked at him beneath long lashes, wondering what drove this man to be the person he was, and saw him grip his fork. Within the breadth of a second, a cloud of some indefinable—but deep—emotion crossed his face. Aunt Nettie's inquiry had hit upon a nerve.

"I managed. Spent time with different families." The smooth inflection of his words didn't reveal his uneasiness.

He was certainly adept at keeping his feelings hidden, Shay thought. Too good. But he had allowed her a glimpse into his past the night they had sat on the porch.

Her stomach fluttered with sympathy. No one deserved such a lonely existence. Despite the problems within her own family, she couldn't imagine life completely without loved ones. His lack of family must be the reason for his distance.

Nettie looked contrite. "I'm sorry. I shouldn't have asked."

"It's all right, ma'am."

"Have you done much traveling?"

"You might say I've been around. But I like it that way, doing what I want. The most important thing to me is my freedom."

"Do you plan to stay long on Twin Creeks then?" Nettie asked.

"Long enough."

His voice, deep and masculine, ebbed through Shay, down to her nerve endings. Something tightened in her lower regions. She reached for her glass and took a sip of water, needing to distract herself from what she was feeling.

And as if her response to Breland wasn't bad enough, she found him looking intently at her.

Shay felt the need to say something—anything to dispel the tension. "Sally's the best cook I know."

What a silly thing to say, Shay thought. But it was the best she could do. Every time he regarded her in that lazy manner, her brain seemed to jumble all her thoughts like scrambled eggs.

Cale took a bite of mashed potatoes and gravy. "Best meal I've had in a long time." A drop of cream gravy lingered on his lip. He licked it off.

To her horror, Shay realized she had been staring, and she dropped her gaze to her plate. Aggravated, she clutched her fork.

Tarnation! What was wrong with her? she wondered miserably. If she wasn't more careful, he'd be able to tell she wasn't as unaffected by him as she professed.

She clutched her fork tighter. He wasn't the first man to kiss her, but it was the first time she had ever enjoyed it. That admission could come back to haunt her. She didn't know if she could withstand a rejection, should it come to that. She'd already been rejected by her father. Once was enough.

Shay's gaze darted to her aunt. Thank God, Aunt Nettie didn't seem to notice what was going on. Shay would die of embarrassment if her aunt—or anyone else, for that matter—discovered her fascination with the man. Rattled, Shay gave up all efforts at conversation.

Silence followed as the diners devoted their attention to the meal.

Shay tried to keep her eyes on her plate, but some puissant force drew her gaze upward. Breland raised his fork to his mouth. As she watched him take another bite of food, her gaze lingered on his mouth, and she remembered how firm and sensual those lips had felt on hers. Their eyes met. His smile wrapped around her like warm sunshine.

Her gaze dropped back to her plate.

Coward! her mind screamed. What was wrong with her? Could she be running a fever? Yes, that was it, she told herself. That's why she felt so odd. He probably didn't give a damn if she were at the table or not. He'd only come because Aunt Nettie had asked him.

She couldn't have been further off the mark.
Cale was all too aware of her presence.
She wore her hair loose, the red skeins falling

gently down her back in soft curls. The light from the lantern cast golden highlights throughout her silky mane. The overpowering impulse to run his hands through that glorious wealth of hair tore at Cale. Through great willpower alone, he fought the urge. He nearly lost the battle as suddenly, and forcefully, he wanted her with an explicit response that only a man's body could manifest.

Cale knew he had to leave. He couldn't sit there a minute longer with his mind conjuring up pictures of Shay Alexander, acquiescent and eager in his arms. It was more torture than a man ought to endure.

She fidgeted in her seat as if she wanted to bolt. He suppressed a smile. He was the one who needed to leave. Now.

He laid his napkin beside his plate. "Thanks for supper, Mrs. Grisham, but I'll be going now."

Nettie's mouth turned down in disappointment. "So soon? You haven't had dessert yet."

"No, thanks, ma'am. Dawn will be coming soon enough, and I had better turn in."

"If you insist," Nettie said.

After Cale left, Nettie began gathering dishes. "I like Mr. Breland."

Shay, only too glad to have something to do, helped her aunt clear the table. "Why? He's just another cowboy," she said, tight-lipped, annoyed with herself for having acted like a fool all through supper. And just because of one man.

"I sense he has special qualities."

Shay certainly didn't need her aunt pushing her toward Cale Breland. "Oh, Aunt Nettie, you just feel sorry for any stray that comes along."

"You're wrong, Shay. There's something different about Mr. Breland. I feel deep down inside he's a good man."

Deep down inside, Shay felt something else, and she didn't know whether it was a blessing or a curse.

Chapter 6

Tired and cranky from lack of sleep, Shay rose before dawn. She had lain in bed for most of the night, staring at the shadows scampering across the moonlit ceiling and walls of her room. It irritated the blue blazes out of her that she couldn't get Cale Breland off her mind.

He made her feel things strongly within herself she had never known before: now she knew what it was like to desire and long for a man. Because of the fiasco of her parents' marriage, she had told herself that she didn't need—or want—a man in her life. But since Cale Breland's arrival, she'd begun to doubt her previous resolution.

She laughed dryly. If he knew of her fascination with him, would he return her feelings or would he turn away from her? The thought of caring for a man spooked her.

Her mouth turned down in a frown. This was silly, she thought to herself. He probably didn't find her attractive at all.

Shay walked to the window. The night had been warm and sultry, and the cotton of her nightgown stuck to her. She pulled the fabric away from her heated skin in an attempt to catch a stray breeze.

She looked out across the yard, past the barn and the gently sloping hills, and envisioned the creek beyond.

Refreshing water called to her, tempting her to indulge in an early morning swim. She smiled. Just what she needed to take her mind off . . . She didn't finish the thought.

In no time, Shay had dressed, left a note for Sally, grabbed a towel, and was out the door, headed for the barn.

Ten minutes later, Shay rode across the landscape in carefree abandonment. She loved the feel of the wind in her loose, flowing hair and against her skin. She seldom got the chance for such wicked freedom with so many men near, but since only one was left behind, she could do anything she wanted and not worry about being discovered.

The broad limestone formations of the Edwards Plateau spread grandly across the land, fringed with broken, cedar-studded hills.

The sun peeped above the horizon, casting a pinkening glow to the sky. Dew clung to the ground.

Shay wove her way through the cedar-choked land until she found a tree-lined trail leading to a cypress-shaded knoll. She followed the waters of the meandering creek. Monstrous trees loomed above, their roots intertwined in torturous loops fighting to maintain their grasp on the eroded banks of the waterway.

Cottonwood and pecan trees spread their limbs across the rippling water, creating a serenity that smoothed the jagged edges of Shay's nerves.

Dismounting, she tied her horse to a tree. She inhaled the sweet scent of morning. Overhead, early morning light filtered through the canopy of tree limbs and bathed her face in soft light.

She made her way down the ledge that led to the water, holding on to rocks, using her legs as leverage to control her descent.

Upon reaching the bank, she sat on a large, flat rock and quickly undressed, removing all but her chemise. She hung her clothes on a nearby bush before wading into the water.

The cool water felt heavenly as the gentle current flowed around her at waist level. Scooping water with both hands, she sent it flying in silver waves into the air. Her laughter filled the quiet.

Shay waded farther into the depths, where she dived into the creek. Surfacing with a toss of her head, she brushed her hair away from her face.

She frolicked in the cool stream, playfully slicing through the water, diving, surfacing, then diving once more. Time became suspended in her watery playground.

At last, growing tired, she swam on her back toward the bank. She had started to rise from the water, when suddenly she was yanked back, pain stabbing her scalp.

"Hell's bells!" she said, realizing her hair was caught on a cypress root.

Twisting and turning this way and that, Shay tried every way to loosen her hair from the grip of the tree. The more she moved, the worse the tangle became.

Shay ceased her struggles and sat dejectedly in the shallow water. If this didn't beat all, Shay moaned to herself. Here she sat, half in and half out of the water, wearing only a chemise. And to make matters worse, no one could hear her cries for help. How long would she have to suffer in this ignominious position?

Until someone finds you, you ninny, Shay berated herself. She knew who that person would be—the one person she didn't want to see—or to see her like this.

Her vision blurred from unwelcome tears. Wouldn't Breland have the biggest laugh, finding her in such a humiliating predicament?

She sat there, trying to think of some way to free herself, but there was no apparent solution. Frustrated, she worked at her jumbled hair until her fingers hurt.

"Damn," she breathed aloud, and hit the water with her fists.

"Having trouble?" Cale chuckled, appearing by the creek bank.

A scream congealed in her throat. Her arms jerked up as she crossed them over her breasts. She jumped, feeling a thousand pinpricks march across her head like angry ants.

When her heart slowed its frantic beating, sweet relief rolled over her. Help was here. In just a few moments, she would be free. . . .

Then a dark, ugly suspicion displaced her relief. How the devil had he discovered her absence so quickly?

She drew a burning breath and slowly twisted her head around to meet his eyes, careful not to pull her hair again. "How long have you been lurking here?"

"Long enough."

"You snake i-i-in the grass," she stuttered.

"How could I let you just ride off without an escort? That wouldn't be doing my job, now would it?"

"A convenient excuse."

Cale's eyes crinkled at the corners. "You get yourself in more trouble than any female I've ever known."

His nearness more than disturbed her. She was painfully aware of how his gaze swept over her, taking in every inch.

Shay pinkened beneath his regard. "Just keep your comments to yourself."

"Always in a temper."

"Because you put me in one."

"That temper's gonna get the better of you one day."

"What do you care?"

He shrugged. "No concern of mine."

"Leave me alone." She gnashed her teeth in frustration.

"Now, if I was to leave you alone, who knows how long you'd be forced to sit out here?" He looked at her with a warmth in his blue eyes that made her entire body feel overheated despite the coolness of the water. "Like that." His gaze dipped below the water's surface and she wondered just how much of her state of undress he could see.

Shay's blush deepened to red, staining her neck and the tips of her ears. His eyes told her. Enough.

Her muscles were beginning to cramp from the strain of remaining in one position. "You going to help me or not?"

Cale leaned closer and bestowed upon her a sensual smile. "I didn't hear you say please."

He didn't move a muscle, yet she felt a physical fondling as surely as if he had touched her.

Shay fought the effect of his drugging nearness. "Of all the nerve," she fumed. "You're a black-hearted varmint."

Cale reached out and caressed her cheek with the back of his hand. "Oh, I've got my soft spot when it comes to you." His voice, rich as velvet, floated across her tingling skin.

The tensing of nerves and muscles made her shift her body restlessly. He was bolder than a brass spittoon. "I just bet you do."

"You know it's true."

She inhaled raggedly as one fingertip lazily traced a path from the side of her neck to her collarbone. His touch then outlined her lips. Shay's senses vibrated, down to her nerve endings, at his nearness, so potently masculine and vibrantly powerful.

"Stop that." She swatted at his hand, but quickly regretted the jerky motions as her scalp was yanked again. She grimaced.

"I reckon if you don't want my help, then I'll be on my way."

His throaty chuckle annoyed her. "You mangy coyote! Don't you dare leave me!"

"And who's to stop me?"

"You can't just go."

"Watch me." He started for his horse.

Her bottom hurt from the rocky creek bed, her teeth chattered from the cold, and her muscles ached unbearably from the strain of keeping herself submerged as much as her trapped hair would allow. If she didn't accept his help, she had no idea how long she'd be forced to remain where she was.

Shay twisted her head just enough to get a glimpse of Cale. "Oh, all right," she said begrudgingly.

He stopped and looked over his shoulder at her.

One side of his mouth turned up. "I'm sorry. I didn't quite catch that." Humor tinted his words.

Shay swallowed what pride she had left—which was precious little. Darn him! "All right, all right. Will you help me?"

Retracing his steps, Cale hunkered down beside Shay. "I didn't hear you say please."

His fingers drifted close. Shay closed her eyes in anticipation of his touch and her stomach tightened. Seconds ticked by, but nothing happened. Disappointment mingled with frustration. She opened her eyes.

Oh, what she wasn't going to do to him when she got loose! Shay fumed silently.

"Please." She forced the words past cold lips. "Just get on with it."

He waded farther into the stream to get better access to the offending cypress root. In a matter of minutes, Cale successfully freed Shay's tangled hair.

Slowly, she tried to stand, but her cold limbs wouldn't support her. She couldn't stop herself from leaning into him. An involuntary sigh escaped her as he wrapped his warm, strong arms about her. In her state of mind, hovering somewhere between reality and displaced emotions, she didn't care that Cale Breland held her practically naked in his arms. He was the first man for whom she had felt the sweet, melting female ache to yield, yet to succumb to her desire would be weakness.

He cupped her chin and forced her to look up at him—into those damnable blue eyes. She knew he meant to kiss her, but nothing prepared her for the effect of his lips on hers. She might have been able to resist if his kiss had been bruising and demanding, but this dizzying, lazy seduction undid her. Time became weighted in chains as their lips melded.

His hands moved to her breasts. The feel of his callused palms through the wet cotton of her chemise was sweet torture. She grew hot—then cold—then hot again.

Their bodies pressed closer, her breasts rubbing against the fabric of his wet shirt, the damp crush of material washing her with emotions so tantalizing that a shudder passed through her that had nothing to do with her chilled limbs.

"Shay," he whispered.

Even the way he said her name, his voice low and husky, added to the erotic confusion of her senses. She climbed out of the recesses of passion and forced herself to think clearly. It was the hardest thing she had ever done.

"Let go," Shay rasped against his mouth.

The kiss continued for a lingering moment, then Cale drew back, looking down on her. "If that's what you want."

With distressing design, his gaze slowly traveled up the slender curve of her neck. His carefully blank expression revealed nothing as he studied the graceful feminine line of her cheeks and jaw; her small, upturned nose, sprinkled with freckles; before journeying over her long, lush lashes, clumped with water. Finally, his gaze rested on her lips. All the while, he traced the creamy bareness of her left shoulder and collarbone, catching droplets on his fingertip.

The combination of sensations assaulted Shay, leaving in their wake a rapidly beating pulse. She struggled to find her voice. "I think you've done enough today."

Determined to salvage part of her dignity, she lifted her chin and started for the bank, but her foot slipped on a rock. She tumbled backward into the water.

"Let me help you," he responded with a laugh, and offered her his arm.

She pushed wet hair from her face. "How kind," she said sweetly. Too sweetly.

She accepted his hand—and pulled hard. He toppled into the water beside her.

He came up, sputtering his astonishment. "Why, you little—"

She smiled again. "Now we're even."

Rising, Shay strategically tried to cover certain parts of her body, but she didn't have enough hands. Why concern herself with modesty now? He'd already seen an eyeful. She wouldn't give him the satisfaction of witnessing her embarrassment.

She straightened her shoulders and stomped out of the creek and onto the bank. Maintaining a proud lift of her chin, she walked to the bush where her clothes hung.

She had once called him a devil. What else was he to make her want him with only a touch? She sensed they played a dangerous game. He was like no other man she knew—smart, determined. Her defenses were in jeopardy of being stripped away by his tactics of perseverance.

Grim-faced, she began dressing as quickly as her trembling limbs would allow. She concentrated on buttoning her shirt, rather than dwelling on Cale Breland and his ability to make her forget herself with only his touch.

* * *

Nearly an hour later, Shay, in dry clothes, sat with Cale at the kitchen table while Sally served them breakfast.

Shay was hungry, but she hadn't wanted to suffer sitting through another meal with Cale. Neither of them had spoken on the ride back, which only added to the growing tension. But if she had refused to eat, Aunt Nettie or Sally would have suspected something, and that was the last thing Shay wanted. No, she wanted to be as far away from Cale Breland as she could get. Distance would keep her from making a bigger fool of herself.

Sally spooned up large portions of scrambled eggs, grits, and thick-sliced ham, served with flaky hot biscuits swimming in butter and honey. Cups of steaming black coffee finished the meal.

"I've been keeping this hot for the two of you," she said, setting plates in front of Shay and Cale. "Now enjoy."

"Hope it was no trouble," Cale said, appreciatively eyeing the food.

Sally's face was wreathed in smiles. "The only thing I loves better than cooking is seeing people eat."

Cale raised his cup of coffee in salute. "And a mighty good cook you are."

"If you're trying to get on my good side"—she chuckled—"you just did."

Turning her back, Sally went about washing up the dishes in the sink.

Shay looked daggers at Cale. Now he was trying to butter up Sally. As if he sensed her scrutiny, he glanced up. She felt like choking when he smiled at her a little too brightly.

She dropped her gaze. Despite her earlier hunger, she only pushed the food around on her plate.

She drew a fortifying breath, knowing she'd just have to make the best of the situation.

Upon hearing footsteps, she glanced up as a smiling Aunt Nettie strolled into the room. "I see Mr. Breland found you, Shay." Nettie went to the stove and poured herself a cup of coffee.

"You sent him after me?" Shay struggled to keep the surprise from her voice.

Nettie sat down. "Yes, dear. You know I don't like you swimming in the creek alone. Think of all the cottonmouths this time of year."

Shay paled slightly, her mind flashing over her accusation that Cale had been spying on her. Well, she'd be damned if she'd apologize to him, not after the way he had behaved. He should have revealed his presence sooner than he had.

Nettie addressed Cale. "Thank you for going."

"No trouble, ma'am."

Shay detected his tone of amusement. He was insufferable! Her palm itched to slap his face.

Cale finished his breakfast, rose, and handed his plate to Sally, who stood at the sink. "Thank you. That just hit the spot."

Sally's face split with approval. "Seconds?"

"Best not. I've got chores to do." Cale inclined his head in Nettie's direction. "Morning, ma'am."

"Morning, Mr. Breland," Nettie returned, thoughtfully watching his departing figure.

She hadn't missed the exchange of looks between Shay and Mr. Breland. Their body language had told her a great deal. Something was going on between the two of them, but she couldn't put her finger on it. Oh, Shay would vehemently deny any attraction if asked, but Nettie knew her niece better than anyone.

Nettie hid a smile behind her hand as she

watched Shay finish her coffee. She sensed her niece had finally met her match. Shay's experience with men was, at best, limited: those who did seek her company had either been intimidated by her frank, tomboyish ways or frightened by her beauty and intelligence. Whatever the circumstance, Shay always sent them packing.

But Mr. Breland was different. He wasn't the type to be molded to Shay's expectations, or to be put off by her attractiveness and sharp mind, or her less than refined manners. The look in his eyes had been one of a man inexorably drawn to an irresistible woman. Nettie knew the look well, having been married to a very loving, attentive man. It pained her to see her niece deny her feelings and close herself off from affection. Nettie knew, even if Shay did not, that this isolation cost her a great deal. Shay had not yet allowed herself to become a passionate woman, willing to return the right man's love, or to take a chance on what lay ahead in the outside world.

Nettie's inner voice told her that Cale Breland was that man. She approved. She'd do whatever she could to encourage this relationship. After all, Shay didn't have much time before her father's return and her impending marriage to Cotton. What Shay and Mr. Breland needed was time—alone.

That afternoon, Cale, bearing an armload of firewood, came upon Sally in the kitchen.

Her face dusted with flour, she looked up from her task of making dumplings. "Just put it in the box."

"Yes, ma'am."

Sally paused, her inquisitive eyes keenly on Cale. "Why you always calling me ma'am?"

"I was taught to respect my elders," Cale replied casually, filling the wood box adjacent to the stove.

"Even if that person is colored?"

Straightening, Cale turned around and shrugged. "A person's skin makes no difference to me. Hate to see anyone treated unfairly. Guess that's why I fought for the Union."

"I reckon it is. It's just that not too many white folks takes that opinion of blacks."

"I'm not most folks."

Sally laughed. "I can see that."

Cale glanced at the water bucket near the door. "Mind if I have a drink?"

"Help yourself."

"Thanks." He drank deeply from the dipper. Finished, he wiped his mouth on his rolled-up sleeve, then strolled over to the table and pulled out a chair. His arms draped atop the back, he straddled the chair with his long legs and watched Sally.

She rolled out the dough to just the right thickness and cut it into wide, inch-long strips. She then dropped the doughy ribbons into the pot of simmering chicken stock.

"Nothing like good dumplings," she said, appreciatively sniffing the rich aroma.

"Can't argue with that," Cale returned. "Nothing's worse than soggy dumplings, but nothing's better than light, fluffy ones. My stomach's rumbling now, just thinking about them." He smiled broadly.

"You know, there's a trick to making dumplings." Sally chuckled. "And even if I says so myself, I gots the touch."

"Yes, ma'am."

Sally shuffled over to the flour bin and retrieved

another cup of flour. Next, she picked up a bowl brimming with dewberries. "Picked these early this morning. We're gonna have ourselves a juicy cobbler to go with them chicken and dumplings."

"You know, a person could get spoiled around here."

"If a person was wanting to." Sally looked intently at Cale. "You thinking about staying?"

Cale returned her direct gaze with one of his own. "A person needs a reason for remaining in one place," he said somberly.

"That they do." Sally's practiced hands began mixing pie dough. "Seems to me you've got one."

Cale frowned. "Now hold on."

Sally clucked her tongue like a mother hen. "Don't go getting all bothered. I'm just telling it like I sees it."

"Maybe you're not seeing things right. Maybe you're seeing what you want to."

"Not likely. I've got eyes and I've noticed the way you and Miss Shay looks at each other. You're only fooling yourself if you think otherwise. Your liking for that girl is written on your face as plain as your nose."

"Is that so?"

"Yes, sir. As plain as the nose on your face," Sally repeated, a faint smile lining her generous mouth.

Intent to end this conversation, Cale rose. Sally cut off his retreat. "I'm not finished and you ain't going nowhere. Sit." She indicated his chair with a wave of the rolling pin.

Cale had never taken to being told what to do, but he liked and respected Sally, and so he sat back down. "You always ordering people about?"

"Only when I sees they're headed in the wrong direction."

"Is that what you think I'm doing?"

"Not thinking. I knows."

"And just what is it you know?"

"That you and Miss Shay is meant for each other. And the two of you shouldn't be fighting it so hard."

"You might have been right in the past, but you're wrong this time."

"There you go again. Denying what's slap-dab in front of you. You'd think a cannonball landed on you and left you touched in the head."

Cale sighed uneasily. "What do you want from me?"

"The same as I wants for Miss Shay—happiness."

"What do you call meddling in a person's affairs?"

"It ain't meddling when people need a little nudging in order to do the right thing. Sometimes folks are their own worst enemies, getting in their own way."

Cale couldn't imagine Shay listening to this advice. "What did Miss Shay have to say about your words of wisdom?"

"I was hoping to talk some sense into you first, and let you do the right thing by that girl. That child has never had much loving from her pa, and she's not much trusting of men, but the right man could change all that. She needs someone to be gentle and patient, but strong enough to set her straight when she's wrong. And she needs someone to love her like she's never been loved before, leastways by a man." Her words took on a gentle emphasis. "You're that man."

Cale threw up his hands. "Wait a minute. She and I can't go five minutes without trying to kill each other. It would never work. I'm not the person she needs. Besides, I'm not ready to settle down. With her, or any other woman."

Sally settled an accusing eye on Cale. "I've read all the signs and you two belong together, and nothing you say is gonna change what's written in heaven."

"You expect me to believe that?" Cale snapped, despite his best intentions to remain calm.

"Do you want to see Miss Shay married to the likes of Cotton? Could you sleep at night knowing she'd be miserable? 'Cause that's what's gonna happen if you don't do something."

"What happens to Miss Shay is none of my business. I'm all wrong for her. Nothing good could ever come out of it. Besides, I'm not ready to settle down. The last thing I want is a wife."

Sally opened her mouth to refute him, but Cale didn't hang around to listen. He felt as if the wind had been knocked out of him. He made a mental inventory of his thoughts, filing away all emotion except one: anger. He was angry because Sally had forced him to examine his interest in Shay, forced him to realize that his interest went beyond physical attraction. He reined in his thoughts. When had he started to think of Shay in terms other than desire?

That evening after supper, much to her surprise, Shay found Aunt Nettie playing checkers in the parlor. With Cale!

Brows drawn, Shay stood in the doorway. Oh, wonderful! she fumed to herself. This is just what she needed. If she didn't know better, she would have thought Aunt Nettie was deliberately trying to wrangle her into Cale's company.

She covertly watched her aunt and the intruder. The two were engrossed in their game and paid her no attention. She'd have to admit that he was a handsome devil, looking especially so with the soft lantern light falling across his rugged features. His good looks could warm the heart of any unsuspecting female. At least, something in Shay's lower regions grew heated at the sight of him.

But damned if he didn't get her hackles up—because her attraction for him grew each time she saw him. She tried to fight his frightening allure with anger.

Perhaps she could slip away unnoticed. She'd already turned to leave when her aunt's voice stopped her. "Shay, darling, come and join us. Mr. Breland plays a challenging game of checkers."

Shay's mind scrambled for an excuse to decline her aunt's invitation, but Nettie's next statement thwarted the effort. "I was telling Mr. Breland how well you manage the piano. He'd like to hear you play."

She squared her shoulders. Trapped with no way out. "I just bet he would," she mumbled past stiff lips.

"What did you say?" Nettie asked, jumping one of Cale's red checkers.

Cale looked up. He had the damnednest way of staring straight through her with a gaze that squeezed her insides. Her contrary side wanted to refuse her aunt's request, but her practical side couldn't refuse her aunt anything.

With a stiff set to her spine, Shay walked over to the piano, in one corner of the room, her eyes

locked on Cale, silently daring him to say something. "I didn't say anything, Aunt Nettie."

"What do you think, Mr. Breland, something
lively?" Nettie asked.

"That'd be just fine. I'm sure Miss Alexander
can play a spirited piece," Cale interjected, immense enjoyment etched in the masculine lines of
his face.

Shay didn't need Sally's abilities at fortune-
telling to catch the meaning of his words.

Flexing her fingers, Shay sat and eyed the keyboard. Her mind searched for a song, then seized
upon an appropriate choice. A wicked smile
spread across Shay's lips. She'd give him something brisk all right—something that would con-
vey just how much she welcomed his company.
She attacked the ivory keys in a forceful rendition
of "Dixie."

All her frustration flowed through her hands,
down to her fingertips, giving dramatic flare to the
selection. With each pass of her hands across the
keys, Shay imagined she was exorcising Cale Breland from her life.

Finished, Shay raised her eyes, feeling quite
pleased with herself. The pinched expression on
Aunt Nettie's face cut short her satisfaction.

"Shay, where are your manners?" Nettie
breathed, clearly scandalized by her niece's choice
of music.

Apparently in the hog trough, Shay thought to
herself. It had seemed a good idea at the time.
Shay could only shrug her shoulders.

Nettie turned to face Cale across the checker-
board. "I'm sure she didn't mean anything by it."

"No offense taken," Cale said smoothly.

Shay's hands curled into fists on her lap. This

was too much! She didn't want or need Aunt Nettie defending her actions to that man. She was a grown woman capable of speaking for herself. "Aunt Nettie, you don't have to make excuses. I played what I felt like playing." She hit Cale with a direct look.

He didn't flinch as he returned her regard. "I'm sure Miss Alexander never does anything she doesn't want to."

If Shay had any doubts as to what he meant, his assessing gaze dispelled them. The skunk! She ground her teeth in mute anger. He had no intention of allowing what had taken place between them to be forgotten. Horse poop! Every time she looked at him she couldn't help but remember their ardent embraces.

If those heated memories weren't bad enough, a tingling sensation tiptoed down her spine when he came to stand beside her.

She didn't help matters by allowing her eyes to meet his. His heated gaze washed over her like warm sunshine, melting her resentment. "Play 'Greensleeves.' "

Unsettled by the blossoming feeling in her stomach, Shay snapped in an undertone, "I don't know that song."

Cale leaned down, took her hands, and moved them to the keyboard. "I'll teach you."

"Where'd you learn to play piano, Mr. Breland?" Nettie interjected.

"In a saloon, ma'am," Cale replied.

He was close, too close, his face only inches from hers, and Shay felt his warm, moist breath stroke her cheek, between the silky play of his fingers atop hers.

Tarnation! Did she have to hit him in the head

for him to understand she didn't want him near her? "I'm sure Aunt Nettie is tired by now."

"Nonsense, my dear. Humor Mr. Breland."

Shay nearly groaned aloud at her aunt's support of Cale's request.

He turned his face toward hers, their noses practically touching. "Yes, humor me." His soft voice drifted across her. It was as if he turned the full force of his potent charm on her.

Slow heat rose from her neck to her cheeks, causing her skin to feel as tight as her nerves. Shay fought the impulse to flee. At that moment, she wanted nothing more than to run away from him—and from the feeling inside her.

Swallowing, Shay could only stare at the mouth so temptingly near hers, the firm lips parted slightly in amusement.

"Shall we begin?" Cale guided her trembling fingers through the motions. "Relax," he coaxed.

To her surprise, that's exactly what she did. At his warm touch, the tension left her shoulder blades and she released her breath in a soft, feathery sigh.

She wanted to be thinking of ways to escape his nearness, but her thoughts drained away, like water through a sieve.

Before Shay realized it, the song had ended and, to her astonishing disappointment, Cale had reseated himself at the checker table.

Closing the lid on the piano, she glanced at Cale. How cool and unaffected he seemed as he resumed his game of checkers with Aunt Nettie with not so much as a glance in her direction.

Disappointment and resentment boiled, hissed, and spewed like a forgotten coffeepot. His curt dismissal of her was a bitter brew to swallow. Well, she hoped he choked on his conceitedness, because the devil could have him for all she cared. Or so she told herself.

Chapter 7

Sheriff Harper looked up from his papers as the door of his office opened and slammed back on its hinges. Jared and Henry Slocum stepped inside. He noted their grim expressions, and he knew they weren't pleased with his progress in finding their father's killer.

"I reckon I know what you boys want and I don't have nothing new to tell you. All I can say is that I'm working on it," Harper said, hoping to pacify them.

Riled, they could be mighty dangerous. And reckless. When the Slocums wanted something, they let nothing stand in their way.

Tall and sturdy, blond-haired and green-eyed, Jared Slocum spoke. "You've had long enough."

Pushing his hat back on his head, Harper leaned forward, his arms atop his desk. "Now, Jared, you know these things take time. I've got some leads that I'm checking out."

He had purposely dragged his feet, knowing by the witnesses' accounts that the elder Slocum had been cheating and had fired the first shot. Self-defense wasn't a crime, and he hadn't wanted to arrest Slocum's killer.

A slightly shorter version of his older brother, Henry entered the conversation. "We want the man who murdered Pa." He sat on the corner of the desk and reached out to grab the front of Harper's shirt. "We want him real bad. Understand?"

"Yeah, I got that." Sheriff Harper looked Henry squarely in the eye. "Now get your hand off me."

Smiling, Henry released the older man. "Good to see we understand one another."

"I understand you better than I'd like to," Harper said.

Henry looked at his brother. "Maybe Jared and me will just take care of this piece of business ourselves." Henry's regard returned to Sheriff Harper. "Our boys done told us that there were two of them. But we didn't get any names." Henry's hand came to rest on the butt of his revolver. "Just tell us what you know."

Harper adjusted his shirt. He looked at Henry, then at Jared, who stood next to the door. Harper didn't envy the poor bastard they were after.

The sheriff cleared his throat. "The one who lost his arm was named Brad Alexander."

"And the other?" Jared asked.

"No one knew," Harper responded.

Jared walked to the bulletin board, littered with wanted posters, and stared momentarily at the sketches. Then, slowly, he turned. "Where's this Alexander from?"

"Somewhere around Austin."

"Did he murder Pa?"

"No. His partner fired the shot that dropped your pa."

Jared stroked the butt of the revolver strapped to his side. "Then he's the one who's gonna pay."

"Yeah," Henry chimed in. "With a bullet through his gut."

Jared's mouth twisted in a chilling snarl. "Shooting may be too easy. A hanging might do better." His gaze went flat and hard. "Hanging's slow. Don't want him to die too quick."

Leaning over a table in the living room, Shay ran a rag across the polished wood. Dust motes danced on morning sunbeams.

She hated cleaning. Aunt Nettie kept trying to teach her domestic ways, but Shay knew it was no use. She'd much rather be riding her horse or mending fences.

Sighing, she looked out the window. Nature tugged at her. It was a beautiful day, not a cloud in the sky. What she wouldn't give for a ride in the pasture.

What she wouldn't give to toss this dust rag away.

On the other side of the room, Nettie stood on a stool, dusting drapes. "Shay, when we're finished here, I'd like to start on the upstairs."

Shay pivoted. "All right. But next time, why don't we hire a local Mexican woman to come and help? I worry about you overdoing things."

"That's what your father says, but I enjoy having something to do other than needlepoint and such."

Shay grinned. "You'll never change."

"I don't intend to." Nettie stood on tiptoe to reach a high place.

"Let me do those top shelves."

"I can manage."

Suddenly, the stool tipped and Nettie crashed to the floor.

Shay ran to her aunt and knelt beside her. "Are you all right?" she asked breathlessly, her heart pounding.

Nettie blinked. "Goodness, I don't know what happened."

Shay helped her aunt to a sitting position. "The stool slipped out from under you."

"Such a silly thing."

Shay placed her hands beneath her aunt's arms to lift her. "Let me help you to the settee. Maybe you should lie down."

"Nonsense, I'm fine," Nettie answered.

Nettie steadied herself on a nearby chair arm and pushed herself up. Standing, she smoothed the hair from her face. She breathed deeply. "See? I'm fine."

She took a step. Agony contorted her face.

"What?" Shay asked, alarmed.

"My ankle," Nettie gasped. "I've twisted it."

Shay pushed the chair toward her aunt. "Sit down."

Nettie did.

Anxiety colored Shay's voice. "You need to stay off your feet. I'll get Sally. We'll have to carry you up the stairs to your bedroom."

She found Sally in the kitchen, along with Breland. He stood talking to Sally, firewood in his arms.

"Sally, I need your help. Aunt Nettie's fallen."

Sally's eyes widened with alarm. "Dear Lord."

Breland dumped the mesquite into the wood box. "Maybe I can help."

Shay didn't argue. Her only concern was her aunt. She headed for the living room. Sally and Breland followed.

In obvious pain, Nettie cradled her head in one hand.

Shay moved toward her aunt, but Breland shouldered past her. Shay started to protest, then decided against it. No need to upset her aunt further.

Breland knelt beside Nettie. "Where does it hurt, Mrs. Grisham?"

Nettie's voice quavered. "My ankle."

Breland glanced at Shay and Sally. "Will one of you take off her shoe and stocking so I can get a closer look?"

Shay immediately set about removing the articles. When she took the stocking off, she chewed her lower lip. The ankle had begun to swell considerably.

She moved away and allowed Breland to make his inspection.

"I'll try not to hurt you," he said, gently probing the injured area.

Tears moistened Nettie's eyelashes. "I trust . . . you, Mr. Breland."

He smiled reassuringly, then bent his head.

Tears now flowed freely as Nettie suffered his handling.

"Sorry." Compassion threaded Breland's voice, as he watched Nettie's face cloud with pain.

Shay observed Breland's treatment of her aunt. Strange how a man with such large hands could be so gentle. His sensitivity struck a chord within Shay.

"Nothing's broken. I think you'll be fine if it's wrapped and you stay in bed for a while." Breland scooped up Nettie. "Put your arms around my neck and I'll carry you to your room."

"I'll get her bed ready," Sally said before disappearing up the stairs. Shay followed close behind.

Inside the bedroom, Breland eased Nettie onto the bed.

With her back propped up with pillows, Nettie whispered haltingly, "Thank you, Mr. Breland. You've been very kind."

Shay could have sworn he reddened beneath his tan, but she was too busy tending to her aunt to give it much thought.

"I'll go so Miss Alexander can wrap your foot," Cale said.

Nettie looked at the door momentarily, then at her niece. "We're lucky to have Mr. Breland around."

Sally eased off Nettie's dress and slipped a gown on her.

"We sure is," she chimed in, also looking in Shay's direction.

"Well, I'm not so sure, but I am thankful he was nearby this time." Shay acknowledged his patience and gentleness in dealing with her aunt.

Half an hour later, having wrapped her aunt's ankle and waited until she drifted off to sleep, Shay crept downstairs to the kitchen.

Her stomach growled and she realized it had been a long time since breakfast. She sliced some cheese and bread, poured herself a glass of buttermilk, and sat down to eat.

Slowly chewing her food, she allowed her thoughts to drift. Cale Breland was certainly a mystery—hard and domineering at times, gentle and attentive at others.

She sipped her buttermilk. He was different from the other men she knew—painfully blunt and direct. She couldn't imagine him saying something he didn't mean, or doing something he regretted. Her instincts told her he would never make a promise he couldn't—or wouldn't—keep. His pride demanded no less.

Finished with her light meal, Shay went to the porch and sat in the swing. From across the yard, she saw Cale sitting inside the barn mending a bridle. She tried to look away, but she found her gaze irresistibly drawn to him. Memories, like tinkling wind chimes, floated about her. Something drew her to him. Something nameless, but nevertheless powerful. At that moment, she wanted to be with him.

Not knowing what she would say or do, and against her better judgment, Shay walked to the barn.

Upon hearing footsteps, Breland glanced up. Surprise—and wariness—registered in his eyes.

Now that she was there, she suddenly felt foolish. What would she say? She thought of what he had done for her aunt. "I wanted to thank you for your help," she said, almost shyly.

"Your aunt is a nice lady." He returned to his mending.

Although he offered no further conversation to encourage her to stay, Shay felt the strong compulsion to remain.

Sitting on a nearby bale of hay, Shay plucked a straw and stuck it in her mouth. "She means the world to me."

"You're fortunate to have her."

She tilted her head to the side, observing the neat stitches in the leather. "What do you mean?"

"She cares a lot about you."

"And I love her."

His voice, low and soft, hung in the air. "Then you're luckier than most."

He intrigued her. She wanted to know more. "How so?"

"Some folks never have anyone they're close to."

"And you're one of them?" she inquired impulsively. Her eyes widened. What had possessed her to ask such a personal question? Yet, on some level, she wanted very much to know the answer.

His hand stopped and he raised his head. Within that lapis-colored gaze, she saw a brief flash of vulnerability before he shadowed it. "I don't need anybody." Mild hostility edged his words. "Especially a wife."

Shay wanted a glimpse behind Cale's steely exterior. She was determined to find the crack in his armor of aloofness. "Everyone needs someone," she persisted.

"People just think they do."

His masculinity intrigued her. Boldness, previously foreign to Shay, infiltrated her being. "What do *you* think?" She removed the straw from her mouth.

He frowned. "That you've asked enough questions for one day."

Despite his obvious reluctance to talk, Shay felt compelled to press on. The intuitive sense that something was going to happen between them— something wonderful and completely unknown— pushed her to learn more.

She leaned forward, her face inches from his, and whispered, "Then what do you *need*?"

Jesus, Cale groaned inwardly as he watched a dreamy sensuality infuse her face. Was she aware of what she did to him? Did she realize how tempting she looked with her lips parted in unknowing invitation? Her eyes were lit with an inner beauty matched only by her physical loveliness. He was very much aware of the graceful lines of her face, throat, and breasts. Suddenly, he wanted her with an earthshaking urgency. Disturbed, he breathed deeply, knowing that too much desire could ruin all his plans.

Damn. How could any man resist her? How could *he?*

His body urged him to kiss her, while his common sense pleaded for restraint. Desire displaced the blood in his veins and moved hot and thin through him. He had never wanted a woman as much as he did Shay. The need to be with her overshadowed all else.

His eyes betrayed his feverish emotion. "What I need is you in my arms." His voice, though low and hushed, bordered on urgency.

They both stood.

"I think I'd better go," Shay mumbled, knowing it was dangerous to remain with him. She turned to leave.

Cale reached out and stopped her with a hand on her arm. "No. Don't."

Shay moistened her lips. "I . . . shouldn't stay." His touch was doing crazy things to her insides.

"You're the one who came looking for me, remember?"

"I know." How well she knew, and now she was caught in a trap of her own making.

"Ssh," Cale whispered.

He pulled her into his arms, her breasts a soft warmth pressing against his chest. His lips—full, fiery, demanding—devoured hers. The feel of her mouth against his sent a bolt of sensation crackling through him. The manifestation of his desire pulsated as she leaned into him.

He kissed her until her breath came in tiny, punctuated gasps of pleasure. Her will became suspended on wings of intense emotion. Nothing mattered except the feel of him. She felt strength, heat, flesh and blood.

Their lips cleaved together feverishly. Her fingers clutched his shirt front, opening and closing. Her blood sang through her veins. Her body was reduced to a tingling mass.

Cale left her mouth and touched her warm forehead with his moist lips. Next, he lightly kissed her eyes, her cheek, her ear. There, he lingered, darting the tip of his tongue in and out, rendering Shay incapable of thought, word, or deed. Yet never had she felt so alive.

"You're so beautiful," Cale breathed, his voice coming warm and damp against her neck.

She closed her eyes and moistened her lips. "Cale." The single syllable drifted from her mouth like a soft breeze.

"I know."

She tilted her head back and gave him access to her neck. He laved and gently nipped the skin along the slender column. She moaned.

He brought her hands to his mouth and lightly ran his teeth across her knuckles. It was an exotic feeling, one Shay had never experienced, but she liked it. Immensely. She kept her eyes shut.

His fingers worked their way into the band of her trousers, pulling her shirt free. They traveled beneath the chemise, upward until he discovered the soft underside of one breast. Her breath came quickly and sporadically. She held it each time he moved as if she awaited the pleasure his touch promised. His touch did not disappoint her as his fingers stroked her breast and then molded themselves about the fleshy globe. Slowly, he squeezed it, teasing the nipple into an aching point with his thumb.

His mouth drew near hers, his breath stirring the tiny hairs curling at her temple. "God, I could kiss you all over."

He kissed her again, while his hand played havoc with her senses.

His touch all but reduced her to liquid. She didn't feel as if she had a bone in her body, or a stable muscle to support her frame, or blood that wasn't pounding through her.

A curious feeling began in the pit of her stomach—fanning down her body. She didn't know or understand what was happening to her, but she didn't care.

Cale sensed Shay's near surrender. She was so soft, so warm, so alive. The knowledge excited him yet, at the same time, sobered him to the seriousness of the situation. What the hell was he doing? He was about to make love to his friend's niece, his mind shouted.

He had never regretted taking what women offered him, but he would regret causing Shay pain. Had Shay been an experienced woman, he would have swept them both into the heady realms of pleasure. But she was innocent, undeserving of a casual romp in the hay. And neither was he ready for marriage.

He thought that he had secured his desire, but the taste of her tentative, sweet lips made passion glow with near-blinding light, pleading, yet demanding.

At that same moment, Shay came to her own

conclusions about the propriety of the situation. Passion dissipated like so much smoke, clearing her judgment. Shamelessly, she had ignored normal restraints when the headlong urgency of desire had taken hold. As she yielded to that driving need, diffident acceptance transformed into fervent reaction.

But it was Cale who broke the contact first and backed away. "I don't want to hurt you, Shay. I think you'd better go."

Shay stared at Cale. Passion hardened the lines of his face. She had no trouble reading what was plainly written in his gaze. He wanted her. And, heaven help her, she wanted him. She pondered the conflicting emotions whirling inside her, more violent than any twister.

When she managed to find words, Shay forced herself to speak with as much dignity as possible. "I'm sorry I bothered you."

They stood, staring at one another, and the already racking tension in the barn escalated to unbearable levels.

For the briefest moment, she thought he meant to extend his hand in supplication, but Cale seemed to sense her probing eyes, and he kept his arms stiffly at his sides.

"What happened was my fault. It won't happen again," he said softly.

Shay knew his admission must have cost his pride dearly. She turned her back on him.

With slow steps, she walked toward the house. She knew what she had allowed to happen was wrong, but being in his arms had felt so right. Shamefaced, she admitted that she had never experienced such intense emotions—emotions which left her drained, but strangely wanting more.

Shay felt cold—then hot—then cold again. Her body trembled with depressed emotions as she continued toward the house. Oh, she was headstrong and unpredictable all right. But she had never in her life done anything so daring, or allowed a man such brazen liberties. And while she had felt closer to Cale than she'd ever felt toward any man, Shay had never felt as alone as she did at that moment.

How could she look at Cale without remembering what had transpired between them? She couldn't. No more than her body could forget.

Just when she'd thought Cale couldn't surprise her any more than he already had, he did. She had all but offered herself to him and he had refused to take advantage of her. He must care about her more than she dared to hope.

In that moment of honesty, Shay's inner voice told her to stop analyzing her thoughts and to trust her feelings. Despite everything that happened, she wanted him. She had glimpsed what life could be like with Cale. The joy she felt being in his arms far outweighed any trepidations about the unknown she might have had. His essence filled an empty void inside her, making her feel alive and whole. She had missed too much of life already because of her father. She wouldn't waste what time she had left. When Cale left Twin Creeks, Shay intended to go with him.

Propped up with mounds of pillows at her back, Nettie smiled at Cale. "Mr. Breland, I sent for you because I have a favor to ask."

Hat in hand, Cale smiled. "Yes, ma'am?"

"Sneed left me with instructions to purchase new dresses for Shay." Nettie smoothed the sheets with one hand. "And as we both know, I'm unable to leave this bed. I was wondering if you'd take Shay into Austin and see that she buys suitable clothing."

Cale cleared his throat. "Ma'am? I'm not sure I heard you right." At least, he hoped he hadn't.

"I'm afraid you have. Now you're probably thinking why don't I ask Sally to go. The truth is, I can't. I need her here to help me. Although it's not exactly proper having you take Shay to Austin, it would be less proper having you assist me with my personal needs."

"Why not wait until the men return?"

"Sneed left specific orders to have those dresses for Shay. Besides, he did leave you in charge, so to speak."

"If that's the way you want it," Cale said stiffly.

"I know I can trust you, Mr. Breland."

Cale gripped his hat tighter. "Who's going to tell Miss Alexander?"

"You leave that to me."

Cale groaned to himself. It was going to be one hell of a day.

Shay's head pounded unmercifully as she rode alongside Cale in the buggy. It seemed Cale took great pleasure in hitting every rut and pothole in the road, jostling her against him and the side of the conveyance. She'd probably be black and blue by the time they reached Austin.

Rounding her shoulders, she tried to relieve the tension from the fatiguing hours they'd spent in the jarring surrey. Even with the black top shading them, perspiration trickled down the sides of her face, making curly red tendrils stick to her temples. She lifted her arms, attempting to catch a draft to cool the clammy skin beneath her shirt. She felt as if someone were sitting on her chest as she tried to breathe in the dry, hot air.

It didn't help matters that Cale hadn't spoken a word since they left Twin Creeks. She had given up any effort at conversation fifteen miles back. Clearly, he wasn't happy about escorting her into town.

Shay stole a glance at Cale. She intended only a glance, but her gaze strayed to his mouth. She remembered the feel of his lips against hers. A rash of color stained her cheeks.

She forced herself to concentrate on the landscape. Only after several minutes of struggling with herself did Shay manage to steer her thoughts from Cale.

At last, they reached Austin.

"The dry goods store is not much farther." She pointed straight ahead to the intersection of East Sixth Street and Congress Avenue. "There on the corner."

In the middle of the thoroughfare, Shay observed heat waves rippling across the landscape. Surely this was the hottest day of the year.

Moments later, they pulled in front of Rutherford and Rector's store.

Cale set the brake, wrapped the reins around the wooden handle, and climbed out of the buggy, reaching out for Shay's hand. He helped her to the ground, careful their bodies didn't touch.

Shay frowned. He certainly wasn't going to make this easy.

They walked across the wooden sidewalk and went inside the mercantile. Pausing in the doorway, Shay inhaled a variety of smells: cheese, pickles, coffee beans, cured beef jerky, and a host of spices.

Along each wall was a long, wooden counter, backed with rows of shelves filled with a myriad of items, from canned goods to packets of seeds. Atop the counters were jars filled with an assortment of candy. At the ends of the counters were various bins filled with coffee beans, flour and other staples. The table of yard goods was to the rear.

Shay walked past the barrels of crackers, apples and pickles positioned in the center of the store, to the fabric.

"Why, Shay Alexander, I haven't seen you in a long spell," crooned Rudella Holcomb, a tall woman with a generous figure.

"It has been a while," Shay returned.

"What can I do for you?" asked the clerk.

"Papa wants me to have some new dresses. I need to purchase some yard goods."

Mrs. Holcomb's brown eyes brightened. "For how many dresses?"

"Aunt Nettie said four."

"Come right over here. I've got some lovely bolts of fabric to choose from."

Shay followed Mrs. Holcomb over to a large table near one wall. The two women proceeded to choose a cream-colored muslin, a lavender cotton, a green and white gingham, and a blue calico. The task went quickly with Mrs. Holcomb's assistance, and Shay was glad she didn't have to deal with such unimportant matters any longer than necessary.

Finished, Shay paid for her purchases and bid the Holcombs good-bye. Unexpectedly, Cale, whether consciously or not, placed his hand on the small of her back and guided her toward the door. Shay was only vaguely aware of reaching the buggy. All she knew was the pressure of his fingers against her back and the tingling sensation darting up and down her spine.

From a distance, Shay heard Cale's voice. "Any other stops to make?"

"The dressmaker's."

Cale escorted Shay to the seamstress's establishment down the street. Forty-five minutes later, Shay was through with the ordeal of making arrangements to have the gowns made.

Stepping out of the shop and onto the sidewalk, Cale asked, "Now where to?"

Shay looked at him over her shoulder. His blue eyes were speculative, his expression slightly guarded. She was determined to seek a truce. Her plans would be ruined if he continued to be cautious around her.

"I'd like some lemonade. There's a café across the street," she heard herself say.

The café was small, boasting several small, round tables with matching chairs. Red gingham curtains framed the two windows.

Cale hung his hat on a wall peg. They sat near the door and soon enjoyed a glass of lemonade.

Sipping her tangy refreshment, Shay peered at Cale from beneath long, sooty lashes. He quietly watched her, his brow drawn, and she knew without any words being said that he was thinking about what had happened between them in the barn.

His gaze told her all she needed to know. He desired her. Even in her naïveté, Shay would have to be blind not to recognize the longing. Dear Lord, she returned the feeling.

She drained the last of her lemonade and set the glass down. Needing to fill the silent void, she said, "That was delicious."

"Would you like another?"

"No, thank you." She toyed with the rim of her empty glass, thinking of ways to draw him out. "I've never had much time or opportunity to enjoy an afternoon like this."

Cale finished his own drink, but said nothing. He looked impatient and Shay knew he wanted to leave.

Bracing herself with determination, she reached out and covered his fingers with her hand. "I'm glad you brought me." There, she had made the first move. The next was his.

His hand tensed beneath her touch. "We'd best be going."

Shay schooled her features to hide her disappointment. She had to get him to talk to her. "Can't we at least be friends?" She pushed the words past suddenly dry lips.

"Is that what you want?" His eyes darkened and his bold stare made her feel vulnerable.

In the pit of her stomach she felt a dull, sweet ache for which she knew no name. "Yes."

He remained thoughtfully quiet. Shay heard no other sound—except one—the soft beating of her heart. She also knew something elemental, a fragile bond, was being woven between them, connecting them.

At last, he said, "I didn't mean to hurt you."

"I know," she whispered too quickly, too breathlessly.

Rising, Cale settled his hat on his head and extended his hand to Shay. She accepted his offer and they left the café.

He lifted her easily into the surrey, then climbed in himself. With a sharp slap, he brought the reins down across the rump of the gelding and they left Austin.

Later, in the waning afternoon light, they reached a bend in the Colorado River, having decided to take the shorter way back. On a strip of flat, dry sand a few feet from the water's edge, Cale pulled the gelding to a halt and looked thoughtfully across the rippling waters.

"Why are we stopping?" Shay asked, tucking a loose strand of sweat-damp hair behind her ear.

"You're going to have to see to the horse," Cale responded, climbing out of the surrey. "Maybe we should've come back the same way we came. I don't like having to cross so late in the day. Can't make the water out clearly." He removed his boots and socks before easing into the river. "I'm going to walk ahead and check the riverbed for soft spots. I'll mark a path with sticks. You drive the rig between them."

He waded farther into the water.

"Be careful." Shay shuddered at the sudden feeling of impending disaster.

The only sounds were the running water and the pounding of her pulse in her ears. She said a quick prayer.

Looking ahead, she saw the pecan branches Cale had planted intermittently into the riverbed.

He turned and shouted, "Don't stop for anything. Keep the horse moving."

Shay got out of the rig and removed her boots before grabbing the lead rein. Breathing deeply, she stepped into the river. As she navigated her way among the markers the murky water swirled around her, grabbing greedily at her legs, trying to pull her under. She felt the river bottom shift beneath her feet, sand oozing between her toes.

Midway the gelding began to drift off course, nervously stepping sideways into an uncharted area. She yanked on the leather.

Suddenly, the horse panicked and reared, slicing the air with its front hooves. Before Shay realized what was happening, she felt something strike her near the temple. There was a brief, blinding explosion of pain inside her head, then nothing.

She never knew when she slipped beneath the water's surface.

But Cale did. He had turned around just when the horse struck her.

"Damn," he gasped, and dove into the water. He couldn't distinguish between the sound of rushing water and the pounding of his heart.

He berated himself for not handling the horse himself as he cut through the water with swift, strong strokes until he reached her. He located her near the bottom. Grasping one arm, he pulled Shay to the bank. His stomach plummeted as he looked down at her unconscious form.

Stark terror gripped his neck in an unrelenting hold as he turned Shay over and forced water from her lungs. Then he eased her onto her back and pressed his hand to her nose. He felt the faint stirring of her breath. He released his own pent-up breath.

With trembling hands, he brushed her wet, tangled hair from her face.

A bruise was already forming near her right temple. Luckily for Shay, the blow had been only a glancing one, causing no serious damage.

"You should've been more careful, Shay Alexander. Look at me, dammit!" he growled, unable to separate pain from a feeling of helplessness.

With water trickling from her mouth, Shay coughed and opened her eyes. Realization slowly dawned in the green depths as she looked up at Cale. With a tentative hand, she touched her head and moaned.

"You're going to be fine." It was all Cale could do to keep his voice even. Concern swiftly gave way to anger—anger at the dangerous situation. "I should've tended to the horse myself."

"Then it might have been you."

Droplets of water fell from his hair onto her face. "You could've drowned."

She touched his cheek with wrinkled, cool fingers. "But I didn't, thanks to you."

Cale enfolded her in his strong embrace. Never had Shay felt safer or more content than she did in that singular moment.

Chapter 8

Dusk had fallen by the time Cale located the horse and buggy.

"Damn," he groused. "Of all the luck."

She came alongside Cale and looked at the buggy, which had a broken rear axle. "Could have been worse."

"Not much." He raked his fingers through his hair. "We don't have any food or water. The roan picked up a stone bruise, and it's a long walk to Twin Creeks."

She placed a hand on his arm. "I know all the neighbors around these parts. In the morning we can reach the nearest place." She shivered from her damp clothes and the cool night air.

"Yeah, but in the meantime, I'm going to hunt us some food. Do you think you can get a fire going?"

Shay forced a smile. "Of course I can. I'm not helpless."

Cale laughed. "I'm well aware of that." On a more serious note, he added, "I'll be back as soon as I can. There are matches wrapped in oilskin in my saddlebags."

She wasted no time in gathering wood, and

shortly she had a small fire going. Stretching her fingers toward the welcome flames, she relaxed and enjoyed the warmth as it penetrated her chilled skin and soggy clothing. She grew tired and sat, leaning her back against a tree trunk. Her eyelids grew heavy. She dozed off.

Shay didn't know how long she'd been asleep when she awoke. Sitting up, she gingerly touched the side of her head, and she squeezed her eyes shut against the throbbing in her temples.

"You feeling better?" came Cale's voice.

"Yes. I think so." She opened her eyes. Cale was hunkered down beside the fire, cooking something on a spit.

An appealing aroma drifted to her. Her stomach growled. Licking her lips, Shay said, "That smells good. What is it?"

Cale looked up. "Squirrel."

Her mouth watered as she watched the small animal turn on the spit. She felt as if her stomach were shaking hands with her backbone.

Shay sat next to Cale, her feet tucked beneath her. "How much longer 'til it's done?"

"Right now." Cale slid the squirrel off the stick and onto a flat rock. He cut it into pieces with his knife, then handed Shay a portion. "Careful, it's hot."

She held the fare with her fingertips and blew on the meat until it cooled enough to eat. Then she attacked her portion with barely curbed ferocity.

Cale glanced up from his supper and laughed dryly. "Hey, slow down or you'll choke."

"It's just that I'm so hungry," she said between bites.

Cale only shook his head as he went back to his own food.

By the time they had finished, Shay felt colder. She inched closer to the fire.

Orange and yellow flames were a stark contrast against the backdrop of night. She bent her head against her raised knees and closed her eyes, lulled by the circle of heat.

A shiver racked her body and Shay coughed hoarsely.

Cale glanced at her. "I'll get something to warm you." Momentarily, he returned from the wagon with a bottle in hand. He handed the whiskey to her. "Here, you'd better drink this. It'll ward off the cold."

She stared at the offered liquor. How many times had she cursed her father for living by that vile bottle? she silently wondered. Hundreds? Thousands of times? She'd lost count over the years. She pushed the thought to the background of her mind. She knew she couldn't refute the necessity of having a drink. Besides, knowing Cale, if she didn't have some, he'd probably pour it down her throat.

Unaccustomed to liquor, Shay tentatively accepted the whiskey and took a small drink. The fiery liquid made her sputter and gag as it went down her throat.

Eyes watering, she held the bottle out to him. "That's . . . awful," she wheezed.

"Depends." He pushed the bottle back at her. "You haven't had enough to do any good. Take a bigger drink this time."

"I don't want to get drunk."

"What you don't want is to get sick."

"Well . . ." She coughed again, the sound coming from deep within her chest.

"Now."

She knew there was no use in arguing with him by the absolute, implacable tone of his voice. She brought the whiskey to her lips, tilted the bottle up, and closed her eyes.

Well, here goes, she thought, and swallowed—more liquor than she intended. When it hit the bottom of her stomach, she gagged and coughed at the bite of it, her face turning beet red.

Momentarily, her breathing returned to normal and she looked up at Cale. "Satisfied?"

"For now." His gaze roamed over her in slow perusal, making his words oddly sensual. Then his gaze caught hers. "You'd best get out of those wet clothes before you catch something worse than a cold."

Her mouth dropped open. "I can't. I've got nothing to wear."

Cale remained thoughtfully silent. A second later he pulled his shirt from his waistband and began unbuttoning it.

Shay's eyes grew round. "What are y-y-you doing?" she stuttered in a thin, trembling voice.

"Giving you something to wear." He gave her a lazy grin and handed the shirt to her "You can change behind that bush."

"I can't take your shirt," Shay protested, her mind whirling with possibilities and consequences.

"It's that or go naked. But I'm not going to let you catch pneumonia."

She couldn't refute his logic. Convention seemed less important when confronted by necessity. Garment in hand, she headed for the bushes, where she undressed, all except her drawers, as quickly as her trembling fingers would allow. She spread her damp clothes on the bushes to dry. She shrugged into the shirt, rolled up the long sleeves to her elbows, and buttoned it to her neck. The coarse homespun was still warm from Cale's body heat, and she enjoyed the sensation against her skin. But she was painfully aware of her exposed legs, from mid-thigh to toes. Shay bit her lower lip. There was nothing to do but make the best of the situation—if that were possible.

She squared her shoulders and returned to the circle of light. Cale stood beside the fire. He looked directly at her. Firelight reflected off his tanned, muscular chest. Never had he seemed so imposing, or so threateningly masculine. Her stomach clenched as his eyes traveled over her in a slow, heated pattern.

He moved closer. "Better?"

Her breathing grew restricted. She could only nod.

He moved even closer. "I thought so."

She tried to swallow against the sudden constriction in her throat, as she looked up at the tall, hard length of him and into his blue eyes.

Reaching out, he lightly traced her cheek with the backs of his fingers, and she trembled. She felt his body heat, his warm breath on her face, along with a building awareness of him that threatened to overwhelm her.

Yet he had done nothing, said nothing, threatening. All he did was look at her. She must be running a fever. Why else were her thoughts becoming fuzzy?

"I appreciate the shirt," she said lamely.

"I know." His words flowed over her like golden honey and coated her senses in titillating sweetness.

She stared at the breadth of his shoulders, the

hard flowing muscles of his arms, and his large strong hands. She shuddered. Did he know what he did to her? she wondered miserably.

Cale knew what she did to him. He was hard with desire. The elegant line of her legs and calves, down to her trim ankles, almost pushed him over the edge of constraint.

He wanted to see more of her. So very much more.

He wanted to do more than look at her.

He wanted to make love to her. All night.

What was the matter with him? His body trembled from desire, while she trembled from cold. He couldn't allow himself to forget that she wasn't the woman for him. He didn't make a habit of seducing virgins. He cursed beneath his breath.

Cale picked up the whiskey and walked to the far side of the fire. Raising the bottle to his mouth, he took a swig and rolled the liquid around his tongue before swallowing.

He stretched out beside the fire and drank more. His hand tightened around the bottle's neck as he stared at the glowing embers. He'd have to keep his distance from Shay or he couldn't guarantee what would happen.

Shay, on the other hand, though relieved, was puzzled at Cale's sudden withdrawal. She sank to the ground and sat cross-legged, tucking the shirt over her lap.

She struggled to turn her thoughts from Cale, but her determination faltered. His closeness, the heady man-smell of him, mesmerized her. At that moment, she neither knew nor understood herself.

She forced her gaze from him, but it willfully strayed back to his virile form. She experienced an almost irresistible impulse to go to him, to make him stop this turmoil inside her as she instinctively knew only he could do.

A cleansing breath quelled her apprehension. Dawn would be a long time coming, she thought woefully.

Another chill seized her, and she coughed. Cale rose, walked over to Shay, and offered her the bottle of whiskey. She accepted the liquor and drank deeply. She didn't gag this time, so she drank again. The whiskey warmed her entire body as it traveled through her veins. She stared pensively into the flames and felt herself relax. Tired and sore, she groaned as she stretched her arms.

Cale had returned to the far side of the fire, and her gaze slid to him. The dancing firelight threw his body into relief. There was something irresistible about him that attracted her.

She indulged in the whiskey a third time. Liquor trickled down her chin and she drew her hand across the spill. She lowered her head and intently studied the bottle she held.

From the shadows, Shay felt Cale's gaze on her. She bent her legs to hug her knees, cradled her head in the fold of her arms, and gingerly held the whiskey in one hand. Turning blurring eyes toward the fire, she smiled as the liquor worked its magic in the ensuing moments.

Time became distorted, and Shay had no idea how long she sat there, staring into the fire.

How strange she felt. Her thoughts became loose, along with her tongue. "Have you had a lot of women?" she blurted out.

Cale's head came up and he looked at her across the fire. "Now, that's an interesting question." There was soft but unquestionable humor in his voice.

"If it's so interesting, then answer me."

"I'd hate to shock a lady such as yourself," he drawled.

Shay giggled. "It might be fun to be shocked."

"What do you want to know?"

"Why don't we start with numbers? How many women have you bedded?"

"Let's just say I've had enough to guarantee I know what to do, and how to do it."

"And did all those women find it pleasurable?"

"I didn't have any complaints."

"Not once?"

"Well," he drawled, "maybe the first time. I was through before she began, seeing how I was only twelve and she was an experienced whore."

"Have you paid most of the ... uh ... women you've been with?"

"Oh, I've had my share of those who didn't make a living on their backs."

"Did you ever want to marry any of the women you'd slept with?"

Cale didn't answer for a long time, and when he finally did, he spoke in a low voice, no more than a rustle of sound. "There was one woman. But that was a long time ago."

"Who was she?"

"That's enough questions for a while." His answer was terse.

"I think you're afraid to answer me."

The reservation in his tone faded into dry amusement again. "What I think is that you've had enough to drink."

"Have I?"

"I gave you that to chase away the chill. Not to get you drunk."

"I don't know ... about these things, but I think it's ... too late for that."

"Give me the bottle."

"No." She hiccuped. She tried to clear her mind, but couldn't.

"Shay, I said give me the whiskey." His voice was woven with patience.

"And I said no." Another sensation wound through her system to curl around her senses. She wanted him to take her in his arms. "If you want it, you'll have to come and get it."

"If I come over there, I'll want more than the damn bottle."

Shay grinned. "And what would that be?"

"You."

The syllable broke over her in soft waves. She remembered his kiss. Perhaps it was because she had enjoyed the feel of his mouth on hers, or perhaps it was because she wanted him to kiss her now.

Whatever the reason, she asked, "Why?"

Cale rose slowly to his feet and walked to her. "Because I've wanted you since the first time I saw you."

"Have you?"

He reached down and pulled her to her feet. "Oh, I've told myself plenty of times that you're not for me, but that hasn't stopped me from wanting you. And right now, there's nothing I'd like better than to be between your legs."

"Do you always go after what you can't have?"

Cale slid his hand through her hair to the nape of her neck. "Can't or shouldn't?"

Shay strained backward, her gaze fastened on his mouth as it came closer and closer, and she couldn't hold a thought. "What?"

"We both know I could have you now, so it's not a question of can't. Whether I should is another matter."

"What if I said you should?"

"Then maybe we're both fools." Cale groaned. "What am I going to do with you?"

"I don't know, but I'm sure you'll think of something."

"You're a damned pain in the ass."

"Am I?"

"Yes."

His mouth moved over hers with slow practiced ease. She wrapped her arms around his neck and her fingers entwined themselves in his silky hair.

He released his hold on her nape and caressed her back. His hands crossed to her chest. His fingers closed around her breasts, and he lightly squeezed the soft mounds. His mouth trailed a wet, burning path from her lips, to her throat, to her earlobe.

A strange, feverish pounding in her temples spread like a drumbeat through her body. Shay whimpered, and he supported her weak, trembling body with one arm.

Cale forced himself to release Shay and step away from her. He would have liked nothing better than to continue kissing her. No, that wasn't true. He would have liked to have made love to her a damned sight better.

But the fact that Shay was drunk—and the fact that she was a virgin—reminded him of some of the reasons he should stay away from her.

She stood there and looked at him in confusion before she lowered her gaze. Her slender shoulders drooped.

Acting on an impulse to comfort her, he said, "I think you've had enough kissing for one day."

Speechless, Shay sat on the ground. She didn't understand her actions or his responses. She shouldn't have encouraged his advances, but she hadn't been able to stop herself. It must be the liquor, some part of her mind tried to convince her. But a deeper part of her knew she was lying.

Moments passed until drowsiness overwhelmed her and she lay down, resting her head in the crook of one arm. She drifted off to sleep.

When Shay awoke the next morning, her head pounded unmercifully and her mouth felt dry as cotton. Slowly, she sat up and looked dolefully at Cale, who stood by the horse.

He must have sensed her regard, because he turned and looked at her with a shrouded expression. "How do you feel?"

"My head hurts."

"It's no wonder, what with that blow to your head and your overdoing the whiskey."

She expected to hear sarcasm in his voice, but instead it was laced with compassion. His empathy heightened her own sense of remorse. "You're right. I don't know what made me behave that way."

"I've seen grown men do mighty strange things. Your not being used to liquor made it easier to set you back on your . . ."

She smiled. "Rear?"

"Something like that." Cale returned her smile. "You'd best get dressed. We've got to get back to Twin Creeks." He returned his attention to the horse.

Shay ducked behind a bush and quickly donned her dried clothes, tucking her shirt into her brown canvas pants, which emphasized her tiny waist and long legs. She shook her boots out, then tugged them on. Next she brought some order to her riotous mass of hair.

Just as she finished, Cale called to her. "Ready?"

Shay moved into the open. "Yes."

"Let's get going. Time's a wasting."

At midday, they arrived at Twin Creeks. They had ridden double on a borrowed mount, with their injured horse in tow. Shay swung off the animal's back and dropped to the ground, Cale following.

Before facing her, he tied the roan to the fence. "I'll go to the house with you."

"That's not necessary."

"If you've got a notion about trying to keep me from getting fired, forget it. I'm not hiding behind a woman's skirts." His gaze passed over her, settling on her hips. "Or pants."

"No one's at fault. What happened to the horse and buggy was an accident."

"Still, I was in charge and I'm responsible."

His dominant tone made her bristle. "And I'm telling you that you're not. I can handle this myself."

"Like you handled yourself last night?"

Her mood darkened. "You've got your nerve. A gentleman wouldn't bring that up."

His foul disposition kept abreast of hers, and he snapped, "And a lady wouldn't have behaved that way."

"I'll never try to help you again."

"I didn't ask you to."

"No, you never ask. You're too busy giving orders."

"Being a major in the infantry for four years, orders come easy."

"It wouldn't hurt you to try and get along."

"Why should I?"

Frustrated, Shay threw up her hands. "You're the most pigheaded male I've ever come across."

"Coming from you, I'll take that as a compliment."

"I don't care how you take it. Or anything else."

Cale moved closer. "Does that apply to yourself?"

Shay blushed from the roots of her hair to her toes.

She opened her mouth to protest, but Cale cut her off. "Save it."

No sooner had Cale and Shay finished their exchange than Sally came out the back door, hurrying toward them. "Where have you two been? Your aunt's been worried sick. Not saying nothing about me." Sally stopped beside Shay, almost out of breath from her brisk pace.

"It's a long story," Shay said. "But the short of it is, we broke an axle, the horse picked up a stone bruise, and we had to walk to the Millers' place to borrow a horse."

Sally's brows drew downward. "It's a good thing your pa isn't here. He'd skin you both alive for being alone together all night."

Shay's heart seemed to stop, then beat again. Sally was right. Her papa would take his shaving strap to her if he knew what had taken place. "Well, he's not here, and there's no way he's going to find out if none of us tells him."

"How you gonna explain the buggy being busted and the horse lame?" Sally asked, hands on her ample hips.

"They'll be taken care of before anyone finds out," Shay responded calmly, although unease tramped up and down her spine. "I figure we've got another couple of days before the men are back from roundup."

Shay turned to Cale. "Return the Millers' horse as soon as possible and get the buggy." Her tone dared him to dispute her.

Cale gritted his teeth, obviously biting his tongue.

Shay smiled sweetly. "You'd better get started."

With a stiff set to his shoulders, Cale walked to the barn, leaving Sally and Shay alone.

"What happened between you two?" Sally asked.

"Nothing."

"Now, Miss Shay, look me straight in the eye."

"Oh, Sally, that worked when I was a child, but not now."

"Look me in the eye."

With a great deal of effort, Shay met Sally's gaze. "Satisfied?"

"When you'll stop lying to yourself." Sally waved her hand when Shay started to say something. "No need to say more about Mr. Breland." Not yet placated, Sally persisted. "What if Mr. Miller should say something to your pa?"

Hooking her arm with Sally's, Shay guided her mother hen toward the house. "Papa hardly ever sees Mr. Miller. We'll just have to take that chance."

Later that afternoon, the sounds of riders broke the stillness. Sally looked up from plucking a hen, and Shay put down her half-eaten apple.

Their eyes met.

Shay bit her lower lip. "The men."

"Just act like nothing happened," Sally said.

Shay nodded and walked to the door. "Here comes Papa." Moving away from the door, she sat back down at the table, picked up a knife, and resumed peeling potatoes.

Sneed strolled into the kitchen, the back door banging against the wooden frame in his wake. "I sent Breland to fetch some strays on the west range." He placed a hand on Shay's shoulder. "Everything all right here?"

Shay moistened her lips. "Aunt Nettie's been in bed with a twisted ankle."

"Anything else?"

"Mr. Breland took me into town so I could order the dresses you wanted me to get." Shay took a fortifying breath and looked her father directly in the eye. "Other than that, nothing happened, Papa."

Sneed glanced at Sally. "I'll expect supper at the usual time." He headed for the library.

Shay's thoughts, like a windmill, whirled inside her head. "Do you think he believed me?"

"You know your pa. If he'd thought anything was wrong, he'd have exploded." Sally added thoughtfully, "Let's just hope, for all our sakes, Mr. Breland got that buggy fixed."

In the distance, storm clouds, their black bellies ripe with rain, rode the southern skyline. The still, oppressive air hung like a pall over the land.

Shooing flies from her face with the wave of a hand, Shay sat in the front porch swing. Aunt Nettie occupied a chair next to her, and Uncle Brad lounged on the steps.

Brad puffed on his pipe. "I missed you two."

Shay pushed off and began swinging. "Not as much as I missed you."

"Seems y'all had your share of excitement."

Shay looked at her aunt, then back to her uncle. "What do you mean?"

"Why, Nettie hurting herself and all."

Nettie smiled faintly. "I assure you I didn't plan it."

"I never know what you two will get into." Brad lowered his pipe. "At least I didn't have to worry about you with Breland here."

Shay nearly groaned aloud. If he only knew the half of it, she thought.

"Why do men think that women can't manage without them?" Nettie asked, piqued at his remark.

Pipe clenched between his teeth, Brad threw up his hand. "Now, don't go getting your tail feathers ruffled, Nettie. I didn't mean anything by it."

"Just making sure," Nettie returned.

Brad looked at Shay. "Don't you trust me?"

Shay stopped her swinging. "I could never keep anything from you."

"And don't start now," Brad said between puffs, patting the spot next to him. "Let's talk."

Shay left the swing and settled beside her uncle.

He put down his pipe and placed his arm around her. "Don't get mad at your aunt, but she told me what happened with Breland."

"Then what's to tell?"

"Your side."

Shay leaned her head against his shoulder. "He didn't take advantage of me, if that's what you mean."

"I know him to be an honorable man, but I wanted to hear it from you."

"Shay, it's just that we were both concerned about you . . ." Nettie's words trailed off as she stared past Brad.

Shay followed the direction of her aunt's gaze. Her heart leaped to her throat as she saw her father coming toward her from the direction of the barn. The slight sway to his steps told her that he had been drinking. Never had she seen such a murderous expression on his face. In that instant, she knew he'd discovered her secret. She tensed.

Brad looked at her. "Don't worry, Pumpkin. I won't let him hurt you." He stood and faced his brother. "What's wrong, Sneed?"

"What I've got to say, I'll say to Shay." Sneed reached out, grabbed Shay by her arm, and jerked her off the steps. "Explain the roan's stone bruise and the missing buggy."

Despite her intentions of remaining unemotional, Shay became defensive. "It wasn't Cale's fault—"

"So, it's Cale now," Sneed scoffed, releasing his hold on Shay. "Since when are you on such friendly terms with the hired hands?"

As if the weather was cooperating with the tension, thunder rumbled in the background, announcing the coming storm, which was no less threatening than the one brewing between the Alexanders.

Brad stood and placed himself between Sneed and Shay. "Why don't we go inside and calmly talk this over."

Sneed shoved Brad out of the way and onto the ground. "Keep your nose out of my business."

Shay knelt beside her uncle. "Are you all right?"

Slowly, Brad rose with Shay's assistance. "I'm fine, Pumpkin."

Shay couldn't bear for her father and uncle to argue. "Papa, it's not what you think."

"Breland is off this ranch as soon as he gets back."

"Papa, you can't do that."

"So you're defending him." The veins along Sneed's neck stood out as his expression darkened. "How long were you alone with that man?"

"Sneed, if you're going to blame someone, blame me. I told Mr. Breland to take Shay into town," Nettie interrupted.

Sneed directed his wrath at his sister-in-law. "Stay out of this!" He leveled his gaze on Shay.

The air crackled with tension. In the distance, thunder boomed like cannon fire.

Shay held her ground against her father's hostility. He'd controlled her life long enough.

"All night," she said in a steady voice, despite her inner turmoil.

"Whore!" The word exploded from Sneed's stiff lips, and he delivered a stinging blow to the side of her face.

Shay swayed, but somehow she kept her balance. She squeezed her eyes shut against the hot tears that threatened. When she opened them, she stared at her father through a misty veil. She didn't know if she could continue to endure her father's cruel treatment.

She placed a hand to her stinging cheek, and she drew a quavering breath. "I did nothing wrong."

"You're alone all night with a man, and nothing's wrong?" Sneed roared. "I'll teach you right from wrong."

Sneed lunged toward Shay, but Brad hurled

himself at his brother. Both men crashed to the ground.

Horrified that her uncle and father should be fighting over her, Shay screamed, "Stop it!"

Disadvantaged by the loss of his arm, Brad was taking the worse of what his brother had to give.

She tried to separate them, but she only succeeded in getting knocked to the ground by her father. Scrambling out of the way, she stood on trembling legs, watching in anguish as her father continued to rain blows upon her uncle.

Her chest heaved with emotion. "Please, Papa! Don't!" Her fingernails dug into the palms of her hands.

Sneed didn't heed her words, nor did he cease his assault on Brad.

Frantic, Shay raced into the house, and seconds later she reemerged, carrying a pistol. She skidded to within inches of the men and fired a shot into the air.

Brad and Sneed froze. When their gazes focused on Shay with a smoking gun in her hand, they staggered to their feet. Blood streamed from cuts on Brad's face, staining his shirt crimson.

Anguish steeled her determination. "If either one of you lays a hand on the other, I swear I'll shoot."

"You think you'll stop me with that?" Sneed twisted his head around and glared at Shay, spitting blood from a split lip.

"Don't make me use it against you, Papa."

Sneed wiped the blood from his mouth on his sleeve. "Look at you. Whore! You're no better than your mother."

Shay's face mirrored her horror in degrees at her father's accusations, and her lips trembled with torment. Her hopes of reconciliation with her father were trampled beneath the heel of his belligerence.

The gun slid from Shay's cold fingers to the ground. With a fist raised to her mouth to muffle a sob, she fled to the barn. While she hurriedly saddled her mare, tears freely flowed down her cheeks as she thought about her father and Uncle Brad. How much more would this family have to suffer? Shay wondered miserably as she cinched her saddle, then dropped the stirrup. And at whose expense would the hostilities continue?

Minutes later, she rode out of the yard toward the hills, leaving Nettie, Brad, and Sneed watching.

Sneed started for the barn, but Brad stopped him. Sneed leveled a baleful glare at his brother.

Brad's chest rose and fell rapidly from the exertion of their struggles, and he returned Sneed's hostile stare with one of his own. "Leave her alone."

"You've interfered for the last time." Sneed clawed at the impeding hand on his arm. "Turn me loose."

Brad's hold tightened. "Not until you listen to reason."

"What am I supposed to do when she admits to being alone all night with that blue belly?"

"You don't know what happened."

"Her reputation is ruined, and I'll be the laughingstock of the entire county."

"Is that all you're worried about?" Incredulity caused Brad's voice to rise. "What about your daughter's feelings?"

"I don't know that she's my daughter."

"You treat your horse better than you do your

own flesh and blood. And that's what she is. You don't know how many times I wished Shay was mine, but Lela was never unfaithful to you. If you'd stay sober long enough, you might be able to see things clearly."

Growling, Sneed jerked free from Brad's grasp and marched into the house, slamming the door behind him.

Brad looked into the distance where Shay had ridden. "I'd better go after her."

"No," Nettie said, a meaningful look in her eye. "We both know where she's headed."

Chapter 9

Shay rode hard, trying to outdistance all of her father's hurtful accusations. A pulse throbbed in her temple, and her throat ached with raw emotion. Dear Lord! Why couldn't her father love her?

A compelling urge to be with Cale displaced Shay's anger and pain. The need to have him hold her in his arms drove her now. He was her only chance at happiness.

Shay gave the horse its head, and she stretched out low over the Appaloosa's neck. The wind whipped the mare's mane against Shay's face as she continued her break to the west.

Thunderheads, accompanied by loud claps of thunder, rolled sullenly across the sky. The heavens opened and released a drenching downpour.

Shay fought for control of her frightened mount. Suddenly, her horse stumbled to its knees. Caught unaware, Shay flew over the mare's head. She hit the ground with a bone-jarring thud. Air raced from her lungs. Rain stung her face as she lay there, trying to catch her breath.

Slowly, Shay struggled to her feet. She cupped her hands over her eyes and looked around. Lightning illuminated the landscape briefly. She saw her fallen horse and hurried toward the still form. Sorrow caused her breath to come in a sharp, painful rasp. Kneeling, she swallowed convulsively as she ran a hand gently over the Appaloosa's twisted neck.

"Why?" Her lips soundlessly formed the single word.

The lump in her throat grew until she felt she would suffocate. This was her fault. If she hadn't ridden out into the approaching storm, her horse would still be alive.

Only after thunder followed on the heels of lightning, and the ground seemed to shake from the heavenly cannon blast, did Shay gather her thoughts. She'd have to find shelter—and soon.

Hampered by the slashing downpour, almost deafened by thunder, Shay thanked her luck when she reached an outcropping of rocks and discovered a cave carved from the limestone. Ducking inside, she sat down and huddled against one stony wall. Shivering from the cold, she clenched her teeth together, trying to stop their chattering.

Her hair hung down her back in red waves, and several tendrils were plastered to the sides of her face. Her sodden clothes clung to her body, and she hugged herself to maintain body heat.

Nothing to do but wait until morning, she thought miserably, as she offered a quick prayer that Cale would find her. Fighting a feeling of desperation, Shay knew it would take a miracle for him to locate her.

She curled into a tight ball and fell into a fitful doze, losing track of time as the cold numbed each of her senses.

* * *

A peal of thunder boomed overhead. Shay jerked upright, clapped her hands over her ears, and squeezed her eyes shut. Momentarily, she opened her eyes. She screamed. A man stood at the cave's entrance, his figure silhouetted fleetingly by a vivid flare of lightning.

Jagged flashes continued to rage against the black sky beyond him. The wind-driven rain pelted the sides of his face, left unprotected by his hat. With each luminous burst, the hair touching his collar appeared shot with silver, and each raindrop that trailed off his slicker sparkled brilliantly.

Merciful Lord, she was going to be murdered. She scrambled to the back of the cave. Maybe she could hide.

In the quiet following the thunder, Shay heard a man's ragged voice. "Shay, if you're in there, answer me!"

Cale. Dear God! He'd found her.

Relief washed over her. "I'm here." She hurried forward.

He moved inside the mouth of the cave. Rain poured off his slicker and hat and pooled at his feet.

"You're here." She threw herself at him, knocking off his hat, and wrapped her arms around his neck. "I prayed you'd find me." She kissed him full on the mouth.

A brief second passed before his arms gathered around her, and he hugged her. With a deep passion that rocked her to the soles of her feet, Cale returned her kiss.

To Shay, it felt as if only a heartbeat had passed before he broke away and cradled her head between his large hands. "I was looking for shelter from the storm when I came across your dead mare not far from here." The sharpness of his voice was interrogating. "What the hell were you thinking?"

"I had to find you."

"Why?"

"Because I needed to be with you."

"Do you know how lucky you are that I found you? What, in God's name, would make you ride out in a storm like this?"

Her joy plummeted at the anger in his voice. She pulled away from him. "I had a fight with Papa."

"Over what?"

"Us. He came after me, and I had to tell him the truth about being alone with you that night." Her features fell into lines of anguish. "He flew into a rage, said he was going to fire you, and struck me. I couldn't stay there, not when he called me a whore."

Cale growled low in his throat. His hands clenched at his sides. "Damn him! If I'd been there, I would have killed him."

Shay placed a placating hand on his arm. "Don't, Cale. Papa can't help himself. It's the liquor." Her gaze searched his. "Nothing matters now that I'm here with you."

She smiled tentatively at him, but he didn't return her gesture. Instead, he turned abruptly and walked outside.

What had she done? Her mouth still tingled where his lips had been, and she felt painfully exposed. Only moments ago, as he had held her within his embrace, she had felt wonderfully alive. Even the air she breathed had seemed sweeter. All that changed with one look—his look of regret.

Cale returned and deposited his gear on the

rocky floor. He removed his slicker and hat and tossed them to the side of his saddle.

He gathered small pieces of wood and dry foliage that had blown inside the cave and built a fire. A soft glow filled the darkness, and a small plume of smoke curled upward, caressing the ceiling. He sat a few feet from Shay, leaned against his saddle, and stretched out his long legs.

His face was unreadable. "You'd best get out of those wet clothes." He tossed her the blanket from his bedroll.

Shay tried to lighten the oppressive mood, despite the fact that her mind shied away from the thought of undressing in front of him. "Seems you've told me that before."

He gave her a wry smile. "Seems that way."

Biting her lower lip, Shay looked around for some place to disrobe and decided on the rear of the cave. "Will you turn your back?"

Wordlessly, he granted her request.

She moved to the darker end of the cave, and with shaky fingers, she undressed. The woolen blanket felt scratchy against her skin as she wrapped it around herself and tucked the edge firmly beneath her armpit. She squared her shoulders and turned to meet his gaze. A muscle in his jaw tightened, then relaxed again.

Shay felt the urge to have him hold her in his arms and comfort her. She knelt in front of him. "What have I done?"

"Nothing." The word was hard and implacable.

She'd already been through enough emotional hell. She couldn't take Cale's indifference too. "There's got to be something," she cried. "Why else are you acting like I've got smallpox?"

"You shouldn't have come after me."

His softly issued words were her undoing. She had wanted to hear him tell her that everything would be all right now that they were together. Tears spilled down her cheeks, and her anguish settled in her chest like a heavy, cold weight.

The turmoil of the last few hours left Shay drained of all emotion except one: bewilderment. It was true, he hadn't said in words that he cared for her, but his actions said otherwise. Harboring a lingering hope that she could soften him, she vowed she wouldn't give up. Not now. "Why don't you want to be with me? Don't you care for me?"

"It's not you," he said wearily. "It's me. I'm not ready to make a lifelong commitment."

Shay wiped the tears from her face with the heel of her hand. With fierce pride, she told herself to remain strong. "I'm not asking you to marry me. Only care for me."

"And if I tell you that I feel something, what then? We're two different people from different worlds. We weren't meant to be together."

Shay drew strength from his impassioned words. "We're not so different. We've both had to grow up without the love of our parents. We're both searching for something out of life. Why can't we find fulfillment together?"

"You'd come to regret it someday."

"Let me be the judge of that."

"I can't. A man's responsible for his actions."

"And a woman's not?"

"I won't do something that would cheapen you."

"It wouldn't be that way."

"You don't understand men."

She leaned closer. Her heart pounded against her rib cage. "I know enough."

"You don't know the half of it. Not when it comes to what a man will do when he wants a woman."

She moistened her lips. "Then teach me."

His blue eyes became guarded, speculative. "You don't realize what you're asking."

Shay hardly heard what he said. She was too aware of the way his eyes stayed on her, hard and glittering. Her hand self-consciously crept upward to brush the loose tendrils from her face, and the blanket gaped open slightly.

Her heartbeat quickened as she watched his expression change. His eyes moved over her in a slow, heated pattern. Suddenly, the cave seemed smaller than before.

Cale stood and pulled her up with him. Her breathing became constricted as she looked at the tall, hard length of him and into his blue eyes.

He raised his hand to touch her smooth, soft face and caressed the cheek her father had struck just hours ago. "I don't want to hurt you."

"Pushing me away hurts me more."

He gathered her to him and rested his chin atop her head. Myriad sensations assailed him: the scent of roses mixed with rain; the feel of her soft skin, contrasting with the scratchy material of the blanket.

Cale never wanted to release her, but he feared the depths of desire and need that he felt for Shay. His need went beyond what he had held for Janet. What he felt for Shay was mature passion— relentless in its power and potency—not youthful affection. At that moment, he wanted nothing more than to bury himself, without regard for the consequences, in that sweet, tempting body of hers.

But his attraction to her was dangerous.

They could never have a life together. He owned nothing except the clothes on his back, his horse, and his gear. Very little to offer a woman who deserved so much more. He didn't want to watch her grow old before her time from childbearing and hard work.

But more important, he didn't know if he was capable of giving her the love she so desperately craved.

"I'll take you back in the morning," he said at last.

"You're going back after Papa fired you?"

"I've got a job to finish."

"Is that all you can think about?"

"I'm trying to think about you, dammit!"

She turned pleading eyes on him. "Then give me tonight."

"Shay, I don't have much except my name and my honor. How could I make love to you, knowing I'd be dishonoring you and your family? You're asking more than either one of us is capable of giving."

"I'm only asking for tonight. There's no tomorrow for us. There's only now." The world narrowed down to the man who stood before her. "I'm not going back."

"You can't hide from your problems. You've got to face your father."

"I can't—"

"You've got to."

"You don't understand."

"I understand better than you think." A fine tension honed his words. "How will you survive?"

"I don't know, but anything is better than the life I've been living."

"I've seen worse."

"And I've lived through the hell of having an abusive, alcoholic father. I doubt anything I find out in the world could be much worse."

"There are people who would take advantage of you. You have no idea what's waiting out there."

"Maybe not, but I'm willing to take that chance. I wasn't before." Her voice became a ragged whisper. "Not until I met you."

The feel of him, hard, warm, assured, awakened so many yearnings within her. But even more, he made her long for a life filled with love and laughter.

"Don't base an entire lifetime on me."

The impatience in his voice caused Shay to flinch. "Why? It's all I've got."

Outside, the raging storm had died down to a steady rain. Inside, a bleak silence ensued, broken only by the crackling and hissing of the fire.

"You have a great deal more than I could ever offer you."

She felt the heat radiating from his body, his warm breath against her face. "What are you saying?"

"I can't give you anything beyond tonight. I'm not capable of the marrying kind of love, if that's what you expect."

"I'm not asking for anything past this moment."

"Doesn't it matter to you that no man will marry you, knowing you've been with another man?"

Shay wasn't thinking beyond her immediate yearning. She knew only that she wanted to be a woman in all things; she wanted him to make her *his* woman. "All I know is that I want you, if only for one night."

Tension rode high across his features. "Well, it matters to me."

She countered his hardness with a soft tone. "What matters to me is having this night with you."

"You don't deserve just one night." His voice fell upon her like velvet mist. "You deserve to have a husband who will spend all his days and nights with you."

Shay looked at the breadth of his shoulders, the hard, flowing muscles of his arms straining against the fabric of his shirtsleeves, and his large, strong hands. He smelled of leather; tangy sweat, both man and horse; and rain. Her gaze was drawn to his strong, sensual mouth.

She reached up and traced his soft, warm lips with a fingertip. "I've never known anyone like you. Ever since you came to Twin Creeks, my life hasn't been the same. I've never known what it was like to be loved by a man. This may be the closest I come to it. Don't turn me away."

"Shay." He cupped her face between his hands and gazed into her face. "You're looking to me for a love I'm not sure I know how to give." His eyes darkened until the lapis color of his irises was nearly eclipsed. "I've never had that kind of love. I don't know how it feels. I don't know how to be the person you need. Our making love would be a mistake. For both of us."

"You're taking my right to make my own choices away from me. How do you know what I need?"

"What you *don't* need is me."

"Do I have to beg?"

He looked at the beautiful outline of her face, contoured by the glow of the fire, and recognized the stubborn set to her chin.

Cale clenched his teeth against the primitive response of his body. "I won't make love to you."

The stricken look on her face nearly broke his resolve. It was all he could do not to take her in his arms and comfort her, but he knew they'd be spending a few hours based on false expectations. If she wasn't thinking straight, then he'd have to think for her. He hoped someday she would understand his reasoning.

He didn't know how the hell his life had got so complicated, but he knew exactly when—the day he laid eyes on Shay Alexander.

"Lie down." He fought his frustration and forced a gentle tone into his voice. Shay had gone through enough today. "We both need some rest."

She looked at him, her throat working, but she didn't argue further. Instead, she stretched out beside his saddle and turned on her right side, with her back to him. She slipped one arm beneath her head.

Cale eased down beside her and lay on his right side. He listened for the soft meter of Shay's breathing that signaled she was asleep before he allowed himself to gently stroke her hair. He wished he had met her at a time in his life when he could have still learned to love.

He closed his eyes.

Cale slept fitfully that night, and dreamed.

A soft backside snuggled against his groin. . . .

Strong, tanned hands stroked a warm spine. . . .

Slender white fingers caressed a corded bicep. . . .

A firm mouth possessed. . . .

Parted lips quivered. . . .

Shay's sweet face . . .

Her naked body pressed full against him . . .

Cale felt a current of desire rising up his spine.

He pressed his mouth to hers and kissed her passionately. Hungrily, impatiently, her lips fused with his. Her tongue darted inside his mouth.

He wrapped his fingers in her red hair. Strands the color of a fiery sunrise streamed past her slender shoulders as his lips trailed across her soft cheek. She whimpered low in her throat while his mouth sought her eyelids and temples to brand her as his alone.

Her warm breath fanned him like a hot, humid breeze, and the sensation tickled. She writhed against him. He sought her mouth again, urgently now, demandingly. Her tongue plunged between his pliant lips and filled him with desire, while his hands, still tangled in her mane of thick hair, gripped her tighter.

With that kiss, their souls joined.

Hovering in a state between wakefulness and sleep, Cale pulled Shay closer to him. His long, hard frame molded to her back. Her soft bottom pressed intimately against his groin, and he grew hard. He sighed and inhaled the sweet, warm scent of her skin.

Still half asleep, he placed his hand on her hip and snuggled closer to her, his lips touching her hair. Shay murmured and turned into his arms. Her warm body beckoned to him, and he pulled her leg over his hip to place his maleness at the entrance of her waiting womanhood. His senses began to spiral upward as he thought how wonderful it would feel to slide within her and lose himself. His hand moved over her hip, his palm settled against her bottom, and he pushed her against him as the tip of his hardness begged entrance.

The discomfort of his intense desire, and the increasing awareness of his hands upon heated skin, woke Cale. He slowly opened his eyes, and after several moments of confusion, he realized he hadn't been entirely dreaming.

He found himself looking at Shay. She had wiggled out of the blanket sometime during the night and now rested naked in his arms. He swallowed hard. Oh, God, he wanted to finish what his body had begun.

Shay's eyelids fluttered open, and she gazed at him with a drowsy sensuality. A smile curved her lips, and she sighed softly. Her hand drifted to his mouth, and her fingertips skimmed across his lips.

Groaning, Cale grabbed her hand, yet he didn't remove it from his mouth. Instead, he kissed her fingertips, then sucked each finger—slowly, tantalizingly—one by one.

His hands framed her cheeks to maneuver her face close to his. His lips whispered across hers, causing warm, delicious sensations to erupt within her, leaving her with a consuming longing for more.

Deepening the kiss, he urged her lips apart with his persuasive tongue. Instinctively, she opened her mouth wider, and Cale plunged his tongue in farther, exploring the moist, warm recesses within. Her hair flowed over his arms in damp waves as he slid his hands lower and pressed them against the small of her back, urging her against the proof of his desire.

Overwhelmed by the flesh and blood texture,

the tantalizing taste and heady smell of the man who held her, Shay thought she'd swoon. She pulled her mouth free and gasped for air.

Casting aside her virtue, Shay could not deny the power of Cale's sensuality. Only one thought presented itself: surrender. She wanted this moment—perhaps to cherish for a lifetime.

Desire flared in Cale's heated gaze. But other equally powerful emotions—tenderness and compassion—tempered the urgency he felt. Never had he seen such untamed, proud beauty as Shay's. He rested his palms briefly upon her strong, smooth shoulders, then outlined the curves and lines of her slender, graceful arms, and finally laced his fingers with hers. He lowered his head and his lips brushed her temples, the sensitive, tingling skin beneath her ear, the hollow of her throat.

He untangled her fingers from his and lightly ran his hands down her sides. Splayed fingers skimmed the contours of her rib cage, dipping down to her softly rounded hips and her shapely thighs, rising to her breasts, where his hands molded themselves around her fullness. His touch lingered, shaping her soft breasts to fit his roughened palms. Next he traveled the sensuous line of her spine, then the splendid curves of her buttocks, before his hands rested on the soft underside of her backside.

When she moaned, Cale trembled with need. "I should stay away from you." He watched the rapid pulse at the base of her throat.

He released her, and running his fingers through her wealth of soft, damp hair, he draped her breasts with a generous section of her thick mane.

As her gaze locked with his, she could see Cale's internal battle. Desire struggled with honor, need warred with decency, yearning grappled with integrity.

"You're a temptation I'm not sure I can resist."

"Then don't try," she whispered.

Rising, Cale shrugged out of his clothes, then reached down with trembling hands to pull Shay to her feet.

Her gaze traveled over his lean, muscular body. She wasn't prepared for the rigid proof of his manhood, and her eyes widened at the sight. She knew the details of animals' mating, but she trembled at the thought of drawing Cale deep within herself.

He must have sensed her uncertainty. "I'll try not to hurt you." His words, rich and warm, held a promise of lavish sensuality. "Will you trust me?"

She swallowed and nodded.

He reached out, circling his fingers about her delicate wrist, and pulled her closer to him. Their bodies pressed together. The feel of him, large and pulsating, sent shock waves through Shay. Had she been less frightened, she would have enjoyed the texture of his body against her, from the smooth, rippling muscles of his chest, to his powerful biceps, to the imposing strength of his legs.

But the only part of his body that registered to her was flagrantly pressing into her stomach.

"Don't be afraid," he reassured her.

How could she not be afraid? she wondered. She'd never been with a man. But the feeling that she had waited her entire lifetime to be with Cale gave her comfort. She had secretly dreamed of a man like him taking her into his strong embrace;

kissing her with warm, persuasive lips; touching her with hands capable of giving pleasure.

Not waiting for an answer, he pressed his mouth to hers and sought to lay claim to her with the consuming persistence of his lips alone.

Time became suspended on wings of desire until he ended the kiss and knelt before her, pressing his face against her taut stomach. His tongue ringed and laved her navel before journeying upward to her breasts. He left in his wake a trail of damp skin, mapping his possession, until he traversed the valley between her satiny globes and climbed the tempting peaks. His mouth took dominion over each breast, lavishing fervent, moist attention. Heat rose in her body like a hot summer day. She drew one shuddering breath, then another.

He stood and planted his feet wide, pulling her between his legs. His fingers whispered across the curve of her hipbone, then down to her inner thigh, parting the budding flesh he sought.

Shay gasped with pleasure and swayed in his embrace. A steadying hand at her back kept her from falling. When his fingers touched her dewy warmth, her eyes closed, and her head lolled back.

Once more, he knelt in front of her. Hands gently but firmly on her hips, he pulled her closer until his lips kissed her silken curls.

Her eyes flew open and she gasped in startled, shocked pleasure, trying to pull away from his scandalous, sinful mouth.

His hold tightening on her hips, Cale glanced up. "There's more." His black hair brushed sensuously against her quivering skin.

Determined yet tender hands held her hips prisoner as he repositioned himself between her thighs. Slowly . . . very slowly, he thrust his tongue deep into her waiting, pulsing warmth. Her body grew taut and quivered at the caressing intrusion. Then at the moment of splintering release, Shay gasped aloud, her breath coming in shallow spurts.

Shay had never known a man could do such wonderfully mischievous things with his wayward tongue and mouth. She was drowning in a sea of ecstasy.

After long moments, Cale lifted his head and quietly said, "I haven't ever been this hard for a woman. See what you do to me?"

Shay wouldn't open her eyes, afraid of what Cale would see in her gaze.

He issued a soft command. "Look at me."

Slowly, her eyes opened and she gazed downward. She trembled at the sight of his arousal.

"I want you like I've never wanted a woman before." His voice flowed with seduction. "I want to touch you in all the right places. I want to feel you beneath me, your skin against mine." Cale stood. "Now I want you to touch me."

Tentatively, Shay began her own exploration. Beneath her fingertips his skin felt warm, a film of perspiration covering it. Her hands investigated the breadth of his strong shoulders; the corded, sinewy length of his neck; the smooth, muscular expanse of his chest; his nipples that came alive beneath her touch. Her hand strayed lower, but stopped on the fringes of his stomach.

"Feel me, Shay," Cale whispered against her hair.

She was shocked at the warmth and softness of his swollen, smooth flesh as her hand moved over it, and she flinched from the contact.

"Don't be afraid." He guided her hand back to his pulsing shaft.

Her gaze met his. "I can't—"

"Yes, you can."

He held his breath as her fingers gently wrapped themselves around his fullness.

"That's . . . right," he groaned.

Slowly, she slid her hand over his length. When he didn't object, Shay grew bolder and glided her fingers up . . . then down . . . his arousal.

Cale stopped her. "Enough. If your sweet hands don't stop, I'll lose it right here."

Her brow furrowed. "Did I hurt you?"

"More than you know," he said in a hoarse voice.

Her pulse leaped as his thumb moved to her mouth, parted her lips, and slid across the ridges of her teeth. His tongue then probed with delicate inquisition. She circled his strong neck with her arms, and boldly, she met his tongue with hers. Her low moan escaped in a breathy, feathery exhalation.

Cale locked his hands behind the small of her back while his lean hips danced seductively against her soft curves. His ragged breathing fell upon her cheek. The taste and feel of him whetted her appetite until she hungered for more.

Shay's senses floated as his tongue slid along her throat to her earlobe, and she felt the hardness which promised ecstasy against her stomach. Her eager hands massaged the warm, tanned skin of his back.

He reached out and softly touched her cheek with his fingertips, then her mouth and throat. Delicately, he brushed downward until his palms caressed her taut nipples. He watched the enjoyment on her face as his hands moved back and forth.

He lowered his head, and his mouth moved over her swollen nipples, his tongue playfully flicking, then circling. Suddenly his lips closed tightly over one, drawing hard, and he reveled at the sound of Shay's gasp and the feel of her body's trembling beneath his hands.

Balancing on the dizzying brink of the unknown, Shay whispered, "Please."

"Not yet."

His hands urgently fondled, massaged, caressed her breasts, her buttocks.

Shay's skin burned from the onslaught of her emotions. She throbbed from wanting to draw Cale deep within her and hold him tightly therein.

Letting her go, Cale knelt to spread the blanket on the ground and drew her down beside him.

Determined to arouse her as slowly and as gently as his aching body would allow, he eased her onto her back and settled between her legs. He bestowed his full attention upon her breasts and showered them with kisses. Taking each in turn, he suckled and fondled them until she writhed madly beneath him.

He hesitated at her opening. His body yearned for release, but his concern for Shay demanded he proceed slowly.

He eased into her tight passage. She gasped, breathless and startled, as the thin barrier of her virginity gave way to his insistent manhood. Tensing, she buried her face in his shoulder to hide her pained grimace.

"I'm sorry," he said.

Cale withdrew and saw the virginal blood. He gazed down at Shay. Softly brushing the sweat-dampened hair back from her face, he saw the discomfort lingering in her eyes.

Lost as she was in her own emotions and the burning throbbing between her legs, Shay didn't see the tenderness in his gaze. How could anything preceded by such delectable sensations be so painful? Her breath came in a tiny shudder.

Cale cupped her chin and gently forced her to meet his eyes. "I want you to have your pleasure. It's not supposed to hurt as much the second time."

He began slow, gentle movements, sliding against her sensitive flower, but stopping short of entering her again. All the while, he kissed her tenderly, wooing her participation with the gentle persuasion of his lips. Her cooperation soon came, and she responded to his kisses with growing eagerness.

Though he burned to possess her, he lifted her buttocks and eased into her tender flesh. When she flinched and moaned in pain, he tensed and looked down at her.

"You know I wouldn't intentionally hurt you. The pain will go away." He groaned. "I can't stop." He threw back his head and grimaced as he buried himself deep inside her.

Cale withdrew, only to slide again into her dewy warmth. With each thrust she grew more receptive. She clung to him, melted against him, and undulated her slim hips to take him deeper.

Within the next pulse beat, he thrust deeply and filled her with his pulsating white-hot seed. He cried out his pleasure and collapsed atop her, damp and slack with contentment.

She squirmed, but his weight pressed her down.

"Don't move. Not yet," he whispered softly.

Raising up on his elbows, he stared down into her flushed face. "I'm sorry I couldn't wait for you. A body like yours won't let a man take it slow." He looked pleadingly at her. "Do you understand?"

She shook her head, not trusting herself to speak. She trembled, her own passion not yet slaked, the fires of her desire still banked, hotly burning.

"No woman has ever made me spill myself so quickly. When I'm inside you, I can't think of anything except filling you—completely."

Shay turned away, unable to look at him after his provocative admission. He caught her chin and forced her head around. He gazed deeply into her eyes, and Shay recognized the rich promise of sweet fulfillment shining from the blue depths. He stretched out her arms to her sides and placed his hands atop hers, palm against palm, his long fingers curling around hers. His chest rubbed against hers. His skin felt hot. So very hot. She sucked in her breath, her stomach becoming concave, and she felt him settle deeper inside her.

"I would stay like this, planted deep inside you, all night if I could," he whispered.

He withdrew from her and rolled onto his back. He gathered her to him and she rested her head within the fold of his arm. The scent of their passion wafted from his heated skin and filled her nostrils, acting as an erotic stimulus to her over-taxed senses. A primal part of her was glad she gave him such intense pleasure.

"You're so fierce, so proud. Every inch an Alexander," Cale said.

The reminder of her father caused stricken tears to gather in her eyes. She felt the sticky reminder of their joining between her legs and shuddered to think what her father would do to her if he knew she had given herself to Cale.

Cale tensed as if he realized his blunder. "I didn't think."

Suppressed tears roughened her voice. "I'm fine." She released her breath slowly, voicing what was utmost on her mind. "You don't have to take me back. I'll face Papa on my own."

"What are you going to do, walk all the way back?" He laughed.

Shay's face fell. "I forgot about my horse."

Cale's expression turned somber. "I can't say I'm sorry for what's happened between us. I am sorry for what I know you'll have to face. But you won't have to face it alone."

"Most men would leave a woman to her own devices." Shay touched his face. "But not you. You're unlike any man I know."

Cale's eyes crinkled at the corners. "So you've been telling me ever since I arrived at Twin Creeks."

Shay returned his smile. "So I have."

She sat up and instinctively crossed her arms over her breasts. She wanted to laugh at her silly gesture. Why bother with modesty now?

"What do you want, Shay?"

"Someone to love me."

Cale, too, sat up and regarded her. "I can accommodate you on that matter," he said in a soft, hushed drift of words.

She shivered at the implied meaning, and the small flame of desire inside her flared brightly once more. Her gaze lowered, and her eyes widened at the sight of his maleness swelling once more.

He grinned. "Usually it takes a man a while before he's ready again. But just thinking about making love with you, sweet Shay, is all I need."

This time he was patient and thorough, determined to leave her well satisfied. It was as if the thought of Shay's ever being with another man made him determined to put his brand on her so deeply, so completely, that she could never forget him. No more than he could forget her.

Holding her trembling legs apart with his hands, he paid homage to her womanhood, his tongue flicking and circling, then dipping into her. The startling pleasure was more intense than the first time, sending shock waves of pleasure rippling from her moist center, obscuring all thoughts of morality.

Her body sang beneath his touch, pleasure echoing throughout her blood, desire reverberating throughout her whole being. He must love her—he couldn't touch her like this if he didn't.

But even as she asked herself these questions, he thrust his tongue more deeply into her. Her world narrowed to the hot, moist attention of his wicked mouth, of breath and heat, depths and wet surfaces. His tongue imitated actions of his manhood's earlier possession, and her breathing became irregular as desire focused into a whirlwind of sensation beneath his lips and tongue.

As she teetered on the brink of release, he moved to stretch his body atop hers. His mouth claimed hers in a hot, evocative kiss that cut off her moaned protest.

He broke off the kiss and raised himself on his elbows. "How do you feel?" He lowered his dark head and drew one aching nipple between his teeth, playfully nipping.

"Wonderful," Shay confessed shamelessly.

"Hmm. Then you'll like the rest."

He raised himself and, with large hands encircling her waist, brought her to her knees in the middle of the blanket.

"What are you doing?" Shay asked, bewildered as he moved behind her.

"You'll see."

"I—"

Her words were cut off as his chest pressed against her back and his arms came around her to fondle her breasts, which were hanging like precious fruit for his picking.

When Shay thought Cale couldn't shock her anymore than he already had with his touch, he proved her wrong. She sucked in her breath when his hands separated her legs and he placed his maleness between her long limbs, rubbing himself against her silken curls and soft buttocks.

Not a single inch of flesh went unattended by Cale. His hands were everywhere, coaxing, fondling, caressing. In the wake of his touch, Shay's body had never felt so alive, so vibrant, so anxious to receive him again.

His palms settled on her shoulders and he turned her around to face him. "Just a while longer."

With his comment, he sat, his legs straight out, and pulled Shay onto his lap, positioning her to receive his throbbing desire.

"Open your legs, sweet Shay," he huskily commanded.

She complied.

With his hands on her bottom, he pressed her against him. Her muffled moan of discomfort was lost on his lips as his mouth lowered to kiss her, and he slid fully into her waiting softness. Her nails dug into the flesh of his back, but he didn't seem to notice as his lips touched her brow. His breathing, harsh and ragged, fell against her ear; his heart beat solidly at her naked breast. In a welter of shock and arousal, she felt her body expand to accommodate him.

"Now wrap your legs and arms around me."

Holding fiercely on to her with strong arms, Cale showed her how to ride him in a gentle rocking motion. He filled her entirely and Shay felt him tremble beneath her, leaving her giddy with her newfound sense of power.

As their rhythm increased, Shay arched her neck and leaned her head back to give him access to her throat and breasts, reveling in the feel of his hot mouth against her warm, moist flesh.

With his hands securing her waist, her body bowed, her hair streaming wildly about them, he sampled her flesh until she thought she'd die of want.

Her need for release soared, but Cale didn't allow his own release until she was ready. As he thrust deeply to coat her womb with life-giving fluid, they found fulfillment together.

Shay leaned forward and rested her forehead against Cale's. Quivering from the force of her deliverance, Shay felt herself expand briefly, then contract around Cale's dwindling flesh. It was as if her being had been splintered apart, and only now was slowly reassembling itself.

Every lesson in morality she had ever learned scattered like dust on the wind. What had taken place between herself and Cale was a wonderful act, and Shay basked in the aftermath.

Cale lifted Shay from him and she stretched out

atop the blanket. He tenderly brushed the hair from her face and kissed her cheek before settling himself beside her.

Fatigued, both emotionally and physically, she snuggled close to him and drifted to sleep.

Cale listened to the soft rise and fall of her breath. God, why couldn't he have remained strong and avoided the temptation of making love to Shay? He groaned. But all his good intentions had disappeared faster than a jackrabbit being chased by a coyote when he had awakened and found her soft and willing in his arms. His mind had been drugged with sleep and passion, and he hadn't been able to think clearly. He had only been able to feel.

But he was thinking straight now. There'd be hell to pay when they returned to Twin Creeks.

His jaw tightened. Shame wasn't an emotion he regularly felt, but he felt it keenly now. What had he done? He'd made love to his friend's niece and ruined her chances of ever having a happy life with a man she could call her husband.

Marriage skipped across his agonized thoughts. Why would any woman want to marry him? He had nothing to offer except a hard existence in a rugged land.

So why did it hurt so much to think of not having Shay in his life? Because he wanted Shay with every breath, every fiber of his being.

He knew what he had to do, but he didn't like it. He had to deny his attraction and growing love for Shay and take her back to Twin Creeks.

Cale eventually found sleep. There were no more dreams that night, only echoing remembrances of what had been.

Chapter 10

The following morning, as Shay watched Cale saddle his horse, she sensed a certain tension in his movements, and she was gripped by a numbing ache of dread. His distant behavior confirmed what she had suspected: he'd made love to her simply because she had been willing. His gentle and patient attention to her inexperience had been a kind gesture, but it forged no lasting bond between them. More important, she now doused her fervent hope that he would change his mind about marrying her. Obviously, she had been mistaken. Cale had entered her life, changed it dramatically, and soon would be gone.

The creaking of saddle leather and the jangling of spurs broke into Shay's misery. She raised her head and met his gaze. She knew nothing would keep him from returning her to Twin Creeks.

As if he had read her very thoughts, he said, "You've got to face him, Shay. You'll never be free if you don't." He leaned over in his saddle and reached out for her.

"I know." She breathed deeply and clasped his extended hand.

Effortlessly, Cale lifted her in the strong curve of

his arm, his muscles flexing, and placed her astride the saddle in front of him. She grimaced at her soreness.

His arm brushed hers as he reined the bay around and touched its flanks with his spurs. The horse broke into an easy canter, pushing Shay back, her shoulders rubbing the muscular wall of Cale's chest.

Shay hazarded a backward glance at the entrance to the cave and experienced a remorseful pang at the memory of the intimacy they had shared there, joined in total abandonment. Every awesome, incredible, reckless moment of their lovemaking swept her, and she hugged those thoughts close to her heart.

She forced her gaze ahead. There was no use in looking back at what had been. They had reveled in the moment, but it was gone. Only the present remained.

She closed her eyes, losing herself in the feel of Cale's muscular thighs branding the backs of her legs. She knew on a deeper level that what she felt for Cale went beyond physical attraction. She loved him with a passion that was soul-shattering and conclusive. In that moment of realization, Shay had never known such joy. Whatever happened, no one could strip her of her love for Cale. He would always be with her in her heart.

Relaxing a bit, she leaned back against his chest, feeling each smooth, liquid motion he used to steer and control his mount. Their closeness, the way their bodies moved in easy rhythm with the bay's strides, produced a profound sensuality.

Shay turned her head slightly and peered at his face under the concealing sweep of her thick lashes. A day's growth of black stubble emphasized the strong, masculine lines of his jaw and chin.

She wondered if she would ever see Cale again—and within that same breath, she knew the answer. If he left without her, he would not return.

Pushing the melancholy thought away, she concentrated on the pounding of the horse's hooves and the wind blowing in her face.

The breeze tugged at her hair, sending silky tendrils flying across Cale's face. He breathed in the sweet scent of the sun-kissed skeins and knew a moment of regret at not being able to take her with him. He ground that foolish notion between the steel jaws of conviction.

For all the wrong reasons he wanted her.

For all the right reasons he must leave her.

As they continued on their way, Cale's right hand moved to the top of her thigh. Her breathing quickened at the gesture, tiny tremors rippling her stomach muscles. She would always remember his masterful touch that commanded her body's compliance. And his tenderness that ruled her soul.

Miles later, they reached Twin Creeks. As they rode closer to the house, Shay trembled in dread. Cale's arm tightened around her waist, pressing her closer to his chest. The steady beating of his heart through the fabric of his shirt gave her reassurance.

Shay grew painfully aware of how the hands stopped their chores and stared at them, but she wasn't prepared for the hatred gleaming from Cotton's eyes. But then what had she expected? Shay forced herself to return his antagonistic regard with cool indifference.

At the main house, Cale swung agilely from his

horse and reached up for Shay. With her hands on his shoulders, she slid down the length of him until her feet touched ground. For a brief moment, their gazes locked, and within his lapis stare, she found strength.

"I'm coming with you," he said.

Resolve infused her with fortitude, and determination took the place of fear, pumping courage through her body. "You don't have to. I can handle this on my own."

His knuckles brushed her cheek. "I know you can, but I'm not leaving you to face this alone."

With his hand at the small of her back, Cale offered support to Shay, as she led the way to the library, where she knew she would find her father.

The look Sneed shot her from behind his desk would have brought Shay to her knees had it not been for Cale's steadying hand at her back.

In that moment, she knew she had entered hell.

She couldn't hide from her father's wrath, nor from the hurt lodged in her heart at his cruel treatment. She answered his silent challenge with a lift of her chin, pushing back the tears that lurked behind her eyes and ached in her throat.

The tense silence in the room throbbed with ripening tension and charged emotions.

Then the moment shattered.

Sneed pinned Shay with an insulting glare. "How dare you come back here after what you've done!"

"I had to, Papa. We need to talk." Her voice was raw with apprehension.

"About what? How you've become a slut, staying the night with a man, not once but twice?"

For the breadth of a second, their gazes locked—his hostile, hers determined.

She shuddered, but she didn't avert her eyes from Sneed's accusing glare. "I know I'm a disappointment to you, Papa," she said, her voice unsteady despite her efforts to control it. "I didn't intentionally hurt you."

Her repentance provoked him rather than appeased him. "Don't insult me by lying. You've always taken great pleasure in rebelling against me. I just never realized to what levels you would sink." Sneed strode from behind his desk, his rigid carriage further evidence of his rage. "My God, to think I gave you everything money could buy, and look at how you've repaid me. I ought to take a whip to your hide." He raised a fist to Shay's face.

Cale stepped in front of Shay and grabbed the older man's arm. "Don't try it, sir. Not if you want to see tomorrow."

Sneed tried to pull away from the restraining hold. His free hand balled into a fist, and briefly Cale thought Sneed meant to strike him. Then he felt Sneed relax and he sensed the immediate challenge was gone.

The rancher's lips twisted with derision. "I should've thrown you off Twin Creeks the first time I laid eyes on you. Knew you were no good, bein' a nigger lover and all." His gleaming gaze shifted to Shay. "What I didn't know was how easily my so-called daughter would spread her legs for you."

Shay couldn't suppress a gasp of outraged anguish.

"I've killed men for less provocation than you've just given me. I wouldn't push your luck, Mr. Alexander." Cale's fingers tightened their hold ominously. "Because at this moment, there's nothing I'd like better."

Sneed shook Cale's hand from his sleeve and turned to Shay. "If you wanted to leave Twin Creeks, you've certainly gotten your wish. But you'll do it by marrying him, or I'll give you that beating you deserve—and take great pleasure from it."

He stomped over to a nearby table and splashed whiskey into a glass from a crystal decanter. Tossing his head back, he downed the liquid in one swallow. He nearly shattered the glass as he slammed it down atop the mahogany table.

His face was distorted with malevolence. "If you want to act the slut, Shay, it's too late for me to do anything about that. But I have to think of my good name. I won't be laughed at behind my back because you slept with a man, who then left the damaged goods."

His seething gaze went back to Cale. "I knew it was a mistake to have anything to do with you. Should've known it when my brother first came dragging back home with you. What kind of a man seduces innocent women? Whores not good enough for you?"

"What I know is that you don't deserve Shay for a daughter. You've probably lived with the bottle for so long, you've forgotten how to treat her decent. I feel sorry for you."

Sneed's nostrils flared. "Don't you dare give me your pity!"

"It's the only thing keeping me from killing you where you stand."

Sneed assumed a threatening position. "You can try."

Cale clenched his hand, aching to smash Sneed's face with his fist, but Sneed must have sensed the immediate danger and remained where he was.

"You're a no-good drifter." Sneed's gaze shifted to Shay. "And *you* belong in the gutter. Unless you have something to say for yourself?"

Shay swayed as if her father had physically struck her. "I don't have an excuse for my behavior," she said, clinging to her tenuous composure with effort. "But neither am I sorry for what I did. I found what happiness I could. I'm sorry if you can't understand that."

"What I don't understand is how you could forget everything you were ever taught. Why couldn't you have turned out to be decent?"

"Damn you!" Shay cried passionately. "Ever since you turned to the bottle, you've been quick to believe the worst in me. Well, I'm not going to take it anymore! Staying here doesn't matter anymore because you've already condemned me." Plunging an emotional knife into her own heart, she finished softly, "Because I'm my mother's daughter."

Sneed's regard shot to Cale and he taunted, "You gonna stand there and hide behind a woman? You're not man enough to take responsibility for your own actions. A wedding would go a long way in soothing my pride."

Cale listened to Sneed's words with volatile emotion as powerful as Sneed's anger—but far more dangerous for being held in check.

His jaw grew taut, his mouth hardened into a cruel, menacing line, and his expression darkened with cold contempt. "I'm not shirking my obligation. I have no intentions of leaving her with the likes of you. I'll take care of her."

"You understand this, you marry her or else she'll pay dearly for her indiscretion. I'll not raise your bastard. Or have your seed sully my reputation."

Bastard? Shay's throat tightened as her mind stumbled over the word.

"What's going on in here?" came Brad's bitter voice as he walked into the room.

"Do come in, dear brother. We're discussing Shay's wedding plans. It seems she decided virtue means nothing to her these days."

Cale turned to Brad. Tension clasped the back of his neck. This was the one moment he had dreaded most, having to confront his friend.

Cale tried to relax a fraction. "Sorry things turned out the way they did."

Anguish etched Brad's features at his sense of betrayal. "For a few moments of pleasure, you've ruined my niece." His voice rumbled with inner turbulence. "How could you do that to her? How could you do this to me?"

Cale glanced at Shay, and their gazes met and held. In the knowing depths of her beautiful green eyes was the bleak knowledge that she was an outcast to her father forever.

With icy dignity in every line of her being, Shay turned away from Cale to address her father. "What happened was my fault. I seduced Cale. There's no need to blame him for my actions. He gave me no false promises," she said in an even tone.

She paused as if to find strength to finish. "It's best that I pack my bags. I've been enough trouble to you already, Papa. I don't want you to have to listen to the town gossips talking about your fallen daughter."

Her voice swelled on a note of self-worth, her gaze sweeping the three men. "Despite what you all think, my life isn't ruined. I intend to see that it's only just beginning." The lines of her face hardened marginally. "Besides, I've never wanted a husband. Not after the way you treated Mama."

Sneed exploded with disbelief. "Don't fool yourself, girl. No decent man will knowingly have you. And those that would are the kinds of men who would make your life a living hell."

Shay swallowed convulsively at her father's condemnation, a lump of pain forming in her throat. She had apologized for hurting her family, but she'd be damned if she would beg her father's forgiveness for something she had no power, or wish, to change.

Brad listened to Shay's impassioned words and witnessed her inner pain. His own pain simmered to the top of his control and spewed dangerously.

Brad turned on Cale and pulled him to a corner of the library, away from Shay and Sneed. "See what you've done?" he asked in low, urgent tones.

A muscle worked in Cale's jaw. "I didn't intend to ruin Shay." Each word was curt, succinct.

Brad's brow knotted. "What then? If not for pleasure, then money?"

Regret eclipsed Cale's expression. "I thought you knew me better than that."

"I thought I did, too."

A tense moment ticked off as the two men glared at each other, and the hostile tension in the room thickened.

White lines framed Brad's mouth. "You can't do this to her." His eyes searched Cale's for some sign that he was getting through to him. "You've got to do the right thing by Shay. She cares for you."

"Caring isn't all it takes to build a lifetime together," Cale said, a hard edge to his voice.

"But it's a start."

Frustration rankled Cale. "I wouldn't be a good husband."

"You could learn," Brad argued in a furious undertone. "You can't turn your back on Shay! Not when she needs you."

Cale looked past Brad, his gaze focusing on Shay, studying the taut lines of her proud face. Her eyes had lost their luster. He drew one raspy breath, then another. His shoulder muscles bunched with stress as her pain infiltrated his being.

Shay's clothing was crumpled and dirty, and her hair hung in windblown disarray about her shoulders and down her back, but she seemed to maintain fingertip control over her dignity. The admiration he felt for her grit was matched only by his desire.

His gaze refocused on her eyes—so wide, so troubled. She looked so vulnerable. And so alone.

Cale grimaced. He felt as if someone had reached inside his chest and squeezed his heart.

The abandoned boy inside him, remembering what it was like to grow up alone, reached out to Shay.

He moved closer to her. He unraveled his temper and resentment. "If Shay wants me, I'll marry her." His eyes swept past Sneed, then settled on Shay.

Her face paled. Wasn't this what she had wanted? she asked herself. But the cold look on his face made Shay want to retreat a step. This wasn't the man she loved, but a stranger.

Color slowly returned to her features. He was only doing this because he was being coerced. Those terms weren't acceptable to Shay.

"I'm not asking for a sacrifice. You don't have to," she said contritely.

"You should know that I don't do anything I don't want to," Cale answered roughly.

Her eyes narrowed. She couldn't bear—and didn't want—his pity. She had fought to maintain her dignified bearing during this encounter, but his charity would be her undoing.

First, her father had dominated her, now Cale was stepping forward to rectify her actions. She wanted to live her own life, not have a man make her choices.

At that moment, she hated her father; she hated her uncle; she hated Cale. More important, she hated herself for allowing them to control her.

"Y'all are so concerned over righting my wrong and salvaging your manly pride. You're treating me as if I don't have any pride or a brain in my head," she cried bitterly. "I'll decide what's best for me." Inhaling a shuddering breath, she looked back to Cale. "I'm better off being ruined than forcing you into marriage."

Brad came forward. "Everyone's temper has gotten the best of them. We all need to calm down and talk about this later."

Brittle emotions threatening to shatter her into a thousand pieces, Shay forced herself to speak in an evenly metered voice. "I'm going to my room."

Spine erect, steps stiff, she crossed the library. She left without looking back.

Brad turned to Sneed. "I have something to say to Cale—alone." His tone brooked no argument.

His chest swelled with agitation, Sneed left the room, leaving Brad and Cale in silent confrontation.

As soon as the door closed behind his brother,

Brad growled, "If you hadn't saved my life, I would have already shot you for what you've done to Shay."

Tension etched Cale's face. "And if I hadn't saved your life, I wouldn't be involved in something I don't like."

"Which part don't you like? The ruining of Shay, or facing the consequences of your actions?" Brad asked flatly, fighting the urge to throttle Cale where he stood.

"Why is all the blame being laid at my feet?"

"Because she was an innocent, and you damned well knew it!"

Genuine contriteness displacing earlier wariness, Cale conceded, "If I could take away the pain I've caused Shay, I would. But I don't regret having lain with her and I won't forget it."

"You've had more experience. You should've known better."

"Yes, I should've, but I didn't. Having her so close made it damned difficult to think."

"And so you gave no thought to the repercussions and made love to her."

"Yes." Cale shrugged with an indifference he didn't feel. "I wish you could understand."

"How could you have allowed it to happen? I thought I could trust you. Instead, you hurt the one person I love more than anyone else in the world and you expect me to understand. If this is what an honorable man does, then heaven help me against a dishonest one."

"You've never been with a woman who made you forget yourself and throw caution to the wind?"

Brad's eyes went flat for a moment, then he said softly, "Yes."

"Then you know as a man I couldn't stop what happened any more than Shay wanted me to stop." When Brad nodded, Cale finished. "I've been honest. I can't marry her."

Brad was relentless. "Can't or won't?"

Cale growled low in his throat and turned his back. Brad's question struck a nerve that Cale hadn't wanted to feel. As a result of that vibrating nerve, an unanticipated, overwhelming need reverberated through him. Shay.

Damn, just thinking her name caused his body to react.

He didn't need her in his life, he reminded himself. He could ride away from Twin Creeks and not look back.

Who was he fooling? He frowned. Rather, what was he afraid of?

One answer came to mind with stark clarity—love.

Cale braced himself and faced Brad. "Why is everyone from Mrs. Grisham to you to Sally so eager to have me marry Shay?"

"I don't know about the women, but I thought you'd be good for Shay. But what you've done to her is inexcusable."

"I'm not making excuses." Cale's frustration and anger surfaced into one unfounded, heedless thought. "Maybe she planned this whole thing just to get me to marry her."

The fragile control Brad held on his temper snapped. Without warning, he swung furiously at Cale. "You bastard!"

Brad knew a moment of satisfaction as his fist met Cale's face, the connecting thud of flesh and bone echoing in the room.

Cale swayed, then straightened, but made no retaliatory move. He rubbed his jaw. "I'll give you that one."

Later that day, Shay found Cale on the front porch. He stood at the far end, staring out across the landscape. Noting that he was heavily preoccupied, she left him to his thoughts and struggled with her own.

On the one hand, her mangled pride demanded she leave Twin Creeks, and current circumstances provided an immediate solution. On the other hand, the cold look in Cale's eyes made the thought of leaving with him almost unbearable. He didn't love her, that much was plain. She didn't want to escape from one contemptuous man only to end up with another.

Uncertainty seared the edges of her raw nerves. His anger had never been directed toward her, but she sensed that if his fury were ever to be unleashed upon her it would be unmerciful.

Shamefully humiliated by the scene in the library, Shay stood, wondering how best to approach Cale. Never had she felt so helpless as she watched him raise a hand and massage the taut muscles in his neck, his features settling into a stony mask.

He must have sensed her presence, for he turned to look at her. "You don't have to stand over there. After all, we're going to be married," he ground out.

Shay's lips twisted with pain, but she fought to control her rioting emotions. She carefully schooled her features into a facade of calmness.

With determined steps, she joined him. "I thought we should talk."

"So talk."

Shay lifted her chin at his curt tone. "Why must you make this harder than it already is?"

"Why should I make it easy?"

She had hoped he wouldn't take his aggression toward her father and her uncle out on her. She had been wrong, although she couldn't blame him for being angry.

Nevertheless his caustic words stung her pride. "Maybe it would be better if we discussed this later."

"Waiting won't make it better."

Shay gave up all pretense of calmness, her raging emotions surfacing. "You're the one who offered to marry me, remember?"

He faced her, his gaze burning bright. "Wasn't it you who said she didn't want someone else making choices for her? And that she'd rather be a ruined woman than be forced into marriage?"

"Yes, because I don't want you saying or doing anything you don't mean."

"What was I supposed to do? Throw you to the wolves?"

"You don't have to do anything. I told you I could take care of myself."

"Not according to your family."

"What do you care what they think?"

"Because your uncle's right. I have an obligation to you that I can't ignore. I thought I could just walk away from you, but nothing's ever been that easy when it comes to you."

Humiliation burned her throat. "I'll save you the trouble by refusing to marry you. There, you have no obligation to me. You're free to leave whenever you want."

"Really? You think you can just wish away everything that's happened?" His voice hardened, along with his expression. "Well, you can't. Your father's going to see to it that we're married, or he'll take his anger out on you. And that's something I can't allow."

"Uncle Brad and Aunt Nettie will see after me until I can leave. Papa won't be able to hurt me anymore."

"Knowing him, if he gets in one of his drunken rages, he'll beat you within an inch of your life and no one will be able to stop him. I can't take the chance of that happening. Marrying you is the only way I can be sure you'll be safe."

Unconsciously, Shay reached out to him and placed a hand on his sleeve. "I don't want you to hate me." Unshed tears shimmered in her eyes. "And that's what would happen if you married me out of some misplaced notion of obligation."

As he'd stood alone on the porch, Cale had searched his mind—and conscience—for a reason not to marry Shay. He'd also made a mental list of all the reasons she shouldn't marry him. Answers abounded: his lack of possessions, the harsh life they'd have to live in Wyoming, his uncertainty about being a good husband, his urgency to return to Wyoming before he lost his claim on his land holding.

He also hadn't considered the possibility that his child was growing inside her at this very moment. Having been orphaned, the thought of a family secretly thrilled him, while at the same time it terrified him. He'd never been responsible for anyone other than himself. Briefly, he wondered what it would be like to have someone who belonged completely to him, then promptly squelched the notion.

It would seem that by making love to Shay, he'd

inadvertently, but irrevocably, changed both their lives. For better or worse.

Now that Shay was here, looking at him with soulful eyes, Cale knew he'd never be able to walk out of her life, whether he wanted to or not. But he also had to return to Wyoming. His land was the only thing he had to call his own. She'd have to go with him.

His expression softened as he tucked a loose strand of hair behind her ear. "What are you going to do if there is a child as a result of our union? Or hadn't you considered that possibility?"

"I don't know what to say other than I'd raise my child the best that I could."

His hand fell away, and his features hardened once more. "Our child," he said with guilt-ridden certainty.

Shay recovered sufficiently to say, "Yes, of course, the baby would be ours. I'd be happy if I were pregnant." Her gaze dropped, along with her voice. "Would you?"

Cale didn't give her the answer she sought, but rather said in a detached manner, "Brad said the preacher's coming in the morning. We'll leave right after the wedding."

As she watched him walk to the bunkhouse, a shadow crossed Shay's heart. If she refused to marry him, without giving love a chance to grow, she knew with conviction she'd grow old with bitter regret.

Was she doomed to a loveless marriage like her mother? Perhaps. But denying her heart's yearning to be with Cale, and never knowing what could have been, would be far worse. She'd take a chance on their future happiness. She'd waited her entire life for this opportunity. And Cale.

Her love for him had made her a whole woman—with all the joy and pain involved. She was willing to suffer the pain for the chance to experience the joy.

The shadow lifted from her heart. With the same certainty that she knew she loved him, Shay knew that marrying Cale would be the right choice.

She knew what she had to do. She'd make him love her.

Chapter 11

Having left Shay behind on the porch, Cale walked around the corner of the barn on his way to the bunkhouse. He hadn't meant to be curt with Shay, but the day's events had fermented in his mind, and he had taken his frustration out on her. His harsh treatment of her wasn't fair, but then life wasn't fair.

With his thoughts on Shay, he never saw the shovel until it smashed against his skull. The impact knocked his hat off, forced his head back, and sent him to his knees.

Dazed, he started to rise, his body directed by involuntary reflexes. Another glancing blow caught him hard in the stomach. Groaning, he dropped again to his knees, rocking back to his heels. He held his head between his hands. He squinted, trying to clear his blurred vision, to see his attacker. Slowly, Cotton's form came into focus.

"Southern men don't hold with having their women insulted. I'm gonna give you a lesson you won't forget." Cotton spat and cocked the shovel back to deliver another blow.

Years of relying on his survival instincts saved Cale. He raised his arms as the shovel descended and knocked it from Cotton's hands. The tool clattered against the barn wall.

Cale staggered to his feet. He breathed deeply against the pain. He straightened to his full height. "I made it too easy for you the first time." Derision hardened Cale's voice. "Let's see if you're man enough for a fair fight."

"I'm man enough to best you, Yankee lover."

Cale looked Cotton over from head to toe. "You hold a high opinion of yourself."

"You're no better than me." With that Cotton threw the first punch, but Cale raised his forearm and deflected the jab.

"You'll have to do better than that," Cale taunted.

He channeled all the day's aggression, anger, and pain into his hands. The bone-jarring thud his fists made as they landed on Cotton's vulnerable face and midsection caused satisfaction to rush through Cale's aching body, infusing him with energy.

Slowly, Cotton straightened. Hatred twisted his features as he glared at Cale. "When I get through with you I'm going to kill you. And with you out of the way, I'll still marry the whore."

Rage traveled up Cale's spine, flowing into every muscle, every cell of his body. A vision of Shay's face swirled through his brain. Fury hammered at his temples, replacing the pain in his head with deadly intent.

A cry sprang from his throat and erupted through his lips, and he threw his full body weight at Cotton. They crashed to the ground amid a thud of bodies and dust.

Rational thought fled Cale, leaving only the need to inflict pain. At last the red haze lifted.

Chest heaving, Cale reviewed his handiwork, clenching and unclenching his aching, bruised hands at his sides. He had accomplished his intent—very capably.

Cotton lay sprawled unconscious on his back, hands extended at his sides. Blood streamed from deep cuts above his brow, his nose, and his mouth. Where one eye had previously been was now a swollen-shut mass of flesh. Cale knew Cotton was still alive by the shallow rise and fall of his chest.

Cale swallowed the bile rising in his throat, but he felt no conscious regret or remorse. The son of a bitch had gotten what he deserved.

At that moment, Roper came around the corner. He stopped in his tracks and looked first to Cale, then to his fallen friend. "What the hell?"

Wordlessly, Cale shouldered past Roper, but heard Roper call, "You're gonna be sorry."

Cale spun on his heel, picked up the shovel from the ground and smashed it against a nearby tree trunk.

Tossing the two broken halves at Roper's feet, he said, "You're lucky you're not burying him with this."

The next morning, after visiting Aunt Nettie, still nursing her ankle in bed, Shay went to the kitchen for breakfast.

As she sat at the table, eating a thick slice of bread with fresh butter, she talked to Sally, who stood at the stove frying eggs and ham. "I wonder if everyone is as nervous as I am before they get married."

Sally ladled eggs from the frying pan onto a serving platter. "Child, I'd be nervous, too, if everything that's happened to you fell on me." She turned and looked at Shay. "Remember, God gave you broad shoulders because he knew you could carry the load."

"I wish I could be sure," Shay said between bites.

Finished with her cooking, Sally wrapped her apron corner around the skillet handle and moved the frying pan from the fire. "No cause for fretting, child. You'll come through this just fine. The angels are smiling because you're marrying the man they sent you."

"How can you be sure?" Shay asked, finishing the last of her bread and butter.

"Because it's written in heaven and the heavenly book don't lie."

"I wish I hadn't lied to myself." The pupils of Shay's eyes grew wider, revealing more of her soul. "But more than that, I wish I hadn't hurt my family."

Sally walked to where Shay sat and put her hand on the younger woman's shoulder. "Those who love you will always love you, no matter what you do. Don't you knows that by now?"

Shay's lips trembled with a faint smile, and she put her hand atop Sally's. "I know. Aunt Nettie said the same thing. I just wish I hadn't made such a mess of things."

"Child, things have been a mess around here for years, and that's got nothing to do with you."

"What about the differences between Cale and me? He's angry because Papa all but forced him to marry me."

Sally removed her hand, took Shay's head between her palms, and cradled Shay's face near her bosom. "That man wouldn't do nothing that he don't want to. So don't go and think he don't want to marry you because in his heart he does. His head just might not know it yet."

Shay pulled away from Sally and looked up at her friend, her eyes wide with emotion. "But when will he know?"

"When he gets past his pride." Sally cupped Shay's cheek with her hand. "But you'll have to do some pushing, because he's gonna sit back on his hind legs like a mule."

"Do you think I can?"

"There's no one else for that man but you. When he talked about you, I saw in his eyes that he's scared of having somebody near his heart." Sally brushed a strand of hair from Shay's forehead. "He's got to have someone be patient with him and teach him the ways of love, because he's never had none, him being an orphan at such an early age." Sally smiled. "And God gave you a heap of both love and patience."

Shay stood and walked to the door to gaze out across the yard. Melancholy wrapped its arms around her. "I'm going to miss you all. I doubt that Papa will ever let me come home again."

"Remember, child, your pa ain't hisself. Liquor does his thinking and talking. Someday I feel he's gonna find hisself again. On that day, you'll be able to come home. So don't lose your faith."

Shay turned and looked at Sally. "I've never given up hope on Papa, only had it run a little thin at times."

Sally smiled widely, her ebony skin contrasting with her white teeth. "You'd better get yourself upstairs. It's about time you were making yourself ready for that wedding of yours."

The next few hours were a kaleidoscope of memories, fears, hopes, and expectations as Shay went through the motions of bathing and packing, then dressing.

At last, she stood in front of her bedroom mirror, regarding the reflection of herself in her mother's wedding gown. Slowly, she ran her fingers over the folds of satin, still remarkably white despite the years. A flower wreath held the floor-length veil in place.

She glanced from her figure in the mirror to her aunt's in the background. "It's so lovely."

Nettie hobbled over to stand beside Shay and linked her arm with her niece's. "It's you who makes the gown lovely. You don't know how much you remind me of your mother."

They both turned their heads to look at each other. Their gazes held for a tender moment before returning to the mirror images.

"What do you think Papa's going to do when he sees me in Mama's dress?"

"If he knows what's best for him, he'd better not say anything."

"I only wish that were true." Shay changed the direction of their conversation. "What are you going to do, Aunt Nettie, after I'm gone? Will you stay at Twin Creeks?"

Unable to put much weight on her ankle for any length of time, Nettie maneuvered to a chair and sat. She inhaled deeply, then released her breath slowly. "I've asked myself that question a hundred times over the last twenty-four hours. I don't know how many times in the past I've wanted to leave, but now that the time for decision is here, I've made up my mind to stay." At Shay's inquisitive gaze, Nettie shrugged. "Someone's got to look after your Uncle Brad."

"I was hoping you'd say that." Shay walked

over to her aunt amid a rustle of stiff petticoats and knelt beside her. She reached over to Nettie's lap and placed white silk glove-covered hands atop her aunt's folded ones. "As soon as I can, I'll write."

"You'd better." Nettie smiled reassuringly.

"Don't worry about me. I'll be fine."

"I know Mr. Breland will take care of you."

Shay's eyes lit with enthusiasm, lending a lighter tone to her voice. "In some ways, I'm frightened of leaving, but in others, I'm excited at the thought of such an adventure, traveling all the way to Wyoming."

"Yes, quite an adventure. Marriage alone will be different from anything you've ever known."

"I just wish mine wouldn't be off to such a rocky start."

"Marriage is not always easy, regardless of the circumstances bringing the couple together." Nettie paused and caressed Shay's cheek, then continued. "Base your marriage on honesty and trust, but don't be a man's puppet. Always think for yourself and hold true to your beliefs."

"I will."

'That's my girl." Nettie's eyes filled with tears and she hugged Shay. In a moment, she released her niece. "It's time."

As they descended the stairs, Shay couldn't help but wonder what her future held. She wanted to engrave the sweet memories of her home in her heart, and forgive and forget the pain.

They stopped at the parlor door, where Brad joined them, taking Shay's hand and placing it in the crook of his arm. "You're a beautiful bride, Pumpkin." His eyes grew misty as his gaze traveled over her gown. "Especially in your mother's dress."

Shay returned his smile. "Thank you, Uncle Brad." Then her face clouded. "Isn't Papa going to walk me down the aisle?"

"No. I wanted that honor. He and I had a discussion, you might say. We finally saw eye to eye. He's caused enough pain and trouble." Brad winked. "Ready?"

"As ready as I'll ever be."

"Keep your chin up, Pumpkin."

The parlor was empty except for her father, Reverend James, and Aunt Nettie, her only attendant. But it was the man who stood in front of the preacher who commanded Shay's attention.

Cale was dressed as usual in his pants, homespun shirt, and bandanna, with his hair combed over his collar. But somehow he seemed more broad-shouldered and powerful, and she thought no other man on the face of the earth was as handsome.

As her uncle escorted her toward the waiting men, her aunt played the wedding march on the piano. Shay's attention focused on Cale. She nearly gasped aloud at the sight of his bruised face. Who had beaten him? Her previous joy plummeted to the bottom of her stomach. Her anxiety wasn't relieved by Cale's cold expression. Had she made the right decision? She swallowed.

Her uncle delivered her to Cale's side and stepped back. Unthinking, wanting to give comfort, her hand drifted close to Cale's face. Her hand was seized in a firm, yet painless, grip that was no warmer than his expression.

That moment seemed frozen in eternity as her mind whirled with uncertainty. She loved this man more than life itself, but was her love enough to warm his feelings toward her? For a craven moment, Shay considered flinging down her bouquet, hiking up her skirts, and bolting.

Reverend James's voice broke into her thoughts, cutting off any avenue of escape. However, soon her mind lost contact with his words as the ceremony began.

She heard only bits and pieces of the vows.

". . . to join this man . . . and this woman . . .

". . . in sickness and in health . . .

". . . Do you, Shay Elizabeth, take this man . . ."

From somewhere, she heard herself answer, "I do." She then heard Cale's rigid, "I do."

At some point, in between all the words, she felt a cold band being slipped onto the third finger of her left hand.

"I now pronounce you husband and wife. You may kiss the bride."

Slowly, her gaze came into focus, and she looked up at Cale. His expression hadn't changed, although a light shone from his eyes that hadn't been there before. And for the briefest moment, she thought that light was affection. Then the emotion dimmed as quickly as it had appeared. He settled a brief kiss on her.

Cold reality set in as Cale steered her out of the parlor. "I want you to go upstairs and get your things. I want to leave here as soon as possible."

Shay tried to coax some warmth into her suddenly cold lips. "I—"

"Just do what I say," he snapped, then turned and walked away, leaving her standing in the hallway.

Repressing a sob, Shay fled to her room for the last time.

Nettie came to assist her. "Give him time, Shay. He's angry now, but that will change."

"I can't help but wonder if I've just made the biggest mistake of my life," Shay half-cried, half-sobbed as she stepped out of her gown.

"The biggest mistake would have been not to marry him." Nettie gripped Shay's shoulders and pulled her around to face her. "Remember what I told you about following your heart's advice. Your heart is never wrong."

Shay rested her forehead against her aunt's shoulder and closed her eyes. "I've staked my happiness on that advice."

Nettie pulled away and lifted Shay's chin. "Don't look for love to come in only one package. It can come wrapped in many ways."

The two women hugged and kissed before Shay picked up her saddlebags. She gave her room one last look, wondering if she would ever miss this corner of her life. No sense dwelling on such thoughts. She had a new life awaiting her.

With a stiff spine, Shay went downstairs and outside to where Cale waited with the horses.

She looked for her father, but he was nowhere to be seen. Although she had hoped he would soften, his absence came as no surprise.

Again, Shay hugged her aunt, then turned to her uncle.

She wrapped her arms around him. "I'll miss you so much," she whispered in his ear.

"Not half as much as I will you, Pumpkin."

They parted, and Shay mounted her blood bay. She looked at her aunt and uncle. Their love for her shone from their eyes.

Don't cry, Shay told herself. You've done enough of that lately.

With a wave and a forced smile, she reined her horse around and followed Cale and the packhorse.

Leaving was harder than she had anticipated. After all, this was the only home she had ever known. Yet excitement also stirred within her breast. She recalled Sally's earlier words: *You're gonna give up what you love for something you'll love more*. She would not look back, but only forward to her new life with her husband. Her leaving was more powerfully rousing to her blood than she had ever imagined.

Shay had no further time to think as Cale set a brisk pace. Her adventure had begun.

Hours later, Shay shifted in the saddle, trying to relieve some of the misery from the weary, bone-shaking hours on the dusty trail. Sweat ran in rivulets down her back, neck, and face, forming dark patches under the arms of her cotton shirt. The garment now stuck to her like a second skin. Her horse wasn't spared the heat either. Lather clung to the blood bay, and its sides heaved from the effort of breathing in the dry, hot air.

Although Shay wore her hat pulled low across her forehead, her green eyes squinted against the intense glare, straining as they scanned the arid landscape ahead. Native mesquite trees that dotted the terrain were dwarfed by ancient Spanish oaks, their gnarled limbs lifted heavenward. Muted shades of green and brown mingled subtly together, creating a picture of sparse beauty under the cloudless blue sky.

The hooves of the mare clipped against the rocky surface of the fault line as Shay continued to follow Cale and the packhorse he led.

Grueling minutes passed into hours as horses and riders kept up their brisk pace.

Shay kept her gaze trained on Cale's back. Occasionally, he'd turn in his saddle to check on her. Resolved to demonstrate her mettle, she set her jaw more firmly beneath his gaze. As she rode, she tried to justify Cale's indifferent behavior and concluded that he was venting his anger in the vigorous gait. Well, better he take out his frustration on the trail than on her.

In the distance, heat waves rippled across the expansive terrain while the sun viciously beat down on them. Although she was used to living a vigorous life, the bracing tempo exhausted Shay, her tired muscles cramping from the strain. Her shoulders burned from the unrelenting onslaught of the sun and her arms and hands throbbed from gripping the reins.

Despite her exhaustion, Shay refused to utter a complaint and upset Cale further. Her backbone wasn't going to turn to jelly just because he set a fast gait. She'd show him. His foul temperament wasn't going to get the better of her. If he could withstand the grueling pace, so could she.

She raised a small, slender hand and removed her dusty hat, sending her thick red plait tumbling down her back. After wiping her tired eyes on a sweaty sleeve, Shay retucked the tangled braid under her hat and pulled the hat down over her forehead. The sand-filled wind pelted Shay's face, causing her to squint. She dug in her heels to keep up with Cale, forcing her body to stay upright in the saddle by sheer willpower.

Some time later, they halted beside a small creek. Its banks were lined with cottonwood and pecan trees, and only an occasional bird disturbed the peace that surrounded the area. Trees spread their shadows across the water, creating a serenity that smoothed the rough edges of her nerves.

Cale dismounted and led his mount and the packhorse to water. He looked at Shay, but said nothing, as if he didn't trust himself to speak. However, his gaze stayed on her, probing, searching. For what?

At last, he said, "We'll rest a few minutes."

Dismounting, she led her horse to water. She removed her hat and hung it on the saddle horn. A gentle breeze drifted across the water. She sighed. Bending, she cupped her hands and brought water to her heated face, the cool moisture trickling between her fingers, down her wrists to her elbows. Wincing from tight muscles, she filled her canteen.

As she straightened and capped her canteen, Shay sensed Cale's scrutiny. Their gazes locked. She read the desire she had come to know so well in his compelling blue gaze. Joy surged through her at the knowledge that he still wanted her. Then his gaze became cold, and his mouth hardened into a disapproving frown. He returned to adjusting the cinch on his mount.

For a moment, she teetered on the brink of tears, partly from exhaustion, partly because she wanted things to be right between them. Why couldn't he talk to her? Were they going to make the entire journey to Wyoming without a civil word or action? And what about later? This was their wedding day. Would there be a wedding night?

With trembling hands, Shay led her mare from the creek and tied the blood bay to a nearby bush, then sat on a large, flat rock near the water's edge.

She closed her eyes. Thoughts fell into step with memories of their lovemaking that stormy night in the cave. They had been lovers, patient, gentle, trusting. Now distrust lingered in Cale's expression and gaze.

Drawing a ragged breath, Shay opened her eyes. A single tear trickled down her dirt-streaked face. Their marriage was off to a very shaky start. She only hoped it would grow firmer, based on love and faith.

Shay abhorred self-pity in anyone, much less herself, and she resolved to make the best of their trip. If Cale wanted to be distant, she wouldn't seek him out. But neither would she discourage any advancement of their relationship—in whatever form it might come.

Chapter 12

Late that afternoon, Cale halted to make camp for the night on the south side of the Pedernales River.

Shay dismounted and uncapped her canteen. As her mouth and throat were coated with trail dust, she drank slowly, the water warm but tasting delicious as it slid down her parched throat. She wiped her mouth on a sleeve, then recapped her canteen and secured it on the saddle horn.

Looking around, she placed her hands on her hips and bowed her body backward, relieving the tension from the day's long but brisk ride.

Cale walked by, leading his gelding and the packhorse. "We'll cross the river in the morning when the horses are fresh. Best rub your horse down."

"I was—" Shay straightened and clamped her mouth shut. He didn't have to tell her how to take care of her horse, but it was wiser to keep quiet.

Wordlessly, she tied her horse to a tree. After she unbuckled the cinch, Shay pulled the heavy saddle from her horse's sweaty back and deposited it, back end up, upon the ground. She hobbled her mare.

Glancing around, she spied Cale near the stream as he watered his horses. She watched him for several minutes before he raised his head and looked at her, his expression somber.

Exhausted and hungry, Shay was beginning to doubt her wisdom in marrying Cale. Why did she have to love a man who took great pains to avoid her?

She chewed her lower lip. Even if he didn't want her, she wanted him. No power in heaven, or on earth, would change that, she thought miserably. She blinked back tears. From early in life, she'd learned that crying was tantamount to weakness. She was determined not to let him use that weakness against her.

Turning her frustration into resolve, Shay felt new energy infuse her lagging body. She'd do everything she could to make their journey pleasant. Maybe then Cale wouldn't be so withdrawn and obstinate, and again would become the man she'd grown to love.

Love. Would he seek her out tonight ... their wedding night?

Cale was wondering the same thing as he led the horses from the stream and staked them out to graze. Why had he been crazy enough to agree to marry Shay? The first hard winter in Wyoming and she'd hightail it out of there. Then where would he be?

Even as his mind finished the thought, his gaze drifted to the woman who was both the wife he didn't want and the lover who roused fierce desire within him. Could he ever reconcile his conflicting reactions to her?

He clenched his jaw. No, he might have married her, but he wouldn't fall in love with her. That way, if she left him he wouldn't get hurt. Theirs was an arrangement of convenience—nothing more. He'd married her to protect her and give their baby a name—if she were pregnant.

Shay didn't further analyze her feelings or Cale's actions, so she went about tending her mare. She groaned as tired muscles tightened in protest when she pulled up clumps of spear grass and vigorously rubbed down the blood bay.

By the time she finished, Cale had a fire blazing. The aroma of simmering food wafted to Shay on a southerly breeze, and she sniffed appreciatively. Her stomach growled.

Tossing her hat atop her upended saddle, she walked toward the fire. Her mouth watered as she looked at the beans in the frying pan.

She sat cross-legged beside Cale. "Umm. Smells good."

"Where are the plates?"

Shay reached into the burlap sack near Cale's feet and pulled out two tin plates when a thought struck her. If she could prove her usefulness, then she might convince him that he needed her.

Shay reached for the spoon. "Let me do that."

He gazed at her with a measure of resentment. "I've done for myself long enough. I reckon I can see to both of us."

It wasn't easy being married to a man who regarded her as a nuisance. "I'm not some pampered woman from back east. I want to, and can, do my share."

"If I want your help, then I'll ask for it. I don't take to being dependent on anyone."

"But we're not talking about just anyone." She recalled her determination to be congenial. So much for resolutions, she thought as she snapped, "We're talking about me—your wife!"

"I don't need you to remind me of that fact, and I certainly don't need you to fawn all over me like some lapdog."

Shay was too angry to be hurt. "I would think you, of all people, would see the necessity of relying on each other while on the trail. But if you're going to be pigheaded, don't let me stop you."

She practically swallowed the beans whole, she ate so quickly. Standing, she tossed the dirty plate at his feet.

Shay smiled at him with all the sweetness of a lemon. "Since you didn't ask for my help, I won't wash it."

She whirled, not giving him time to reply, and stomped over to her saddlebags, withdrawing a towel and a bar of soap. Her scowl stabbed the distance between them.

"I'm going to bathe." She wrinkled her nose. "You could use a bath yourself." Lifting her chin, she headed for the river, leaving him to eat alone.

With each step Shay took, anger pounded inside her. No matter how hard she tried, he thwarted her every effort to reestablish a peace between them. Cale made it very obvious that he didn't want her close to him, and he intended to make her pay for trapping him in a marriage he didn't want.

Perhaps in the future they'd be able to go a day without fighting.

Perhaps . . . but Shay seriously doubted that day would come any time soon.

Reaching the river, she stripped and hung her clothes on a bush. She undid her braid, shook out the red mass, and massaged her scalp with her fingertips. Tension began to ebb from her.

Vowing to enjoy the quiet reprieve from her troubles, Shay waded into the Pedernales. As cold water touched her skin, goose bumps cropped out along her arms. She took a deep breath, then ducked below the water's surface, emerging seconds later. She smoothed the hair back from her face and blinked the water from her eyes. It was heavenly to rake her fingers through the dust-covered skeins and feel the dirt lift and float away. She inhaled the sweet lavender scent of the soap. She intended to use it freely, lathering perfumed suds over her body and through her hair.

Just as she raised the soap to her face, she thought she heard a splash. She glanced behind her, but she saw nothing. She shrugged, then rubbed the soap vigorously across one hand, raising a cloud of perfumed suds. Closing her eyes, she lathered her face, then submerged herself in the stream.

Shay's stunned expression when she surfaced with Cale's arms around her should have made Cale feel a measure of satisfaction. But when her surprise turned to annoyance, he grew angry. He didn't like the idea that she didn't want him near her.

Hadn't she made a great show back at camp of getting his attention? And now that she had it, she didn't welcome his interest. He'd be damned if she was going to play him like a puppet. They might be married, but there were no strings attached to him. If anything, she would dance for him.

"What are y-y-you doing?" she stuttered, as she always did when angry.

"Following your advice."

"When I said you needed a bath, I didn't mean for you to take yours with me."

Cale judged the determination in Shay's voice and knew this would be a contest of wills. Well, to the victor went the spoils. He intended to win this skirmish, if not the war.

"You can't have any objections to a husband swimming with his wife," he said, his tone lazy.

At his words, Shay's eyes narrowed, her delicate nostrils flaring slightly, and Cale knew she refrained from a stinging reply. He couldn't contain the grin that spread across his face. "Nothing to say?"

"This isn't a good time for you to be here," she said in a measured tone.

Cale eyed her sleek, wet nakedness. "Oh, but I think it's a perfect time."

Her expression was colder and bleaker than a blue norther. "I find it strange that earlier you didn't want my company, and now you do."

His arm encircled her waist, and he drew her to him. "I changed my mind." Actually, Shay had changed his mind with her sweet, enticing allure that he was powerless to ignore.

"And they say women are fickle."

His thumb traced the outline of her wet lips. "That's not all they say about women."

Although she trembled beneath his touch, Cale recognized her fight to control her responses in the tight set of her jaw.

"What else do they say?" she asked evenly.

Cale cursed himself for allowing her to tempt him so unmercifully. "That they were placed on earth to please men," he said.

And that's just what he wanted her to do—

please him—in every way. After all, she was his wife in the eyes of the law and God. Until death do us part. The pleasure Shay had given him was unique, exquisite, making him forget his previous determination to stay away from her.

She arched a brow. "Oh, really. And next you're going to tell me that we should all be like Ruth and meekly follow. Men always interpret situations to suit their needs."

Oh, she suited his needs all right. More than she knew.

One side of his mouth lifted. "I see you more as Eve, tempting me in the garden of delight."

Shay saw him as the snake, enjoying his bedeviling ways, but she kept her opinion of him to herself. "If you think of me as Eve, then maybe you need spectacles to improve your bad eyesight."

"There's nothing wrong with my sight, or my other faculties. I'd say my sense of touch is particularly good, wouldn't you?" He laid a hand to her breast, her softness molding to his palm.

"Damn you!" Shay spat out, even though her nipple ached against his hand.

With a slow, secret smile, he understood her body's response. Cale lowered his head, nuzzling the side of her face, and nipped her sensitive earlobe.

"Then there's my capable sense of taste." His lips whispered across her mouth. "You're sweet."

His mouth left hers. "Which leaves us with my powers of hearing. I particularly enjoy hearing your cries of pleasure." His smile had a spark of eroticism. "Yep, I'd say there's nothing wrong with my senses." He regarded her. "What do you say?"

Her pulse spurted, then slowed, as she pondered. "What would you like to hear?"

"How you feel."

"I admit your prowess in handling women is more than capable."

"Was that so painful?" His voice broke with huskiness.

"Yes, because I don't like thinking about the women in your past." Tension honed the edge of her voice.

The sensuous curve of his mouth became more pronounced at the impact of her words. "As long as you're with me, that's where they'll stay. There'll be no other women." The gleaming blue light in his eyes also promised that she'd never need or want another man.

In response, her own gaze lit with joy and excitement.

"I've decided that, as my wife, you should perform certain duties that would be pleasurable to us both."

She nibbled her lower lip, thrown into a quandary by the lush assurance in his voice, and by a longing to have him make love to her. "Such as?"

"Washing my back." Beneath the water's surface, a fingertip traced the curve at the base of her spine. "At least, that's where you can start."

"Go to the devil!" Frustration and agony throbbed in her voice.

"Didn't you want an attentive husband?"

She nodded curtly, frustrated that he could so easily extract such responses from her.

"Well, now you have one." What he didn't say was just how attentive he intended to be.

The fading daylight cast Shay's features in fiery, molten copper, highlighting the soft play of mus-

cle beneath her fair skin. The combination of alluring femininity and equally enticing beauty stirred
his blood deeply. The thought of Shay running her
hands over his body fanned his desire, but he
clamped down his passion. For the time being.

"It's going to be a long trip to Wyoming. We
might as well make the most of the time and get
to know each other," Cale said, his gaze conveying
rich promise. "Very well."

Her frown accentuated the annoyance she felt
with herself and him. "I see. When you feel like it,
you throw me a few crumbs of attention."

"I certainly do feel like it. I don't want you
starved for attention."

"We may be married, but I don't have to grovel
for you to notice me." There was defiance in her
tone as well as subtle challenge.

They stared at each other across a sudden throbbing silence.

"You're free to leave at any time." Neutral
shades carefully tinted his response.

She kept her bearing stiff and proud, but confusion ruled her body, mind, and spirit. "Do you
want me to go?"

His voice drifted into a hushed whisper. "Not at
the moment."

Their gazes locked as their breathing came in
unison. A long, delineated moment passed.

Offering her a sudden, arresting smile, he released her and presented his back to her. "I'm
ready."

Shay's gaze went from his broad shoulders and
well-defined back muscles to his tapered, trim
waist.

Cale turned his head to look at her. "I'm waiting."

With lavender-scented soap in hand, she began washing his shoulders, then between his shoulder blades. There were no sounds other than the slow running water, the gentle rustle of wind-fanned leaves—and the steady beating of Shay's heart.

Despite her initial annoyance, Shay found she liked the combined sensations of warm, supple flesh; light, frothy lather; and cool water beneath her fingertips as her hands passed over the smooth expanse of Cale's tanned skin.

She found she wanted to feel more of him. Much more.

Suddenly, he pivoted. "Now the front."

Shay wanted to blow the suds covering her hands into his arrogant face rather than comply with his wishes like an obedient dog, but somehow she couldn't.

Instead of voicing her irritation, she asked, "I trust from your satisfied smile that I'm doing all right?"

"Just fine." His rich voice cascaded over her in shimmering, dark waves.

She washed his neck and throat. Yet, when she touched his chest, her hand lingered, her nerve endings registering the feel of his strong heartbeat and the ripple of tight-knit muscle. On some level, Shay tried to resist him. But the overwhelming visceral tug of his virility defeated her aggravation.

Several moments passed before Shay asked, "You must still think I'm doing well because you haven't stopped grinning."

Too well, Cale thought as he inhaled deeply at the sound of her soft voice. He struggled to control his body's primitive arousal as her hands continued to whisper seductively across his skin.

His struggle for control didn't go unnoticed by

Shay, and she thrilled in her womanly strength over him. If her touch could stir his desire, then she had a chance of balancing the power in their struggling relationship—and making their marriage work.

Yet despite all the pleasurable sensations, Shay felt the need to prove that she was unaffected by his touch. "Tell me about Wyoming."

"What do you want to know?"

"What part are we headed for?"

"Jackson Hole."

"What's the lay of the land?"

"Some of the most beautiful country God ever created. Snowcapped mountains, tall trees, and sparkling rivers that take your breath away each time you see them."

"Sounds wonderful. . . ." Her words trailed off as her hand met the water's surface.

He gave her an indolent, seductive smile. "Don't stop."

"But—"

He wrapped his arms around her and pressed her tightly to him. "You're not finished."

She felt every wet, sensuous, fluid line of him. Especially that rigid length which begged attention. It pulsed, hot and hard, against her stomach. She wondered how much more of this sweet torture she could endure.

Cale saw through her transparent thought. The fact that he was the virile man who was the source of her torment excited him.

Shay wrapped her fingers around him. Her touched elicited the heady thought of slipping his shaft of living steel into her receptacle of sweet warmth, and he groaned in response.

"Cale, what's wrong?"

Seconds passed before his intense need lessened and he could breathe once more, enabling him to answer. "Nothing."

Nothing was wrong. To the contrary, everything was right. He conceded her the victory in this first battle of wills and desire.

But a second contest was to be waged.

"Now it's your turn," Cale said.

Cale's hungry stare devoured Shay—and made her extremely nervous. "That's not necessary."

"Oh, but it is."

The underlying sensuality and hidden nuance in his words caused Shay to back away. "Really, that's—"

"I insist." He gave her a smile that made her want to run for her life. "After all, who should know what you need better than your husband?"

Shay swallowed. She offered a quick prayer for mercy. When it came to his wicked touch, he seldom showed any mercy.

A strong hand took the bar of soap from her. In the span of a heartbeat she felt a tiny pulsing within her womanhood.

His long finger traced her lips. "You're going to enjoy every minute of this."

Of that, she had no doubt. What she feared was where all this would end. And in what condition she would be left. The tip of her tongue moistened her lips where his finger had been.

He lifted a section of wet hair away from her breast and moved it to trail down her back. "I want you to relax." His breath fell like a soft mist on her skin.

She tried to relax, but it was hard with him so near.

He moved behind her. "Close your eyes and tilt your head back."

With surprising gentleness, his fingers softly sank into her hair and began lathering the thick mass, working the dirt from her scalp and her tresses.

A moment later, she heard Cale say, "Now rinse."

She submerged herself, then surfaced, tossing her head back in a spray of water. A hand settled on her shoulder and turned her around to face him.

Her breath caught in her throat when he lathered her neck. She slowly released her breath as his hands skimmed her collar bone. Then her breathing became rapid as his fingers soaped her ribs, her belly. But when his touch rested on her breasts, his strong fingers kneading her soft flesh, her breath untangled in shuddering gasps.

As he continued his movements, a peculiar weightlessness came over her. She groaned softly and allowed her head to loll back in relaxation.

"Feeling better?" he asked in a husky voice.

"Hmm."

Had Shay opened her eyes, she would have seen Cale's heated smile and known desire throbbed through him as well. But she kept her eyes closed.

"Did you enjoy my attention?" he asked, wrapping her long hair about his wrists several times.

"Yes," came the single hushed word.

He gently tugged her hair, bringing her yet closer to him. "In case you haven't noticed, it's nearly dark."

Slowly, Shay opened her eyes. Deep purple hues

descended over the landscape. "So it is," she managed to say.

He unwound her hair from his wrists and let the wet strands trail atop the water's surface.

Wordlessly, they waded to the bank. Cale dressed in plain view; but strangely, Shay felt a twinge of modesty, which made no sense after the intimacies she'd shared with her husband. She hadn't become used to exhibiting her sexuality so openly. She ducked behind the bush that held her clothes.

Shay dressed, then hurried back to camp. She put away her soap and hung her towel to dry before she joined Cale beside the fire. She noticed that he had spread their bedrolls on the ground.

"I'm not sure I'll ever understand you." She looked at the fire, then at him. "But I suppose I should learn to control my temper." She stopped short of apologizing.

Cale broke a stick across his knee and tossed it onto the flames. "I don't expect you to figure my thinking."

"How's that?"

A vertical line creased his brow to the bridge of his nose. "Being orphaned, I learned not to expect much from people."

"You can expect loyalty and honesty from your wife, of all people. I can't blame you for being angry about our marriage, considering you were pushed into it. I also understand how you must feel about not having a choice in a wife." His silence plucked at her nerves. "I just wish you wouldn't take your anger out on me. I may not be what you expected in a wife, but I can still be a good one if you'll let me."

"You're a perfectly fine wife, just not for me, because I can't be the husband you want."

"I wish we could start over, change the circumstances," Shay said wistfully.

Cale's expression revealed no lingering sign of the desire that had burned so brightly in his gaze a short time before. "No sense in wishing for something you can't have."

"Why can't we begin anew?" Shay persisted.

"It's too late for that. There's been too much hurt. Too much said."

"I suppose you're right." Her gaze held his. "Do you regret marrying me?"

"I don't regret keeping your father from hurting you."

"That's not what I asked."

"Don't you understand?" His hand clenched. "I don't want to be the one to hurt you now."

"But are you sorry?" Her words were emphatically underscored.

"I've given you the only answers I can."

She lowered her gaze, not wanting him to see her unhappiness. It would take time to make things right between them, only she didn't know how much time she had.

Her gaze lifted. "What do you want from a woman?"

For an instant wistfulness stole into his expression. "Strength to take whatever comes, but softness to warm my bed."

"And I'm not that person?"

"I don't know," he said with quiet emphasis.

A melancholy frown furrowed her forehead. "When will you be sure?"

"I may never be."

"But you won't give up on me until you're positive, will you?"

The hard set of his mouth, the familiar display of impatience in his gaze, the frustration etched into every line of his body, testified to his inner turmoil.

Yet, somehow, she couldn't quit their marriage. Her life lay ahead of her in Wyoming, not behind her at Twin Creeks. She was sorry that Cale viewed her as an unwanted burden. He admitted his uncertainty as to how she figured into his life. But she would find a way to earn a place in his heart. Somehow.

"We'll learn to be friends. Who knows, we might even learn to love each other. I'll show you that I've got grit enough to survive wherever you take me, or whatever we face. Surviving is the one thing I've learned to do best," she said.

The intensity of his probing gaze was intimidating, but she refused to cower before him. She'd done enough of that with her father. She only wanted him to understand why she longed to be a wife in all ways. True, he hadn't wanted this marriage, but they *were* married, like it or not. Would he ever try to understand her? She dropped her chin atop her chest and sighed.

Cale, having grown up alone, understood her better than she imagined. Against his better judgment, he took her into his arms. He pulled her close and rested his chin atop her head.

Neither spoke as Cale continued to hold her.

Only a strong woman would be able to carve a life for herself out of the rugged country of Wyoming. Was she strong enough to receive his love—the way he wanted to love a woman?

Was Shay that woman? He wished he knew.

How could he make her understand how much his land in Wyoming meant to him? As an orphan he had had nothing to call his own and was shuffled from place to place until he was old enough to make it on his own. His land was the security he had yearned for as a child. It was the only thing that wouldn't ever forsake him. But if he didn't reach Wyoming and finish paying off his holding in time, he'd lose the home he'd worked for his entire life.

If she thought he was too hard, she had no idea of what lay ahead. But Cale did. Storms, harsh winters, disease, poisoned water, poisonous plants and reptiles, wild animals, outlaws, and Indians had claimed many settlers. And he knew that, for her own good, he could show her little kindness.

He released her and stepped back. "I've always been honest with you."

"Sometimes I wish you weren't so painfully direct," she murmured, then her voice grew stronger. "But, has it ever occurred to you that I'm different from most people you've known?"

Unexpectedly, his sudden smile, a brilliant flash of white teeth against tanned skin, was as startling as a burst of sunshine after a thunderstorm. "I'm well aware of that fact."

At the sight of his disarming smile, she wanted to wrap her arms around him and kiss him with all the emotion she felt.

Just as suddenly as his smile had broken across his face, it disappeared behind a clouded expression. "You'd best be turning in. We've got a long day ahead of us. I'll wake you before daylight."

She couldn't go to sleep without knowing the answer to the question foremost on her mind. She moistened her lips. "Will you be sharing my bedroll with me tonight?"

Cale turned away from Shay and threw more wood onto the fire.

It seemed a long time before he faced her again. Their gazes met—and held for an even longer moment.

By the rigid set of his shoulders and jaw, she knew he held a close check on his emotions.

"No." He exhaled harshly. "Now go to sleep."

"But I thought—"

A tic developed in his cheek. "I said go to sleep."

Shay lay on her side atop her bedroll and spread her saddle blanket over her. With her arms folded beneath her cheek, she looked at him.

"Are you going to be able to sleep?" she asked.

Cale crouched beside her and stretched his arm out, and for one wild, dizzy moment, Shay thought he meant to touch her, until his hand settled on the rifle that rested against the food sack behind her.

He lifted the lever-action Winchester and stood, staring down at her. The lines around his mouth deepened, giving him a look as lethal as his weapon.

"Will you quit talking, dammit?" he growled.

With his free hand, he picked up his blanket and moved to the far side of the campfire.

Shay raised herself onto an elbow and looked at him over the tops of the flames. "Good night, Cale."

He breathed out a brusque "Good night, Shay."

Chapter 13

The aroma of strong coffee awoke Shay. Her nose twitched at the familiar smell, and she slowly opened her eyes.

It was the hour when night slowly surrenders to the coming of the sun, and the sky lightens in gradual, soft shades of dawn.

Shay inhaled again, savoring the anticipation of a cup of the steaming brew. Rubbing the sleep from her eyes, she uncurled herself and stood, first bending her long legs, then stretching her slender arms. Every stiff muscle of her body reminded Shay that it had been a while since she had slept beneath the stars on an unyielding bed of earth and rock. Or since she had ridden a good twenty miles in under a day.

Since they would be crossing the river, she saw no point in changing into clean clothes, so she straightened the ones she had slept in before she shook out her boots and tugged them on. Next, she tackled the task of combing and braiding her unruly hair. Last, she brushed her teeth, using water from her canteen to rinse. Having finished with her limited grooming, she felt more confident of meeting the challenge of a new day.

But was she ready for the challenge of facing Cale?

She found him frying bacon in a black cast-iron skillet. At the edge of the fire, biscuits baked in a covered container buried in the ashes on the fire's perimeter. To one side, the coffeepot steamed. The lid rattled from the bitter brew boiling and spewing inside, and steam rose from the spout.

He must have heard her, for he glanced up. "Breakfast?"

His distant expression told her what kind of day she could expect—a very vexing one.

Shay smiled tightly. "And good morning to you." She grabbed a cup, poured herself some coffee, and sat on the ground.

His dark expression didn't change except for a raised brow. "Do you want to teach me a lesson in manners, or do you want breakfast?"

Her mouth thinned. "Breakfast, please."

Shay wished she had the gumption to take her coffee and throw it right in his face. He was the most irritating, flustering man she'd ever known.

Too bad, she thought. She might have been able to convince herself that she really didn't love him if it weren't for the soft feeling in the pit of her stomach whenever she looked at him.

She also knew with certainty that if she ever lost Cale, a part of her soul would be lost, too. Somehow they were two parts of a whole. And that's the way he made her feel when they were together—whole, alive.

Inhaling deeply, she held her breath briefly, then released the air slowly. It would take time to fix things between them. She'd have to have patience—a great deal of it.

They ate as the sun rose above the eastern horizon to touch the landscape with golden fingers. Sipping her coffee, Shay glanced at the river. Steam rose from the warm water into the cool air.

Finished eating, Cale stood. "I'm going to the river to shave." The deep timbre of his voice vibrated in the morning quiet. "You can clean up." With that he got his grooming items and headed for the riverbank.

Shay sat fingering the rim of her tin cup for a long moment, staring at the space where Cale had stood. Remember, she told herself. Time. And patience. She then tossed what remained of her coffee into the ashes and set about breaking camp.

Having extinguished the fire and put the foodstuffs away, she gathered all the items that needed washing and headed for the river.

As she reached the downside of the riverbank, Shay saw Cale. He stood at a pecan sapling, stripped to the waist, soap cup in one hand, brush in the other. He was looking into the small mirror he had hung on the young tree.

Slanting sunlight rimmed his figure in living gold, highlighting his height and build, and the angles and planes of his face. She was struck again by how handsome he was. The first time she had seen him shave, back at the bunkhouse, he had been a stranger. Now, she looked at him through the eyes of a wife who took pleasure in the sight of her attractive husband. It was all Shay could do not to walk over to him and run her hands across the expanse of his muscular chest she had come to memorize with her touch.

Sighing fretfully, she walked to the water's edge and deposited the dirty articles on the ground. As she washed the items, Shay had never been so aware of Cale's presence.

Suddenly, she was struck by the absurdity of the situation. She was his wife. She had every right to touch her husband—whenever and wherever she wanted.

With a singular purpose, Shay left the utensils where they lay and walked over to Cale.

He lowered his razor. "Yes?"

Shay pointed to a fallen tree log. "Sit." Her tone was authoritative, her gaze steady.

He frowned. "What are you up to?"

"I'm going to shave you."

An arched brow indicated his surprise. "Why?"

"Because I want to." Impatience peppered her voice. "Don't argue with me." She stuck her hand out. "Just give me the razor and sit down."

Amazingly, Cale handed over his razor without another word. Satisfaction that, for once, she'd known just how to handle him brought color to her cheeks. If she could say anything about herself, she'd say that persistence was a hallmark of her character.

Shay retrieved the soap cup and worked up more lather, then applied the fresh coat to Cale's face with efficient, circular motions.

Amusement wrinkled his voice. "Where'd you learn to shave a man?"

"Where do you think? I have a father and an uncle, you know."

The reminder of her family stabbed Shay's heart, but she forced the emotion to the shadowy corners of her mind.

Satisfied with the layer of lather now in place, she set about shaving the broad angles of Cale's face. She stood in front of him and leaned forward to apply the sharp edge to one cheek.

Intent on her task, Shay didn't realize how close her breasts were to Cale's face.

But Cale did. They were level with his mouth and so close he could flick out his tongue and touch them. Which was precisely what he would have liked to have done. Only through sheer will, tenuous at best, did he refrain. He squirmed on the log.

Shay stopped to admonish him. "If you don't sit still, I'm liable to cut something vital—like your throat."

She leaned forward once more and continued her self-assigned chore, unaware of the torture her nearness was inflicting on Cale. Had she known, she would have been secretly glad. As it were, she missed having that small measure of satisfaction.

Minutes of absolute torment went by for Cale until he couldn't stave off his body's yearning.

His hands came, large and firm, to Shay's small waist, causing her to drop the razor as he pulled her to him.

"Come here," he commanded in a low, husky tone.

No words were necessary, her hands rising of their own accord to twine in his thick black mane. The clean scent and silky texture of his hair filled her senses as she leaned her cheek against the top of his head.

Cale's hands performed a different task. He efficiently unbuttoned her shirt with one hand, and with the other he parted the material and stroked her thinly covered breast. She moaned, deep in her throat, as his forefinger and thumb commanded the nipple to life.

In her ecstasy, her grip on his hair tightened and

he flinched, but he didn't leave off his painstaking attention.

His hands encased her hips and held her a heartbeat away from him. "God, I can't stop."

She opened her eyes and looked down at him, understanding and acquiescence in her gaze, even as his hands pushed her shirt off her shoulders, down her arms, to her waist. She felt the erotic sensation of his silky hair and the lingering soap lather against her skin as her camisole followed the way of her shirt and he bared her breasts.

"What are you doing to me?" Cale murmured as he pressed his face to her chest.

For Shay, it wasn't a question of what she did to him, but rather what he did to her. And what he was doing was sinful and heavenly at the same time.

His hands cupped her ripe, beckoning breasts and gently kneaded the proud, firm flesh until her nipples ached. The throbbing traveled lower ... until it settled in her warm, vibrating center. Then, as if to lay claim to her flesh with his touch, he ran his splayed hands down her rib cage to her waist, across her flat stomach, back up again.

Profound delight streaked through her when his mouth captured one breast, marking it as his possession. Her fingers curled reflexively in the richness of his shoulder-length hair. She pressed his face closer in wanton demand.

Her breath came out in a feathery sigh as Cale sought ownership of the other breast. The sensation extracted a ragged, brazen plea from her moist, parted lips. Her legs became liquid and she would have sagged to the ground had it not been for the support of Cale's large, strong hands anchored at her waist.

Feeling as though she were being swept along by a powerful river current, she surrendered completely to the pleasure Cale was agonizingly inflicting on her more than willing body.

Between spurts of her erratic pulse, Cale's possession of her breasts stopped and he abruptly released her.

Unable to stand, her legs buckled and she dropped to her knees between his widespread legs. He steadied her with firm hands on her shoulders.

"Cale, make love to me," Shay begged, dignity forgotten in the name of desire and love.

Cale was caught in finely meshed emotions. Every fiber of his being yearned to do just that. But he knew that if he took her now, she would give herself to him body and soul. He didn't know what he could give back to her—except an impossibly hard existence in Wyoming. They spent most of their time arguing as it was. How would it be when she finally realized what kind of life—and man—she'd committed herself to?

"Not now," he said in a raw, throbbing voice.

She placed her hands atop his thighs, her fingers digging lightly into his muscles, and whispered a broken plea. "Please."

It took all his willpower not to take her in his arms. The sight of her wide, stricken eyes and the sound of the sob that escaped her branded themselves in Cale's memory.

Absorbed in her own pain, Shay didn't see the spasm of regret flit across Cale's face before he rose, pulling her to her feet with him.

Their labored breathing tangled, becoming one sound.

Vaguely, Shay was cognizant that Cale pulled

her camisole up her arms and settled it about her shoulders. Stepping back, she looked at him, her eyes wide with simmering pain and confusion. She wanted to face him in calm defiance, but her trampled spirit caused her body to vibrate with intense emotions.

When he reached out for her, she whispered furiously, "Don't touch me." She adjusted her clothing with trembling fingers.

Behind his taciturn expression smoldered a barely controlled rage that was best heeded.

Had Shay been in a more coherent frame of mind, she would have done just that, but she wasn't thinking clearly. She'd offered herself to her husband, allowing herself to become vulnerable. All he'd had to do was accept her—all of her. But he had turned her away.

Shame, outrage, and humiliation churned inside her. Shay had to release her raw emotions or burst. She bent and scooped up river mud with both hands, hurling the muck at him as she straightened.

The ensuing seconds ticked by . . . with each beat of her heart. Shay had never seen such fury as she stared at Cale's mud-splattered features. Panic overrode all other emotions and she bolted for camp.

The harsh rasp of air streaming through her lungs muted the stark bellow behind her. "*Shay!*"

Had she been able to distinguish the nuances in the single word, she would have recognized all the desire and anger in Cale's voice.

As from a great distance, the sound of pounding footsteps registered on Shay. Fear drove her to greater speed, but to no avail, as Cale tackled her from behind.

Sights and sounds twisted into one suspended moment as they hit the ground with a thud.

Shay lay breathless, her lungs burning, fighting for air. Slowly, she opened her eyes. She blinked to clear her vision, only to discover Cale glaring down at her as she lay beneath him.

Panicking at the brutal set to his mouth, she tried in vain to buck him off.

Cale effortlessly secured her wrists on either side of her head. Her chest heaved with each ragged breath she took, and her body trembled. Yet she summoned her courage and glared at her husband, who held her prisoner.

The early morning light outlined his mud-splattered face into craggy lines and angles. She swallowed.

"Let me up." Her voice faltered as the fathomless depths of his blue eyes struck her like a physical blow. "You don't own me," she ended on a serrated whisper.

Clenching his jaw, he slowly released her and stood. He wiped the mud from his face with his sleeve. Her gaze never left him as she struggled to her feet.

Although Cale spoke with a deliberate calmness, there was no mistaking the hard edge to his voice. "God help you if you push my temper any more than you already have."

Shay retreated two shaky steps from Cale's scorching scowl, steady and dark with a singular anger. But the humiliation burning brightly within her gave her a sense of bravado.

"Don't threaten me, you bully! I have no intention of taking orders from you."

Cale clenched his hands until his knuckles grew white.

When Shay made the mistake of blinking, he bridged the distance between them in three long strides.

Caught unaware by his speedy pursuit, Shay choked on astonished outrage as his relentless fingers clamped about her wrist. Cale sat on a tree stump and dragged her across his lap.

"Let me loose, you flea-bitten son of a biscuit-eater," Shay said, panting as she kicked her legs and swung her arms wildly.

He repressed her struggles by throwing a muscular leg over the backs of her knees, trapping her limbs between his. "Not until you've gotten what you deserve," he said, tight-lipped. "I've never wanted to strike a woman before—until now."

The fight drained from Shay as vivid memories stung her mind, like so many blows from her father, and she went limp.

Face down across his lap, Shay couldn't see how the fire was doused from his gaze, leaving smoldering anguish in its ashes, leaving no doubt that he couldn't hit her no matter what she'd done.

Shay squeezed her eyes shut, waiting. She didn't think she could bear the pain of what Cale threatened to do to her. Like Papa.

What seemed an eternity later, Cale stood and Shay tumbled to the ground.

He stared down at her. "What am I going to do with you?"

The query was spoken so softly that Shay didn't know if he posed the question to her or himself.

Yet, the indignity of Cale's treatment of her imbued Shay with a sense of purpose. She'd had enough of men and their hurting ways.

"Don't treat me like some unwanted piece of

goods." She rose, her dignity badly bruised. "Papa treated me that way most of my adult life."

Cale advanced; his gaze was steady with determination.

Eyes wide with mistrust, Shay retreated until the trunk of a large oak blocked her way.

"Don't compare me to your father," he growled.

He leaned into her, so firmly that Shay could feel the warmth of his breath on the bridge of her nose. The hard, lean length of his body sent primitive signals to the softness of hers as he imprisoned her by bracing himself against the tree, one hand on each side of her.

She fought the attraction and angled her chin at him in defiance. "And why not?"

An earthy essence emanated from his skin. "I've never mistreated you."

"If what you just showed me was affection, then Lord spare me from your indifference."

His face hovered near hers. "Shay, I'm warning you. No more childish tantrums."

"Oh, yes, it's always my fault," she said breathlessly. "A moment ago you were no better than my father."

His gaze skimmed her eyes, her shoulders, her breasts. "No better, am I? I married you, didn't I?"

The arrogance in his voice sharpened her senses. Sick of his playing the martyr, she snapped, "Don't try to switch topics on me. I'm the one who should be furious for the way you treated me."

His facial muscles tightened with impatience. "And just what did I do?"

"What did he do, he asks." She directed her fury at Cale with a force begot from ragged emotions. "I all but begged you to make love to me, and you turned me away like I was a whore you didn't want to pay, instead of your wife."

"You came to me, or have you forgotten?"

"How can you be so cruel?"

"No more cruel than you, tempting me like a shameless wanton."

"And who's made me that way?" she cried. "I knew nothing about men until I met you. If I'm wanton, it's your fault." She stabbed the air with an accusatory finger.

If she hadn't been so furious she would have felt breath-stealing fear from the look he leveled on her.

"I only took what you were willing to give." Each word coiled tighter, like a rattler poised to strike. "But because of your family, I've paid dearly for what you gave away."

"If I act like a shameless whore, then I want to be paid like one. Then, at least, I'll have something to show for my trouble."

Cale's firm lips curled with contempt—and genuine pain. "If that's the way you want it. From now on, money for services rendered. Nothing more." He laughed, the sound void of humor. "Why not? I've already bought you with my name, the price being my freedom."

"Our getting married was a mistake."

"I'm glad we see things eye to eye."

Shay ground her teeth in anger and frustration. "Bastard."

Cale's expression darkened like a gathering storm. "If you're with child, that's what our union would have brought if I hadn't married you."

"I could have taken care of myself—and a baby."

"Like you've taken care of everything else?"

"Maybe I can do things without you. True, I gave you my body. But I didn't give up my dreams." Her throat constricted in vexation. "Why do men think women don't have aspirations and plans of their own?"

"Because most women don't know what they want."

"Right now, I want to be as far away from you as I can get."

"Until I know if you're carrying my child, you're staying with me."

"Why do you care?"

"Because I lived my life alone—not having known my family. I intend to know my own child."

His unvarnished honesty gave her reason to pause—but only briefly. "Not unless I want you to."

"You belong to me now," Cale said, revealing straight, white teeth. "And nothing's going to change that unless I want it to."

"And what about me?"

"You got what you wanted. Your father saw to that."

Shay was incensed. "I'm not some mare to be traded at will, or a piece of property to be staked for claim."

"The law says you're my wife. You belong to me. To do with as I please. I'm just waiting to see if, besides my name, you bear my child."

She fixed him with an accusing glare. "What makes you think you're man enough to father a child?"

His jaw tensed as if he waged an inner battle for restraint. "Many reasons." The wind, and his heated words, blew across her. "Which I intend to show to you. In many different ways." His gaze promised things she both dreaded and craved.

She couldn't bear his nearness. She despised her vulnerability. She hated the shivers that seized her and the way her blood flowed thin and hot through her veins.

Tears sparkled on her thick lashes. "You hurt me, but I swear you'll never do it again."

For a timeless moment they studied each other, two prideful, independent wills locked in silent combat.

A muscle constricted in his jaw, then relaxed again. He pushed away from the tree, turned on his heel, and strode toward camp.

Shay stood absolutely still, watching him. She felt as if her heart were being torn from her chest.

Damn your black soul, Cale Breland, she thought. Despite everything, I love you.

Half an hour later, they struck camp and crossed the river to begin the second leg of their journey.

With each subsequent mile, Shay breathed life into her outrage whenever it threatened to die, forcing pain into the background of her heart.

How long before anger came too easily? And stayed too long?

Cotton pushed open the swinging doors, stepped inside the saloon, and slowly walked to the bar. He didn't think there was an inch of his body that didn't hurt from Breland's beating.

He dipped two fingers into his vest pocket and fished out a coin.

Slapping his money atop the smooth, worn wood, he called to the bartender at the other end of the counter. "Beer."

A large, portly man, with sweeping gray sideburns that blended into a handlebar mustache, walked to the middle of the bar and drew a mug of draft. He set the frothy drink on the counter and, with a push of his meaty hand, sent the beer sliding down the counter to Cotton.

As Cotton took a drink, the man chuckled. "What happened to you? Your face looks like hell."

Cotton grimaced as he wiped the foam from his swollen upper lip with his sleeve. He glared at the man. "Why don't you mind your own business before I tend to it for you?"

"Don't get all riled. Just asking." The barkeep snickered, then returned his attention to his other customers.

Cotton leaned forward on his elbows and raised his mug to his mouth. Even having a drink hurt.

Damn that bastard Breland. Cotton knew what he'd like to do if he ever got a hold of that nigger lover again. The next time Breland would never know what hit him.

With that satisfying thought, Cotton casually turned his head toward the entrance when he heard the doors swing back on their hinges. Two strangers entered and walked up to the bar.

They leaned back against the bar, pushing their hats off their blond heads to hang by cords between their shoulder blades.

The taller of the two produced money and called over his shoulder to the bartender. "Whiskey."

The barkeep complied and poured two jigger glasses of rotgut.

Cotton turned his head and seemingly gazed at his beer, but from out of the corner of his eye, he continued to study the men. Covered as they were with trail dust, they sure must have been riding hard. White sweat lined their mouths and eyes. His gaze dropped to the guns they wore slung low on their hips. Colts—and expensive ones at that.

The cowboys downed their drinks, then called for another round.

This time they sipped their whiskey, all the while studying the saloon patrons. Then the shorter man motioned the bartender over.

The cowboy turned sideways, his hip against the bar, and said, "We're not from around these parts." He pulled out a crisp Union back and held it between his fingers in the bartender's face. "Was wondering if you might be able to help us."

The bartender pocketed the money, then wiped off the counter as he talked. "What can I do for you, boys?"

The taller man spoke. "We're looking for two men. Only know one's name though. Brad Alexander. You heard of him?"

The barkeep kept his gaze lowered, although his wiping motion slowed. "What y'all want with Brad Alexander?"

"That's our business." The stranger leaned forward. "You heard of him, or not?"

The bartender swallowed when pinned by the cowboy's intense regard. "He and his brother run a spread, called Twin Creeks, about twenty miles from here."

"We heard he might have traveled home with another man. Know anything?"

"I—" the bartender began.

"He don't," Cotton said as he turned to face the two strangers. With mug in hand, he smiled. "But I might. Let's go where we can talk in private."

The three men moved to a secluded corner table.

The shorter cowboy looked at Cotton. "Who are you?"

"The name's Cotton. I'm the foreman at Twin Creeks."

The taller man raised a brow. "So?"

"So, I know who you're looking for." Cotton was hard-pressed to hide his smile as he had the travelers' full attention.

"There might be something in it for ya if we get a name."

"First, tell me why you're looking for him."

The shorter cowboy looked at the taller one, then back to Cotton. "We've got business with him." His hand rested atop the butt of his Colt. "He gunned down our pa, and we mean to see to it that he pays."

Cotton couldn't believe his good fortune. Lady Luck was smiling down on him. He would have his revenge on Breland and Shay, and not have to do any of the work or share in the blame.

"His name is Cale Breland." Cotton's voice smacked with satisfaction.

The taller man punched the other's shoulder. "Let's get going."

"Hold on," Cotton drawled, intending to enjoy every minute of his satisfaction. "He's not at Twin Creeks. He left yesterday, heading for Wyoming with his new bride." His eyes narrowed at the thought of Shay. "I reckon you boys would be right interested in which trail they're traveling." He grinned. "Isn't that right?"

"Yeah, that's right," the taller cowboy replied, peeling off another Union back from a roll of money in his pocket. "It seems we all just hit the jackpot today."

Cotton's breath came tight and hard. Breland.

The bastard. Fury replaced a portion of the ache in Cotton's battered body as he remembered the beating Breland had given him. Breland would get what he deserved.

Chapter 14

Cale and Shay came upon an elderly couple
stranded in a buckboard on the side of the
road.

The woman sat on the seat, holding the reins,
while the man gripped a rear wheel, straining to
use his weight as leverage. The buckboard didn't
budge in the sand.

Cale dismounted, tossed his reins to Shay, and
walked toward the pair. "Looks as if you could
use some help."

Straightening, the man pulled a bandanna from
his vest pocket and wiped his palms, then extended a hand. "Josh Owen."

Shay observed Mr. Owen as he and Cale shook
hands. He appeared to be in his late fifties. He had
a ruddy complexion, long face, and square jaw. His
cheekbones were high; his eyes were deep-set. His
appearance taken as a whole was a kind one.

Mr. Owen left off the handshake and motioned
toward the woman. "This here's my wife, Minnie."

Cale touched the brim of his hat. "Ma'am. Cale
Breland." He inclined his head in Shay's direction.
"My wife, Shay."

"I'm so glad y'all happened our way. Josh's not

getting any younger. We're obliged." Mrs. Owen smiled, wrinkles deepening in her pleasantly plump face. "Trying to get back home with supplies, but we're not having much luck."

Shay took an instant liking to Mrs. Owen, with her voice, smooth as worn leather, and her gentle regard. "We're happy to be of help," Shay said.

Mr. Owen glanced at the wagon over his shoulder, then mopped his brow beneath the rim of his hat. "Can't seem to make any headway."

"We'll have you clear soon enough." Cale took hold of the front wheel spokes. "Ma'am, you lay down those reins across the backs of your horses when I give the word."

Mr. Owen positioned himself at the rear wheel. "Whenever you're ready, young man."

"On the count of three," Cale said. "One." He gripped the spokes tighter. "Two." He planted his feet and set his shoulder to the wheel, muscles bunching. "Three."

In one choreographed act, Mrs. Owen drove the team forward and the two men put their backs into their task. Moments later, the buckboard pulled clear of the sand.

Once his breathing had returned to normal, Mr. Owen said, "Don't like being indebted. You two come home with the missus and me. Looks as if you could use a good night's rest and a home-cooked meal. Minnie's the best cook in these parts." He smiled at his wife.

She returned his compliment with a half-snort and half-laugh. "Josh always was a bragger."

Mr. Owen winked. "No brag, just fact."

The Owens' gentle teasing tugged at Shay's heartstrings. What would it be like to share such a good-natured moment with Cale? she wondered.

"We wouldn't want to put you to any trouble," Cale said, taking his reins from Shay, clearly wanting to be on his way.

"Won't take no for an answer," Mr. Owen returned. "We're having a barn raising this afternoon. Tonight there'll be lots of eats and a dance."

Cale looked up at Shay. Unable to hide a smile of delighted anticipation, she asked, "Oh, could we, Cale? It's been so long since I've been to a dance."

Did she imagine his expression softening before he faced Mr. Owen?

Cale shrugged. "Looks like I'm outnumbered."

"You just might enjoy yourself." Laughing, Mr. Owen slapped Cale's shoulder with a work-roughened hand. "Our place is just down the road."

The Owen homestead was typical of small Texas farms, boasting a modest white frame house surrounded by a picket fence with a vegetable garden to one side. A row of cedars served as a windbreak on the north side of the house. Oak and pecan trees dotted the perimeter. To the rear of the house, a blackened patch of earth bespoke a once-existing barn. Guinea hens flapped their gray-and-white wings and raced around the yard, crying shrilly at the approaching riders and wagon.

Mr. Owen halted the buckboard at the white picket gate and helped his wife down from the wagon.

"Young lady, you go inside with my wife. Your husband and I will see to the horses," Mr. Owen said as he took his seat again on the buckboard.

Mrs. Owen led the way inside the farmhouse. Shay found the dwelling to be rustic—and totally charming. A dogtrot bisected the building into two halves, allowing for a southerly breeze to flow freely down the hall. Living and dining rooms and the kitchen were to the left, with sleeping quarters to the right. Furniture was sparse but made to last a lifetime. Colorful quilts draped the backs of chairs and the single settee.

Mrs. Owen untied her blue calico bonnet and hung it on a peg near the front door. She smoothed several strands of gray hair from her face and patted them into place at the knot she wore at the nape of her neck.

Somehow the simple gesture made Shay aware of her dusty appearance. She removed her Stetson, the hat dangling by a cord from her fingers.

After she hung Shay's hat on a peg adjacent to the one that held her bonnet, Mrs. Owen took Shay's hands in her own. "You remind me so much of my daughter."

"Does your daughter live here?" Shay asked, grateful for an avenue of conversation.

Mrs. Owen's face clouded. "She died from the fever some years back."

"I'm sorry."

"You had no way of knowing." Mrs. Owen's expression brightened as she squeezed Shay's fingers. "But I'm not one for dwelling on the past. It'll be nice having a young woman in the house again—even for a night."

Her hands still clasping Shay's, Mrs. Owen stretched Shay's arms out to the sides to get a better view of her figure. "You look to be just about Nancy's size. If you'd like, I have a gown you can wear to the dance."

Although she had never been one for dresses, the thought of Cale seeing her gussied up once more caused Shay to feel soft inside. She wanted to be an alluring woman tonight. For Cale.

"Thank you, Mrs. Owen. I'd like that."

Mrs. Owen released Shay and stepped back, waving an age-spotted hand. "Call me Minnie. Everybody else does."

"But—"

"Do you like me, child?"

"Oh, yes."

"And I feel the same about you. Friends use Christian names."

"All right." Shay laughed. "Minnie."

"Good. Let's wash up and get to fixing some food. There'll be lots of hungry folks coming soon."

"What happened to your barn?" Shay asked.

"It was hit by lightning and burned to the ground. But, thanks to all our friends, we'll have a new barn in a jiffy," Minnie answered.

Arm in arm, the two women walked into the kitchen.

Working side by side, they became lost in conversation and cooking until they heard Josh's voice at the back door. "Wagons coming."

Minnie wiped her hands on her apron. "We'll be out directly," she called out.

After Minnie removed her biscuits from the oven, she and Shay joined the folks outside.

Buggies and buckboards were left on the fringes of the yard by the cedar trees, while single horses were tethered to the fence. Men converged on the spot where the barn was to be built, while women gathered closer to the house. Shortly, the sounds of voices, saws, and hammers filled the air.

Shay was soon swept along in greetings as

Minnie introduced her to the women. The hours passed in domestic conversation.

At one point, Minnie asked Shay to take water to the men. Shay found herself missing Cale, and she was glad for the opportunity to see him.

As she made the rounds, she felt as if someone were staring at her. Slowly turning, she discovered a man who appeared to be in his mid-twenties assessing her—boldly, openly. How dare he! Irritation caused hot color to stain her cheeks.

Before she could move away, he called to her. "Miss, water please."

Intent on giving him a piece of her mind, she opened her mouth, but then her eye caught Minnie looking at her.

The man called to her again, but louder this time. "Miss, water, *please.*"

Certain Minnie had heard him, Shay knew she couldn't embarrass her hostess by ignoring the man—despite his impertinence. She wove her way through the workers until she stopped within a foot of the stranger.

Wordless, she handed him a dipper of water. He drank deeply, then wiped his mouth on his rolled-up sleeve and returned the dipper to her.

"More." He had the audacity to smile. "Please."

Shay gritted her teeth as she ladled more water for him. She thrust the dipper at him, splashing water in the process. "I'll thank you to stop staring at me."

The corners of his brown eyes crinkled. "Why? You're a beautiful woman."

"Because I'm a *married* woman. I'm Mrs. Breland."

"Matt Clayton." He brushed a lock of chestnut

hair from his forehead. "You're still beautiful, Mrs. Breland."

"Maybe you'd like to tell my husband that."

"I didn't know you were married, but I'm sure your husband knows what a lucky man he is. I meant no offense. I only wanted to talk. I won't bother you anymore."

To her amazement, Shay found her irritation dwindling at his charming, soft-spoken manner. He had rudely stared at her, but in his defense, he hadn't noticed her wedding ring. Her actions had been no less rude. Perhaps she was being overly sensitive.

She extended her hand. "If you're finished, I need to see to the others." She attempted a more civilized tone of voice.

He laid the dipper in her open palm. "If your husband doesn't mind, maybe you can save me a dance tonight."

Her fingers closed around the dipper's blue enamel handle. "Maybe." She walked away.

Shay came upon Cale sawing planks. He must have sensed her presence, because he stopped and looked up.

Shay smiled as their gazes met. "Minnie asked me to help. I thought you might like some water."

Cale straightened and wiped his brow with his forearm. "I could use some." He took the dipper from her and drank the cool well water.

She started to tell him about Matt Clayton, but when he looked at her with a possessive light in his eyes, she decided against it. No sense in causing trouble. Mr. Clayton would no doubt find himself another woman to pursue at the dance.

* * *

That evening, as Shay helped the other women clear away supper dishes, Minnie pulled her aside. "The men are around back cleaning up for the dance. I want you to get yourself in the house and do the same."

"But I'm not finished."

"You're coming with me and that's the end of it."

Shay knew by Minnie's tone of voice that it was useless to argue. "All right."

"Good." Minnie laughed, a knowing glint in her eyes. "I reckon you'll be wanting to look nice for that handsome husband of yours."

Shay's stomach tightened. She wanted him to be proud to take her in his arms and dance with her. Her thoughts stopped short. Could he dance? She knew so little about him.

An hour later, the two women emerged from the house.

Pausing at the back door, Minnie gazed at the blue satin and white lace creation that Shay wore. "I remember how excited Nancy was when she got that dress. It came all the way from Saint Louis." She patted Shay's hand. "Everyone worked hard today, now it's time to have some fun."

The smell of fresh-sawed lumber greeted Minnie and Shay as they entered the new barn. The warm glow from numerous lanterns cast the interior in a festive atmosphere. The day's hard work was forgotten as men and women, young and old, were infused with a spontaneous gaiety and new energy.

From the far end of the barn came the spirited sounds of guitar, banjo, fiddle, and mouth harp. Soon dancers took to the floor.

Minnie directed Shay to the right and a long table laden with pies and cakes and a large bowl of punch.

Seeing all the sweets, Shay groaned. "So much food after we've already eaten."

"Folks around here know how to celebrate."

Josh walked up and kissed Minnie on the cheek. "Looking pretty as always." His gaze swept Shay. "And you're mighty fetching too, young lady."

Shay curtsied. "Why, thank you, kind sir."

Josh indicated the barn with a sweep of his hand. "Minnie, isn't it wonderful to have such good neighbors?"

Minnie hooked her arm in the crook of her husband's. "The good Lord's blessed us."

Shay scanned the crowd, then looked at Josh. "Have you seen Cale?"

Josh rubbed his chin. "Not since we cleaned up."

"Don't worry, Shay. I've noticed the way that husband of yours looks at you when you're not watching. His eyes followed you all afternoon," Minnie said. "He won't leave you by yourself long. Not in a barn full of men."

Josh smiled. "Cale don't strike me as a man who would let others horn in on what's his."

Shay couldn't keep the disappointment from her voice. "I just thought Cale would have—"

"Would have what?"

She turned, at the sound of his voice, to face Cale. How handsome he looked, freshly washed and shaved, wearing clean clothes.

"Been here by now," she said slowly, almost breathlessly.

He grinned. "Well, here I am."

His slow perusal of her appearance warmed her. His eyes told her how beautiful he thought she was. Never had she wanted him to take her in his arms and kiss her more than she did at that moment.

Since yesterday she had nursed her bruised pride with anger. But as he gazed at her with desire gleaming from the soulful depths of his eyes, she forgot her anger. She knew only love.

Minnie poked Josh in the ribs. "We'd best be making the rounds."

"Should've done that already," Josh said, leading his wife away.

Pinches of laughter and dashes of conversation mixed in the air. A sprinkling of music added to the evening's enjoyable ingredients.

"Would you like to dance?" Cale asked, his hand closing warmly over hers.

Shay felt as giddy as a filly at the intimate touch and the soft look on his face. She wanted nothing more than to spend the evening laughing and dancing with her husband.

"Oh, yes," she said, all her joyful anticipation of a wonderful evening revealed in her smile.

"Good." Cale squeezed her fingers. "Because I've been wanting to hold you." He guided her onto the dance floor.

Shay put a hand on her husband's broad shoulder, felt his hand at her waist as he guided her among the other dancers.

The tune was slow, and Cale held Shay close to him—so close that she felt deliciously out of breath. She also felt a luscious tingling everywhere his body touched hers. Her senses vibrated with awareness.

This was the gentle, virile man who had won her love.

"Shay, is something wrong?"

"What?"

"You look as if you don't feel well."

Feel, she thought. That's all she could do. "I've never felt better."

"Good. I want you to enjoy yourself."

"Do you?" Her voice was rife with emotion.

"Yes." The look in his eyes matched the rich promise in his voice.

The merrymaking of the other dancers was infectious, and Cale and Shay were caught up in the revelry.

Suddenly and unexpectedly, Cale lifted Shay by her waist and swung her around. Their laughter blended into the gaiety surrounding them.

The next few hours were heavenly. They danced; they laughed. They looked; they touched. Shared moments to be cherished.

Eventually, Cale pulled Shay over to the refreshment table. He picked up a cup. "Punch?"

"Yes, please." Shay brushed a strand of hair from her forehead and smiled. "I can't ever remember dancing this much." She accepted the cup and sipped the cool punch.

The approach of Matt Clayton interrupted any further conversation. "Could I have this dance, Mrs. Breland?"

Shay turned to Cale. "Do you mind?"

"No." The lines around Cale's mouth deepened. "Why should I?"

She walked onto the dance floor, followed by Matt Clayton. They took their positions in line for the Virginia Reel.

His fists clenching and unclenching, Cale watched Shay. He was completely unprepared to deal with the sight of Shay in another man's arms. She was his. And he didn't like sharing her.

Cale saw Clayton say something and Shay tilt her head back to laugh. His jealousy soared with each beat of the music. Damn! He had to leave before he walked onto the dance floor and strangled Matt Clayton where he stood. Cale spun on his heel and left.

He walked out into the night with no clear intention of where he was headed. Eventually he found himself sitting beneath an oak tree with the bottle of whiskey from his saddlebags.

Cale closed his eyes and leaned his head back against the tree trunk. The air in his lungs burned as he breathed deeply.

"Been looking for you."

Cale opened his eyes and saw Josh standing in front of him. "Well, you found me."

"Only because you wanted me to."

With his teeth, Cale uncorked the bottle and brought the whiskey to his lips. Cale spat out the cork, then drank deeply from the bottle. The aged liquor warmed a path across his tongue, down his throat, to his stomach. "I don't know what you're talking about."

"When I saw you leave the barn, I figured you might want some company."

Cale's lips drew back from the bite of the bourbon. "Save your concern for someone who needs it." He wiped his mouth on his sleeve.

Josh eyed the bottle Cale held. "Is that good bourbon?"

"Yeah. So?"

Josh smiled. "All the more reason not to drink alone."

When the older man sat down beside him, Cale shrugged. "It's your place. I can't tell you what to do." He passed the bottle.

"Is everything all right between you and the missus?" Josh asked before taking a healthy swallow.

Cale gave a humorless laugh. "Maybe you should ask her."

"I'm asking you."

"You're asking the wrong person then."

"Not the way I figure it."

"You figured wrong."

Josh shook his head good-naturedly. "You're better than most, I'll give you that."

"What the hell are you talking about?"

"Hiding your feelings."

Growling, Cale snatched the whiskey from the other man's grasp and took another long drink.

"Yep, I was right. But you won't find any answers in that bottle."

"Not looking for any."

"Son, you can fool yourself if you want, but you're not fooling me. I've seen the signs before. If I don't miss my guess, I'd say you've been a loner most of your life."

"What makes you think that?"

"You stayed to yourself most of the day. Like you're not comfortable with lots of folks around."

"Is that a crime?"

"It is when you let it get in the way of other things. Because you've kept to yourself most of your life, it's real hard for you to trust anybody." Josh retrieved the bottle from Cale and took another drink. Then, sighing his appreciation, he continued. "And it scares the hell out of ya to care for someone."

"I like you, Josh, but I'd appreciate it if you'd keep your nose in your own business."

"And you get real touchy when anyone gets too

close or tells a truth you don't want to hear. You're afraid to have anyone see the man inside."

Cale's head snapped around. "I'm warning you, Josh, you're going too far."

"Somebody's got to make you see daylight. Shay is too fine a young woman to lose. You'd regret it the rest of your life. What it all boils down to is you don't know how to love a woman. You can't show that wife of yours that you love her." When Cale opened his mouth to say something, Josh silenced his objection with a wave of his hand. "Don't bother denying it. We both know it's true."

"How do you know so much?"

"Because thirty years ago, I was you. It took the love of a good woman to bring me around. But thank God she did. I would've missed a helluva lot of life by keeping to myself. You can't be afraid to take chances. Love's worth gambling on."

Cale raised the bottle to his mouth and groaned before swallowing more bourbon.

"Don't use the liquor to hide," Josh said.

"But it helps me forget."

"Why would you want to forget Shay? Even for a moment? I don't know anything about the women in your past, but that girl's your future."

Tension clasped the back of Cale's neck. He massaged his throbbing temples with two fingers on each side of his head in small, circular motions. "But am I the man for her?"

"Can't say. But you're the man she wants. Her love for you is written all over her sweet face."

"That's what makes it hard. I don't want to hurt her." Cale's tone conveyed his uncertainty and frustration—and something more.

"I think you owe it to her to let her make up her

own mind about that. Your Shay's a lot like my Minnie. They're the kind of women who don't like being told what to do. They want a say in their lives. You've got to respect Shay enough to give her that."

"I don't know—" Cale passed a weary hand across his eyes. "I'm not sure I'll ever understand her completely. She won't listen to reason. She's stubborn. She acts before she thinks most of the time."

"Aren't you attracted to her for all the reasons you find so damned frustrating? Be honest."

Cale fingered the bottle rim. "Talking about stubborn, she's got nothing on you."

"But you're beginning to understand. A man and a woman apart are just that—separate parts. But when they come together they become a special whole."

Cale grimaced. "I'm not sure I'm capable of giving myself completely to someone. I don't want to hurt her, and I don't want to be hurt again." His face twisted in anguish. "I don't think I could bear it if Shay ever left me. This way, if I'm hard, I can protect myself."

"It's too late for that. Don't push her away."

"I couldn't even watch her dance with another man without wanting to wrap my hands around his throat—and squeeze."

Josh laughed. "Maybe your jealousy is your way of letting her know you care."

"How the hell am I supposed to go through life fighting the impulse to kill any man who even looks at her? It drove me crazy just seeing the way all the men in there watched her."

"I used to feel the same way about Minnie. I'd get mighty jealous if anyone got too close to her.

But I forgot the most important part—she loved me. There was no other man for her. Then I decided that others could look, but she was mine to hold and kiss. My Minnie would never be unfaithful. Once she gave me her heart, it was mine for life."

In his mind, Cale knew Josh's words were about Minnie, but in his heart, he knew that Josh had been talking about Shay.

Cale struggled to find words. Why couldn't he admit his true feelings aloud?

Because he was afraid of loving Shay.

Afraid that someday she wouldn't love him in return.

Josh must have sensed his inner turmoil. "I'm not an overly religious man, but you've got to trust in the Lord that everything will work out the way it's supposed to." He placed his hand on Cale's shoulder. "And you've got to put your faith and trust in your wife. Regret won't keep you warm at night, or keep you company in your old age. Don't hold back from life. You've got to live it. With her."

"It's not religion that's gone to your head, but the whiskey."

Josh looked up at the star-filled sky. "You just think about what I've said."

Cale handed him the bottle. "Here, old man. This is the only way I'm going to shut you up."

"Ssh. Don't tell Minnie. She's been trying for years to do just that."

Both men laughed.

The next morning, Shay approached the waiting Owens, feeling melancholy over leaving her friend

Minnie and the place where she and Cale had shared a few precious moments of happiness.

Minnie hugged Shay. "I'm going to miss you, Shay."

"And I'll miss you."

The hug ended and the women separated.

"Thank you for everything." Shay looked at Josh. "Both of you."

"Weren't nothing," Josh returned.

Cale came to stand beside Shay. He extended his hand to Josh. "Thanks."

"We're glad you two stayed," Josh returned.

Cale looked at Shay. "Time to go."

They mounted. As they rode away, Shay turned in the saddle and waved a final good-bye.

Chapter 15

Shay tilted her head back and looked upward, squinting against the sun's glare from beneath the rim of her hat. With their wings spread wide, buzzards soared in dark circles on wind currents. The stench of decaying flesh and blood caused her stomach to roil, but she said nothing to Cale. She kept her inner turmoil to herself.

As they neared the death scene, wisps of smoke drifted on the wind, rising in small columns from a burned wagon. Scorched, blackened wood hissed and popped.

Cale reined in his horse. Shay stopped beside him and looked at him. A muscle worked in his cheek.

"Looks like they didn't have a chance." His voice came out as a slow hiss of words.

Cale nudged his mount in the flanks and guided the gelding around an outcropping of rocks skirting a dusty road. Shay followed.

Broken and mutilated bodies littered the blood-stained ground. Mangled flesh and muscle took the place of recognizable faces. Shay pressed the back of her hand to her mouth to keep herself from choking on the bile rising in her throat. The

foulness of singed hair and flesh filled the air—
and Shay's heart. How could anyone do this to
other human beings?

"Comanches?"

Cale turned in his saddle and gazed at her. "No,
Apaches, by the signs."

"How do you know?"

"When you've traveled as much as I have, you
learn the different tribes and how best to keep
your hair."

Shay spied a burned book on the ground and
dismounted. Picking up the volume, she lightly
ran her fingers over the scorched edges, the text
still warm to the touch. Her heart wrenched when
she opened the book.

Cale dismounted and came to stand beside her.
"What's that?"

A tear tracked from the corner of her eye down
her cheek. "Someone's Bible."

Cale put his arms around her. "Don't, Shay."
Compassion threaded his voice. "Don't look anymore."

Clammy perspiration covered her skin, and
Shay wondered if she would be sick. She swallowed.

"I've seen too much already. How can I close
my eyes to this?" Shay asked in a small voice
against his shoulder.

She then pulled away from him. A faraway look
glazed her eyes. "Why does God allow these
things to happen? Surely these people didn't deserve to die such horrible deaths."

"I wish I had an answer, but I don't."

"Look at all of them." Her gaze swept the scene.
"How can we bury them all?"

Cale walked to his horse. "We don't."

"How can you be so callous?" Her voice conveyed her outrage and disbelief. "They might have been strangers, but they deserve a decent Christian burial."

Cale tensed, then turned and walked purposely toward her. He grasped her shoulders and stared into her eyes.

"I care. But anyone looking for our trail would know we came this way if we bury them." His tone exuded restrained patience. "Or do you want to leave a calling card for the braves who did this?"

"I didn't think," she said simply. "I'm sorry." She turned her head, and her gaze returned to the carnage. "What are we going to do?" Her words trembled past stiff, cold lips.

"Put as much distance as we can between us and them." Cale's eyes narrowed as he, too, looked again at the bodies strewn on the ground. "In the open, we're no match for Apaches."

Shay reached out and touched Cale's forearm. "We'll get through this, won't we?"

"I didn't survive the war to get scalped by Indians."

Once they were mounted, Shay said, "You won't let them . . ." She felt the color drain from her face. "Let them touch me, will you?" Her eyes widened. "I mean . . . you'll take care of me before they could . . ."

Adjusting the leather reins between his fingers, Cale said between clenched teeth, "If it comes to that, I'll see to you."

Cale touched his spurs to his mount's flanks, urging the gelding forward, carefully picking his way between the corpses with the packhorse in tow. Shay trailed behind.

The ensuing miles and hours became an indistinguishable blur for Shay. Mentally and physically exhausted, she no longer had any idea where they were, or where they were headed. Cale spoke only when necessary, and she dared not ask further questions.

The night air was chilly, and her dust-covered clothes chafed her tender flesh. All she could think of was having something to eat and getting some rest.

She raised herself in her stirrups, trying to relieve some of the tension from her weary body. Years in the saddle hadn't conditioned her for the brisk pace that Cale maintained, or for the mentally draining terror of running from Apaches.

She concentrated on Cale's broad, rigid back in front of her. He exhibited no signs of fatigue. She didn't know how he did it. Mile and mile, he remained ramrod straight in the saddle. With a sense of dogged pride, she resolved that if Cale could maintain their pace, so could she.

Cale separated his thoughts from his weariness, concentrating on outdistancing the Apaches. By the signs, he had figured the band was headed for northern Mexico, but one could never accurately forecast what Apaches would do. So, instead of riding in a direct line for San Angelo, he had begun, several miles back, to widen their circle of travel, to lessen the predictability of their destination.

Pain twisted in his gut. Only Comanches treated their captives worse than Apaches. His mouth hardened. He vowed they wouldn't take Shay—alive.

Cale glanced over his shoulder at Shay. By her pinched face and her slumping body, he knew she was near the breaking point, but he couldn't slacken their speed.

A molten red sun sank behind the western horizon. The breeze died with the coming of night, and the air grew cooler. Overhead, the sky's dome darkened into indigo. Cottonwoods spread their branches against the twilight sky, and giant oaks stood like dark sentinels against the heavens.

Shay slid off her horse. When her feet touched the ground, her legs sagged from numbness. She clutched the mare's mane to steady herself. Presently, the blood returned to her legs, and she could stand on her own.

She walked stiffly to a nearby cottonwood, sat, and leaned against the trunk. She inhaled the sweet fragrance of the night air. It was the first peaceful moment of the day.

Her gaze shifted to Cale as he cut branches and interlaced them to form a crude shelter.

After he tended the horses, Cale knelt beside her. "Sorry. Can't take the chance of building a fire tonight." He offered her several strips of dried meat.

She removed her gloves and, with aching fingers, accepted the food. She was so tired she could barely chew the jerky, but somehow she managed to swallow several bites.

Sighing, she leaned her head back against the tree and closed her eyes, a forgotten piece of jerky dangling between her fingers.

Cale must have seen the uncontrollable shiver that chased its way down her spine, because he retrieved his blanket and wrapped it around her.

"Lie down in the shelter. You'll be warmer."

She opened her eyes and nodded.

When Shay started to move, her calf muscle cramped, making it impossible to walk. She collapsed on the ground and grabbed her leg.

Cale knelt beside her. "What's wrong?"

She grimaced. "Cramp."

He removed her boot and sock and pushed up her pant leg. His hands skimmed over her limb. The calf muscle was corded and hard beneath her ivory skin.

Cale gripped her ankle and pulled Shay horizontal on the ground. "Try and relax."

He knelt before her, placing the foot of her aching limb against his chest, and leaned forward to apply pressure while massaging the tight muscle.

Slowly, the cramping subsided, and Shay relaxed. She threw an arm across her forehead and closed her eyes as she allowed Cale's fingers to work their magic on her throbbing limb.

The lines that framed his mouth deepened. His motions slowed with each pass of his hands over her leg, his fingers softly kneading the tightness from her flesh. The temptation to divest Shay of her pants and rub more than her calf was nearly impossible to ignore.

With considerable effort, he starched his voice with nonchalance. "Feeling better?"

"Umm. Much."

His desire grew with each progression of his hand over her shapely leg. He cursed himself for his reaction, yet he couldn't stop himself. He wanted to laugh. It seemed he seldom had control when it came to Shay.

Perspiration broke out across his forehead as he imagined easing her pants down her rounded hips. His movements slowed.

"Don't stop," she whispered. "It feels wonderful."

Cale stifled a groan. Stopping was the farthest thing from his mind—and body. He wanted to nudge her legs apart, ease his silken steel into her warm softness, and have her accept him completely as he spewed himself deep within her, time and time again.

Moving his hand from her calf, he removed her other boot. He massaged her soles with his thumbs, while his fingers stroked and kneaded the tops of her feet.

Soft, mewing sounds escaped from Shay, and she stretched her body like a contented tabby, unknowingly pressing one foot against his groin.

Desire pierced Cale. He tensed.

"Cale?"

Moments passed before he could form a coherent thought. "Yes?"

"Are you all right?"

Cale fought to curb his desire. "Don't worry about me." He muttered a curse and yanked her pant leg back down to her ankle. "I think you'll live."

Shay's arm fell away from her face, and she gazed up at him. Anger flared inside her at his abrupt tone. "I'm sure I will. But thank you nevertheless."

"If you think I'm going to play nursemaid to you all the way to Wyoming, you'd better think again."

"I never thought you would." The recurring hostility was too bitter to swallow. "Nor do I want you to."

He bent and scooped her into his arms. "Enough talking. It's time you got some sleep." He carried her over to the makeshift shelter and deposited her inside.

Cale took his bedroll and spread it on the ground nearby. "Just shut your eyes." He stretched himself out and covered his face with his hat.

Shay lay on her side and regarded him. Damn him. He wouldn't always be able to keep her at arm's length. Sooner or later, she'd get past his defenses.

She sighed. No use in wasting energy by fretting. She closed her eyes.

That night, Shay tossed and turned in her sleep as images of the murdered settlers haunted her dreams.

Her anguished cry woke Cale. He left his bedroll and settled beside her in the shelter. Gathering her in his arms, he crooned softly in her ear. Her scent, carried on her warm skin, invaded his senses.

He touched her pale cheek, then traced the soft column of her graceful neck, delicately etched with faint blue veins. He listened to the soft, easy cadence of her breathing as she settled into a peaceful sleep.

She deserved her rest.

She deserved more. More than he could give her.

Cale grimaced as he tried to staunch his tender feelings. He should insist she leave him for her own good, he knew that. The rugged land of Wyoming had claimed much stronger people than she. And if she were pregnant? Such a hostile environment was no place for her or a baby. Yet, the thought of her leaving caused a sharp pain in his chest.

Sweet Jesus, he couldn't allow his feelings to cloud his judgment. He must make her see reason.

Dawn peeked above the horizon when Shay felt something tickle her. She scratched her nose and snuggled deeper in the warmth of her blanket.

Seconds later, something brushed her cheek, and she passed a hand across her face. Slowly, she rubbed the sleep from her eyes and opened them. What she had thought was the warmth of her blanket turned out to be Cale's arm around her. The tickling sensation was his shirt and strands of his long hair rubbing against her face.

Her heart soared. He cared for her. Why else was he lying next to her with his arm tenderly draped around her?

Her illusions of reconciliation were shattered the moment she looked up at Cale's visage. His gaze was flat, his features grave, his mouth a thin, hard line.

Throbbing silence stretched between them until it took on a life of its own.

Shay disengaged herself from Cale and sat up. She pushed the hair from her face. "What do you want from me?" In her words, she bared all her hopes and fears.

"You had a nightmare last night." Cale's aloofness reinforced his solemn countenance. "I didn't want you spooking the horses. I had to quiet you somehow."

"Damn you! Why show me any kindness at all?"

Cale moved out of the shelter and stood. "A good question." Coldness, more biting than a blast of arctic air, frosted his words. "You'll regret having an unwilling husband more with each passing day."

At midday they stopped. Shay was sitting beneath the shade of a mesquite tree, eating her cold rations, when she thought she heard a moan. She grew still and cocked her head to one side. She heard only the horses munching the sparse grass.

Shrugging, Shay returned to her noon meal. As she finished the last bite of her food, she imagined she heard the moan again.

Shay scrambled to her feet and hurried over to Cale, who stood near the horses. "Did you hear something?"

"No, why?"

"I thought I heard a moan." Shay pointed to the boulders she had been sitting by. "It sounded like it was coming from behind those rocks."

The low sound drifted on the wind, sounding more distinct this time.

Shay tensed. "There! Did you hear it?"

"Yes."

They ascended the rocky incline until they reached the top and could look down the other side. At the foot of the limestone formation was a covered wagon. The team of horses was tethered on a line nearby. Beside the wagon there was a campfire with a large kettle suspended over the flames.

Close as they were, they clearly heard a woman cry out in pain. At that moment, a haggard-looking man swept open the canvas flap at the rear of the wagon and climbed down. He walked with weary steps to the fire.

Shay touched Cale's sleeve. "We've got to help."

She started down the incline, using her feet and hands to slow her descent. Cale followed.

A small shower of pebbles and dirt alerted the man to her presence. "Who's there?" the man called out as he grabbed his rifle, which had been standing at the ready against the rear wheel.

Reaching the ground, Shay walked to him, her arms outstretched. "My name is Shay Breland." She nodded over her shoulder. "That's my husband, Cale. We heard someone moaning. Can I be of some help?"

The man looked warily from Shay to Cale, obviously trying to judge their intentions.

Shay sensed his apprehension. She attempted to put him at ease. "We only want to help. Is there something we can do?"

The woman moaned again—the low, agonized cry of a creature in agony. The man's tall, thin frame seemed to droop several inches as his shoulders sagged at the sound.

He propped his rifle against the wheel once more. Dragging his fingers through his unkempt hair, he said in a thin, flat voice, "My name's Jeb Logan. My wife, Sarah, is in the wagon. She's been in labor since before sunrise. The baby just won't come. I'm afraid something's wrong and I don't know what to do."

"May I see your wife, Mr. Logan?"

"I'd welcome any help you could give. I'm at the end of my rope."

Shay stopped beside him and laid a comforting hand on his arm. "I'll see what I can do. Cale will stay with you."

Shay climbed up on the tailgate and crawled into the shadowed interior of the wagon.

She inched her way forward, softly talking the

entire time. "Mrs. Logan. I'm Shay Breland. I'm here to help."

Shay had to strain to see any movement as the woman weakly rolled her head to look at Shay. Mrs. Logan clutched her distended stomach and cried out weakly.

Kneeling beside the pallet, Shay got a better look at Mrs. Logan. Dread chased its way down her spine at what she saw. Sweat plastered straight brown hair to the woman's temples. Against a chalky complexion, her eyes appeared as two sunken holes, her blue irises barely discernible. Her parted lips were swollen from her biting them against the pain and flecks of dried blood speckled her upper lip.

Dear Lord! Never had Shay seen such suffering. A thought flashed through her mind, and she wondered, if she were pregnant, would she suffer the same fate as this poor soul? She pushed her misgivings aside and concentrated on Mrs. Logan. She knew a great deal about birthing foals. Shay just prayed she could extend her knowledge to help this woman.

Shay held one of Mrs. Logan's hands. Her flesh was cold to the touch. "I'm going to ask you a few questions. Don't try to talk. Just squeeze my hand if you can. Once for yes. Twice for no." Shay leaned closer to Mrs. Logan, making sure she made eye contact with the woman. She summoned a smile. "All right?"

Mrs. Logan feebly squeezed her hand once.

"Good. You've been in labor since before sunrise?"

Again, a light squeeze.

"Is this your first baby?"

Another feeble compression.

Shay smiled and wiped Mrs. Logan's brow with a wet cloth she found in a basin near the pallet. "They say firstborns are always the most stubborn. They come into this world when they're ready. We'll just see if we can coax your baby into coming soon."

She then inched backward toward the flap. "I'm going to wash up. I won't be a minute." She exited the wagon and walked to the fire. "Mr. Logan, I need some hot water and strong lye soap to wash my hands."

Cale came over to her. Concern tinted his voice. "Is she going to be all right?"

"I honestly don't know. I don't know what the problem is yet."

Cale laid a hand to Shay's shoulder. "Have you ever delivered a baby?"

"Lots of 'em. Just not human ones." Shay smiled reassuringly. "See if you can get Mr. Logan to eat something. He looks as if he's going to faint on the spot."

Mr. Logan brought Shay the requested items and she nodded her thanks. She then rolled up her sleeves and scrubbed her hands and forearms with the harsh cleanser.

Finished, Shay reentered the covered wagon and reassumed her position beside Mrs. Logan. She turned up the wick on the single lantern.

"I want you to relax as much as possible," Shay said.

She drew back the sweat-drenched quilt to examine Mrs. Logan. Gently, she placed her hands on the swollen stomach and felt with her fingertips to gauge the baby's position. She couldn't tell that anything was amiss.

Another contraction gripped Mrs. Logan. Her

body twisted from the pain, and she clutched her distended belly. A weak whimper came from deep inside her throat.

Shay shared Mrs. Logan's pain. She tried to will some of her strength into the woman.

"With your next contraction, I'm going to help you push. But you must do as much as you can."

Only a faint glimmer in Mrs. Logan's eyes revealed she had heard Shay.

Shortly, another spasm seized Mrs. Logan. The two women worked together until moments later, a baby boy made his way into the world.

Shay cleared his nose and mouth of mucus. She remembered hearing once that you had to spank an infant in order to make it breathe. She delivered one firm whack to the baby's red bottom. The baby's healthy wail filled the wagon.

She washed the child tenderly and wrapped him in a small quilt before placing him in a small wooden cradle. Shay then helped Mrs. Logan expel the afterbirth.

Next, she bathed Mrs. Logan and slipped a clean gown on her, then changed the soiled bedding.

Once that was done, she eased out of the wagon. She wanted to laugh aloud at the stricken looks on both men's faces. She didn't know who looked worse for the wear—Mr. Logan or Cale.

"Mr. Logan, you can see your son now," Shay said, pushing down her sleeves and buttoning them.

Mr. Logan smiled his thanks and hurried to his wife and baby.

Cale came to Shay. His expression still showed scars of some inner battle he had waged.

Shay laughed. "Looking at you, you'd think it was your son being born."

Cale gripped Shay's upper arms. "It's no laughing matter. The entire time I heard Mrs. Logan crying out in pain, I thought of how that could be you."

Touched by his concern, Shay looked tenderly into his eyes. "If I'm with child, and when my time comes, I'll do just fine."

"I hate to think of you suffering such agony because of my uncontrollable desire."

"Our desire. I wanted you to make love to me, remember?"

His severe expression softened. "You did a wonderful thing today. I'm proud of you." He tucked a loose strand of hair behind her ear. "It made me realize what a strong woman you are."

Shay's heart swelled with joy as Cale wrapped his arms around her and kissed her, possessively, thoroughly.

Satisfied that the Logans were all right, Cale and Shay set out on the trail once more. However, they didn't cover much territory since they had lost most of the afternoon.

That night, after they had made camp and had eaten, Shay sat back. Her mind retraced the day's events. She looked down at her stomach. Was a baby growing inside her? She hoped so with all her heart.

A soft smile played on her lips. Perhaps she should make sure there would be a baby. How did one go about seducing an uncooperative husband?

An idea came to her. She retrieved her comb and unbraided her hair. First, she combed out all the dust, leaving the thick mass with some semblance of silkiness. Next, she repeatedly wound a section of her mane between the comb's teeth until the mass was hopelessly tangled. Then she undid the first three buttons of her shirt, certain the tops of her breasts showed above the neckline of her chemise.

Satisfied with her efforts, she sat and waited for Cale to return from checking on the horses.

When at last he reappeared, she called to him. "Cale?"

Frowning, he walked over to her. "What?"

"I've gotten my hair in a mess and can't seem to untangle it." She turned innocent eyes on him. "Could you help me?"

Annoyance peppered his voice. "You sure you can't do it yourself?"

God, he could be muleheaded. "I wouldn't be asking if I could," she said sweetly.

"I'm not so sure about that." Cale's conjecture showed in the tight line of his mouth and so did the doubt that reinforced it.

"Fine. If you don't want to help, I suppose there's only one thing to do. I'll have to cut it."

Cale's answer didn't disappoint her.

"Are you crazy?" he asked sharply, advancing on her with slightly less than intimidating strides.

Standing a whisker's breadth from her, he reached out and lifted a section of hair, letting the silky strands ripple through his fingers. "Cut your hair, and I promise you, you'll regret it." The velvet roughness of his voice somehow emphasized the consternation on his face. "Understand?"

"That you're giving me another order, yes."

The muscles in his face relaxed marginally. "Not an order then, but a strong request."

She gave him a saucy look. "Well, since you put it that way."

Humor blunted his agitation. "Woman, you try my patience."

She smiled. "So you've told me—repeatedly."

He moved to sit on a fallen log. "Come here."

She settled between his legs. She felt two small tugs, then a big yank. Her eyes watered. "Ouch. If I'd known you were going to be so rough, I would have taken my chances by cutting it."

"Whose fault is it that your hair is in this mess?"

"That doesn't mean you have to snatch me bald."

He sighed in exasperation. "Will you just be quiet?"

He hadn't meant to be so rough, but he wasn't used to combing a woman's hair.

Unthinkingly, Cale began to comb her hair after he'd untangled the strands. Even if he had wanted to leave, he was powerless to rise. The cool silk of her hair beneath his touch drugged his senses, sedating him with a sense of euphoria.

Her breath escaped in a feathery exhalation as Shay leaned against his legs and tilted back her head.

His mind cataloged her appearance: the thick cascade of red flowing down her back, the tops of her creamy breasts peeking from beneath her clothes, the delicate line of her neck, the finely sculpted curves of her cheekbones, and the expressive arch of her brow.

He substituted his hands for the comb, and closing his eyes, he slid his fingers through the silken waves. His thoughts filled with longing to have her luxurious mane drape his entire body in velvet sensation.

Yet, even as logic detailed why he shouldn't take Shay, he found himself turning her around to face him, pulling her close between his wide-spread legs.

Uncurbed desire governed his thoughts, his feelings, his actions. It was one thing to tell himself that he wouldn't touch Shay and quite another to make his body obey.

Ageless instinct drove him to frame her cheeks with his hands and draw her face close to his. "God help me, but I can't resist you."

His mouth covered hers in a soft yet compelling kiss, warm and deep.

Their breathing fell into unison, deepening in swift and incessant arousal.

"I can't stand this sweet torture any longer," he murmured against her moist, pliant lips. "I want you. I've wanted you since the first time I saw you. I want you ready. I want you slick with passion."

His hands slid down her back, rested on her shapely buttocks, and pressed her closer to him. He trailed a lavish, beguiling path north and south along the column of her neck.

Breathing in the irregular rhythm of passion, he unbuttoned her shirt; then, hooking his fingers inside the neck of the garment, he pushed the shirt off her shoulders and down her arms until it fell away. His hands returned to gently tug the fabric of her chemise over the fullness of her breasts. Pushing her lush flesh upward with one hand, he pulled the taut fabric over the swelling curves with the other. The soft cotton slid over her aching, stiff nipples, leaving want in its sensuous wake. Cale dipped his head and suckled one nipple before taking the entire aureole in his mouth.

He left off his sweet torture to unfasten his pants, then pressed Shay down and against the smooth leather of his nearby saddle. He knelt between her legs, his lean hips moving in a slow dance of persuasion against her lower body, his roused masculinity throbbing at the apex of her womanhood.

Freeing himself, he unfastened her pants and eased Shay out of them. He positioned her so her back touched the seat of the saddle.

"I can't think of anything except having you. Wrap your legs around me," he said with urgent need.

Her silky thighs locked about his tapered waist as he reached beneath her and lifted her up to him.

She squeezed her eyes shut against the tender yet tumultuous emotions whirling inside her.

"Look at me, Shay. I want you to look at me. I want to see your eyes when I come inside you. I want to know your passion is as strong as mine."

Her mind registered his words, but her senses recorded their seductive tenor. The provocative timbre of his voice seeped through every pore of her skin and into her very soul. Her pulse kept pace with the beating of her elemental desire.

With his hands anchored on her hips, Cale repeatedly glided into Shay's tight, moist passage. "You feel so good. God, so wet and sleek. I don't know if I can keep from bursting right now."

He maintained his rhythm until he gave a savage cry and simultaneously brought Shay and himself to fulfillment.

"How is it you affect me so?" His raspy breath fanned the perspiration-misted hair clinging to her temples.

Shay lay weak and exhausted, even though her heart still hammered a fast pace, and her rushing blood had not slowed. She knew by the slight flare of his nostrils and his tight breath that Cale's gratification had been as great as hers.

"Because . . . I'm your wife," she managed to reply at last.

"Because you're a witch." Slackened passion roughened his voice, yet softened the angles of his face.

He withdrew from her, stood, and fastened his pants as he stared down at her.

Never had Shay looked more beautiful to him than with her skin glistening with the moist sheen of their lovemaking.

Never had his resolve to make her leave wavered more.

Never had he felt so torn.

Cale extended his hand and helped Shay to her feet. Despite the fact that he was showing more tenderness than he deemed wise, he kissed her forehead. "Don't take hope by what just happened, because I haven't changed my mind." He walked away from her.

Shay observed him with an intuitive inner eye. He had changed his mind, all right. He just didn't know it yet. She smiled. It hadn't been a substitute for the wedding night she'd hoped for, but it was a start.

The next morning, having eaten, Shay walked to the riverbank to wash herself and her clothes. She had left Cale sleeping. He had looked so peaceful that she hadn't wanted to wake him until the last possible moment.

She found a secluded spot and undressed down to her underclothes. She dipped her pants, shirt, and socks into the water, and washed them with her bar of soap.

Finished, she spread the garments on the rock before slipping into the water. When she emerged from a brief swim, Shay discovered one sock was missing. She scoured the area, but to no avail.

With shoulders hunched and legs spread wide, she sat on the riverbank and sighed. Damn! Of all the luck! Well, she'd have to find the missing article. It wouldn't do for Cale to find out she couldn't do something as simple as keeping track of her clothes. His lecture would be endless.

She waded back into the water and started downstream. Her progress was slow because of the slippery rock bottom and the painstaking search she was making of all low-lying branches and plants along the river's edge.

She had almost resigned herself to that lecture when she located her sock, wrapped around a jutting limb of a fallen tree. Giving a small cry of satisfaction, she snatched up the article.

Her delight was short-lived; suddenly, the tiny hairs at the nape of her neck raised. She stood still, the pounding of her blood unnaturally loud in her ears above the sound of the river water. She wasn't alone.

Shay turned around slowly. All coherent thought fled her as she stared into the broad, flat features of an Apache—and the wicked-looking knife he held.

Her eyes widened, and her face paled beneath a sheen of perspiration. Scream! her mind cried. Her throat worked, but her vocal cords were paralyzed.

The brave's gaze raked her person, and Shay cringed at the lewd inspection. As if sensing an easy conquest, he sheathed his knife and extended his hand, motioning her closer.

Shay had but one thought: Dear Lord, don't let me die.

By heavenly intervention, Shay found the strength to force her petrified limbs into action. Unthinkingly, she flung the wet sock into the Apache's face, startling him and giving her a moment of grace to escape.

She scrambled for the bank. With her heart pumping wildly, she dashed along the riverbank. Rocks cut into her feet. Her labored breathing deafened her.

She raced for the nearby brush which skirted the area. If she could just reach the bushes, she'd be safe, she thought wildly.

Hazarding a backward glance over her shoulder for signs of pursuit, Shay was caught unaware by a sharp blow to the side of her head. The impact spun her around, and she sprawled to the ground.

Dazed, Shay struggled to rise. As she came to her knees, a hand twisted in her hair and she was viciously jerked to her feet.

The stench of unwashed bodies and horseflesh penetrated her dazed state of mind. As her vision cleared Shay saw two more Apaches. Her heart flew to her throat, then plummeted to the pit of her stomach.

She saw her death written in their cold, flat stares.

But not before they'd had their fill of her.

Fear propelled Shay into action. Acting instinctively, she kicked and clawed at her captor, until he slapped her hard across the face. She slumped against him.

He shoved her to her knees and once more

twisted a hand in her hair, insuring her submission. The second brave tied her wrists in front of her. Her breath came as a mingled gasp and sob. Through tear-swollen eyes, her face contorted with dread as she looked at her captors.

Pain streaked across her shoulders and down her arms as she was yanked to her feet by her wrists. The brave from the river walked toward her. Shay steeled herself as he reached out and fingered the material of her chemise, then her hair. He smelled of excrement, grease, sweat, and horseflesh. Bile rose in her throat, and she gagged.

The Apache said something to the other two in guttural sounds before he shoved her toward a waiting pony and threw her onto its back. Her legs were secured with a rope beneath the animal's belly; a second rope was tied around her neck.

Shay knew her chemise would offer little protection for her inner thighs as the horse's shoulders pressed into her tender flesh. She resolved herself to the inevitable pain.

The braves swung themselves onto their own mounts. The rope around her throat tightened as her horse fell behind the one leading it. Sourtasting bile filled her mouth, and she choked. Pain shot through her, from her neck down across her breastbone, in a paralyzing spasm that left her arms tingling as the rope was stretched taut.

Shay concentrated on remaining upright on the horse. Her thighs quivered from the tension of gripping the pony and her shoulder muscles burned.

Be strong and survive, she told herself as the band traveled across the terrain. Stay alive. No matter what.

Chapter 16

The sun had traveled halfway across the sky when Cale rode out of the shadows of the cottonwoods in pursuit of the Apache raiders.

Long, muscular legs gripped saddle leather as he leaned forward, his body moving in rhythm with his horse as the gelding's gait lengthened.

Roiling hatred and dread centered on the Apaches who had taken Shay. They'd pay for what they'd done.

His mind tumbled across the morning's events. When he hadn't been able to find Shay, he had gone looking for her. Instead of finding her, he had come across signs of Apaches, evidence of a struggle, and pieces of Shay's clothing. He quickly guessed what had taken place. What he didn't understand was why they hadn't come after him.

Every word of advice that Josh Owen had given him returned with a vengeance to ravage his thoughts. Why couldn't he have just listened to the older man's counsel and enjoyed his time with Shay? He loved her more than life itself. Why hadn't he told her? Why had he squandered precious time because of his fears and foolish pride? So many whys and no answers. He was certain of one thing. By God, once he had her safely back, he'd never let her go again.

His thoughts refocused on the morning's events. Upon his return to camp, feeling a ruthless sense of urgency, he had packed extra food in his saddlebags and had tossed Shay's saddlebags across his horse's rump. He had then turned the packhorse and Shay's mount loose, knowing the extra animals would slow him down. Seconds later, he had been astride his gelding. Apaches feared no man, except Comanches, and he knew they wouldn't bother to cover their tracks.

Flecks of foamy lather from his mount covered his skin as Cale maintained his relentless pursuit across the landscape. Fear that he wouldn't find her alive raged within him. He knew what Apaches did to white women. His knuckles whitened beneath his tanned skin as he gripped the reins tighter to stave off the dire images.

Cale wasn't on familiar terms with the Lord, but his lips formed a single word: *Please*.

Shay's knees quivered from hours of gripping the horse's flanks. The loss of circulation at her wrists had long since deadened the feeling in her hands, and she hardly had strength to grasp the pony's mane. Bone-tired and half deadened with pain, she felt drained of all emotion—even fear.

The ground dipped suddenly, and Shay used her limited strength to maintain her balance. The band rode down the middle of a gorge before heading up the other side. Again, with waning ability, Shay clung to her horse, barely keeping herself from sliding off the horse's rump. Pain shot through her legs at the effort.

With each plodding step the animal took, Shay

was miserably aware of the growing distance separating her from Cale. She had no way of knowing if the Apaches had killed him before they abducted her.

All she knew was that she didn't want to die. As long as breath remained, there was still a chance of escape. Survive! The word screamed through her veins. If she removed the stranglehold of fear, she could survive.

By nightfall, Shay was only dimly aware of the throbbing pain in her body and the rhythmic movement of the horses. She could barely hold her eyes open. Her skin was sunburned and blistered from the abusive wind and sun.

The Apaches pressed on relentlessly, alternating their pace from a fast walk to a canter to a bone-jarring trot. Shay felt as if her insides had been taken out and mashed.

Miles later, the riders finally stopped and dismounted.

Somehow Shay managed to pry her fingers from the pony's mane. Despite her previous intention, panic, hot and cold, blew through her as a brave dragged her from her horse. She feebly resisted. The Apache slapped her hard across her face. She tasted the saltiness of her own blood as it trickled from her lip into her mouth.

With her wrists still tied, Shay sank to the ground. Dirt gritted against her teeth, and she was afraid to swallow for fear of choking on her saliva, which mingled with blood and dust. She closed her eyes, emitting a tortured, quivering sigh into the night air.

A spate of guttural Apache startled Shay, and her eyes flew open. She tensed as she stared into the leader's face. He pulled a knife from its sheath and pressed the honed tip against the base of her throat, prickling the tender flesh and drawing a spot of blood. He then slowly, but lightly, traced a line with his knife point from her throat, between her breasts, to her wrists. He cut her bonds. The circulation in her hands was gone, and she was unable to prevent him from shoving her onto her back.

The other braves laughed as she lay in the dirt, staring into her tormentor's gruesome face as he towered above her. He bent and cut her chemise from top to bottom, exposing her to their lewd gazes.

Smiling, he pressed one hand to her breast and stared into her eyes like a snake mesmerizing its prey. He pinched the nipple, extracting a pained gasp from Shay. He grunted his satisfaction. The Apache removed his hand and looked at the braves over his shoulder. The three of them laughed.

Her tormentor jerked Shay to her knees by her hair. He brought his knife to her throat.

Shay lost her sense of reality, distancing herself from her fear. As if in slow motion, Shay's mind registered the feel of the blade pricking her flesh with the simultaneous approach of a figure on horseback. The earth rang with thundering hooves and the rider's bloodcurdling yell as he bore down on the Apache in front of her.

Her eyes widened in recognition. . . .

The charging horse never slowed its speed until Cale was practically atop them. He sawed hard on his reins, causing his gelding to skid to a stop on its hind legs.

Cale leaped off his horse, hit the ground with the ease of a panther, and strode to the Apache leader. Hand signals provided a universal tongue, and Shay instinctively knew the two men were heatedly discussing her.

Communication broke off and Cale walked to her. For the space of a heartbeat, Cale's gaze consumed Shay. "Are you all right?"

"I am now that you're here."

Cale began stripping down to the waist. "I've got no time to talk."

Shay's eyes grew large with fear. "What have you done?"

He pulled off his boots and removed his belt. Momentarily he wore only his pants.

"Made a deal. A fight to the death. It was the only way for both of us to walk away from here with our scalps."

"What about the other two braves?"

"Even Apaches have a code of behavior. They'll honor their leader's word and let us go if I win."

"Oh, Cale. Why did you come? Because of me there's a chance we'll both die."

"My life wouldn't be worth living if I lost you." Withdrawing his knife, he glanced at her. "Be brave just a little while longer. We're going to get out of this."

The Apache leader had stripped as Cale had done. He produced a leather strip approximately three feet long. Each man took one end in his mouth.

Shay stood on trembling legs and watched the scene unfold. She pressed the back of her hand against her mouth to keep herself from crying out.

The two men began to move slowly in a circle. Suddenly the Apache lunged at Cale and his blade slashed a crimson trail across Cale's chest. Grunting his pain, Cale never relaxed his stance, his muscles straining as he tensed to strike.

Within a horrifying split second, Shay's heart flew to her throat. She bit her lip until it bled, but she didn't make a sound. Her gaze never wavered from the struggling combatants as they lunged and retreated repeatedly, each looking for the opportunity to slay his adversary.

By slow degrees, a strange sense of denial seized Shay, robbing her of all thought and emotion except the most primal, elemental impulses. As she watched, she wasn't immune to the savage, primitive excitement that enveloped the men.

By now, blood flowed freely from both men. Red streaks and smears covered their bodies like grotesque war paint. Each man's posture and expression promised death to the other.

The Apache lunged at Cale again. His cold blade flashed in a deadly arc. Cale ducked, then sprang to the balls of his feet and pounced at the Apache. Cale slashed the Indian's hamstring. Howling in agony, the Apache dropped his guard for a heartbeat.

It was all the time Cale needed. He rose, whirled, and thrust, his blade sinking with a soft thud into the Apache's stomach. The brave dropped to his knees, clutching his belly. Cale jerked the Apache's head back by his hair and slit the brave's throat. A soft gurgling sound was heard before the Apache slumped forward, dead.

The two remaining braves took the body of their fallen leader and quietly departed.

Shay had seen plenty of death, in horrifying clarity, since they began their journey. The only emotion that registered on her mind at this moment was agonizing relief.

Cale was alive.

And he had come for her.

Turning, he strode to her and took her into his arms. With sweet thanksgiving trembling on her lips, Shay threw her arms about his neck and leaned into him, pushing her physical discomfort to the recesses of her mind. Fiercely, he wrapped one arm around her waist, while his other hand gently cupped the back of her head to press her close.

He buried his face in her hair. "Oh, God, Shay. I didn't know if I'd find you in time." He released a raw, tremulous sigh.

Tears ran down her cheeks to mingle with the sweat and blood on his chest. "Thinking of you kept me sane."

He kissed her forehead before he pulled back to look at her. "I just about went out of my mind wondering if you were still—"

"Don't say it." She passed her trembling fingertips across his lips. "I told myself to be strong, to survive somehow." She touched his cheek. "But you could have been killed. Why did you come after me?"

"Because, against all odds, I'm looking at what I've been searching for my entire life."

Her chin trembled. "If I had died, I would have wanted our souls joined."

"I've been a fool." He cupped her face between his hands, heedless of the blood staining them, and gazed intently into her eyes. "Everything I want in life is here in my arms." His own eyes grew bright with emotion. "I love you, Shay, and will until my dying day."

Cale supported Shay as she sagged against him,

weak with joy. "You don't know how long I've wanted to hear you say that."

"I'm sorry it took me so long to tell you."

Cale bent down and picked up his shirt. Gently, he turned Shay around, her spine pressing against his chest, and put his shirt over her. His hands glided across her breasts as he pulled the edges of material together and fastened the buttons. He then stepped into his boots and retrieved his belt, gun belt, and knife.

Cale turned her around. "Can you ride?" Concern was deeply etched in the lines of his face.

She didn't want to worry him, and she tapped into the last of her reservoir of energy to keep herself upright. "I'll be fine."

The utter exhaustion that gripped her made Shay feel as if she might faint, but she'd never let him know that.

Stiff, sore muscles protested as she stepped toward the gelding, and her legs buckled beneath her.

Growling, Cale swung her up into his arms and carried her to the gelding. He placed her on his horse before swinging up behind her. He curled his left arm around her waist and took the reins with his right hand. With a touch of his spurs to the gelding's flanks, Cale urged the horse into an easy canter.

Shay leaned against Cale. The wind whipped her unbound hair about her face and over his shoulder. Each jarring step pounded inside her brain and through her body.

She turned her head to the side, partly to draw comfort from his warmth and partly to keep him from seeing her discomfort. With her ear against his chest, she heard the steadying beating of his heart. She was loved and safe. Nothing else mattered. Mercifully, sleep overtook her.

Such a deep sleep claimed Shay that she didn't stir when Cale halted beside a water-carved gully and lifted her from the saddle, laying her down on a soft bed of thick grass near the arroyo. He retrieved the bedrolls and spread a blanket over her.

He drew one raspy breath, then another. Pain at Shay's suffering, and anger at his inability to protect her, twisted his gut. None of this would have happened if he hadn't relaxed his guard.

He brushed her pale cheek with his fingertips, then tenderly traced her mouth. Cale grimaced from self-contempt. He hadn't hurt her, but he had allowed her to be hurt. Would he ever be able to forgive himself?

Sunshine teased Shay into awareness. She blinked against the bright light, wondering where she was. She rolled to her side and grimaced at the painful movement. Nearby, Cale stirred something in a pot over the fire.

He must have sensed her gaze on him for he turned and looked at her. He came to kneel beside her. "How are you feeling?"

"Better." She reached out to touch his stubbled cheek. "But I'm worried about you. Have you gotten any rest at all?"

"Enough."

His haggard appearance caused her throat to tighten with concern. Fatigue chiseled deep grooves near his mouth and across his forehead. Two days' growth of black beard filled out the curves and hollows of his face. And his unruly hair hadn't seen the teeth of a comb in as long. Yet beneath the veneer of fatigue Cale's inner strength shone through. She loved him so much.

His fingers closed around her hand and he turned it over, kissing her palm. "I'm fine." Brushing aside several strands of hair from her face, he asked, "Feel up to eating something?"

"I'm starving."

"Good." He walked to the campfire and filled a plate, then returned to hand her the dish of beans. "While you're eating, I'm going to the water to clean up." He rubbed his chin. "You have to admit I certainly need a shave."

He dropped beside her and leaned over, planting a light kiss on her forehead. "I love you."

Did she imagine his eyes bright with suppressed tears, or was the sunshine playing tricks?

They remained camped beside the arroyo for three days. During that time, Shay and Cale grew more intimate. Shay blossomed beneath the warmth of Cale's attention. Cale, on the other hand, drew sustenance from Shay's love, trying to allow past fears to fade.

On the morning of the third day, they reclined near the water's edge. Cale shifted to his side and teased one of Shay's nipples with a blade of grass until it hardened. She blushed, but she didn't shove his hand away.

She reclined with one leg raised, hands at her sides, and her damp hair spread on the ground above her head. Beside her, Cale balanced on one elbow and stared down at her.

Shay lifted her hand and touched the ends of his silky black hair. "How did Uncle Brad lose his arm? He never told me the whole story." Her hand drifted back to her side.

"Not much to tell. I had gotten into this dishonest poker game. Brad figured the odds weren't in my favor, and he decided to take my side. It was the two of us against a rancher named Slocum and five or six of his hired hands. I called Slocum on his dirty dealing and there was a gunfight. I killed Slocum, and Brad's elbow was shattered by a bullet fired by one of the rancher's cowboys."

"Why would a man risk his life over cheating at cards?"

"Some men think they're above the law. From what I understand, Slocum owns about half of Dallas County. Brad and I didn't stay around to find out how close a friend the sheriff was to Slocum."

Cale leaned down. "Enough of that. Have I told you today how much I love you?"

"Not in the last hour."

"I love you," he whispered.

"And I love you." Her tone grew more serious. "It's funny how easily I can say that now. In the beginning I was so afraid you wouldn't want me. And then our marriage confirmed my worst fears. You were so distant."

"If it were within my power, I'd take back every angry, hurtful word I've spoken to you. What you have to understand is that I was afraid of wanting you and not being able to have you."

His voice dropped to a whisper. "I still carry with me childhood scars of being rejected by one family after another. I remember how I hated holidays. There were never any Christmas or birthday presents for me. I kept hoping against hope that someone would want me until bitterness had replaced possibility. If anyone took me in, it was because they needed me to work. I grew up not having been truly loved by anyone—until you."

Shay looked past the ruggedly hewn features of her husband to glimpse the lonely child he had been. Her heart swelled with poignant tenderness.

Wanting to give comfort, she raised her hand to his cheek. "I'll always love you. Perhaps in time, you'll be able to leave those painful memories in the past," she said in an aching whisper.

"Promise me one thing, Shay."

"What?"

"You won't ever leave me."

"I promise."

Cale smiled. He couldn't remember ever having felt so content.

"What are you thinking about?" he asked, as he massaged the tension from Shay's furrowed brow.

"About whether there's going to be a baby or not."

"Only time will tell."

"That's just the sort of thing a man would say."

Cale grinned. "Well, I'm a man."

She playfully batted away his hand as it moved down her throat. "Yes. And a persistent one at that."

"I'd say there are several parts of me that are persistent."

"Will you make a good father?"

"Don't you think I should work on being a good husband first?"

She returned his heated gaze, and desire rose yet again within her. The far-reaching rays of morning lit the edges of his black hair until his ebony locks appeared nearly blue, and she wanted to run her hands through them. She also wanted to taste his lips on hers once more.

As if reading her thoughts, Cale bent his head. Shay sighed when his lips melted obligingly and temptingly into hers.

"I want you," she confided, her small tongue tracing an enticing path over his bottom lip, "inside me."

"It would seem my wife is quite brazen."

"Only when it comes to you, sir."

The corners of his eyes crinkled. "Then I suppose I am obliged to honor your request."

She giggled and rolled over, taking him with her. She felt a blissful rush of pleasure as his arousal flirted with her thighs.

Her hair spread about them like a velvet cloak, and she took a handful and rubbed it seductively across his chest.

"If I didn't know better, I'd wonder where you learned such things," Cale teased.

"From an expert." She lowered her head. "Let me show you what else I've learned."

She took his dark nipple in her mouth and flicked her tongue across the hard button.

"Witch." Cale groaned and switched positions again.

His heart slammed against his ribs when Shay sighed her contentment as his mouth found her parted, moist lips.

Cale nipped her earlobe. "Shall we see how powerful your spell is?"

"If you dare."

"Oh, I dare all right."

Cale rose, and Shay groaned her disappointment.

"Where are you going?"

"You'll see," he said over his shoulder as he

walked to the gelding and fished something out of his saddlebags.

He dropped to the ground beside her. "Take this"—he handed her a small container of scented oil—"and rub it on your body."

"Why do you carry this?"

Cale laughed. "You don't have to know everything."

She raised a delicately arched brow. "We'll see about that."

"Stop talking and do what I said."

"There you go again with your orders."

The lines about his mouth deepened pleasantly as he said, "Please."

Shay gave him a very seductive, feminine smile as she poured a small measure of oil into her palm and rubbed it into her skin, beginning at her neck.

The living gold of morning highlighted the soft planes and pleasing curves of her body and her delicately sculpted face. Cale experienced a moment of immense joy at the sight of her magnificent form, knowing she was his. He looked forward to having the rest of their lives to make love to her. He knew that his love for her would never dwindle. For the first time in his life, he looked forward to growing old.

Her full breasts beckoned like ripe fruit when she raised first one arm, then the other, to apply the fragrant mixture to the soft undersides.

His mercurial gaze watched her every move, caressed every luscious curve of the perfection of her body.

"Now, your breasts." Only the incandescent spark in his eyes belied the lazy drawl of his words. "And do it very slowly."

She smiled once more. "Whatever my husband wants."

"Oh, but your husband wants more." The light in his eyes glowed brighter. "So very much more."

Pouring oil into both hands and rubbing them together, Shay applied the warm substance to each breast in sensuous, circular motions. She saw his arousal and knew how much he wanted her.

She intended to tempt him—a great deal more.

Her heart thrummed in anticipation.

She rose and presented the swell of her bottom, the languid curve of her hip. "Is this to your liking?"

"More than you know."

Mesmerized by those hot, compelling eyes, Shay stepped closer. "Where should I apply the oil next?"

A singularly masculine smile curved the handsome mouth that she longed, more than ever, to feel against hers. "All over."

Shay shivered at his heated words, underscored by his even more heated look. The lower regions of her body hummed with expectation.

She closed her eyes as she rubbed oil over her shoulders and arms, stomach and hips, with slow, erotic strokes. Feeling more than a bit wicked, she bent and applied the scented liquid to her ankles, inching slowly to her calves, then to her thighs.

A light sheen of perspiration covered Cale as he sat transfixed, his breathing rhythmically matching his spurting pulse, his groin aching intolerably.

Unable to stand another minute of this sweet torture, Cale rose and covered the distance separating him from Shay.

He reached out to stroke her hair. "I think you've tempted me enough." Winding several strands about his knuckles, he pulled Shay closer until her upturned face nearly touched his. "It's time to do something about it."

Cale released her hair and lifted her hands, turning them palms up. He poured oil into each, then guided her hands to his rigid manhood.

Shay knew without words what he wanted, and she obliged him by thoroughly covering his throbbing length.

He pulled her down to the ground with him.

His voice, rich with promised pleasure, came in short breaths, bathing her cheek in warmth, as his body moved over hers. "I can't wait."

His lips, warm and compelling, covered hers. His tongue was a hot, wet extension of his manhood as it thrust deeply inside her mouth.

Shay arched her body against his, wanting. . . .

For Shay, to be one with Cale was to be one with herself. Never had she felt so replete with emotion, so loved. The world held no meaning. There was only Cale.

Her hands stroked his firm, supple back muscles, and his pulse galloped like a wild stallion at her touch. Impatience rippled through him, until he could stand no more.

"I want release, but I want to go slow and bring you pleasure," he groaned.

"Don't hold back," Shay urged.

With each stroke, he increased his tempo, quickly propelling them into ecstasy.

Moments passed as they remained joined, their breathing slowly returning to normal before Cale kissed Shay and moved from her. He pulled her against the curve of his side, her head on his shoulder. The scent of their passion, mingled with the aroma of the perfumed oil, clung to them.

Shay wasn't surprised when, minutes later, Cale began anew his seduction of her. His lips journeyed across her delicate shoulder blades, to the hollow at the base of her throat, to the coral tips of her full breasts. There, they lingered, laving their full attention on her flesh. His mouth claimed hers again in a kiss that tickled her senses with anticipation.

Cale raised himself on his elbows and stared down into Shay's flushed features.

How could he have denied his love for her? He had only hurt them both by asking her to surrender to his will. She was capable of making her own decisions, and she had chosen him. She had also proved herself to be a survivor. The last cobwebs of doubt had been cleared from his mind.

Her touch had the unequaled power to bring him to his knees. He welcomed the hold she had on his heart. For an instant, Cale held Shay with the force of his gaze alone. She watched him in return, her eyes wide with desire.

He knelt before her and pulled her up to her knees. Only a breath separated their bodies. His hands settled on her upper arms, then traveled up and down her slender arms in slow motion.

His fingers wound themselves in her silky hair, and he brought the rich mass to his face, breathing deeply of its fragrance. He gently tugged her head back, exposing her slender throat to the lazy attention of his tongue.

He raised his head and kissed her, demandingly, urgently. Gossamer strands of her hair caught between their lips.

Cale pulled away. Her rapid breathing blended with the morning sounds and the sighing wind, becoming part of the beauty of the wild land.

"This will be the wedding night we never had." Cale looked into her eyes—and deep into her soul.

The morning light made Shay's eyes burn with a mixture of green and gold that flared brighter and hotter than fire. Shay could only nod as her emotions formed a hard lump of passion in her throat.

"We'll remember this time together." He cupped her face between his hands and traced the outlines of her lips with his thumbs. "Forever."

"Forever," she softly echoed.

He inhaled her ragged breath, then exhaled their mingled air, and she felt it drift across her heated flesh. She gazed into his flushed features, his eyes like a slate-blue sky, his upper lip and forehead dotted with perspiration.

"Quit talking," she murmured.

Shay leaned into him, wrapped her slender arms about his neck, her fingers twining themselves in his thick, silky hair, and fully pressed herself against him. She ran the tip of her tongue across the ridges of his teeth before drawing his lower lip into her mouth and sucking gently.

"I want you to be as wild as any untamed creature, to wrap your legs around me and meet my every move."

Delicious expectation coiled tightly inside her, then spiraled upward at the explicit look in his eyes.

Cale pressed his lips against the side of her neck while his touch roamed across her shoulders, her breasts, her arms, before his hands cupped her buttocks.

She tasted him. She felt him. She heard his ragged breathing. She had seen the desire burning hotly in his gaze. Her eyes closed in lazy sensuality.

When his hands teasingly journeyed down her hip, then parted her legs and sought the soft flesh of her inner thigh, she moaned. But when his fingers traveled wickedly higher, stopping at the opening of her womanhood, her breath caught in her throat.

His fingers parted her and slid into her moist warmth. She placed steadying hands on his shoulders to keep herself from swaying, so great was the violent trembling of anticipation. As the sweet, steaming need for release built inside her, her fingers clutched spasmodically at his shoulders, her nails digging heedlessly into his flesh. She writhed against his hand, her rhythm building apace with her demand for deliverance.

She was only dimly aware that Cale had directed her to lie on the blanket, but then she felt him settle between her legs and lift her hips to his awaiting mouth. His tongue slid into her with shocking, seductive intent. Her fingers clutched his hair convulsively, and she opened her legs wider.

He tasted her honeyed warmth as she writhed beneath the onslaught of his penetrating, provocative tongue. He felt her thighs quiver about him before she cried out as climactic pleasure swept her.

Cale raised himself and looked down at his wife. Her eyes were closed in sated fulfillment, and her breasts rose and fell with her short, rapid breaths.

His heartbeat quickened until its tempo matched that of his pulsing manhood. He lowered himself atop her and paused, tensing his muscles, controlling his movements.

He shifted against her, the tip of his maleness begging entrance to her womanly core. His mouth smothered her groan as he entered her like silk and steel. Her feet locked against his taut buttocks. Her hands clutched at the bunched muscles of his back, and her head fell back. He moved slowly . . . so very slowly . . . until her wet, heated womanhood molded itself around his swollen length.

Their bodies one, Cale moved in a leisurely rhythm that Shay readily matched. She arched against him, riding each satiny thrust of his body.

She was as wet and sleek as he—and achingly aware. Raw ecstasy streamed through Shay's veins while spasms racked her body.

The moment she cried out, Cale no longer denied himself, and he shuddered deep within her with a force that made his body convulse. He covered her cheeks and eyes with kisses. He stayed inside her until he felt himself grow soft, and he withdrew slowly.

Content, Cale rolled to his back. Exhausted and spent, Shay lay against him, and he held her tight, his hand below the sweet curve of her breast. He inhaled her scent and knew that he would love Shay until his last breath.

Chapter 17

That afternoon, Cale came to Shay. "Can you shoot?"

"Some. Papa never approved of my handling guns. But Uncle Brad would take me occasionally to practice when Papa wasn't around."

"Can you hit what you aim at?"

"If it stays still long enough."

Cale took her by the hand and began to lead her to a rock formation. "We've got some work to do. You've got to be able to hit a moving target."

She stopped in her tracks. "You mean a man?"

He turned and looked deeply into her eyes. "Yes. What happened with the Apaches made me realize that I won't always be around to protect you."

Cale set large pieces of wood on the rocky ledge, then walked back to Shay.

He pulled his army revolver from its holster and moved to stand behind her. He reached around and placed the gun in her hand. The sweat-darkened walnut handle was smooth to the touch. The feel was strangely reassuring, reminding her of Cale's own strength. She inhaled the musky male scent of his warm body so close to hers. Silence enveloped them, broken only by the whisper of Cale's breath against her ear, and the soft beating of her heart.

"I'll talk you through it," came Cale's low voice. "First, sight your target."

Shay pointed the muzzle toward one of the intended targets.

"Second, use your other hand to steady the gun."

She rested the gun butt against her palm.

"Third, cock the hammer back with your thumb, and fourth, squeeze the trigger slowly."

The metal was cool beneath her fingertip, reminding her of the cold bloodiness of killing, but she swallowed back her feelings. She knew it was for her own good that she learn to shoot.

"Don't shut your eyes when you fire. Keep an eye on your target at all times."

She pulled back the trigger the rest of the way. The revolver recoiled against her hand as the air reverberated with the sound of the pistol shot. Bits of limestone flew as the bullet slammed into the rock above the wood.

Shay lowered the weapon. "I missed."

"Not by much." He moved to her side. "You've got to learn to use the sight on the gun. Now try again. By the time we're finished, you're going to be able to hit your target three out of five times. Both still and moving."

What Cale didn't tell Shay was that his instincts were nagging him. He'd lived by his intuitive senses too long to disregard them. He just didn't know in what form, or when, the trouble would come.

* * *

Jared Slocum rose from his kneeling position, having examined the campfire remains, and slapped his thigh with his hat in irritation. "Shit!"

"Nothing?" Henry asked from atop his horse.

"It's like Breland and the girl just disappeared. Three horses came in. Then two went in one direction and the third in another." He rubbed his forehead. "It just doesn't make sense."

"What now?"

Jared paused to deliberate. "We follow the one that headed due west. Deeper prints. Might mean a double rider." He settled his hat atop his head and pulled the brim down low.

"Damn. I hate losing time. Just when we were close," Henry said.

Jared swung up into the saddle. "If we ride hard, we can make up the difference. The bastard's not that far ahead of us." He jerked his reins to the left and kicked his mount in the sides.

As they rode toward San Angelo, warm winds fanned Shay to sleep. Cale circled her small waist with one arm and held her close to him. He felt the definition of sinewy muscles beneath his touch. His thighs and legs molded themselves around her curved hips and pressed against her shapely buttocks. He was glad she slept. He'd managed to act as if nothing in particular was wrong, but it'd been damned hard. He hadn't wanted to worry Shay.

His gut tightened like a bowstring pulled taut. His instincts had been right. Someone had been on their back trail for some time now. He'd seen a telltale cloud of dust in the distance across the flat expanse of West Texas terrain when he and Shay had stopped for food and water earlier in the day.

Cale noticed a larger swirl of dust ahead of them. It had to be a trail drive of sorts to raise such a big cloud. An idea came to him. He'd flank the drovers and the herd, allowing his tracks to mingle with those of the animals. Just maybe he could buy them enough time to get to San Angelo ahead of whoever was tracking them.

Finding the herd, he was enveloped in a sea of swirling color. A multitude of horses in all shades—browns, black, gray, yellow, and red—filled the plains.

The air was filled with the smell of horse sweat and excrement, mingled with thick dust particles that floated overhead. Dense swarms of horseflies hovered above the animals in droning clouds.

Shay awoke, coughing. "Where are we?"

Cale looked down at her when she turned her face toward him. "On the edges of a horse herd."

"Why?"

"No reason," he said nonchalantly. "Just passing 'em on our way to San Angelo."

That evening, Cale halted the gelding on the outskirts of San Angelo. He lowered Shay to the ground, then dismounted.

"Why are we stopping?" Shay asked.

"Something's wrong with the horse."

Cale ran his hand down the horse's right foreleg, then turned and, positioning the hoof between his bent knees, he leaned over for a closer inspection. He ran his gloved fingers over the rim of the horseshoe.

"Damn." He released his hold, stepped away, and straightened. "Just as I thought. Loose shoe." He let his breath out slowly. "We're going to have to get the gelding reshod."

"Would a delay be so bad?" Shay asked, her eyes wide and full of worry.

Cale forced himself to shrug. "I just didn't want to stay in San Angelo any longer than necessary."

"Why?"

"It's not important. We've got to spend the night anyway. Blacksmith, or dry-goods store for that matter, won't be open until morning."

"Do you think we could sleep inside tonight?" Hope tinted her voice.

Cale was hard-pressed to deny her request. Especially when she looked at him with her beguiling green eyes. He cupped her chin. "Why not? But I'm afraid we'll have to stay at the saloon. Rooms are cheaper."

She threw her arms around his neck. "I don't care so long as I can sleep on a real bed."

Cale groaned as he held her to him. He loved her so much. The thought of impending danger nearly broke him.

Cale led the horse as they walked the rest of the way into town, stopping in the alley adjacent to the local saloon. He tied the horse to a crate.

"You wait here. I'll get us a room," Cale said, then disappeared inside.

He reappeared moments later. He pulled his rifle from its scabbard and tossed their saddlebags over his shoulder. With the lever-action weapon under his arm and his hand at her back, Cale directed Shay toward an outside flight of stairs leading to the second story.

As they ascended the steps, Shay turned to look at Cale. "Our room is up here?"

"Told the bartender that I wanted a private room for my new bride. This is just a back way into the building."

"I see."

The uncertainty in Shay's voice made it clear that she didn't completely understand, but Cale wasn't going to tell her otherwise. The less she knew, the better off she was.

At the top of the stairs, Cale moved around Shay. "I'll go first and light the lantern."

The flare of a match, then the soft glow of a lantern dispelled the darkness. Sulfur drifted to her nose as she entered. The room contained only a bed and a shabby dresser. She passed in front of the cracked mirror and looked at herself in it. Her mouth turned down at her reflection. She ran her hands over her dusty clothes, face, and hair.

Cale came to stand behind her. His hands settled on her shoulders, and he looked at her in the mirror. "I've ordered water." He nodded toward the copper bathtub in the corner of the drab room, a faded screen to one side. "Thought you might like a bath."

"That would be lovely." Shay sighed. She turned around in his arms. "But can we afford it?"

Cale cupped her cheek and smiled at her. "I want you to have some decent food and a hot bath. You'll feel better."

A knock sounded and Cale admitted a shy-looking young girl who brought several large pails of boiling water, a cake of scented soap, and towels.

Shay smiled her thanks as the girl filled the tub, then left.

Soon the girl returned and set a tray of food on the dresser. Shay appreciatively sniffed the aroma of steak and potatoes, and a loaf of crusty sourdough bread.

Cale and Shay sat on the floor, much like they

were having a picnic, and ate. Little conversation passed between them as they did justice to their food.

Cale finished first and leaned back against the side of the bed. Reaching out, he ran his finger down Shay's cheek, leaving a tiny trail across her dust-covered skin.

Between bites, Shay glanced into his face. She remembered the day they spent by the arroyo and how she had admired his body, sculpted arousingly into a graceful, sensuously lean frame. Her love for him struck a chord of harmony within her.

Cale stood. "I'm going to take the gelding to the livery stable and see about buying another horse. I'll be back as soon as I can. Lock the door behind me. I shouldn't be long." He placed his revolver atop the dresser. "I want you to have this. I'll take the rifle."

Shay laughed. "Why all the fuss? I'm sure I'll be just fine."

Cale's mouth tightened. "Don't take strange surroundings for granted, Shay. And don't stay in a room with your back to the door."

"All right," she said softly.

Shay watched the door close slowly before she moved behind the screen. Stepping out of her clothes and undergarments, and pinning up her hair, she slipped into the tub. The water, which by this time had cooled to the perfect temperature, lapped about her waist, and she closed her eyes, savoring the penetrating warmth on her cramped muscles. She had found a corner of heaven.

She began to leisurely lather herself with the scented soap, her body glistening in the soft lantern light. She stretched a long, slender leg atop the tub's rim and scrubbed vigorously. Water dripped from the sponge to bead the floor. She leaned her head back against the tub and closed her eyes. Time blurred as she became lost in her contentment.

Then she snapped her eyes open. She'd forgotten to lock the door. She started to rise when a furious Cale walked through the door, slamming it behind him.

She braced herself as he strode purposefully to the tub. "I thought I told you to lock the door," he said between gritted teeth.

Her large green eyes met his gleaming blue ones. "I was just about to when you came back."

Cale had been scared when he'd found the door unlocked. Fear channeled into anger. Anyone could have entered. Including whoever was following them. She didn't know the potent danger stalking them.

"Shay, do you know what could have happened to you during the ten minutes I was gone?"

"I'm sorry."

He raked his fingers through his hair.

"You're keeping something from me, Cale. What is it?" Irritation tightened her voice.

"Nothing. Just feels funny being under a roof again."

He had already discerned from the tension in her face that she suspected something was wrong. The slight trembling of her lips told him that fear was replacing her annoyance.

No, he wouldn't give her cause to worry.

His gaze roamed over her. The perfection of her form was exposed to him above and below the water. He saw where her sunburned skin, a deepening red, met her untouched flesh, flushed pink

from the warmth of the bathwater. Droplets of
moisture ran in slow rivulets between her breasts.
Her slender hips tapered to the long, shapely
thighs and calves he'd come to know so well. His
anger melted. He loved her too much to stay angry with her.

Damn. He should leave her to her rest, but just
the sight of her stirred his blood. His regard returned to her face, and he saw an invitation of her
own shimmering in her eyes.

It was an invitation he couldn't refuse.

Leaning over, Cale entwined his long fingers
about Shay's delicate wrists, and he felt her steady
pulse as he pulled her to her feet and helped her
step gingerly from the tub. His gaze traveled hungrily over her as she stood before him, her small
feet planted between his booted ones. His other
hand slid over her hipbone, and he drew her
closer until her silky thighs grazed against his
pants.

The sense of urgency he felt at the sudden
thought of anyone else touching her intimately di-
luted his desire. "Shay, you've got to trust me and
do what I tell you."

"I promise I will." She wrinkled her nose. "Now
why don't you get in the tub? And we'll finish this
conversation when you're done."

When her lips parted enticingly, and she ran her
tongue seductively across her teeth, Cale knew
how he would spend the next few hours.

"Just wrap yourself in a towel." He patted her
rear. "Keep things warm for me."

Cale released Shay. He watched as she picked
up a towel and swaddled herself in it. The corn
husk mattress sagged beneath her as she sat down.

He undressed, each piece of clothing dropping

to the floor in a heap. He felt the heat spiraling from her gaze as she watched.

He submerged himself in the tepid water. As he washed himself, Cale wondered if he was doing the right thing by agreeing to stay the night. But what could he do? The smithy couldn't reshoe the gelding until morning. He couldn't afford to buy two mounts, and they hung men for stealing horses. Besides, they were low on supplies, which meant waiting until morning for the mercantile to open.

And what could he possibly tell Shay if they abruptly left?

He had lived constantly with uncertainty for a companion, as an orphan and then during the Civil War. If Shay weren't along, he would have lain in wait for the tracker. His hands curled into fists beneath the water.

Cale finished sponging himself off, rose from the tub, and wrapped a towel about his midsection. He walked to the edge of the bed and stood in front of Shay.

She opened her legs and pulled him between them. Dipping her fingers into the top of the towel, she tugged. The length of cotton dropped to the floor. She reached up and ran her hands across his chest, then down to his lean midsection.

"I've been waiting." The top of her head grazed his stomach muscles as she lowered her mouth to the proof of his desire. "To do this." Her lips encased him, and she sucked gently.

Cale groaned and cradled the sides of her face to press her closer. He shut his eyes, and his head dropped back at the agonizing delight of her mouth sliding over his swollen flesh. He became lost in a blur of sensuality as she licked, sucked, and gently nipped his arousal.

When she withdrew her mouth, he looked down. She turned her face up and smiled impishly at him, then pressed her lips against him again.

Watching her take him into her mouth repeatedly aroused him until he thought he would burst. "Mercy, woman. Or I'll spill myself."

Shay raised her face. Cale sank his fingers into her wealth of hair and tugged, sending hairpins flying across the room. He then put his hands on her shoulders and pressed her into the mattress. With one strong, swift motion, he yanked the towel from beneath her and tossed it aside.

He lowered himself slowly atop her and stretched out until his body covered hers completely. He twined his fingers with hers and pulled her arms out to her sides, all the while nibbling the sensitive area where her neck joined her shoulder.

Laughing, Shay craned her neck and bit him playfully. "Let me loose."

Cale raised himself on his elbows and stared down at her. "What?"

"You heard me. Let go of me." She shoved at his chest and rolled him over.

Still laughing, she straddled him. "You taught me to shoot. Can you teach me to ride as well?"

Cale wrapped a section of hair around his wrist, pulled her face closer to his, and kissed her. He spoke against the lushness of her mouth, strands of silky hair caught between their heated lips. "Depends on what type of mount you want. One that's tame, or one that bucks." He arched his hips against her.

She sat up and tossed her head back, her hair

settling about them like a fiery cloak. "A bronc has to be ridden long and hard to be broken."

Cale pressed his palms against her breasts. "Some have to be ridden more than once to bring them around."

"Or shall I choose between a gelding and a stallion?"

"Stallions have greater stamina." He smiled wickedly. "And they usually cover more ground."

"Umm. Let me see." She reached beneath her and settled her hand against his fullness. "Most definitely a stallion." She leaned forward, took his bottom lip between her teeth, and sucked gently before whispering, "Now that my mount has been chosen, shall we begin with my lesson?"

"The first thing is to ease into the saddle," he said huskily.

Shay raised up, then lowered herself slowly onto his erection. She moved her hips in small, circular motions until she absorbed him completely. "Now what?" She moistened her lips.

"You adjust the reins between your fingers."

She settled her hands on his taut stomach. "All right."

"Then you urge your mount into whatever pace you want."

"Such as?"

"If you want an easy canter, you'd nudge the mount in the ribs."

"Like this?" She skimmed her hands across his rib cage, then pressed her fingertips lightly into his skin.

"Now fit your bottom firmly against the saddle and let your body roll with the rhythm of your mount."

She began to rock gently atop him. He matched

her movements with a tender cadence of his own. She felt him deep inside her, his manhood filling her completely, and she knew intense pleasure.

Cale increased the power and speed of his upward thrusts. Shay moaned. Her inner muscles quivered about him, slick and hot.

Their ardent gait intensified until their breath came in punctuated gasps and soft cries, their skin moist and heated.

Together, they rode the passion-covered plains of desire.

Cale awoke with a feeling of dread, though only the increased tempo of his heartbeat betrayed his anxiety. Four years of sleeping in enemy territory had taught him to control his every response. He sharpened his mind by focusing on his surroundings. Easing his free hand beneath his pillow, he retrieved his revolver and lay it beside him on the mattress. Repeatedly during the night, he awoke to the slightest sound, only to drift back to sleep when no threat presented itself.

Sounds of pedestrian and horse traffic filtered through the plank walls, but no footsteps fell on the stairs. He took a deep breath, then released it slowly. They were safe—for the time being.

Shay was still snuggled against his left side, her head resting on his shoulder and her soft breath falling lightly against his chest. She looked so peaceful. He hated to rouse her, but they should have been on the trail hours ago. He shook her gently.

Her eyelids opened, then fluttered closed, then opened. She uncurled her body from beside him and stretched. "I can't remember sleeping so well." She flopped onto her stomach and closed her eyes with a sigh.

Cale stood, retrieved his discarded clothes, and began dressing.

He shoved his shirttails into the waistband of his pants, then reached over and playfully swatted Shay's bottom. "We should have been gone from San Angelo already. Get dressed. I want to be out of town in an hour."

Shay groaned and opened her eyes. "Why the hurry?"

"The sooner we leave Texas, the sooner we'll be in Wyoming."

"Just a few minutes more."

"Now. Or I'm going to drag you out of bed."

Shay smiled drowsily at him and managed to roll off the bed. She walked to the dresser, poured water into the basin, and washed her face, letting the cool water revive her. She was soon dressed.

Cale slung the saddlebags over his shoulder and picked up his rifle. He motioned with the tip of the barrel toward the door. "Let's get going."

They descended the stairs and stopped in the alley.

Cale retrieved a piece of paper and money from his shirt pocket and handed them to Shay. "Go to the mercantile across the street. Fill the list and meet me back here. And don't draw any undue attention to yourself."

Shay looked at him with a puzzled expression. "What's that supposed to mean?"

Cale forced his tone to be less abrupt. "I just don't want any man gawking at my wife."

"Aren't we going to eat breakfast? I'm hungry."

"We'll eat on the trail. Daylight's wasting." Cale gave her a shove against her backside.

She glanced over her shoulder at him. "All right. I guess this is what happens when you don't have your morning coffee."

Hearing his impatient growl, she smiled. Some things would never change about Cale. She liked it that way.

She looked both ways before crossing the busy thoroughfare and headed inside the general store.

A clerk greeted her. "May I help you?"

Shay handed her list to the young man. "I need these supplies, please."

"Yes, ma'am." He set about filling her order.

While she waited for her purchases, Shay bought a piece of licorice and walked around the general store eating her candy. She stopped at the aisle which contained women's toiletries and looked over the wares. Various perfume bottles littered the counter, and she smelled each one in turn. She wrinkled her nose at some and sighed in appreciation of others.

Behind her, she heard the door open and close, followed by heavy footfalls approaching her. She turned and glanced in the direction of the newcomer.

A tall man stopped at the gun counter several feet from Shay. By his disheveled, dirty appearance, he'd been riding hard. He removed his hat, revealing matted blond hair, and beat at his clothes, raising small puffs of dust.

An older man made to help the stranger. "Yes, sir. What can I do for you?"

"I need ammunition. And some gun oil."

"What caliber cartridge?"

"Forty-four."

The newcomer leaned his folded forearms against the counter and spoke to the clerk while the man retrieved the requested items. "Say, I bet you pretty much know the coming and going of strangers around here."

"Most. But this is a busy town. More strangers all the time." The clerk readjusted his glasses on his nose. "Why?"

"My brother and I've been tracking a man by the name of Breland who murdered our pa."

"Breland?" The clerk shook his head. "No, I don't recall anyone coming in here by that name. But you might ask at the saloon."

"He's tall, with black hair and blue eyes. He'd be traveling with his wife. She's got red hair and green eyes."

"Haven't seen anyone looking like that either." The clerk took the man's money and gave him his articles. "Sorry."

"If you or anyone remembers anything, my name's Slocum. My brother and I will be around for a while. There could be money in it for the person who has the right information."

Shay felt her insides grow cold, and she stood rooted to the spot. Slocum. The name flashed across her mind like a grass fire. That was the name of the man Cale had shot in self-defense. But this younger Slocum had called her husband a murderer. She had to warn Cale. Thank God she hadn't removed her hat. She only prayed the stranger hadn't gotten a good look at her.

She barely heard the young man when he finished her order and asked for payment. She shook herself mentally. "I'm sorry. How much did you say?"

"Two dollars and a bit."

She handed him the money and scooped up her supplies. She thought her legs would buckle beneath her, but she managed to reach the door and step outside without drawing attention to herself.

Disregarding the possible danger to herself, Shay hurried across the street, weaving in and out of moving riders and conveyances. She reached the alley, but Cale was nowhere to be seen.

Suddenly, a hand clamped down atop her shoulder from behind and spun her around, causing her to drop her bundle of supplies and knocking off her hat. A lump of raw fear threatened to choke her as she stared into Slocum's face.

Pushing his own hat back on his head, he leered at her, hatred burning in his gaze. "You thought I didn't notice you, Miss Alexander." He stepped closer. "Or should I say Mrs. Breland?"

Stay calm, Shay told herself. She had to think clearly.

She inched away from him until her back pressed against the saloon's wall. "You must have me confused with someone else. My name is—"

A tic worked in his cheek. "Don't lie to me, bitch. I recognize you from the description your father's foreman gave me and my brother."

"Really, mister." She made her voice as steady as possible. "You've got me confused with someone else." Hands behind her, she began feeling her way along the wall, not daring to take her eyes off Slocum.

He stretched out a hand to her. "Come with me quietly, and I won't hurt you."

"I'll scream."

"Open your mouth and I'll cut your fucking tongue out."

"You'll never get away with this." She kept inching along the wall toward the street.

"Get away with what?" His gaze raked her. "I

only want you to tell me where your murdering husband is. After that, you're free to go."

Shay knew he was lying. Her stomach knotted with dread. Her gaze shot sideways as she sought some avenue of escape. Slocum stood between her and freedom.

Trying to calm her racing heart, she decided to change her tactics. "What if I told you that I was forced to marry Cale Breland? That I didn't really want to be here?"

Slocum clucked his tongue. "I'd say that was too bad."

"If I help you find Cale, will you see that I get home?"

"If you make payment of some kind for my help." He jerked his thumb over his shoulder. "I haven't had a woman in a spell. Why don't you show me how grateful you'd be?" He moved closer.

She tried to dart to one side, but he lunged for her and grabbed her by her shirt front. In desperation, Shay slammed her knee into his crotch. Howling, he released her and crumpled to the ground.

Shay bolted for the street. She had to find Cale. As she ran, her panting echoed in her ears. Perspiration coated her skin, and she developed a stitch in her side. She dashed into another alley. Stopping to catch her breath, she doubled over and leaned against the side of the alley. Her body shuddered as she inhaled large amounts of air.

Above the pounding of her heart, she heard Slocum's voice. She pushed off the wall and struck out again. Her legs felt like lead, and her muscles burned, but still she pressed on.

She heard Slocum's labored breathing, could almost feel his hot breath. Suddenly she was grabbed by the scruff of her neck and wrenched to a halt.

Slocum wheeled her around and delivered a stinging blow to the side of her face. "You're gonna pay for what you did."

The distinct sound of a revolver's hammer being pulled back could be heard. "Let her go or I'll kill you where you stand." Cale spoke in a deadly, calm tone.

Slocum released Shay, and she stumbled toward Cale.

Tension rode high on his features. "Are you all right?" His gaze remained trained on Slocum.

"Yes," she gasped. "I was trying to find you to warn you."

"The horses are tied in front of the hotel. I want you to wait there for me."

"My brother will see you," Slocum spat out.

"Not likely. I already checked on his whereabouts. Right now, he's bedding a whore at the saloon."

"You might get away now. But next time you won't. You're gonna pay for shooting my pa in cold blood."

"I caught your pa cheating at cards. He drew on me first. Ask anyone who was there. They all saw what happened."

"You'd say anything to save your neck. When Jared and I catch up with you, you're gonna dance on the end of a rope." Slocum's lips drew back in a sneer. "But before you die I'm gonna have your wife, right there in the dirt, before your eyes. She owes me."

Fury, black and potent, washed over Cale. He

raised his gun and pistol-whipped Slocum. The younger man sagged to the ground.

Cale holstered his revolver and walked to Shay and the horses.

Wordlessly, they mounted. Amid the soft thud of hooves, the jingle of bit chains and spurs, and the creak of leather, they rode out of town.

Shay prayed the Slocums wouldn't follow.

With her next breath, she cursed the brothers, knowing they would.

Chapter 18

Shay shoved her hat off her head, allowing it to dangle down her back by its cord, and wiped the sweat-damp hair from her forehead with her sleeve. Cale had led them into some cliffs hewn from weathered rock, limestone spires rising against the late afternoon sky. A small stream tumbled down limestone boulders into the narrow channel it had carved from the rock. Altitude, the stream, and the abundant vegetation protected them from prying eyes.

She dismounted and gripped the stirrup, resting her forehead against the buckskin's warm, sweaty neck. Her mount tongued its bit, thirsty and tired.

"I know I've asked a lot from you today. Thank you." Shay breathed, then stepped back to rub the buckskin's velvety, moist nose.

With slow, stiff movements, she unsaddled the mare. She then upended the saddle and draped the saddle blanket atop it, and rubbed the horse's sweaty back with clumps of grass. She followed Cale's example and hobbled her horse near the stream.

Cale walked over to her. "I'll build a small fire. We'll have something hot to eat."

"Should we risk it?"

"The way the wind swirls down these cliffs makes it hard to know exactly which direction smoke is coming from. But just in case, I'll douse the fire an hour before sunset."

From rote, Shay cooked bacon, then made corn dodgers and fried the mixture in the grease.

As they ate, she couldn't keep her fears to herself. "Do you think they'll catch us?"

Cale looked up from his food. His gaze was steady and direct. "I know they'll die trying."

Her appetite left her, and she set her plate down. "Which means you'll have to kill them." Shay inched forward on her knees and took Cale's hand in hers. "I'm making things more difficult for you, aren't I?"

Cale brought their clasped hands to his mouth and kissed her knuckles. "What you do for me is make life worth living." He withdrew his hand from Shay's. "I'd best put the fire out now. Sun's setting."

That night a coyote's howl pierced Shay's veil of sleep. She bolted upright on their pallet. Unconsciously, she placed her hand over her chest and felt the frantic thumping of her heart. Coaxing moisture into her dry mouth, she ran her tongue across her lips.

She started when Cale rested his hand on her shoulder. "What is it?" He sat up.

She twisted around to look at him. Darkness draped his features. "Didn't you hear it? Someone screamed."

"It was only a coyote."

"Are you sure?"

"Coyotes can sound almost human at times."

"It seemed so real."

Cale eased back on their pallet and pulled Shay to him. She rested her head against the pillow of his shoulder.

"Ssh. Everything's all right. Go back to sleep," he crooned in her ear.

Plains Indians said that when the coyote roamed, deceit and trickery followed. He wondered how much time they had before the Slocum brothers caught up with them.

If he'd been alone, he could have dealt with the Slocums in one of two ways. He could have backtracked and surprised them at their own camp, or he could have stayed where he was and waited to pick them off when they got close. But he couldn't do either without endangering Shay. Instead he'd have to outwit the brothers. Which meant staying one step ahead, sleeping with one eye open, one finger on the trigger, one ear to the ground. He'd find some way to keep Shay safe.

Shay felt as if she had just closed her eyes when Cale shook her awake.

Not wanting to draw unwelcome attention to themselves by lighting a campfire against the predawn darkness, they breakfasted on cold corn dodgers and canned peaches. Shortly after, they broke camp.

After two days they crossed into New Mexico, the landscape changing little from that of West Texas. Agaves thrived among the limestone formations. Cacti and low-lying scrub brush littered the arid grassland. Giant cottonwoods grew intermittently with stands of oak and big-tooth maple.

Cale alternated the pace between a hard gallop and a fast canter, taking advantage of the lead time they had on the Slocums. They would ride relentlessly until the horses' coats became dark with sweat, lather streaking their shoulders and flanks, and Cale was forced to slow the pace to a walk.

Sleep came in snatches. Not risking campfires, they ate cold food.

Each grueling day that passed left Shay leaner and more hardened to the rigors of trail life. She had difficulty remembering a day when she hadn't stayed in the saddle from sunrise to sunset. Her life at Twin Creeks became only a memory.

Shay learned the painful lesson that southern New Mexico was a tortured land. Hardships awaited them at every turn: scarce water sources, arduous stretches of rocky terrain, and extreme temperatures, not to mention a variety of snakes, scorpions, and other poisonous creatures.

Shay rubbed her eyes, rimmed with crusty sand particles. A foreboding weighed heavily on her spirit, darkening the corners of her mind with thoughts of losing Cale. These endless stretches of terrain made ambush a very real threat. Behind which boulder, stand of trees, or dense brush, would they find the Slocum brothers? She would never allow Cale to see her fear, but inside she died a little each day.

As they continued their flight to the north, Shay hoped fervently that they had outrun the Slocums.

In her heart, she knew they hadn't.

Cale and Shay approached the Pecos River from the east. Dismounting, they led their horses up an incline to the limestone caves nature had carved from the land. One large chamber provided shelter for both horses and riders.

With the two horses in tow, Cale disappeared at

the rear of the cave. Moments later, he reappeared at the opening, holding his rifle.

"I'll keep watch." He looked at Shay. "You get some rest."

Cale checked the rifle's firing mechanism, then settled the weapon in the crook of his arm as his gaze swept the terrain below.

Glad for the respite from the glaring sun, Shay wet her bandanna with water from her canteen and wiped the grit from her neck and face.

She soaked the cloth again, walked over to Cale, and handed him the bandanna. "Here. You look like you could use a little cooling off."

"Thanks." He removed his hat and wiped his face with the handkerchief. Sponging off the back of his neck, he said, "Try and get some rest. We'll stay put long enough for the horses to get their second wind."

"What about you?"

Cale returned the bandanna to Shay. "I'm fine." His attention returned to the landscape. "Damn, I wish I had a pair of field glasses."

Suddenly, he tensed, cursing beneath his breath.

Alarmed, Shay's eyes grew wide. "What is it?"

"Move back."

She retreated a step. "The Slocums?"

"Can't tell. I only saw a glint of light reflected off something. Maybe a spur or bridle bit." While his gaze remained fixed on the landscape ahead, he said, "Do what I tell you, Shay, and move."

She retreated several feet, then stopped. The seconds stretched into agonizing minutes as Shay waited and watched.

Down below, a horse snorted.

Cale swore violently and dropped to the ground on his stomach. "Two riders coming up the incline," he whispered while sighting down the rifle barrel.

"Is it them?"

"Can't tell yet."

Another torturous minute passed. Shay felt every muscle in her body begin to quiver from the strain of remaining perfectly still.

Then she heard Cale say in a vicious tone, "Yes."

She stretched out on the ground and crawled over to him.

"Jesus! Shay, get back."

Although she was far from composed, she managed a calm tone. "Give me your pistol."

Instead of arguing, he pulled his revolver from its holster and handed it to her. Steadying the weapon between both hands, she cocked the hammer. Her breathing sounded unnaturally loud in her ears as she waited alongside Cale for the Slocum brothers.

Cale didn't move a muscle; his rifle remained trained on the incline leading to the cave. Shay followed his gaze and saw the Slocums riding up the slope at a canter.

"When I give the word, start firing," he said. "Understood?"

Shay maintained fingertip control over her strained emotions. "Yes."

He levered a shell into the rifle's firing chamber. "I'll take the brother riding behind. If you can't hit the first rider, aim for his horse."

Despite the seriousness of their situation, Shay's sensibilities reared at the thought of shooting a defenseless animal. "But—"

Cale shifted his position slightly, his eyes never leaving his target. "The bastards. The sun must have addled their brains. They're riding straight for us."

Cale squeezed off a shot, the rifle recoiling slightly against his shoulder. A split second later, he fired again.

The rider to the rear howled in pain and clutched his left shoulder, his body swaying in the saddle.

An answering report from the front rider echoed up the limestone walls. The bullet ricocheted, and particles of rock stung Shay's face.

"Now, for God's sake, Shay, shoot."

She closed one eye, aiming down the barrel, and pulled the trigger. The revolver kicked in her hands. Her eye snapped open in time to see the rider kick free of his horse as the animal dropped from beneath him. He rolled to his feet and swung himself up behind his brother. They crashed into the bordering growth of dense brush and trees, disappearing from sight.

Shay saw Cale rise, and she stood also. She noticed his mouth moving, but she couldn't hear anything. Her ears were ringing from the near-deafening roar of the rifle and the report of the revolver.

She watched his mouth and was able to make out some of his words.

"Damn . . . bastards disappeared . . . I . . . get off . . . shot."

Shay reached out and tugged on his arm. "Is it safe to leave?" Her voice sounded as if it came from deep inside a well.

Cale put down his rifle and placed his hands on her shoulders, looking intensely at her.

Her forehead furrowed from the effort of watching his mouth so closely.

His lips formed the words. "Yes. There's a way out back there."

Gathering the canteen and the rifle, Cale guided Shay and the horses out of the limestone catacomb.

To the west, a dark cathedral of clouds gathered. The wind picked up, sending dust swirling around the two riders. The heavens rumbled with thunder as Shay watched the delicate strokes of lightning being painted against the black canvas.

The temperature had dropped with the approaching storm, and Shay reveled in the cool kiss of air against her skin. Closing her eyes, she breathed in the sweet smell of approaching rain. Her lagging spirits lifted. However, her respite was cut short as the wind came in hard gusts, pelting her face with stinging sand. She raised a hand to shield her eyes and looked at Cale. He had pulled his bandanna up to cover the lower part of his face. Guiding her horse with pressure from her knees, she lifted her own bandanna to her face and tied it securely at the back of her head.

The turbulence gained ground on them. Shay prayed that the rain would come soon and that their trail would be lost in the downpour. Shay followed Cale's lead and put on her slicker.

Lightning flared across the flat expanse of terrain, and thunder exploded. Rain pounded the riders with watery fists. The horses ducked their heads against the driving elements. Shay pulled her hat down low across her forehead and huddled inside her slicker.

As they continued, Shay fixed her gaze on Cale's figure ahead of her, blinking against sporadic waves of wind-driven rain. All she could hear above the din of the storm was the pounding of her heart and the rasp of air through her lungs.

Suddenly and miraculously, the gray, misty form of an abandoned soddie came into view. They rode to the side and found a lean-to for the horses. Quickly, they stripped their saddles from their mounts, then carried their gear to the hut.

The door proved stubborn, and Cale shouldered it open. They deposited their gear just inside the entrance. Shay had to swallow a cry of dismay as, through a single window, lightning revealed an interior of dried mud walls and a cobwebbed ceiling of earth and timber. A lone table, two rickety chairs, and a cot situated along one wall were the only pieces of furniture. Faint scurrying sounds came from a corner, and Shay shuddered at the thought of rats.

Remorse plagued her. She should be grateful they had found a haven from the storm. She silently thanked God for the shelter. She straightened her shoulders and lifted her chin. She'd make the soddie right in no time.

Cale built a fire, and soon its warmth reflected off earthen walls and cast a bronze glow about the room.

Shay set about cleaning the hut until the interior took on some form of order. In the meantime, Cale prepared a bite of food for them.

Later, Cale leaned against his saddle before the fire with his arms around Shay's middle. She reclined between his legs, her back resting against his chest, her head against his shoulder. Blankets covered them while their clothes dried on nearby chairs to the side of the fire. They listened to the crackling of wood compete with the pelting rain-drops outside. A few stray raindrops, pushed through the chimney by the driving rain, hissed and turned to steam as they landed on the flames.

Finding Cale's silence oppressive, Shay asked, "How much time did we buy?"

"Hard to say. Maybe a day. Maybe more. They'll have to find a doc to patch up the one I shot. And they'll have to get another horse," Cale said against her hair. He paused a moment before he continued, "Shay, I've been thinking and I want you to hear me out."

His cautious tone caused Shay to tense. "All right."

"It's no good."

"What do you mean?"

"You're in the way."

She angled her body to look at him. "I've never complained."

His gaze skimmed her eyes, her shoulders, the tops of her breasts from above the blanket. He wanted nothing more than to hold her, but he reined in his thoughts. He had to think of Shay's well-being.

"No, you haven't."

"Then what?"

"When we reach Fort Sumner, I want you on a stage for Austin."

"Why?"

"Don't argue. I've made up my mind."

"Since this is my life we're talking about, don't you think I should have some say in the matter?"

His features hardened. He couldn't afford to show any weakness, not when her life depended on his being firm. "No point. Until this thing with the Slocums is cleared up, one way or the other, I want you safe."

"And you call being with my father safe?"

"Better than having a bullet put through you."

"But so far we've outrun them."

"For now, but what about tomorrow? And the day after that?" He cradled her soft face between his roughened hands. "Oh, for God's sake, Shay. Look at you. You can't keep up this pace. With each passing day, I watch you grow thinner, the circles under your eyes become darker. This is no way for you to live."

"But it's the way I chose to live my life. Here. With you."

"And what if something happens to me?" Cale's hands fell away. Frustration roughened his voice. "You'd be alone."

Shay felt the raw energy radiating from his eyes. Her mind raced with thoughts that had little to do with obedience, and everything to do with love.

She placed two fingers against his lips. "I want to stay with you."

"Shay—if you stay with me, you could be killed."

"But you're my life. Don't send me away."

For the space of a heartbeat, his eyes betrayed his wavering resolve. Then his gaze went hard and flat. "You've got to listen to reason."

"No. I don't want to live without you. Not to feel your touch would kill me."

A muscle constricted in his jaw, then relaxed again. "Maybe you're slowing me down. Maybe I could get the jump on them if I didn't have to worry about you. Did you ever think about that?"

Shay rose on shaky legs. "I know what you're

doing, but it won't work." She swiped at her eyes with the back of her hand.

Cale came to his feet, letting his blanket drop to the floor, and took her in his arms. He felt as if someone had reached into him and squeezed his insides.

He forced conviction into his voice. "If I have to drag you screaming and kicking, you're going to get on that stage."

Shay shuddered. "Please, don't do this to us. Don't make me leave."

"I love you too much to take a chance on your getting shot, even killed. I've hurt you enough already."

She pressed her cheek against his chest. "It would hurt me more not to be with you."

Cale shoved her back in anguish. "You don't know . . ." His voice faltered. "You don't know what you're saying."

Shay reached for him and drew him to her. "I know exactly what I'm saying." She caressed his face. "The only thing I fear is living without you."

"You're asking me to be a willing party to your possible death."

"I'm only asking you to love me and let me love you."

"You know I love you, but you've got to listen to reason."

"I'm listening to my heart. I've waited my entire life to find you. You can send me away, but I'll find you somehow."

"I should make you go." Cale drew a burning breath as his voice splintered. He closed his eyes and finished raggedly. "But, God help me, I can't."

He rested his chin atop her head, and he softly stroked the hair framing her face.

If he couldn't outrun the Slocums, or cover his and Shay's tracks, he'd have to outsmart—or outshoot—the brothers. For he knew without a doubt they still followed.

Yet, he did doubt how much time he had left with Shay; each night together was perhaps their last. And so, he cherished every moment with her, and every moment he wanted to cherish her with his body.

She must have read his thoughts, for she said, "I want you to make love to me."

Cale pulled the blanket from her body. Her breath caught in her throat at the near-physical fondling of his gaze. She expelled the air from her lungs in a soft rasp of sound.

His mouth covered hers and thunder echoed in the forceful persistence of his kiss. He pulled her head back with a gentle tug of her hair, exposing her slender throat. He buried his lips in the soft, pulsing hollow of her neck.

With arms entwined and lips joined, they sank to the floor and stretched out atop a blanket, Cale resting on his back and Shay reclining on her side.

She raised on one elbow and looked down at him. "I want to forget the outside world, if only for a few hours." She brushed the hair away from his face. "Pretend this is our cabin in Wyoming. Pretend we know nothing except each other, and the joy of being in each other's arms. There's no yesterday, there's no tomorrow. There's only now."

Cale pulled Shay atop him and craned his neck to kiss her. "I wish it were that simple," he said, groaning against her soft lips.

"It can be if you let it." She anchored her hands in his hair. "There is no one in our world except us." Her mouth drifted close to his, and she kissed him in return.

Thunder echoed in their hearts as they found fulfillment together.

Chapter 19

Jared propped his left shoulder under Henry's right armpit and slid his arm around Henry's back to steady his brother as they stood in the rain. Henry's chin rested against his chest as he hovered between delirium and consciousness.

Jared pounded on the farmhouse door with his fist. He listened. Nothing. He hammered on the door again.

Moments later, he heard a shuffling sound, then the door opened slowly on creaking hinges.

Lantern light spilled through the doorway of the adobe structure into the murky night. The face of a middle-aged Mexican, his wife staring over his shoulder, came into view.

"*Sí, señor?*"

"You speak English?" Jared asked.

"Yes. A little."

Jared shouldered his way past the couple, dragging his brother inside and over to a bench along one wall. He laid his brother down. Henry grimaced from the movement, then grew still. His breathing was shallow and raspy.

Jared straightened and made a quick assessment of the room.

A primitive kitchen, with a fireplace in one corner, along with a table and four chairs, took up half of the room's area. An arched doorway on the other side led to a hallway, hinting at additional rooms.

Facing the man, Jared said, "My brother's been shot. Tell your wife to tend him."

The man in turn relayed the message to his wife in Spanish. She nodded and moved to the table to light another lantern. She put more wood on the fire and swung a kettle over the flames to boil water.

In a few moments, she ladled hot water into a bowl and tore a clean piece of cotton cloth into several strips. Kneeling beside Henry, she washed the wound.

Jared dropped into one of the chairs and asked, "You got anything to drink?"

"Mescal."

The Mexican placed a bottle and a glass in front of Jared. The elder Slocum poured himself some of the liquor, then knocked the drink back with two strong swallows. He drew his lips back at the bite of it and wiped his mouth on his sleeve.

As the woman worked on Henry, Jared grimaced with each agonized moan from his brother.

Half an hour later, the woman stood and spoke to her husband.

The Mexican conveyed her message to Jared. "The bullet passed through. Your brother will live. Must rest at least one day."

Jared poured himself another drink, tossed his head back, and downed the mescal in one fluid motion. He banged the glass down on the table.

The earth would ring with Breland's cries for mercy.

* * *

Following Cale, Shay kicked her mount into a steady canter across the heat-baked trail. The horses' hooves thudded against the rocky surface, leaving little evidence that anyone had passed that way. Only the eyes of an expert tracker would be able to discern the faint marks left behind. There had been no sign of the Slocum brothers in over a week, but Shay knew Cale wasn't taking any chances by slowing their pace.

Endless miles blurred into one another as horses and riders kept up their grueling pace. In late afternoon, they approached a large limestone formation.

Shay urged her horse abreast of Cale's. "Do you think we could stop for just a few minutes?" She blushed. "I need to relieve myself."

"Not here." Cale pointed ahead to a stand of trees. "Over there. I just don't want to take too—"

Rifle fire splintered the silence. Shay's horse broke into a gallop, racing ahead. Cale's horse broke stride and stumbled. Staggering, the mount labored for its balance, but went tumbling down. Cale grabbed his rifle and kicked free of the stirrups before the gelding hit the ground. The horse scrambled to its feet and galloped away.

Two more shots rang out, one thudding into a nearby tree trunk, the other grazing Cale's cheek. His face felt on fire, but he had no time for pain. He rolled behind a limestone boulder.

For breathless seconds, Cale remained motionless, his eyes straining for signs of the Slocums. Time crawled. He touched his cheek. His breath hissed through his teeth as pain flared anew. He'd have a scar, but he didn't think any damage had been done to the muscle or bone.

He fingered the butt of his revolver. Shay had no gun. Damn! He couldn't leave her unprotected. He knew he'd have to act—and fast. He'd have to use every trick he knew, every ounce of strength and cunning to overcome the Slocums. "Cale!" came Shay's anguished cry over the sporadic gunfire.

He glanced behind him. His heart went to his throat. Shay sawed hard on her reins, causing her mount to skid on its hind legs, churning up dirt and gravel. Then she pulled the reins crisply to the left, and the horse reared and whirled.

Damn! He growled. What the hell was she doing coming after him? She was going to get herself killed.

Shay stretched out low over her horse's neck, but didn't slow her pace. Cale gave return fire to draw the Slocums off Shay.

"Cale, give me your hand!" Shay yelled.

Rifle in hand, Cale sprang to his feet when Shay came alongside him, grabbing for the saddle horn with his free hand. But he missed. He hooked his arm around her waist instead, nearly unseating her, but somehow Shay anchored herself with a hand on the saddle horn and managed to keep her balance. Cale swung himself up behind her. The horse missed one stride, but quickly corrected its gait.

More shots were fired, slamming into nearby rock, sending sediment flying as Shay directed her mount around a large rock formation.

On the backside of the boulders, Cale slid off the horse's rump and landed on his feet, rifle in hand. He ran up the rocky incline which canted sideways. Reaching the top, he dropped to one knee and sighted down the rifle barrel.

A stillness came over Cale for the space of a heartbeat.

"Damn," he swore violently, and lowered the rifle.

The Slocums were gone.

He scrambled back down the backside of the rock formation. At the bottom of the incline, he stopped. His stomach knotted. Shay was nowhere to be seen. He clenched his fists and cried out in outrage and pain.

Shay reined in her mount. She held her breath, silencing the harsh rasp of air through her lungs. Her horse labored for its own breath, nearly winded from the sprint.

After she had dropped Cale off, she had foolishly allowed Jared Slocum to cut her off from Cale when she had ridden down the backside of the incline. She knew Slocum wanted to use her as bait to lure Cale out into the open. She had ridden in the opposite direction to thwart Slocum's plan, praying she could give Cale time to find his mount and gain some advantage over the Slocums.

Again came the muffled sound of hoofbeats. Shay twisted around in the saddle and saw Slocum riding across the flat expanse of land. Looking for some avenue of escape, she spied a dense stand of mesquite trees interspersed with cacti. If only she could reach the brush . . .

She laid the ends of her reins to the mare's shoulders. Clouds of sand and dirt went flying as the buckskin galloped headlong for the trees.

A short distance behind her, Jared Slocum thundered across the dry riverbed that butted the dense growth. Losing sight of his prey, Jared reined in his horse sharply, nearly causing the sorrel to lose its footing. The stallion pranced nervously around in a circle, tossing its head from side to side.

Beneath the brim of his hat, Jared's green eyes narrowed. "Damn you, bitch. Where'd you go?" His voice rose in harsh syllables.

He heard retreating hoofbeats and jabbed the stallion's flanks with his spurs. The horse sprang forward.

The glaring sun extended its blinding fingers across the land, giving grotesque shadows to the trees and brush. When she heard a horse, Shay looked behind her. Her heart flew to her throat. Her pursuer was rapidly closing the distance between them. Jared Slocum looked like a demon from hell as he bore down on her. She rode with every ounce of skill she possessed.

Out of the corner of her eye, Shay saw the stallion come abreast of her smaller mount. She raised her quirt to lash out at the sorrel, but before her arm completed its arc, her hat flew from her head to dangle down her back by its cord. She was thrown off balance and grabbed frantically at the saddle horn to keep herself from falling.

With a muffled curse, Slocum fell back as his horse hit a gopher hole and stumbled. Shay seized the opportunity to press her horse to its limits. Lather flecked the buckskin's mouth and sides.

Shay made it to the edge of the brush. Mesquite thorns and cacti tore at her hair and clothes as her horse crashed through the thick growth.

Suddenly, a jackrabbit dashed beneath the buckskin's hooves and the horse reared. Shay felt herself sliding from the saddle. She landed on her back, the jolt knocking the air from her. Her lungs burned from the force of the impact, and she couldn't move. She could only stare into the face of Jared Slocum as he knelt beside her.

He straddled her prone form and pinned her wrists to the ground on each side of her head. Slowly the air returned to her lungs, and she drew a burning breath. She knew it would be useless to struggle, and she forced herself to lie still. Summoning her courage, she glared at her captor.

His eyes raked her sweat-drenched shirt as her breasts strained against the damp cotton with each ragged breath she took.

"I can see you're quite a spitfire." Slocum chuckled. "I like my women that way. Makes things right interesting."

Shay's jaw tensed. "I'm not your woman."

Jared lowered his face near hers. "Mine? Henry's? No matter. I reckon we'll both have ya."

Shay felt her insides curdle from Slocum's sour breath. "You've forgotten about my husband. He'll kill you if you lay a hand on me."

Slocum threw his head back and laughed. Then he stared down at her. "What's to keep me from having ya right here?"

"Nothing but my husband."

"Henry's waiting back on the trail. He's to fire a warning shot if he spots Breland. I haven't heard any shot, have you?"

Shay was terrified, but she told herself that she wouldn't let Jared Slocum know it. She told herself to stare at him with anger—not fear.

Slocum's leer was one of satisfaction. "Didn't take much to flush you out." He reached out and grabbed her right breast.

"Get your filthy hands off me."

"Nope. You're not going to disappoint me one bit." He squeezed the flesh punishingly.

Shamed and degraded, Shay tried to throw him off her.

"I like for a woman to fight me."

Logic forced her to grow still. However, she leveled a look of undisguised loathing at him.

"Why not enjoy yourself?" He kneaded her breast. "I've got quite a way with women."

He lowered his head. Revulsion washed over her as his mouth covered hers with a wet, punishing kiss. In the meantime, he ripped the buttons from her shirt. His hand slid inside to rip open her chemise and latch upon one breast. He rolled the nipple between his fingers until it became a tight bud.

"See here, girlie. I knew you'd enjoy this."

Shay's flesh shrank from his vile touch. He lowered his head, and his mouth latched onto the nipple, sucking like a vulgar pig. He then moved his mouth to her face and slid his slobbering lips back and forth across hers.

Revulsion roiled inside her. She couldn't stand any more. She bit him.

He jerked his head up. "You'll pay for that, bitch."

Her eyes widened briefly before his fist struck her. A thousand pinpricks of light danced before her eyes as darkness descended upon her.

A rough hand on her shoulder roused Shay into consciousness. She raised her head, feeling a twinge in her neck, and blinked against the harsh daylight.

She found herself sitting propped up against a

tree trunk, her hands tied behind her back, her ankles secured as well.

Henry Slocum squatted beside her, his left arm in a sling. He shoved a plate of food at her with his right hand. "Want some?"

A foul smell drifted to her nose from the greasy glob of food on the plate. She swallowed to keep her queasy stomach from rebelling.

"What's the matter, Mrs. Breland? Don't you like my cooking?"

"I'm not hungry." She turned her face away.

Henry grabbed her chin with his good hand, his fingers digging cruelly into the soft flesh, and jerked her head around. "You'll eat it, if I have to force it down your gullet." With a knife, he scooped up some of the greasy concoction and brought it to her mouth. "What'll it be? You gonna eat it, or am I gonna force it down your throat?"

She opened her mouth and he crammed his fingers inside, depositing the glob on her tongue. Shay tried to swallow but couldn't. She turned her head and spat out the food.

Yellow teeth were revealed as Slocum peeled his lips back in a predatory fashion. "You're gonna need your strength before the night's through."

A chill chased its way up her spine at his words, but she kept her gaze steady on him. "I won't struggle. And you won't like it."

"Before I'm through with you, you're gonna beg me to finish you. There are women who enjoy having men rough with them. Maybe you're one. I know lots of ways to inflict pain." His eyes took on a meaningful glint as he wet his lips with his tongue.

Don't show any fear, Shay cautioned herself. She sensed that Henry Slocum was the type of a man who fed on his victim's dread. She wouldn't give him the satisfaction of cringing before him.

Jared Slocum walked over. His regard went from Shay to his brother. "Leave her for the time being. She's got to stay alive long enough to flush Breland out. You can have her in the morning when there's plenty of light. I want Breland to be able to see everything you do to her. He'll come to us."

Laughing, Henry stood. The two brothers walked away.

The sun was setting as Cale tied his horse out of sight at the end of a dry creekbed. Hunched down, rifle in hand, he crept up the sloping incline. He removed his hat and laid down on his belly, peering over the rise.

He scoured the Slocums' camp until he found Shay. She was off to one side, tied hand and foot, leaning against an alligator juniper.

Five feet from her was Jared Slocum, stretched out beside the fire, and beyond him another ten feet was Henry Slocum, urinating on a scrub brush. He could easily drop Henry, but Jared was too close to Shay. Jared wouldn't hesitate to kill Shay if anything happened to his brother. Cale knew he'd have to wait until dark to make his move.

Shay tried to readjust her position, but the painful movement brought a moan to her lips. She closed her eyes against the discomfort, then opened them. Her gaze fell to the ground beside her. Henry's knife.

Her stomach pitched wildly. If she could angle her body away from the tree trunk, she just might be able to get her hands on the blade. But how to do it without drawing attention to herself?

An idea came to her, and she called to Jared. "I have to relieve myself."

He stood and walked over to her. Looking down at her, he said, "So?"

"Could you please untie me?"

He only stared at her.

Seeing his hesitation, she went on. "Where could I run to?"

Jared regarded her for a moment longer before he bent and cut the ropes binding her hands and ankles. Grabbing her upper arm, he pulled her to her feet, then released her.

She rubbed her wrists, wincing at the pain as she walked from camp.

Hearing Jared's footsteps behind her, she turned. "Can't I have any privacy?"

"I mean to keep an eye on you."

She was appalled at his intent, but then she should have known better than to expect any decency from him. Her face felt scorching hot as she sidled around a short bush, watching for snakes as she stepped.

"That's far enough," Jared called.

Her face blushed crimson at the thought of having to drop her pants with that lecherous man watching. But if there was any chance at freedom . . .

At that moment, Henry called to Jared, and the older brother turned from her.

She unbuttoned her pants and began to slide them down when she heard a voice.

"No sudden moves, Shay."

Dear God, was she hearing things? She turned

her head a fraction to her right. Not far from her, she saw Cale lying flat on his stomach.

"Listen carefully," he whispered. "Drop to your knees, then get down on your belly and move toward me. Understand?"

She nodded.

"When you're past me, keep going until you reach the dry creekbed. My horse is tied at the far end. I'll follow as soon as I can. My revolver is in its holster wrapped around the saddle horn. Use the gun if you—"

Jared's voice cut off Cale's words. "Hey, what's taking you so long?"

"Please, just a few more minutes," Shay said.

"Hurry up. Or I'm gonna come in there and get you."

Shay turned her head in Cale's direction, waiting for his signal.

"Now, Shay."

Easing onto her stomach, she pulled herself across the ground with her forearms, then pushed her body forward with her legs. She pulled and pushed until she was fifteen feet from the creekbed.

Suddenly, Jared's voice rang out. "You bitch! Where are you?"

Henry's voice followed his brother's. "Dammit. Where'd she go?"

"Go to the left. I'll swing right. She couldn't have gone far," Jared shouted.

The sound of them crashing through the scrub brush, their boots thudding against the rocky ground, resounded in Shay's ears. She froze. The air in her lungs seemed to turn to ice, making it impossible to breathe. She squeezed her eyes shut.

"Shay. Run!"

The urgency in Cale's voice thrust her into action. She scrambled to her feet and raced for the creekbed, throwing herself over the sloping rise and rolling down the other side. Coming to her feet quickly, she ran for Cale's horse. She jerked the revolver from its holster and sprinted back toward her vantage point.

Shots rang out wildly, as did the Slocum brothers' savage curses.

She crawled up the rise and peered over the sandy, grass-studded edge. Her eyes widened as the Slocum brothers came into view, heading straight for Cale's last position. She saw a flash of light, the sun glinting off Cale's rifle barrel as the weapon leveled on Henry Slocum.

Cale fired quickly, repeatedly levering bullets into the firing chamber without recoil.

Caught by surprise, Henry was cut down by Cale's bullets. Jared swung around and came after Cale from Cale's blind side.

Acting instinctively, Shay scrambled up the sandy bank and leveled her weapon at Jared Slocum. Before her warning cry cleared her lips, Cale spun around and fired at the same time Shay pulled the trigger.

Bullets thudded into Jared Slocum. With his gun still clutched in his hand, he sagged to his knees. His eyes widened as he pulled his hand away from his stomach and glanced at the blood covering it.

He looked at Cale. "This ain't finished." The tip of his barrel wobbled as he took aim—at Shay.

"*No!*" Cale fired again, but not before Slocum squeezed off a shot.

The impact of Slocum's bullet knocked Shay off her feet and onto her back. Her hand burned and throbbed. Dazed, she wondered if she had been been shot. She squeezed her eyes shut against the pain.

Suddenly, she felt Cale gather her in his arms. "No, no." He tenderly brushed the hair from her face.

She opened her eyes and looked at him. "Have I been shot?" she whispered.

First disbelief, then relieved joy, played across Cale's face as he stared at her. He ran his hands over her. "Thank God, no."

He helped her to a sitting position. "But my hand hurts."

Cale examined her right hand, then saw the gun lying next to her. He picked up the revolver. "His bullet must have hit the gun and knocked it out of your hand."

He tossed the gun aside and wrapped his arms around her. "No one will ever take you from me again," he whispered raggedly, and buried his face against her neck. His tears were warm against her skin.

Shay moved to look at Cale, and he raised his head.

"I'll always love you." Her voice was a silver thread of emotion, binding their souls.

She kissed him, tasting their mingling tears on her lips.

Never had life been sweeter, or love more treasured.

Epilogue

My dearest Shay,

It was wonderful to get your letter. We all read it.

Summer won't get here fast enough. I cannot wait to see you and little Alexander. I imagine he's the most handsome child with his black hair and blue eyes. Certainly, his father's son. It doesn't seem as if you've been gone nearly two years.

Your father is doing well and sends his love. You'll be amazed at how different he is since giving up drinking. The two of you will have a lot to talk about. He wants very much to make things up to you.

Give my love to Cale. I know he's working harder than ever now that the spread is growing so quickly.

One last bit of news. Brad and I are engaged. And we want to marry while you're here, so we're looking at a June date.

I'll close for now. Write soon.

Love,
Aunt Nettie

Shay folded the letter and tucked it away in her apron pocket, then wiped the tears of joy from her eyes with her fingertips. Moving to the window, she glanced outside and saw Cale emerge from the barn, heading for the house.

She turned from the window and walked to the stove, adding more wood to the fire. After feeding the stock, he'd be hungry and want his supper.

She had just taken a plate of food from the oven when Cale walked in. He paused at the door to stomp the snow from his boots.

"Ssh." Shay brought a finger to her lips. "Alexander's asleep."

He hung up his hat and coat. "Sorry." He pulled out a chair and sat down at the table. "It's going to be a cold one tonight."

When she set his food in front of him, he reached out and grabbed her hand. "What's wrong?"

"Why?"

"You've been crying."

"Only because I'm happy. I just finished reading Aunt Nettie's letter."

Cale pulled Shay onto his lap. "And?"

"Aunt Nettie and Uncle Brad are getting married."

Cale smiled. "That's certainly good news."

"They're all looking forward to Alexander and me coming in the spring. Including Papa."

"Your father's lucky to have a brother who cared enough to try and help him. I doubt Sneed would have been able to find himself again if it hadn't been for Brad."

Shay nodded. "You'd better eat or your food will get cold."

A wicked glint entered his eyes. "I think I'll just have dessert."

His hand settled on her neck, and he pulled her face close to his and kissed her.

The kiss lingered until Shay pulled away a fraction. "I love you so much."

"I love you, too." He brought her face close once more and rimmed her lips with his tongue. "What do you say we practice making a sister or brother for Alexander?"

And practice they did.

Avon Romances—
the best in exceptional authors and unforgettable novels!

THE LION'S DAUGHTER Loretta Chase
76647-7/$4.50 US/$5.50 Can

CAPTAIN OF MY HEART Danelle Harmon
76676-0/$4.50 US/$5.50 Can

BELOVED INTRUDER Joan Van Nuys
76476-8/$4.50 US/$5.50 Can

SURRENDER TO THE FURY Cara Miles
76452-0/$4.50 US/$5.50 Can

SCARLET KISSES Patricia Camden
76825-9/$4.50 US/$5.50 Can

WILDSTAR Nicole Jordan
76622-1/$4.50 US/$5.50 Can

HEART OF THE WILD Donna Stephens
77014-8/$4.50 US/$5.50 Can

TRAITOR'S KISS Joy Tucker
76446-6/$4.50 US/$5.50 Can

SILVER AND SAPPHIRES Shelly Thacker
77034-2/$4.50 US/$5.50 Can

SCOUNDREL'S DESIRE Joann DeLazzari
76421-0/$4.50 US/$5.50 Can